D0294861

Falling From the Sky

A Thomas Larsen Story

Tim Goodwin

ROBERT HALE · LONDON

First published in Great Britain 2002

ISBN 0 7090 7051 9

Robert Hale Limited
Clerkenwell House
Clerkenwell Green
London EC1R 0HT

2 4 6 8 10 9 7 5 3 1

Typeset by
Derek Doyle & Associates, Liverpool.
Printed in Great Britain by
St Edmundsbury Press Ltd, Bury St Edmunds, Suffolk.
Bound by Woolnough Bookbinding Limited.

Contents

1 November 1958

OUTSIDE, THE GREAT Pratt and Whitney turbojet engines thundered away. Inside, points of light flashed, or shone steadily from the instrument panels; but it was not they that made the cabin pulse eerily with crawling, flickering shafts of livid colour. The whole sky was alight with the aurora borealis: an awesome display of rippling green and white curtains, that seemed to stretch for hundreds of kilometres, changing almost imperceptibly through blue, violet and yellow, then back to green.

'Any improvement, Will?' called the pilot. His voice was rough and echoing as it came over the radio microphone contained within his oxygen mask.

'No, sir,' said the radar operator. 'Sorry, Captain. This stuff in the sky is just ripping the instruments clean apart.'

'They're all over the place,' put in the navigator, with his distinctive New-York-Jewish twang. 'Like Grace Kelly's ass.'

There was a faint swell of laughter.

'How about communications, Bobby?'

'Just noise, sir,' replied the co-pilot. 'I'm getting a fucking earache.'

'That's something,' said the navigator. 'I never knew you could fuck with your ear.'

'Sol,' retorted the co-pilot. 'A guy like you can fuck up anything.'

'Hey, people, give me room to think,' said the pilot irritably. He took a deep breath. 'Take me through that last message again.'

'OK. What we got was that there was heavy cloud, with the tops up to 20,000, combined with strong winds and blizzard conditions on the ground. That applied to round about 69°, then from there the cloud cover became scattered and broken. Basically they recommended us to get above trouble and head straight up the east coast, as far as Scoresby Sund at 70°, then take the crossing to north-west Iceland, before heading back down to Keflavik.'

'Hell of a way round.'

'The reception was lousy, sir. But it sounded like they reckoned on the longer trip as being safer, and you know they seem real concerned about what we're carrying. Don't forget those guys last year that got in trouble with heavy-duty icing on the wings over the Denmark Strait. Not forgetting all those fuel system bugs they were warning us about. Anyway, I think they also said that taking our time would give the snow a chance to clear from Keflavik.'

'Sure, sure.' The captain tugged thoughtfully at his oxygen mask. As usual the strip of exposed skin just above the mask, and below his flight goggles, felt bitterly cold. It was about time someone designed things better. 'Well, we've done it like they said anyway. We must be about over Scoresby Sund now.'

'We're like Bobby, sir,' said the navigator.

'What?'

'Well past it.'

'Funny guy, Sol! How much past it? And I don't want a wisecrack, I want a serious estimate.'

'You're the captain. OK, so an average speed of just under 500 mph from Bluie West One, plus a contrary wind estimated at 60 mph, gives us an average real flight speed of round 440 mph.' The navigator was measuring distances on his map, by a small light. 'It's just short of 500 miles from Cape Farewell to the DEW warning station at Kulusuk, then the same distance again to Scoresby Sund. Add on 100 miles for Bluie to Cape Farewell, and you've got an effective total of 1,100 miles. We've been flying for 2 hours, 47 minutes, which means we've covered 1,225 miles, give or take a few. Time to head east-southeast, sir, I'd say. We must've overshot by a minimum of a hundred miles.'

'OK, that sounds good. Better safe than sorry.' There was a moment's silence, then the pilot's voice came again, his doubt clear even through the poor sound quality of the internal radios. 'Hang on in there, Sol. Did you say you've just made an allowance for us to fly down to Cape Farewell, then back up again?'

'Yes, sir.'

'Jesus H. Christ! We didn't do that – don't you remember? We agreed to cut straight over the ice.'

'But, sir, that wasn't on the flight plan . . .'

'Screw the flight plan. I changed it, Sol. I told everyone.'

'Captain's right,' came the voice of Will, the radar operator, a young, slow-talking, self-effacing man from St Louis.

'Course I'm right. We agreed that as it was only about 60 miles due east, and we'd done it before, it would be OK. For Chrissake, you gave me the course settings, yourself, Sol.'

'Shit! So I did. I'm sorry, Captain. I don't know what got into me. Don't worry, I'll sort it.'

'It's not me that's going to be worrying, Sol. It's you.'

'Excuse me, Captain, but there's something else.' This was the electronic warfare officer, from his seat behind the pilot and co-pilot.

'What?' snarled the captain.

'Well, did I hear Sol say he was allowing for a 60 mph contrary wind?'

'Sure. So?'

'It's a following wind, sir.'

'What the fuck. . . ? Are you sure?'

'Yes, sir.'

'What in God's name is going on in this plane?'

'But, sir,' broke in the navigator. There were no jokes now. 'That just cannot be right. When we left Bluie . . .'

'I did tell you, Sol, not long after we hit the coast.'

'Yeah,' said the captain. 'That's right. I heard that.'

'I didn't hear a fucking thing,' said navigator. 'Who told me? Nobody told me. Jesus, I said my headphones have been playing up. And you didn't get a confirmation of the change from me, did you? You can't have because I didn't give one.'

'Well, no, that's true,' agreed the warfare officer. 'But . . .'

'So then . . .'

'Shut up, Jerry. Shut up, Sol. We'll sort out whose screw-up this is later. Now, we need to recalculate our position. And fast.'

They could all hear the navigator muttering to himself.

'OK, sir,' he said after a moment. 'I reckon if we've managed to keep to our course – and that's something of an assumption – then we should be about 395 miles north of Scoresby Sund.'

'Four hundred miles. Jesus, Sol! We're on our way to the pole.'

'Yes, sir.'

'Brilliant! Charlie Lindbergh could get across the whole fucking Atlantic Ocean without a single hitch in 1927, and thirty years later we can't even do a third of that distance without getting lost. Great. OK. Now, before we go blundering off towards where we think Iceland is, maybe, I want to know just where the fuck we are, and what's under us – sea, mountain, land, ice, whatever. In other words, I don't trust nothing any more. So let's start swinging and dropping the girl.'

'Yes, sir.'

The great plane turned sluggishly, and began to barrel downwards.

'Anything on the radar, Will?'

'No, sir, not so far as I can tell. But the aurora's still screwing up the instruments.'

'What height are we?'

'Twenty thousand, sir.'

'I'm going to keep taking her down.'

'Fifteen thousand.'

'OK. Let's slow it a bit. Anything there?'

'No, sir.'

'Twelve thousand. Eleven.'

'Still nothing?'

'No, sir.'

'Could we be over the sea?'

'Yes, sir,' responded the navigator. 'That's the way the odds lie. The coastline slants a little west after Scoresby Sund. Our course was aimed to be just off the coast anyway, and if we're that far north, then the chances are that we're well out to sea. . . .'

'Except that right now our course is looking like a load of hooey. OK. Let's take her down some more, but real careful.'

'Ten thousand. Nine and a half. Nine. Eight and a half. Still heavy cloud cover. No, wait, there's a gap below us.'

'Can you see anything?'

'Could be water, sir,' said the co-pilot cautiously.

'Let's take her down a little more, so we can see for sure.'

'Eight thousand. Seven eight, seven seven . . '

'I'm pretty sure it's water, Captain.'

'The sea. Great stuff. So we've done something right. OK, we'd better—'

'Mountain immediately ahead sir,' came a high-pitched yell from the radar operator.

Shouts rang over the radio. The plane had barely begun to lurch upwards when a great mass of solid blackness loomed out of the colour-stained night, straight in front of them.

'Fucking hell! Get her over to the port. Get the bitch over!'

It was far too late. There was a deafening screech of torn metal as the tip of one of the 25-metre-long wings caught an outflung crag, and was ripped clean off. The great machine plummeted down in a sickening, twisting spiral, then smashed crushingly into the huge, glistening glacier that filled the valley below.

A few hours later the great water-filled gash, which the plane's flaring engines had briefly melted into the ancient ice, was already beginning to refreeze. The clouds had closed back in, and snow was falling thick and hard.

The long, dark, bitter silence of the high arctic winter returned to the wastes of Iversen Land.

2 Frederik

THE BIG, BROWN-HAIRED man glanced out of the window of his hotel room. Outside it had begun to snow, but it was only wet snow, melting as it fell, nothing that might delay his flight. His bag was packed – he nearly always travelled light – but when he glanced down at his watch, he realized there was still over an hour before the taxi to the airport was due to arrive. Which was also typical – he was always early.

He picked up the telephone and called a number in Copenhagen.

'Yes?' came a woman's voice.

'Hi, Natasha.'

'Frederik. It is good to hear from you. How are things going?'

'Not bad. I'm staying at the Hans Egede.'

'Who died and made you a millionaire?'

He laughed.

'I felt I needed a bit of comfort around me.'

'I thought you were already on your way to the conference.'

'I'm about to fly to Iqaluit. From there it's on to Ottawa.'

'You'll be here on Friday then?'

'*Immaqa*, as we've all heard a thousand times. Maybe. You know what it's like in the north.'

'I know. And I also know that at fifty-six, you are starting to get too old for all this running around. I'm half your age, and I find it exhausting just to listen to your schedule. I don't know how you do it.'

'It's what I like doing.'

'If I was you, I'd maybe think it was time to let other people do the field work. You could sit comfortably in your college rooms, give a few restful lectures and tutorials, and smoke a pipe, while getting some eager young graduates to help you to analyse results, and look for patterns. That's what all the other senior professors do.'

'I don't like pipes. And they're boring people.'

'I won't argue about that. But don't quote me.'

She laughed, and Frederik felt a shiver run up his spine. Natasha Myklund was a thin, quick, soft-spoken Danish woman, with nervous mannerisms, ash-pale skin, and a thick mop of curly brown hair that fell in a disordered waterfall below her shoulders. He had known her for five years, since she had arrived at Copenhagen University as a graduate studying polar biology, and for at least half of that time she had haunted him, like an insubstantial erotic phantom.

This summer he had taken part in an expedition to north-east Greenland with her and three others, spending two months studying the isolated region of Iversen Land. He had hoped that the closeness of the expedition would bring things to a crisis – either destroying his obsession, or providing him with the chance to make it known. Inevitably neither had happened, and his relations with her remained on the same friendly, superficial level they had always been. The level he never dared to endanger by making an overt advance.

'Anyway,' she said. 'What are you calling me about?'

'Just to see how things're going.'

'Good. Though there's been a lot to do, especially when it comes to details of the Iceland gull subspecies – if it is a subspecies. I'm still hopeful that what we have found is a whole new species. . . .'

'Look, Tasha, the whole problem of white-winged gulls . . .'

'. . . is up for discussion. I know that. But I feel in my gut that those birds were neither Iceland gulls, nor an isolated population of Thayer's gull.'

'We'll see,' he remarked, scratching his nose and staring out of the window again. It was still snowing, but without conviction. 'I hope you're right, but it's going to take a lot more work – much of it in the field.'

'Sure, and that's why I'm about to get down to the whole funding thing. Anderssen's sure to be unenthusiastic, but maybe we can bypass him, and sell the project to the real movers and shakers.'

'Let's hope so. We need every scrap of support we can find. Talking of which, how are you getting on with that reel of film from Lake Sølveig?'

'Sorry?'

'Those photographs we discussed. You must remember. I gave you the film.'

'Oh, yes. Sure. Those.'

'You mean you haven't had them developed yet?'

'There's been so much to do.' She paused. 'What exactly was on them anyway?'

Frederik felt a burst of suppressed irritation.

'I told you all this, Natasha. Jens and I saw what looked like the remains of an old expedition, but the point is I spent all yesterday in the library, checking it out. There haven't been any other expeditions to that area. In fact, since Mikkelsen and Iversen discovered the place in 1910, there have been just six documented visits, and not one since 1989.'

'Oh.' Her voice had changed, and he could almost hear her thinking. 'You're sure?'

'Sure, I'm sure. There's something else too,' he went on. 'As you know, Lake Sølveig wasn't in existence when the south-eastern part of Iversen Land was last surveyed. So how could there be any trace of an expedition there?'

'You should have had a closer look.'

'There wasn't time,' he said with hard-won patience. 'We were on the wrong side of the glacier, our supplies were running out, and the weather was turning nasty. I just had enough time to take a couple of ice cores, then get back to Jens. We made about four kilometres before we got holed up in that blizzard.'

'I remember.' She laughed. 'When you finally got back, the two of you looked as thin and pale as supermodels, but a bit less attractive.'

Frederik was not amused.

'Look, Natasha, if you haven't time to check out those photographs, perhaps you could give them to someone else. Or Seana can do something with them.'

'Seana's gone off to earn some money,' said Natasha.

'Seana is obsessed with money,' remarked Frederik coldly. 'She ought to be working in finance, not university research.'

'That's not fair,' objected Natasha heatedly. 'You know her mother was always in debt, and Seana reckons it was the stress of trying to make a living that led to her stroke. Being short of money scares Seana; that's why she always has to make sure she's got some stashed away.'

'Well, anyway, I want to know what's on that film as soon as possible. With Jens and Wendy still out there, they could go and have another look.'

'There's hardly any time left before they're due to leave. You know that.'

'I suppose so, but . . .'

'Anyway, don't worry about the photographs. I remember now – I had a set of copies made for myself, and sent the negs on to Jon Skalli, a photographic analyser I know. He'll find everything in the photos that's there to be found.'

'You always do this, Natasha,' he said, half-relieved, half-irritated. 'You give the impression of not listening to a word anyone says, and then you go ahead and sort everything out without telling them. It's really annoying.'

'Sorry. It's just that it always takes me five minutes to shift my mind from what I'm doing at that moment to something new. I'll contact you straight away if there's some news. Anything else?'

'Not really—'

'I'd better go then,' she broke in briskly. 'I'm meeting Doctor Anderssen in an hour, and I have a strong feeling that he's not going to be as impressed with our provisional report as he ought to be.'

'Why do you think that?'

'Female intuition. I must go – you know how the good doctor hates it if one's late. Bye, Frederik.'

'You will contact me the moment you have any news, won't you, Natasha?'

'Sure. But the funding question won't be decided for some time.'

'I meant about those photos. If there has been another expedition to that area, then it could change everything about the work we're doing—'

'The line's breaking up at this end, Frederik,' she interrupted, blatantly untruthfully.

'No, wait,' he said. 'There's a couple of other things that need doing too, Tasha.'

'Frederik . . .'

'Please listen. You know that if I make an impression at this conference, there's a good chance it will help with our funding. Well, I need some information from the ice core samples you took with you. Specifically the two I've registered as LS – they're the ones from the Lake Sølveig glacier.'

'Frederik, that'll take serious time. We're talking at least a week of work, and—'

'Yes, I know that,' he broke in. 'But a few preliminary impressions might add weight to what I have to say. What I'm particularly interested in are the width and compression of recent ice layers, together with consideration of the oxygen isotopes of course. The physics laboratory has plenty of experience in—'

'Frederik, for Christ's sake!' she interrupted. 'What do you expect me to find in a day or two? There'll probably be some initial evidence which implies the world's been warming up since about 1650, and that the process may be accelerating, especially in the Arctic. That's not going to have people fainting in the streets, is it? We need precise detail to impress a scientific conference. . . .'

'Just have a look at them, then contact me. Please Natasha. There was an unusual quality to some of that ice, and I think you'll find something.'

'Like what?'

'I don't know.'

She sighed.

'OK then. I'll have a look if there's time.'

'The LS samples . . .'

'I heard you. Just. The line's getting bad again. Sorry. Lots of love. Bye, and see you soon'

The phone line hummed very faintly, then went dead.

Frederik put down the receiver and sighed. As so often, while speaking to Natasha, he had a sensation that he was driving through thick fog – which would suddenly, unpredictably, lift up to reveal perfect views in all directions, only to roll in again before he had time to take in his surroundings. It was as if he was talking a subtly different language to her, and neither of them really understood the other, even though they imagined they did, so their communication was tainted with misinterpretation and cross-purposes. And – as with driving through fog – there was always the danger of a full-scale, head-on collision. It had happened three or four times in the past, and no doubt would again. Not that it was all her fault. Not completely anyway.

This time there was something he hadn't told her. In his cold-blooded scientific way, he knew it was essential that he made no attempt to influence the way she – and anyone else – saw the photographs. He had to have an unbiased second opinion before he could go on. But Frederik was almost sure of what he had seen on the edge of the receding glacier – which was why he had cut those particular ice cores. As things stood at the moment, money for a fresh expedition the following year would be hard to come by. But if he was right about what the photographs – and perhaps the ice cores – would show, then everything would change. That was for sure.

He glanced outside again, where the snow had turned into a muddy drizzle. After a moment he picked up the phone again. The line crackled as it travelled over 1,500 kilometres of ice cap, from the hotel room to a small tent in the wastes of north-east Greenland. After half a minute there was an answer.

'Hello?'

'Jens, it's Frederik. I'm in Nuuk. How are you two?'

'We're fine. I'm sorting things out here, and Wendy's just off to check out the long-tailed skua colony, to see if any stragglers remain, and to pay a last lightning visit to the gull cliffs. Luckily the weather's good and settled, so we'll have the camp broken by tomorrow morning, and be at the airstrip in the evening. Mathias is expecting to fly us to Ivtoriseq on Thursday, and I've confirmed we can stay there until the Isafjordur ship arrives.'

'Right. Great.' Frederik hesitated a moment. 'I suppose there's no chance you could make it back to Lake Sølveig?'

Jens laughed.

'It's at least ten hours there, ten hours back, even if the weather's kind – which it sure as hell wasn't the last time. With time spent there taking observations, that's a bare minimum of 24 hours – without sleep. No way can we do that, break camp, and still get the supply plane the day after tomorrow. And you know the next plane isn't for another two weeks – we can't risk waiting that long.'

'I don't see why not,' said Frederik stubbornly. 'We left the departure date open on purpose, to give us flexibility. You've enough supplies to last you, and the meteorology stats show there's been a late autumn for the last three years.'

'It's dangerous to overstay, now that September has kicked in,' said Jens warily. 'You know that. There's a steadily increasing chance of really heavy snowfall, and if we're in Iversen Land when the first winter blizzards hit, then we could be trapped for weeks. We're not equipped to cope with that sort of extended stay. And what's the point anyway, when we'll be coming back next spring?'

'The spring could be off,' said Frederik. 'Natasha reckons that Anderssen is planning to block our funding. Have you got any ideas on someone who could fix a grant for us? A big business looking for some-one to sponsor maybe, or a millionaire who needs to write off some money against tax.'

'I don't know people like that,' said Jens.

'That makes two of us. As you remember, it was hard enough getting the money together originally, and if the university pulls the plug, we'll be totally fucked.'

'But look, it wouldn't be the end of everything if the funding was delayed for a year or so. You've got plenty of stuff to work on, haven't you?'

'Not on Lake Sølveig.'

'I think you're making too much of that.'

'But you agree with me about what we saw.'

There was a pause.

When Jens spoke again, even the poor quality of the contact could not disguise the change in his tone.

'No, Frederik. I don't.'

'But you said—'

'I've changed my mind.'

'What about the pictures? Natasha's given them to a photographic analyser to check them out.'

'I don't think they'll show anything, Frederik. Nothing at all. Listen, I must go. Wendy's calling. Speak to you soon.'

The line went dead. Frederik sighed, and wondered what had happened to change Jens's mind Not for the first time doubts began to creep into his own mind – perhaps the whole thing was just wishful thinking. But Frederik wanted it sorted out, either way. Mysteries – however trivial – always irritated him in the same way as wrong notes in an orchestral piece.

He decided that when he got back to Copenhagen on Friday, he would find the man Natasha had given copies of the photographs to, and talk to him. His mind wandered on to what sort of person this Jon Skalli might be – a boyfriend of Natasha's perhaps. He had known her for five years, and still had no idea of her personal life, of what sort of men she was attracted to.

The hotel room was warm, and there was still at least half an hour before the taxi would come. Idly he lay back on his bed, and drifted into a haze of ifs and maybes.

What would have happened if he had made a play for Natasha in the first few months he had known her? That had been the time. But she was so much younger than him, so much younger. And he had never been comfortable with women. When he lay in his tent, and listened to the snarl of the Arctic winds, or the patter of snow, he often drifted into improbable erotic fantasies, but with real women, he was always likely to head off and away. Just as he did with his life, dropping everything for the chance of another scientific trip, with its simplistic realities of work and survival.

Frederik frowned. Like many Arctic travellers, he was helplessly given to bouts of self-analysis, but they rarely lasted long, and tended to go round and round the same tracks – which in itself gave him a reassuring sense of familiarity.

He turned his mind to the conference on Thursday. There wasn't a lot of time to sort out exactly what he needed to say, and it was important that he put on a good show – there would be some important people there. He sat down on his bed, pulled out his papers and began to go through them.

Perhaps twenty minutes later his mobile telephone rang.

'Hello?' he said cautiously.

'I'm sorry, who is this?' asked a man's voice. A heavy, strong voice, speaking Danish.

'My name is Frederik Dahl. Can I help you?'

'What name did you say?'

'Frederik Dahl. Professor Frederik Dahl. Who are you trying to contact?'

'Sorry. Wrong number.'

The telephone went dead.

Frederik held it in his hand and looked at it doubtfully. After a moment he called up the last caller feature. To his astonishment it showed Natasha Myklund's number in Copenhagen.

Frederik called the number back. It rang for a little while, then he heard Natasha's voice.

'I'm afraid I'm not in just now, but you can contact me on my mobile, or alternatively please leave a message after the long tone. . . .'

Frederik rang off without speaking. There must be some mistake. He considered ringing Natasha at the university, then remembered she would be on her way to her meeting with Doctor Anderssen. In the circumstances it was best to leave her be. He'd ring after arriving in Iqaluit, and find out how things had gone. Frederik glanced down at his watch again. It was time to go.

Two and a half hours after losing sight of Lille Malene mountain, towering over Nuuk airport, and following a brief touchdown under the high, sandy slopes of Kangerlussuaq, the First Air flight left Greenland behind, and headed out over the Davis Strait. Although it was 3 September and autumn was dyeing the tundra red and gold, there was little sign of ice on the dark blue waters, except for occasional flashes of white, marking one of the great icebergs from Ilulissat Kangerlua or the mighty ice shelves lining Melville Bay and the Kane Basin.

Frederik glanced around at the passengers. There was no one he recognized, which disappointed him a little, for he felt like talking.

A young Inuk in jeans, fleece and baseball cap was sitting beside him.

'Going far?' asked Frederik, in Danish.

The young man looked at him, and shrugged.

'I'm sorry, I don't understand,' he replied, his voice pure Canadian.

'I just wondered where you were travelling to,' said Frederik, switching to English.

'My family live in Iqaluit.'

'Not many Canadians visit Greenland,' said Frederik.

'No. I think that's right. But my brother has a job in Kangerlussuaq – as the deputy manager of the Ummimaq building of the Hotel. I've been staying with him for a few days. How about you?'

'I'm catching the connections to Ottawa for a scientific conference.'

'A conference. Sounds important.'

'It's about the preliminary results of a surveying trip I've been leading in north-east Greenland. We've logged some interesting facts about the biological changes in the area over the past forty or so years. It's heating up, like most of the Arctic.'

The young man nodded.

'My grandpa says that. He says the spring thaw comes two or three weeks earlier than when he was a kid, and the first freeze is a couple of weeks later. Pretty good thing, I'd say.'

'Not necessarily,' said Frederik cautiously. 'There's a complex web of consequence involved, and people are still arguing about it. But we've also made some other interesting discoveries.'

The young man stifled a yawn, and tried to look interested.

'What kind of things?' he asked.

'Well, the thing we were most pleased about was a completely new subspecies of the Iceland gull, that hasn't been described before. It may even be a species in its own right, which would be a major find.' He gave a brief smile, then found himself returning to his present preoccupation, almost in spite of himself. 'We also came across what appeared to be the remains of a previous expedition in the area.'

'That's not so weird is it? I mean, I thought everywhere was pretty thoroughly explored these days.'

'That's true. But this particular region is exceptionally hard to penetrate, and I was under the clear impression that I had seen the documentation of all the previous expeditions, so—'

There was a flash of brilliant white light, and a micro-second later the plane filled with searing heat and skull-splitting noise. Bitterly cold air rushed in, fanning the flames. Smoking and burning, great jagged fragments of metal fell out of the sky towards the cold empty waters of the Davis Strait a mile and a half below. With them fell twenty-three small dark shapes – the crew and passengers. One brief lightning strike of horror and pain, not even time for consciousness of what had happened, and dead before the ruined plane even began to fall.

Their bodies, still enfolded in the torn remains of the fuselage, obeying the unbending laws of gravity, smashed into the water approximately thirty-nine seconds later.

3 Conversations and Phone Calls

DOCTOR ANDERSSEN WAS a big, bruising bear of a man, fast-balding, with a thick – though carefully-clipped – beard, and a habit of leaning almost aggressively towards people as he spoke to them. He was Natasha Myklund's head of department, and she did not like him.

Three years before he had invited her to a dinner party in his choice, university-owned lodgings, overlooking the exclusive Christianshavn Canal, with its moored yachts and cabin cruisers, cultural centre and cafés. Only after arriving did she discover that it was a dinner party with a guest list of just one: her. Halfway through the lobster salad, she had felt Dr Anderssen's foot rubbing gently up and down her calf. She hastily withdrew it out of range, but the doctor had not been put off. During the coffee, he had sat down next to her, on his fawn leather sofa, told her how much he admired the work she was doing, and put his chubby, white hand, with its short fingers and immaculately manicured nails, on her knee. Natasha was twenty-three, and not sophisticated. She had gone red, and told him she was glad he thought she was doing good work, and that she thought it was very important to make sure personal matters never interfered with work.

'Sometimes they improve situations,' he had rumbled. 'Good relations with one's more influential associates can smooth problems out. And often open the way to advancement.'

The implied blackmail had almost taken her breath away, but she managed to keep her temper, and replied that while she understood the need to get on with her colleagues, she hoped advancement would come simply from the standard of her work.

'I'm sure that won't be a problem,' he had said, eying her up and down.

'I hope it won't be,' she had agreed.

He smiled at her. Realizing that he was not taking the hint, she bit her lip, went even redder, and finally gathered up her courage to move his hand back on to his own knee.

That had been as far as things had gone. Nothing was ever mentioned again, and their relationship remained scrupulously polite and professional. Nevertheless, she was sure that her rejection of his advance had contributed to the seemingly endless difficulties she met in trying to raise money for projects, and in getting her work published.

Dr Anderssen was, as ever, dressed immaculately – which made Natasha Myklund acutely aware of her own jeans, scuffed Timberland boots, and chestnut brown sweatshirt. It was true she had put on the smart black jacket which represented her interview outfit, and her jeans were expensive – though ageing – Gloria Vanderbilts, but they didn't compare with the doctor's charcoal-grey Italian suit, dark blue shirt and black silk tie.

Today he was at his worst. During her presentation he eyed her constantly, with his small, pale eyes shifting lingeringly up and down her, and the moment she finished, he unleashed his attack.

'You know I was against this expedition from the beginning. Professor Dahl is far too old to go wandering around North Greenland, and you are not experienced at polar field work. . . .'

'I have been to Greenland three times, doctor.'

He swept aside her interjection with a patronizing air that bordered on contempt.

'My dear young lady, you must realize that a week or two sitting opposite a little auk rookery in Disko Bay, or counting Arctic terns round Uummannaq, doesn't even begin to prepare you for a full-scale expedition to an isolated and little-visited region of north-east Greenland. Of course Jens is a good man, but you were forced into far too much dependency on the two undergraduates with you.'

'Wendy and Seana are both graduates, doctor.'

'What did you say?' he snapped irritably. It was well known that his hearing was not good, and was getting worse, but Anderssen was too vain to do anything about it.

'They are both graduates,' she repeated, louder.

'Be that as it may, neither of them has much more on-the-ground Arctic experience than I have in underwater exploration.'

'Seana is a Greenlander. . . .'

He sighed.

'I believe much of her upbringing was here in Denmark, and even you must accept that working in Nuuk for a few years does not prepare you adequately for high Arctic research work. Anyway, this meeting is about your application for university funds to undertake a follow-up expedition next year. If I may speak frankly, Professor Myklund, I would say that there is no chance of such a thing. No chance at all. The university has already disbursed large sums of money on your research, and when all the bills have arrived I suspect the total will not come to an øre under half a million kroner. What exactly has this half a million kroner provided?'

'How about the discovery of the first new bird species to be discovered in the Arctic for fifty years?' retorted Natasha.

'From the information you have provided so far, it looks like just another minuscule variation in a notoriously variable family of species. And if you want my personal opinion . . .'

She didn't, but she knew she had no choice in the matter.

'. . . the present fashion for subdividing birds into innumerable new species has nothing to do with rigorous science, but is simply driven by the explosion of amateur interest in ornithology, and especially the pathetic hobby of collecting new species – twitching isn't it called, or listing, or something? When I studied zoology, different species were defined by their refusal to cross boundaries to mate, or more specifically by their inability, if they did cross species boundaries, to produce viable offspring. Today every bird that looks a bit different instantly becomes a new species. The yellow-legged gull was just a subspecies of the herring gull, until birdwatchers wanted it made into a species in its own right. Ditto Thayer's gull, Pacific diver, Isabelline shrike, Scottish crossbill, and any number of others I could name.'

'You're not being fair, Doctor. What about the British red grouse that has now been recategorized as simply a subspecies of the willow grouse?'

'One of the very few examples you could provide,' he retorted, and relaxed into his high-backed, mahogany and leather, executive desk chair, gently pulling at his left ear, and regarding her challengingly. She had the feeling he was enjoying himself.

'Of course the final decision on your project is not up to me,' he remarked. 'But you may as well know that I shall be recommending strongly that funding should not be renewed for next year.'

'We do have other sponsors, Doctor.'

'Indeed. And if you can raise the money yourselves, so much the better. But I would not be being fair to my department if I did not proceed as I have just outlined. Now, if you could leave the formal application and supporting documentation with my secretary, I have another meeting in a few minutes. Thank you Professor Myklund.'

Feeling almost physically bruised by the encounter, Natasha reeled out of the offices into the sunshine, and went in search of a café. After two large, strong, black coffees, she tried to ring Frederik Dahl for some comfort and commiseration, but she only got an unobtainable tone. Then she remembered he was probably still in the air. Dully, she took a bus back to the modern block where she lived on the western edges of Copenhagen, near Vanløse.

Walking back from the bus stop, along a pleasant, tree-lined avenue, she glanced up. Silhouetted against a cloudy, early-evening sky, she saw a steady stream of gulls flying overhead towards their roosting places around the harbour. It reminded her afresh of Doctor Anderssen's contemptuous dismissal of their work. And of all the things she should have said – and hadn't even thought of.

Her mail box contained three circulars and a letter from the post-graduate club, reminding her that she hadn't yet bought a ticket for the annual fancy-dress party on Sunday evening, despite its ridiculously low price. Every year they tried to sell her an invitation, and every year she ignored their blandishments. Basically, Natasha simply wasn't the sort of person who went to fancy-dress parties, or to any social gatherings that involved putting on clothes different from her everyday wear. As a child, she had cried bitterly if told she must be in the school play, and when the day of the performance came round, she was invariably ill. Really ill – not pretending. In more recent years her reluctance to put on frivolous clothes, get drunk and party had, she reckoned, lost her at least four boyfriends, while her tendency to arrive at interviews in jeans had had a similarly damaging effect on her professional career. But at least it wasn't really necessary in the university. Except for meetings with Doctor Anderssen of course.

She threw her mail straight into the big communal dustbin outside, and went upstairs.

Her home was on the third floor of the block, a pleasant, airy flat with three large rooms, a somewhat cramped shower, and a view over the small park to the north. It was, as always, a mess. One former boyfriend had told Natasha that he knew exactly why she spent such a large proportion of her life arranging and going on field trips – because she didn't have a home, in fact she didn't live anywhere, she just camped wherever she happened to be.

It was true. After two years in this flat, she was still camping. Piles of books lined the walls, clothes were scattered at random, there were dirty coffee cups on windowsills and tables, yesterday's dinner plates were congealing in the kitchen, a spider plant was slowly dying from neglect, and her computer was blinking because she had forgotten to turn it off that morning.

She took off her jacket, tossed it carelessly on to the back of the sofa, then went over to listen to her messages. There were only two.

'Natasha, hi. This is Jens. Just to confirm that we'll be on the Danmarkshavn weather station supply plane on Thursday morning – God and the Greenland weather permitting. There's a hell of a lot to do, so don't bother to call unless it's important. Best to leave it until we're at Ivtoriseq. See you.'

The second was a blank message. She dialled to find out who had phoned her, and saw that it was Frederik, so she tried him again – and again all she got was the high-pitched whine that told her the number was unobtainable. After a moment she looked up a number in her phone book and called Seana.

'Hi,' said a young man's voice.

'I'd like to talk to Seana, please.'

'Who? Oh, yeah. The Eskimo chick. She split months ago.'

'I'm sorry?'

'She was off on some wild trip someplace, and said she couldn't afford to keep the room on.'

'Do you have an address or phone number for where she is now?'

'No way. Like I said, it was somewhere wild, Antarctica, or Africa, or . . .'

'Greenland?'

'Yeah. That's it. Wild.'

'So you haven't a clue where she is?'

'No, man. Sorry.'

A call to the university was just as unsuccessful, and Natasha swore under her breath. It was typical of Seana to forget to give people her new address.

Remembering Frederik's request about the photographs he and Jens had taken, Natasha went over to the pile of folders beside her desk, brushed away an unexpected array of pencil shavings and fingernail clippings, then frowned.

Although her room seemed a chaotic mess, she knew where everything was – or at least everything important, and that meant anything to do with her work. It was one of the reasons she found it impossible to live with anyone else. Just like her mother, they always tended to move her things around, to 'tidy them up' as they called it, and once that had happened, she couldn't find anything at all. People seemed bizarrely incapable of understanding that you could leave things on the ground, or in precarious, untidy piles, and still know exactly where they were.

So she went straight to the correct folder, which was half under one of the curtains, and almost totally concealed by a pair of discarded tights, and looked for the photographs.

Except they weren't there.

The folder contained many miscellaneous pictures of Iversen Land – glaciers, the temporary meteorology station they had set up, studies of birds, animals, flowers, geological strata. But not the ones of Lake Sølveig.

Yet Natasha could clearly remember having put the photographs in that folder. And she had not looked at them since. Nor had anyone visited. She never entertained at home. Her flat was her office, and on the rare occasions that she wanted to socialize, she went out.

Surprised, she began to go through the other folders in the pile, but there was still no sign of the photographs she was looking for. Growing irritated now, she went through all the folders again. Still nothing. A thorough scouring of the room got her no further.

'Shit!' exploded Natasha. She hated losing things, and rarely did.

In an effort to take her mind off it, she ignored Jens's message and rang the expedition in Greenland. It was the the round, spectacled, earnestly optimistic, Australian, Wendy who answered.

'Hi, Tasha,' she said. 'It's a bit hectic with just the two of us, but we should get it all done in time. Jens told me that he spoke to Frederik earlier this afternoon, and there isn't much chance of getting university funding for next year.'

'That's right. But I'm working on an appeal.'

'Why is Anderssen giving us this grief?' asked Wendy.

Natasha felt like shouting over the phone 'because I wouldn't fuck him'. But instead she gave a verbal shrug.

'Who knows?'

'What was it you wanted?'

'Have you got a number or an address for Seana?'

'No. No, I haven't. Haven't you?'

Natasha could hear the underlying comment, 'after all, she's your friend'. Wendy and Seana had not got on very well.

'Don't worry. What I really need is a quick word with Jens.'

'Sure. He's just outside, I'll get him.'

A minute or two later Jens's rough, deep voice came over the line.

'Yes?'

'It's about the pictures you took at Lake Sølveig. Why is Frederik so obsessed with them?'

'God knows!' Unusually there seemed to be a trace of anger in his voice, but it vanished almost immediately. 'I was taking some weather observations, and Frederik went on up the lakeside by himself. When he came back he told me he'd seen something that looked like a camp site, and that he'd taken some photographs with the zoom lens, as well as two core samples from the glacier.'

'That's it?'

'Yes.'

Natasha could visualize the dull frown on Jens's wide-eyed face. He was a pleasant man, an excellent mountaineer, and brilliantly experienced at life in the Arctic, but he had a total lack of interest in anything outside his own speciality.

'You didn't see anything?' she asked.

'Not really, no.'

'But I thought you said . . .'

'I'm not sure. Ice makes weird patterns sometimes, and you can think you see all sorts of things when they're not there.'

'That's true,' she agreed. 'Did you take any photographs?'

'No. Frederik did though. I thought he gave the film to you?'

'Yes, he did. So there aren't any others then?'

'I shouldn't think so. Unless he shot off two films, and kept the second one. Why don't you contact him and ask?'

'I've been trying, without any luck.'

'Try this evening. He's staying the night in Iqaluit, before pushing on to Ottawa tomorrow morning.'

'I know. Thanks, Jens.'

Natasha put down the phone with a faint sense of frustration, then yawned. She ought to be preparing for the appeal for further funding, but there seemed no point until she had discussed things with Frederik. Anyway, the mysterious photographs sat in her head like immovable stones. Eventually she decided to contact Jon Skalli. He had had the negatives for a week – he must have some idea of what they showed by now. She rang him, but there was no answer.

Putting down the phone, she stared out of the window. A great grey wall of cloud was slowly rolling over the sky from the west, stifling the sun. She watched the clouds for a moment, then found herself looking down at a large, sandy-grey BMW that was parked opposite. It had tinted windows, and looked as if it had cost more than her flat.

After a couple of moments, without warning, it started, purred away down the quiet street, then surprisingly swung left into a cul-de-sac. Natasha went over to the little kitchen and made herself a cup of tea. After one mouthful, she suddenly decided that she needed to get some air. Leaving her steaming mug on the table, she snatched up her jacket and went out again.

An hour later she got off the number eight bus on Prinsessegade, and walked down Badsmandsstraede, past the barrier, and a sign, which declared she was entering the '*free state of Christiania*', and warned that while soft drugs were permitted in the free state, there was a Junk Blockade to prevent all use of hard drugs. The sign was rather dog-eared – like the whole concept of Christiania, Natasha thought.

The bright, young social experiment of allowing 'alternative' people to run their own small section of the city, had evolved from a full-scale hippy rebellion against the status quo. But now it was thirty years old, and not much more than another comfortable, money-making attraction, comparable to the Tivoli Gardens or the Little Mermaid statue. Yet Natasha still liked visiting Christiania – and the old fire station, the low-tech experiments with wind and solar energy, and the overall ambience of the area remained refreshingly different from the rest of Copenhagen.

Jon Skalli lived and worked in a large, low-ceilinged attic above a café. Outside the café, which was called Poppin', was a sign that said '*No weapons. No biker gang colours. No bulletproof vests.*' She had once asked Jon if the sign was serious, and he'd laughed.

'It was a few years back, but now we just leave it up for the tourists. It gives them a thrill, and encourages them to pay more for their coffee. We're real capitalists these days.'

Inside, Natasha was told Jon hadn't been around that day.

'Yeah, I know,' said the long-haired waitress, with a vague smile on her long face. 'It's not like Jon, is it? Three or four people have come looking for him, but we had to tell them we hadn't a clue where he was.'

'Can I check out his room?' asked Natasha, after a moment's thought. 'He's got some things of mine I need back.'

The waitress looked at her doubtfully.

'What kind of things?'

'Photographs.'

The waitress cast a quick glance around the café. Except for a couple of young men smoking hash cigarettes, and talking about politics, there was no one there. A tape was playing West African music.

'I suppose I could give you five minutes,' she said. 'Things don't get busy till later.'

She escorted Natasha up the rickety wooden stairs at the back of the café, past three or four other doors, to the very top of the building. The door had no lock, and the waitress opened it, then stood by as Natasha went in and looked around.

The room – which a couple of years ago had been so familiar to Natasha – looked like a thousand student rooms. A purple shade hung round the light, the curtains were black and still drawn, the peeling and stained walls were half-covered in posters – posters for concerts and rallies; posters of rainbows and natural views with green messages; posters of semi-clothed women on motorcycles. There was a mass of books on one wall – alternative healing, crystals, astrology, conspiracy theory, mythical history, mixed with specialist manuals on photography. The floorboards were covered in brightly-coloured dhurris, and the bed – a double futon – was tucked away into a corner. At the far end of the room was a low door.

'That's where he keeps most of his photographic stuff,' said the waitress. 'It's locked.'

'Sure.' Natasha looked about the bedroom vaguely, but could see no sign of the photographs she was looking for. 'Perhaps it would be easiest if I left him a note.'

She discovered a pad of paper, and wrote down: 'Hi. Give me a ring as soon as you get in. It's important. Love, Tash.' She put the note down on a low coffee table, which had been painted with a marbling effect in black, white and pink, held it in place with an old coffee cup and an amethyst geode, then thanked the waitress and left.

On her way out she noticed that Jon's motorbike, a battered old Triumph that he had bought years ago in England and loved like a child, was chained up in its usual place, round the back. The sight was reassuring – he would never leave town for long without his bike.

After a few moments' thought she went on to his favourite bar, but no one she asked had seen him for a couple of days. They simply shrugged. In Christiania people often disappeared. It was the way of things. No one was surprised or concerned, or even particularly interested.

That evening Natasha realized that she was worrying. In an attempt to take her mind off things, she put on Swedish television, which was showing a season of Andrei Tarkovsky films, and lost herself in the bleak, surreal world of *Stalker*, with its underlying sense of a nightmare about to explode, like the prickling of hair on your neck when you hear nothing, yet feel certain that someone – or something – is behind you. Poised to strike.

Her curtains rustled in the slight breeze from the open window.

When she woke up Natasha almost phoned Frederik, then remembered that in Canada it was only three in the morning, so she went in to the physics department, and explained that she wanted to check over some of the ice core samples she had brought in ten days earlier. Ebbe, the old lab technician, looked at her with his usual stiff, puritanical expression.

'Yesterday afternoon Dr Anderssen came in and said that no work is to be done on the samples until independent researchers are available to work on them.'

'What?' Natasha stared at him in disbelief.

'That is what the doctor said.'

'You mean he thinks we're going to fix the results somehow?'

Ebbe said nothing. His expression did not change.

'For Christ's sake,' said Natasha. 'I just want to have a look at two of the samples – it'll take a couple of hours at the outside. You can stay with me if you don't trust me.'

'I have work to do,' said Ebbe, unbendingly. 'And at this time, when the university is not yet in term, there is a lack of staff.'

'Ebbe, please.'

She gazed at him imploringly. His stone face showed nothing, but after a moment he turned away.

'If I had not happened to have been here, I would not have been able to give you the doctor's message,' he said. 'Now I must go and do some essential maintenance work in the electronics block. I will return at midday.'

'Thanks.'

He did not respond, but walked stolidly away.

Natasha waited until he had left the block, then went over to the

great refrigerated storehouse where the ice cores were stored in metal cylinders. She put on an insulated white coat with hat and gloves, extra disposable gloves, and finally a white cup mask which covered her mouth and nose, then went inside. She knew where the samples she wanted were, and drew them out, checking their reference numbers. The labels showed no one had looked at them since she had deposited them.

There were only two cores marked LS in Frederik's characteristic, heavily slanted writing. Natasha pulled out the first cylinder, removed the 13.2 centimetre diameter core from its thick plastic coating, put it in the insulated trough, and studied it for twenty minutes, first by naked eye, then using a fine lens. As far as she could see in such a brief study there was nothing exceptional about it – except perhaps the extent to which the layers had been twisted and distorted by the movement of the glacier, and a faint red staining over some of the most recent ice. Certainly nothing that stood out enough to make a call to Canada about. Later it would be analysed by slicing off tiny sections, and either melting them to establish their chemical make-up, or looking at them in far greater detail, using a powerful electron microscope, but there was no time for that just now.

She packed the first core away again, and pulled out the second, putting it in the trough stand. It seemed very similar to the first sample, with the same faint staining. Working her way down the ice core, she paused and looked closely at a large impurity enclosed within the ice. Initially she thought it was simply a stone – glacier samples often had small stones in them, sometimes ground into bizarre and unlikely shapes by the ice. But this one seemed different.

She got the lens to look closer.

Encased within the ice core was a pinkish-purple object, perhaps an inch long, and half that wide. Suddenly Natasha let out a retching sound, and shook her head violently. There was not the slightest question of what she was looking at. It was the severed tip of a human finger.

4 At the Club

IT WAS DARK in the corners of the large, rectangular room. Closer to the centre, the flashing light show – purple, lime green, rose, indigo, orange – reflected off white formica tables and plastic chairs in a rich kaleidoscope of colour, sending dazzling sparks crawling over the walls and through the air, like fireflies. The air was hot, moist and stale, infected with smoke and the thick smells of beer and junk food. Despite the noisy air conditioning, it felt as if it had been breathed too many times. Bass-heavy music issued from the speakers, which lined the walls, and were mounted in a stack before the small, tight stage, with its old-fashioned mikes on stands, and red lights glowing faintly from the amplifiers. Three geriatric-looking video screens, equally spaced down the right-hand wall, were showing an equally geriatric video of some nondescript American heavy metal group. At the far end of the room was a bar, where people massed, four or five thick, to buy drinks. Alongside it was a food counter, with another – rather smaller – crowd collecting burgers, chips, slices of microwaved pizza, ribs, hot dogs and fried fish.

A small, skinny young man, wearing reflective sunglasses, torn jeans, and a sealskin jacket, climbed up on to the stage and went over to one of the microphones. He began to speak, but the microphone wasn't hooked up, and the music and conversation ensured he was completely inaudible. After a minute or two, a roadie ambled on, and fixed the microphone. There was a deafening roar of noise, followed by an ear-ripping screech of feedback.

'OK, guys and girls,' said the man. 'Getting ready to dance Tuesday night away here at Salo's. OK? OK. But . . . wait a second man, give me a moment . . . there's a couple of things that need saying first. Now you all know that Salo's gives you the finest live music for a thousand klicks, isn't that right? The sharpest, the fastest, the greatest hard rock café in this God's own country of ours. Come on, let me hear you say it, Salo's is where hip's at. OK. OK. Good. Last week it was the legendary Zikasa, and what a set that was. I don't know about you people, but my head's still some other place – and that's where I like it. OK, now for those of you who've been living on the ice-cap for three months and haven't heard, the Saturday after next it's sexy Danish folkie, Claudia, owner of the saddest voice, the longest legs and the tightest arse this side of Nicole Kidman – but don't tell her I told you so, she likes it to come – and I mean come – as a surprise. And after that we can look forward to our old favourites, Sumi. The best rock band in the land.'

'The second best,' someone shouted out from the audience.

'Well, whatever. It's pretty good stuff anyway, huh? Enjoy. But tonight – and tomorrow night too, as you all know – we have two men and a woman who, between them, can make enough noise to wake the dead – and that even includes you guys at the back. Yes, from the waist down. As you know, I'm talking about Ulo, the tip of the harpoon that's going to rip you all apart. And I mean that. But I've got to tell you that they've been held up a bit, and we don't expect the set to start for another hour or so. So get down some beers, get some food, and prepare for a real special, special evening here at Salo's. OK? OK!'

He pointed his finger at the crowd, self-consciously adjusted his sunglasses, then climbed down.

Few people had taken much notice of the announcer, but among those who had was a good-looking boy in his mid-teens, holding a can of Carlsberg with the stubborn air of someone who had spent more than he could afford, and intended his drink to last a long time. He glanced around, then took a bite from his hot-dog. The video screens were now showing Cher's strange, artificially sculpted face, though the music over the speakers was still locked on the previous song.

Three young men, aged perhaps twenty, were standing close by the boy. Their swaying postures and dull eyes showed they had already been drinking heavily, although it was only mid-evening. The boy, his attention drawn by their loud voices, leant back against the wall and watched them, sipping minutely at his own drink.

'So how about it being your turn to get the beers in, Neilsie?' said one of them, who had short, bleached hair and stud earrings, to the smallest of the three, a sharp-featured, nervous-looking man. 'You've been keeping pretty quiet.'

'It's OK, it's OK,' said the third man. He was unshaven, and had a great mop of loose black hair, that hung well below his shoulders. There was a smug, rather vacant smile on his face. 'It's no problem. I've got the money.'

'You, Steen?', said the bleached blond, obviously unconvinced.

'Sure, Josef. Me. And you can get a slice of it, so just you go fight it out at the bar. You see, I'm busy keeping my eyes open for talent. And there's sure some of that around.'

'You mean her?' said Neilsie, nodding at the video screen, where Cher had already disappeared to be replaced by Britney Spears in a red rubber catsuit, declaring – out of synch and apparently untruthfully – that she wasn't that innocent.

'No. I mean real live talent.' Steen brushed back his hair, then reached out a long arm, and pulled a heavily made-up girl in short skirt, crop top, high-heeled slingbacks and leather jacket over towards him. 'What can I get you, honey?'

The girl looked him up and down with calculating eyes.

'What are you offering?' she said.

'Depends how nice you are to me. What's your name?'

'Katinka. And I can be really nice – in the right circumstances.'

'Show me.'

'OK.' She reached up and kissed him hard, and open-mouthed.

'I'm convinced,' said Steen. 'You and me are going to have a good time tonight. We're going to burn money.'

'You said it,' Katinka replied, allowing him to pull her close, and nestling in against him. Steen's large hand ran up and down her back.

'What makes you so rich and successful, suddenly, Steen?' said Josef, looking enviously at Katinka, who gave him a cat-like smile, and wriggled enticingly under Steen's caresses.

The long-haired man shrugged his shoulders loosely, and tried to look cool, but only succeeded in seeming foolishly pleased with himself.

'Don't you worry about that.'

'But I do worry. Last week you couldn't afford to buy a single drink for yourself, and you had to borrow 200 kroner off me. Money you still haven't paid back. What's happened since then?'

'I got smart.'

Josef laughed ironically.

'And a flock of seals flew over my house yesterday. Get real, Steen.'

Steen shrugged.

'Just because you've never seen money like this,' he said, and with a sudden movement he pulled out a fat wad of notes, and flourished them in Josef's face. 'Get real yourself, sonny, and then maybe you'll find out exactly what it does mean to be smart. That is – like me.'

'Hell!' exclaimed Josef, startled. 'Some of those're 1,000K notes.'

'They're all thousand K. Look and weep!'

'Nice,' purred Katinka. 'Very nice.'

'You said it.'

'How the fuck did you get that money?' demanded Josef.

Steen took another large mouthful of beer, and smirked.

'A friend of mine flew in this morning, and thought that it looked as if I needed a bit, so he gave it to me.' He ran his hand over Katinka's neck. 'Just like I'm going to give it to you, honey.'

'Promises, promises,' she said.

'Talk sense,' growled Josef. 'How did you get it?'

'Like I said, I was given it.'

'Crap! Tell me the truth.'

'Oh no, Josef, my boy. I'm not such a sucker.' Steen stuffed the notes back in his pocket, then turned his attention back to Katinka. 'It's going to be a seriously good night.'

'You said it,' whispered Katinka, and kissed him again, longer and harder. Steen's big hand ran up and down her black-stockinged leg.

'Not so fast,' growled Josef. He reached out and gave Steen a sharp push. 'How did a useless prick like you get that sort of cash? I want to know.'

Steen, his arms still round Katinka, came up for air, and looked round at Josef, his smirk back in place.

'Wouldn't you like to know?'

'That's what I just said.'

'OK then. Maybe it's because, like I said, I am seriously smart, and you are a waste of space.'

Katinka giggled.

'That's telling him,' she said.

'Wasn't it though,' said Steen.

'No. It wasn't,' snarled Josef. 'I want the fucking truth, man.'

'Well, too bad.'

'Too bad for you, yes,' gritted Josef. 'You stole it, didn't you, Steen, you lump of sealshit?'

The man with the long hair ignored him, returning to his tight clinch with Katinka.

'Calm down, Josef,' intervened little Neilsie, putting his hand on his companion's shoulder. 'We just came out for a good time – and Steen's having one. That's nothing to get so angry about.'

'So walking off with thousands of kroner is nothing to get angry about? Is that what you're saying?'

'No. Of course not. But—'

'But I'm not going to be patronized by this crooked bastard.' Suddenly Josef grabbed Katinka, and pulled her savagely away. 'Get out of here,' he snarled.

'Piss off!' she snapped back at him.

'What the fuck are you doing, Josef?' growled Steen. 'What business is it of yours how I spend my money?'

'Guys, guys,' said Neilsie, holding out his hands placatingly.

'*Your* money,' said Josef, pushing Neilsie aside. 'Don't make me laugh.'

'Are you accusing me of stealing?'

'Got it, son. Well done. It finally penetrated your concrete skull.'

'Fuck off, Josef!'

'That's what you'd like, isn't it? And I know why, too. Because that way you can forget all about the 200 kroner you owe me.'

Steen laughed.

'If you want some money, then you'd better say please, nicely,' he said, pushing his face towards Josef's.

'Like fuck I will.' Josef lunged out and thrust his hand into the pocket where Steen had stuffed the money. 'I'm taking what I'm owed.'

'In your dreams!' retorted Steen, grabbing Josef's hand. There was a moment's silent struggle, then Josef wrenched his hand away, gripping the wad of thousand kroner notes.

'Give me those back, you thieving bastard.'

Steen drove Josef's arm up behind his back, and Josef retaliated by slamming his forehead into Steen's face. The long-haired man staggered, and loosened his grip on Josef's fist, which held the money. Josef ripped his arm clear, then a moment later let out a shrill scream of pain.

Katinka had driven her stiletto heel down hard on his foot.

The entire wad flew up into the air, and was caught by the draught from the air conditioning. A moment later the air was full of fluttering notes.

Steen gave a bellow of fury, grabbed the hobbling Josef, and punched him full in the face, knocking him to the floor, where he slumped back, blood gushing from his nose.

Behind them there was a wild scrabbling, as first one person, then another, snatched at the money. Steen swung round, let out another inarticulate bellow, and turned on the people who were kneeling on the floor, picking up the money. Within moments the centre of the club had become a seething, struggling mass of people, fighting, punching, clawing, pushing, butting, grabbing for the crumpled notes. One table was knocked over, then someone fell on a second, and it cracked and broke. A chair was flung across the room. Plates of food and cans of beer went flying.

The club announcer hurried back on to the stage, and begged for people to settle down, but no one took any notice.

Ten minutes later the police arrived. While one policeman stood by the door, to prevent anyone getting out, the second – a short, squat, powerful man in his mid-forties strode into the middle of the fight, efficiently pulled apart two or three struggling men, then surveyed the wreckage.

'Right!' he said. He spoke quietly, but all the fifty or sixty people there listened to him. 'That's it for the night.'

'The bastards have stolen my money,' objected Steen, pale-faced and shaking.

'That's true,' shouted out Katinka. 'I saw them doing it. Grabbing his thousand K notes.'

'Your money was in thousand kroner notes?' said the policeman.

'That's right.'

'OK. We'll see then. Everyone gets searched as they go out . . .'

'But the Ulo concert,' objected the club manager, who had emerged from an inner office wearing a suit, bow tie, and harassed expression. 'It's going to start in half an hour.'

'It will have to wait,' said the policeman simply.

'But look, sir—'

'My name is Sergeant Tomas Larsen.'

'Sergeant Larsen, we have to get this concert under way.'

'Not until every person here has been searched for thousand kroner notes, and I have found out just what's been happening. After that, you can have your concert.'

'All that'll take hours.'

'Then you'd better encourage your patrons to settle down and get on with it.'

Half an hour later, Larsen was sitting at the manager's desk. In front of him was the fifteen-year-old boy, still clinging to his all-but-empty can of Carlsberg.

'I didn't expect to find you here, Edvarth,' said Larsen calmly.

'It's the place to go,' said the boy.

'And the place for fifteen-year-olds to drink?'

'Didn't you do it when you were a kid?'

Larsen looked at him thoughtfully, tapping his teeth with the nail of his little finger.

'Don't tell my mum, Tomas,' pleaded Edvarth, abruptly dropping the mask of defiance. 'She'll go nuclear. I'll be grounded for weeks, and with me going to this new school next week, everyone's certain to find out, and then they'll have me down as a total wuss. Christ! It's not easy at the best of times, and this'll kill me stone dead before I've even arrived at the place.'

Larsen continued to look at him without speaking.

'I saw it all,' said Edvarth hastily. 'How the fight started. Everything.'

'Tell me.'

A little later, Larsen was still sitting in the manager's office, but now it was the long-haired Steen who was in front of him. And Larsen was counting out crumpled and torn banknotes.

'Seventeen one-thousand kroner notes,' he said. 'Is that it?'

'No,' said Steen, tossing back his hair angrily. 'No, it's not. I told you before, I had twenty.'

'Since when, you've clearly had a few drinks, son. And maybe so have your friends. I reckon that's where your missing money has gone.'

'No. I should have twenty, for fuck's sake.'

'Don't swear at me, son. We've searched everyone here, even the manager, and seventeen is all we could find. Plus a few in the cash till – which you probably spent. Just be pleased to get seventeen back, and next time don't be such a bloody little fool. There's not much thieving in Nuuk, but if you flash money in people's faces, then some of them are likely to have a go at it.'

He pushed the notes towards Steen. As the young man reached out for them, Larsen suddenly clamped his hand back down on the money.

'What exactly do you do, Steen?' he asked, staring into the young man's open, rather stupid face.

'What's that to do with you?'

'If you want to argue the matter, then we can continue our discussion at the police station,' said Larsen.

From outside came a few crashing chords, as Ulo tuned up for their set. Steen glanced over his shoulder, towards the closed door, then surrendered with a shrug.

'I work at the Spar supermarket on Tjalfesvej,' he said.

'You seem to have an awful lot of money for a job like that,' remarked Larsen.

'I won it in a poker game.'

'You must be very good at poker.'

Steen shrugged.

'I think maybe I was just lucky.'

'Very lucky.'

Larsen raised his hand, and let Steen take his money.

Ten minutes later Sergeant Larsen left Salo's Club. It was dark outside, and there were few people around. A car drove past at speed, swinging from side to side, and followed almost immediately by another.

There was the roar of a third, coming up behind them. Larsen took shelter in the shadow of the next door building, leant back against the wall and thought. He had still not made up his mind whether to tell Risa, his partner, where he had found her son.

Suddenly, light spilled out into the street as the club door opened again, and two girls came out, giggling.

'Aren't you going to stay any longer?' one of them said.

'No. It's best not to push your luck.'

'What do you mean?'

'You know, Leah, I really love these new slingbacks of mine. My mum told me I was out of my mind to get them, that they were a complete rip-off for 800 kroner, but she was so wrong. They've already paid me back, and a lot more.'

'What're you talking about, Katinka?'

'Well, for one thing they're excellent fighting shoes – I took out a guy with just a single stamp. I shouldn't think he'll be walking straight for a week.' There was a laugh. 'And for another, I think maybe they're lucky.'

'Lucky? Like how?'

Larsen could just see them on the far side of the road. They had both stopped, and there was the sound of a zip being pulled down, as one of them reached inside her jacket. Then a gasp from the other girl.

'Bloody hell!'

'Amazing, isn't it. I really can't understand how these thousand-kroner notes got stuck inside my bra. And of course I'd like to give them back, but I don't have a clue who they belong to.'

'But they belong to that boy. They must do.'

'I can't see that. And even if you're right, Leah, for one thing I don't know where he lives. And for another, where did he get it all from?'

'I heard him say that he'd got all his overtime pay in a lump.'

'That's what he said, yeah. But he also told me what he did – he's got a part-time job at the airport, handling the baggage. A friend of mine did the same thing last summer, and you don't earn money like that. Wherever that boy got his cash, it wasn't straight, you can bet your life on it.'

'So . . . ?'

'So let's go spend our share.'

'Well . . . oh, OK. Why not?'

The two girls put their arms round each other, and walked jauntily off along the street. Larsen wondered whether to follow them, but it seemed likely enough that they were right, and Steen had come by the money illegally. Why else should he have told two different stories? Anyway, the incident was over, and despite taking a long list of names and addresses, Larsen had decided not to take any action. Alcohol-fuelled fights were common enough, especially in the autumn.

But the question of where Steen had got his money kept nagging at Larsen. It couldn't have been from working overtime. And not from a game of poker either – the only people in Nuuk who might play poker for thousands of kroner, men who whiled away the long winters in obsessive gambling, were far too smart to allow a dumb kid like Steen to get lucky.

Which left his job. Baggage handler at Nuuk airport. There might be some interesting ways of earning money at that job. And suddenly Larsen wished that he had asked Steen a few more questions.

5 Investigation

CHIEF THOROLD'S FACE was a rock wall, showing nothing. His eyes sea ice.

'I'm seconding you for special work, Sergeant Larsen,' he said abruptly.

'Yes, sir.'

'As you know, just under two days ago First Air flight 608 to Iqaluit, with twenty-three passengers and crew on board, vanished. No trace of it has been found, but the Canadian police have asked for us to provide someone to link with their investigations. As the most fluent English-speaker in the department, I want you to provide that link.'

'Yes, sir.'

'You will be answering to Inspector Philippe Barre. Jette has his number. I would recommend that you contact him immediately.'

'Yes, sir.'

'That's all.'

Larsen left. Two minutes later he was talking to Inspector Barre. The Canadian had a big, friendly voice.

'Good to hear from you, Tomas. Let me bring you up to speed on things so far. First Air flight 608 vanished off our radar screens at 15.27 on Tuesday. The last transmission anyone received from the plane was control at Iqaluit, at 15.09, when the pilot said everything was fine, weather was good, and they expected to arrive in about ninety minutes. There was no mayday, nothing. The radar records are, frankly, a bit fragmented – there's been some intensive electromagnetic activity in the region, and you know what things can be like up here. As far as we can gather, the plane disappeared over one of the deep stretches of the Davis Strait. We have got a Canadian navy fishery protection ship that'll help investigate, but it could be a long while before we know anything solid.'

'What do you think happened, sir?'

'You don't need to call me sir, Tomas. Ray is fine for day-to-day use.'

'Thank you.'

'OK. Now, no one wants to make guesses – and sure as hell we won't be making them in the face of the media – but the theories we incline to all point towards something pretty catastrophic. Planes just don't vanish like that, without any warning at all. So we're not looking for survivors, I'm afraid. What we *are* looking for are explanations. So far the most likely possibilities we've come up with are some disastrous structural failure in the aircraft or its engines, or just possibly sabotage – though no one can think of any reason why that should have happened. There are a few other wild suggestions out there too: a suicidal pilot, or one that had a heart attack; massive radar error; mid-air collision with some other plane that did not register; pilot error, possibly caused by mirage – the Fata Morgana for example. Jesus knows, the easiest explanation of what we have so far is probably missile attack.'

'But, sir—'

'Yeah, OK. Don't tell me – crazy! But we have to be aware that there are a few crazies out there – though hopefully they're not armed with SAM missiles. Anyway, back to the beef. As far as we can tell, the plane vanished in Canadian air space, so we'll be doing most of the investigation, but what I'd like you to do is firstly to check out this list of names – that's the people on the flight who weren't Canadian nationals – and talk to their relations. Nasty job I'm afraid, but most of them will already have been contacted. Secondly, it could be useful to find out something about just who was on the plane – what they did, if they had criminal records, etc. etc. You can guess the kind of stuff I'm talking about. Be tactful, but we do need to look at that side of things, just in case. I mean, to put it crudely, if a top Russian military leader was on the flight, then maybe we've got a reason for what happened.'

'Do you think there was a Russian military leader on the flight?'

Barre laughed.

'I was just using that as an example. Anyway, the third, and probably most important job, is looking into everything you can find out about that particular plane, and the crew. The flight started in Nuuk – so that's probably where you'll want to begin – and then stopped off at Sondrestrom . . .'

'We call it Kangerlussuaq.'

'Well, I'm not even going to try to say that; it'd probably twist my tongue permanently. Anyway, try nosing around there too. I don't know what you might expect to find, but certainly question anyone connected to the flight – OK?'

'OK.'

'I'll fax the relevant stuff straight through to you. Thanks. Be in contact.'

He cut the connection before Larsen had the chance to say goodbye.

The passenger list of First Air flight 608 was nineteen people, of whom thirteen had a note scribbled beside them – Canadian. So that left six: four native-born Greenlanders, and two Danes. Larsen contacted the relevant police stations to check that the relations had been given the news, then went himself to the two addresses in Nuuk.

At the first one, a small house overflowing with young children, he was met with stunned disbelief, then an explosion of weeping. Larsen stayed for over an hour, doing his best to comfort the family. The second was an apartment in a very new block in the suburb of Eqalugalinnguit on the northern edge of the peninsula. The woman there already knew, and was grimly polite. Larsen stayed for barely ten minutes, then returned to the police station.

Although it was getting late, Larsen called up the names of the four Greenlanders on the flight, and checked through the police computer records. Only one appeared: a charge of being drunk and disorderly three years before on National Day, for which he had received a caution. Larsen moved on to the main Danish files for the other passengers. One was a man in his late twenties, who had inherited a substantial fortune from a well-off Danish industrialist, and had seemed to spend it globetrotting. The other, Professor Frederik Dahl, was a well-known biologist, who specialized in the Arctic, and had visited Greenland many times. That was as far as the records went. It seemed there were perfectly valid reasons for both of them to have been on the flight.

When Larsen went home, it was already dark. His small apartment felt cold and empty. He rang Risa.

'Why won't you come and live with me?' he asked.

'You know the answers to that,' she said patiently.

'Remind me.'

'There isn't room.'

'Edvarth could sleep in the sitting room.'

'My son doesn't want to sleep in the sitting room. Edvarth has rights, and what a fifteen-year-old needs is space – space to go and brood and feel sorry for himself.'

'Sure, but—'

'You can't do that in your mother's lover's sitting-room. And you can't do that when you know that your mother and her lover might be having sex just at the time that you're feeling depressed because you're spotty and girls won't look at you.' She rode on, over his attempted interruption. 'All children know for a cast-iron fact that their parents don't have sex, or at least not in the way that teenagers do. But if your mother suddenly finds herself a lover, then that's different. OK? So I'm not going to live with you until we can find an apartment that gives Edvarth his own room. That's final.'

'Final?'

'Final. And if that isn't enough, you know I'm on shift work at the hospital, and you're not the world's best sleeper. With me coming in and out during the night, I reckon you'd start disintegrating round the edges.'

'In other words, as long as you're working at the hospital, you won't live with me.'

'I didn't say that. But it needs thought, Tomas.' She paused, then her voice dropped. 'Edvarth's staying with friends tonight. You can come round if you like, but I'll need to get up at six – so there has to be some sleep, OK?'

Three hours later, Risa was lying on top of Larsen, running her finger absently up and down his nose. He was on his back, his head resting on his locked hands, gazing up at the peeling paint on the ceiling.

Slowly, Risa raised herself up and looked down at him, her breasts brushing gently against his chest.

'All right, what is it, then?'

'Nothing.'

'Nothing,' she repeated, and made a wry face. 'Nothing can be a big problem then.'

He shook his head.

'I don't like bringing home work.'

'Neither does Edvarth.'

'I'm trying to be serious.'

'Trying.' Risa unexpectedly kissed him on the mouth, then pressed herself against him. 'Listen, two days ago I talked about that old man dying of lung cancer, didn't I? Well, today it's your turn. What's worrying you?'

Larsen shrugged, ran his hand down her smoothly sloping back, then slipped it between her muscular buttocks.

'Oh no,' said Risa quickly. 'You're not changing the subject. I know Inuit men don't talk about their feelings, which is probably why we have some of the problems we do.'

'What problems?'

'You're doing it again, trying to deflect me.' With a swift movement she got off him, and knelt on the side of the bed, looking earnestly at his face. 'This is important, Tomas. I don't keep everything tight inside me, and I don't want you to be like that either.'

'It really is nothing, Risa. I was just wondering why Thorold has seconded me to work on the Iqaluit plane crash, that's all.'

She shrugged, and began unconsciously to tie up her hair, recently streaked with the copper-red of henna.

'Because you can speak English pretty well.'

'That's not the real reason.'

'Then because he wants you out of the way. The further you are from him, the easier he can feel about himself. If there's any way to get you out of Nuuk, that's probably what he'll do.'

'Do you think so?'

'Look, Tomas. You've known me long enough to know that I don't say what I don't think.'

'Sure.'

Risa glanced at him, trying unsuccessfully to read his thoughts, then shrugged again. She reached up and turned out the light, then rolled over so that her back was to Larsen.

'I've got to get some sleep,' was all she said.

Within a few minutes of arriving at work next morning, Larsen was phoned by Inspector Barre from Iqaluit. It sounded as if the Canadian had already been up for several hours. In contrast Larsen felt he had barely slept at all – though he could not remember waking, except briefly when Risa had left to go to work – and there was an ache in his left shoulder that was grinding steadily up into his neck, oblivious to the paracetamol he had taken.

'Hi, Tomas. How are you? Any news?'

'Not really,' admitted Larsen. 'All the non-Canadians who were on the flight had reason to be there, and all of them seem to have travelled in the Arctic before.'

'OK, that's fine, Tomas. Good work. Now I have some news: our search group found wreckage this morning, flotsam on the water, so we know pretty accurately where the plane went down. About thirty miles off Cape Mercy. And that was smack on the scheduled course.

Larsen had a sudden, gut-wrenching vision of books, handkerchiefs, love letters, toys, all washing in the bitter waters of the Davis Strait. The last pathetic symbols of their dead owners. A bitter taste filled his mouth.

Inspector Barre was still talking.

'. . . which of course means we're back with either mechanical failure or some form of sabotage. Now, Tomas, I think I'd like you to look into the ground crew that dealt with flight 608. That's everyone – air traffic controllers, mechanics, refuelling operatives, cleaners, baggage handlers, the works. I appreciate it's quite a job, Tomas, and most probably nothing'll come from it, but we have to try. I'm sure you agree.'

'Sure, Inspector.'

'*Ray*, Tomas, *Ray*.'

'Ray.'

'OK. Talk to me soon.'

Six hours later the nascent headache had exploded in Larsen's skull. He had already interviewed thirteen people, totally uselessly it seemed, and there were still six to go. The man in front of him was the shift leader of the baggage handlers; a stolid, long-eyed man, who sat motionless, barely seeming even to breathe, answering questions in a slow, hoarse, reluctant voice.

Larsen rubbed his temples with his fingers, closed his eyes for a moment, then turned back to the interviewee.

'OK,' he said. 'Is that everyone then?'

'All the full-time handlers.'

'What about part-timers then?'

'We employ few part-time staff. You've seen two of them.'

Larsen sighed, and consulted his list. Then he frowned, tracing his finger under a name that he seemed to recognize, but could not place.

'Who's Steen Sanders?'

'He was a part-time worker.'

'Right,' said Larsen, with a great effort. 'And did he work on flight 608?'

'He was at work that day, yes.'

'Then I need to interview him. Where is he?'

'He has not turned up for work for the last three days.'

Larsen stiffened, like a husky smelling a bear.

'Go on. Tell me more about him.'

'He is a young man, aged nineteen, who has worked with us since June. We usually take on some temporary staff over the summer, to cope with the tourist traffic. He was expected to work until the middle of the month, but it seems he has already left.'

'Did he give you any warning that he was going to leave?'

'No.'

'Do people often just walk out on you?'

'Sometimes. Employees know that the job is coming to an end, so they simply leave when they feel like it, or if they find another job. It makes my job very difficult.'

'I'm sure it does,' said Larsen, summoning up the appearance of a little sympathy. 'And Tuesday was the last day he came into work?'

'Yes.'

'Could you give me his address, please?'

'I will have to refer to our files. . . .'

It took nearly half an hour before Larsen had Steen Sanders's address in his hand. And by that time he had realized why the name was familiar. It was the same name – and the same address – that the young man at Salo's club had given. The young man who, the night after flight 608 crashed, had been flashing a lot of money around town. And who had lied about where he had got it.

Larsen went straight downtown, to the apartment block where Steen Sanders lived, and knocked on the door. It was eventually opened by a young man, who looked at the greying-haired policeman with a faintly superior expression.

'Is Steen Sanders in?' said Larsen.

'Steen's gone,' said the young man, with a shrug. 'He left a couple of days ago.'

'Where has he gone?'

The young man shrugged again.

'Who knows? He took what he could fit in a rucksack, and left the rest. He didn't tell me where he was going.'

'Are his belongings still here?'

'Sure.'

'I'd like to see them.'

'Who are you? His old man?'

'I'm a policeman.'

'Awesome,' said the young man calmly. 'OK, have a look. There's nothing to see.'

Larsen went through the shared sitting room, with its large television, video, and music system, and a cloying smell of stale cigarette smoke. Beyond was Steen's room. It was fairly bare, though there were scattered objects lying around: T-shirts, trainers, empty bottles, a full ashtray. On the wall was a poster of the north Greenland band, Anguigaq, and an assortment of haphazardly-mounted photographs, mostly showing young men laughing, showing off, drinking, and with their arms around an assortment of girls. Larsen took one of the pictures off the wall and looked at it carefully. It showed a young man, with a mass of long, thick black hair falling down below his shoulders, and a self-satisfied grin on his face. The man from Salo's.

'Is this Steen Sanders?' Larsen demanded, swinging on the young man who was lounging against the door-post, watching.

The young man glanced at the photograph and nodded.

'Sure.'

'And you've no idea where he's gone?'

'No.'

'Or how long he's going to be away for?'

'No.'

'Did he say anything when he left?'

The young man shrugged yet again. He seemed to like shrugging.

'Not really.'

'Not really?'

'You know, just stuff.'

'What kind of stuff?'

The young man's loose, almost bored face, opened out a little. A hint of feeling crept into his words.

'Just the stuff people are always saying. Especially at this time of year, with winter coming on. About how Greenland's a place for losers, and anyone with any sense would get out of here.'

'Had he said that before?'

'Who hasn't?'

'So you didn't take what he was saying seriously?'

'I took it seriously. That didn't mean he could do anything about it, any more than any of us can.'

'It never occurred to you that he might be about to leave Greenland?'

The young man looked at Larsen with his head to one side.

'Has he left Greenland?'

'That is what I'm trying to find out.'

'Why?'

Larsen ignored his question.

'What about his room? Aren't you worried by the fact that you have no idea when he'll be back – or if he'll be back at all?'

'The rent's paid up to the end of the month. If Steen's not back by then, we'll get someone else in. There's no problem finding people.'

'And you didn't guess he was about to go somewhere?'

'I don't go in for guessing much.'

'I'd like to take this photograph.'

The inevitable shrug.

'It's not mine, man. Sort it out with Steen.'

Larsen prowled around the room for another couple of minutes, looking inside the wall cupboard and the chest of drawers, then he picked up a small book and opened it up.

'An address book,' he remarked. 'People who are going somewhere for any length of time generally take their address book. But Steen left his.'

'Maybe he forgot it.'

'Maybe. Thanks for your help.'

'What help was that?'

'If you hear from Steen, please ask him to contact Tomas Larsen, that's my name, at this number. I'll put it up by the telephone.'

'Sure.'

Larsen knew he wouldn't.

However, it only took a few hours to discover what had happened to Steen Sanders – he had taken a flight to Copenhagen two days earlier. Informed of this fact, Inspector Barre said that it might be helpful if Larsen would see if he could track the young man down. Chief Thorold agreed without a murmur.

As Larsen walked slowly home along the muddy road, the first aurora of the autumn cast a nebulous radiance over the sky above him. The northern lights were rarely impressive in the heart of Nuuk, drained and weakened by the street lights, so Larsen walked over to the west shore, near the museum. There he sat down on some rocks and looked out over the the darkness of the Davis Strait.

Gradually the brightness in the sky grew, and a long banner of pearly pinkish-rose light, unfurled gracefully, changing to clear cut ribbons that quivered, shook and rippled, like seaweed on a rising tide, before transforming into great shining curtains, varying from crimson at the foot to white with the faintest possible hint of pink at the top. Gently the curtains continued the beating motion, then the twisting wall of radiance gradually faded into a few desultory flashes.

Larsen got up and set off home. His mood had changed, and he walked lightly and fast, with the feeling of uplift that the first aurora of the autumn always gave him. As if he had been shown a high beauty which was more than enough to justify himself and his life.

6 Iversen Land

DESPITE HAVING SPENT the previous day carrying all the expedition's remaining equipment across the glacier to the airstrip, Jens found it hard to sleep. After tossing and turning much of the night, he finally gave up the struggle and got up with the dawn. It was cold, clear and silent as he climbed the 230-metre-high hill behind the rough stretch of flat stones that served as an airstrip. The sun was almost at his back as it rose, and on the barren slope below him the two tents, and the stack of boxes and packages, stood out sharply.

The arrival of autumn was already signalled in drifts of recently-fallen snow on the far side of the little creek, where a river came bustling noisily down from the hills to find peace in the deep, cold waters of the fjord. Further south, on the edge of sight, shoals of jagged icebergs drifted idly along, parallel to the shore. Beyond them the mouth of Niakornak was lost in mist.

Jens gazed out for some time, pushed a hand through his longish, ash-blonde hair, then suddenly shivered. His face grim, he turned and strode back down to the camp site.

Wendy was sitting outside, by the stone-ringed fireplace, sipping coffee and talking over the radio.

'Who is it?' asked Jens.

'Mathias. They'll be here in a couple of hours.'

Suddenly she sneezed violently.

'Damn!'

She sneezed three times more in quick succession, then blew her nose loudly as Jens poured out some scaldingly hot coffee from the thermos.

'A bloody cold coming on. I always go down with something the moment an expedition comes towards its end.' She blew her nose again. 'Here, you'd better take over the conversation.'

'Hi,' said Jens, taking over the transmitter. 'It's me.'

'So long as you don't start sneezing,' replied Mathias, his voice coming unusually clearly over the receiver. 'That was like a bomb going off in my ear. Anyway, I was just asking if you were sure that you want to quit now. The weather seems to be set fair for quite a few days, and I seem to remember the original idea was for you to leave on the next flight in two weeks' time – which would coincide with the arrival of the Iceland supply ship.'

'Yeah, it was. But we thought delaying that long might be pushing our luck. And we've done most of what we planned on doing.'

'But you're still catching the Iceland ship?'

'Yeah.'

'So you're going to be staying in Ivtoriseq for a couple of weeks?'

'Yeah.'

'Rather you than me. I prefer the hostel at Nerlerit Inat.'

'Why?' asked Jens, frowning.

'Well, the families are starting to come back from their hunting camps, and that means trouble.'

'What sort of trouble?'

'Heavy drinking. They haven't had a drop for months, so when they get back to Ivtoriseq, some of them put enough away to make up for all they've missed over the summer. And the thought of winter coming on seems to encourage them to drink even more. And that means fights. Lots of fights.'

'In Nuuk there's trouble most Fridays,' said Jens, unimpressed.

'Not like Ivtoriseq,' Mathias assured him. 'Last September I had to fly nine people to Pituffik hospital. Serious knife and gunshot wounds – including two punctured lungs, a woman with a fractured skull, and a man who got three bullets in the belly. He died. The year before last three people were killed, two of them in the same night.'

'Oh.'

'Oh is right. But it's your choice. Incidentally, I've got a passenger with me, so it'll be a bit of squash.'

'Passenger?'

'An Australian guy, Dr Chris Goater. He's something to do with UNESCO – been checking that the grants they've given the Greenland government for the national park aren't being wasted. Though how he can do that in a two-day round flight, I've no idea. Anyway, he seems interested in talking to you. See you in a couple of hours. Signing off.'

Jens frowned, and the fingers of his left hand slowly clenched into a fist. Then he recalled himself, and turned the radio off.

'What was that about?' asked Wendy.

'Apparently Mathias has got some UNESCO rep with him.'

'A UNESCO rep? That sounds promising.'

Jens looked at her in surprise.

'What do you mean?'

'There might be a chance of grants for next year,' said Wendy, with her customary enthusiasm. 'We could tell him about some of the work we've done. What aspects do you think are best calculated to appeal to UNESCO? I don't really know what UNESCO does, do you?'

But Jens was staring out into the surrounding hills, with a lost expression on his long face. Wendy waved her hand in front of his face.

'You OK, Jens? You seem a bit weird.'

He started, and shook his head.

'Sure. I'm fine.'

Two hours later a small, white, five-seater prop plane came bouncing down along the the rough gravel runway.

It had barely come to a stop before Mathias got out and came over to Jens and Wendy. The young Swedish pilot was on a summer contract to fly the twin-engine Piper Navajo on a variety of connecting flights up and down Greenland's east coast, and over the summer they had come to know him quite well.

'Hi. OK?'

'Sure. And you?'

'Not bad.' Mathias gave a grin, adjusted his dark sunglasses, and ran a hand through his already thinning fair hair. 'This is a bit of an invasion, isn't it? What with me, and Dr Goater. I hope you've fixed something good to eat.'

'Soup,' said Wendy.

'There's a surprise.'

Jens was looking over to where a second man was coming to join them. He was tall and lean, but strong-looking, with grey, cropped hair, a lined face that was difficult to age, and what seemed like more than a hint of east in his long dark, slanting eyes. But his accent was pure Antipodean.

'Hi there,' he said, shaking Wendy's hand. He had a firm, powerful grip. 'I'm Chris Goater. Good to meet you.' He turned to Jens, and shook his hand too. 'You know, I was delighted to have a chance of coming out here and seeing how your work was getting on. Delighted. I'm real jealous of you two being able to work here in this magnificent wilderness. Fantastic, it is. Superb.'

Jens had expected Goater to be one of those silent, reclusive men, apparently obsessed with the desire to avoid any human contact, who often end up inside the Arctic Circle. Clearly he was wrong.

'You're from Australia?' said Wendy.

'Jesus no. I'm a New Zealander. With some Maori blood in me too.'

'Oh, I thought . . . I'm sorry.' Wendy blushed. 'I have a terrible natural talent for saying the wrong thing.'

'That's OK. Just don't even dare to think of me as an Aussie again.' He gave a broad, toothy smile. 'Anyway, maybe you know I'm here as part of UNESCO's Man and the Biosphere programme, to compile a report on this great national park.'

'It seems a bit late in the season to be putting together a report,' remarked Wendy. 'The winter storms aren't more than three or four weeks away now.'

'Sure, sure,' said the New Zealander, nodding. 'But this'll only be a brief introductory survey. UNESCO likes to be reassured things are going OK, and its money isn't being wasted. Though if you ask me, I'd say UNESCO is still pretty good at wasting money itself. Not that its intentions aren't good. Anyway, that's no business of mine. But I've been hearing some about the work you're doing up here. It sounds fascinating.'

'It is,' said Wendy, enthusiastically, then hesitated. 'But if you'll excuse me saying so, I can't remember anyone warning us about your arrival.'

'Ah, well.' Goater laughed awkwardly, as if he were making an effort. 'You know what things are like. No one tells anyone anything. But I must say I am surprised that you got no prior information. I hope I'm not too much of a shock.'

He gave another broad smile.

While they were talking, Mathias began loading up the plane with the equipment that Wendy and Jens had stacked near the runway.

'Hey, Matt,' called Goater. 'Leave that. We'll all help after we've had some food, and something to drink.'

'I prefer to get it done,' replied Mathias quietly. 'In the Arctic things change so fast that it is best to be prepared to leave quickly.'

'It's also best to be ready to stay where you are,' said Jens.

Mathias put down the packing case he was carrying.

'OK,' he said.

'Pilots!' Wendy said, smiling and shaking her head. 'They're all obsessed with the weather up here.'

'So tell me how the survey's going then,' said Goater, a few minutes later, as they all sipped mugs of scaldingly hot vegetable soup. 'Have you found anything unusual?'

'Actually we've done very well,' said Wendy. 'What we're most excited about is a possible new species of gull . . .'

'Sure. Sure. But you'll need to check that out, won't you?'

'Yes we will. In fact all our data will need some months of intensive work before we really know how we've got on.'

'That's how it is, isn't it? But what about the unexpected?' He gave another of his pleasant, but slightly embarrassed laughs. 'Something weird usually turns up when you're in the wilds doesn't it? I remember one time I was out in the Caucasus mountains, a hundred klicks from anywhere, and there was a pair of shoes, neatly arranged with the laces done up, just standing on the edge of a river. I mean, what the hell were they doing there?'

'Perhaps someone had taken them off and gone for a swim, then had an accident,' suggested Mathias.

'That's what I thought. But why just their shoes? Where were their clothes? And why were the laces done up? It was weird.'

'It's true,' said Jens. 'Once I found a dead seal, frozen but untouched, an hour's march from the nearest river. I still can't think how it got there.'

'How've things been in Iversen Land then?' asked Goater.

'I love it,' said Wendy, with her customary warmth. 'So pure and untouched.'

But Jens shook his head.

'Once you've crossed the glacier, you're entirely surrounded by ice,' he remarked, speaking slowly and quietly. 'Every now and then that makes me feel like I'm caught in a trap.'

'I know what you mean,' said Mathias unexpectedly. He pushed his sunglasses up on to his forehead, and looked about him. 'I had it one time when I was cut off in Danmarkshavn for ten days. I got this sense that northern Greenland has its own rules, which I did not understand. And that those who do not understand, and cannot get away, will die.'

'No one's died in Iversen Land,' said Wendy.

'How can you be so sure?' asked Mathias.

'We checked back on all the expeditions to the area. A couple of men drowned on the fjord to the east of here, but that was over twenty years ago, and no one's ever died in Iversen Land.' Then she frowned. 'Though Frederik did find what he thought were traces from some other expedition that we had never heard of.'

'What happened?' inquired Goater, leaning forward intently.

'You were with him, weren't you, Jens?'

Jens shrugged.

'I didn't see anything. Frederik took some photographs, that he sent off to be analysed. Natasha must have them I suppose. With the ice cores from the glacier. . . .' His voice trailed away.

'It must have been a terrible blow to your expedition,' Dr Goater said after a few moments, shaking his head solemnly.

'What's that?' asked Wendy.

'Dr Dahl.'

'What about Doctor Dahl?'

Goater stared at her, then put down his soup.

'You mean you don't know?'

'Don't know what?'

'That Dr Frederik Dahl died on Tuesday. The plane he was in, flying to Iqaluit, crashed into the sea, and everyone was killed.'

'Oh my God!'

Wendy began to cry, and covered her face.

Jens was still staring at Goater in disbelief, his face pale and taut.

'Are you sure?'

'Of course. They've found a few traces of the crash, but no survivors. I'm really sorry.'

There was a faint mutter, and Jens turned to see Mathias, his eyes closed, muttering a prayer.

'You're sure?' said Jens again, standing up, though he did not know why.

'There's no doubt, I'm afraid.'

'It's the Arctic,' said Mathias, softly. 'We live here only at God's pleasure. When it pleases him to remove his cloak of protection, then there is nothing left for us. Naked we go forward into the other life that is the destiny of all. The peace that is forever under the gaze of the Almighty.'

'He didn't believe in God,' said Jens, eyes wide open, scarcely aware of what he was saying.

Abruptly, he buried his face in his hands and fell silent. It was as if a dense, enveloping pall had fallen over the camp site, cutting everyone off from those about them.

Half an hour later Mathias went over to the plane, and after knocking off a few fragments of ice that had gathered on the wings, he used the radio to contact their destination.

'Bad news!' he said, rejoining the others. 'Heavy mist has rolled in over Nerlerit Inat, and they're recommending we don't fly today. Apparently it should be OK tomorrow – but then that's what they said yesterday.'

'It's not a problem,' said Wendy, dragging herself back to the present. 'We've still got three or four weeks' supplies, and there's a spare store tent you two can use.'

Once the camp site had been prepared for the night, Goater insisted that Jens take him to see the glacier which cut Iversen Land off from the coast. When they came back, two hours later, Wendy sensed that something in Jens had changed. She looked at him and waited.

'Listen, Wendy,' he said. 'I think maybe you were right. There's no point in hanging around in Ivtoriseq for two weeks.'

'I buy that,' remarked Mathias judiciously.

'If we stay here then we could get some more good, solid research in.'

'I don't buy that,' muttered Mathias. 'It's seriously weird to offer to spend more time out in the middle of nowhere, with winter coming on. But then I suppose you're scientists.'

He sounded as if he was speaking of people infected with an incurable disease.

Jens was still talking, taking no notice of Mathias.

'I think we owe it to Frederik,' he said, and there was a fresh, raw energy about him. A sense that he had made up his mind. 'Aside from the extra work we can do, there's something else. Frederik was fascinated by whatever he saw at Lake Sølveig. I think perhaps we should go and see for ourselves just what it was.'

'Maybe,' agreed Wendy cautiously, trying to adapt to this sudden change. 'But what about all our stuff?'

'Mathias can take most of it back. We can operate with a couple of full rucksacks – and the food we've already stockpiled. And from here we can get to Lake Sølveig via those cliffs where Frederik recorded that unusually large colony of breeding barnacle geese. I know the birds may have left already, but even then we could still survey nesting evidence.'

Less than two hours later, driven by Jens's sudden burst of energy, they had taken their departure from Mathias and Goater, and set off down the fjord. Jens, a large rucksack on his back, led the way to the water's edge, with Wendy, similarly loaded, walking a little behind him. Ahead of them the open spaces of the seashore were speckled with great dark boulders, left there by long-gone glaciers.

It was an exceptionally hot day – the sun shone out of a near-cloudless steely sky, and the going was rough. Among the rocks, silvery-green Arctic willow grew to perhaps half a metre. The birches, which reached a similar height, were already turning brown as they felt the touch of winter on their leaves.

After three or four kilometres of silent walking, a steep outcrop, broken by the deep narrow clefts carved by small streams, forced Jens and Wendy up on to the higher slopes, where stretches of frost-shattered stone were concealed under a wiry, hard-to-penetrate mantle of crowberry, bilberry and red cranberry. The bushes, most of their fruits stripped by birds and lemmings, were also turning before the onset of the brief and severe autumn. Higher, up towards the heights of the mountain that loomed over the northern tip of the bay like a lowering creature, the snow-line was creeping steadily, inexorably, down the steep slopes.

'I haven't visited this area before,' said Wendy, joining Jens. 'Do you know exactly where we're going?'

'Sure,' he answered, wiping his forehead. 'Frederik and me surveyed it last month.'

'Oh, good.' She paused. 'You spent a long time out with Goater. Did you talk to him much?'

'Not really. I don't think he'd been to the High Arctic before, and he just kept looking around him, and saying "amazing".'

'What did you think of him?'

'He seemed OK.'

'Maybe, yeah. But. . . .' She hesitated. 'I felt there was a sort of closed quality to him, as if there were things going on inside that you weren't going to reach. And another thing – I wouldn't have ever thought that he was a New Zealander.'

'Why not?'

'He just doesn't seem like one – not his accent so much, but his attitudes. The whole way he holds himself. New Zealanders are easy-going people, life's OK and there's nothing for them to be scared of. But I used to have a boyfriend who was from Iran, Amir. His family had fled when the Shah was kicked out, and come to live in Australia, but they'd had a rough time before they got away. Goater reminded me of Amir's father. Partly his looks, but also a hardness about him, almost a contempt, as if he'd gone through things that most of us couldn't understand.'

'I didn't feel any of that,' said Jens.

Wendy stared at him for a moment, then shrugged.

'Maybe I just imagined it,' she said.

Jens did not answer, but set off again, walking steadily downhill, back to the shoreline.

After passing a long stony spit, which cut off an arrow-shaped lagoon, they came to the head of the bay, where a whole series of glacier-born streams from the mountain massif to the north, came leaping and pouring together to create a barren delta area of shingle and greyish sandy flats, intercut by many different channels. On the beach, a few small waders – dunlin, ringed plover and turnstone – flew away hastily, while little sanderlings, halfway between their summer colours of handsome chestnut and their winter plumage of snow-white, scuttled like clockwork toys just out of reach of the gentle, slapping waves.

Without looking back at Wendy, who was trailing a little way behind him, Jens strode along rapidly on the uncertain, energy-sapping surface, and then waded through the largest of the streams, yellow-grey with sediment. The water rose a little above his knee, and he was forced to hold on to a large rock to make sure that the torrent could not sweep him away. Beyond, the land opened out into yet more sandy flats, tied loosely together by crawling, deep green plants of purple saxifrage, but the beautiful cyclamen-coloured flowers were long gone, and only brown empty seed-heads remained.

A white bird flew from a sandbank. Wendy instinctively stopped and glanced across at it, but the short wings and heavy build told her it was only a glaucous gull. Some distance out on the water was a raft of moulting eider ducks, drifting among the blue-green ice floes. It seemed bizarre that they were still alive, idly swimming, scarcely a thought in their stupid heads, when the huge, warm, dominating personality of Frederik Dahl had gone for ever.

After a little over an hour, Jens turned inland, climbing a steep slope and swinging west, towards the ice wall that hemmed Iversen Land in. Perhaps four hundred metres up, by a knife-edged ridge that enclosed a small, cottongrass-bordered lake, Jens stopped. He got out his binoculars and scanned eastwards, to a distant, ragged point of brown and grey land, which jutted out into the ice-scattered water.

Wendy caught him up and sat down beside him, breathing heavily.

'You were in a hurry,' she said, after a moment. Then, with barely a pause, she added, 'I can't believe he's gone.'

Jens said nothing.

'He was so fiercely and thunderously alive,' she went on, after a moment. 'That loud voice, and all those desperate enthusiasms, and driving certainties, and raw determination. I used to think that being with him was like experiencing a flow of cold air straight from the ice cap. It was as if he could start you into a new, more extreme state of consciousness.'

'Everything revolved round him,' agreed Jens. 'Without him, we couldn't have done anything.'

'And now he's gone. It makes no sense.'

Jens did not want to talk, but it seemed he did not have the choice. With an effort he overcame the dull resentment he felt at his broken solitude.

'Maybe it's just that we can't see the bigger picture.'

'No,' said Wendy bitterly. 'There is no sense in it. The world is controlled by random dice-throwing.'

'What do you mean?'

'Don't you remember when Frederik left, he only just made the plane connection to Nuuk. If those low clouds had stayed for another half hour, then he wouldn't have got to Nuuk, and wouldn't have been on the plane that crashed. Blind bad luck, that's all it is.' She sighed. 'I reckon the Vikings were right – some folk are born lucky, and others struggle.'

Silence sank over them, except for the hissing of the wind.

'What do you think we're going to find at Lake Sølveig?' asked Wendy suddenly.

'We'll know when we get there.'

'I'm glad we're going. Like you said, it's a sort of gesture to Frederik – what he would have wanted us to do. He was strange about it, wasn't he? Even though he wouldn't talk about it when he got back, you could tell that it was sort of suppressed and bubbling inside him. I'd never seen him like that before, but whatever it was, he certainly thought it was important.'

Jens shrugged, then scanned the area with binoculars again. A long-tailed skua, rakish and piratical, was cruising over the hillside, and he watched it. Gradually his binoculars blurred and grew dark.

Jens pulled them away, wiped his eyes, then looked inland. As he did so, he frowned, then fiddled with the focus. Perhaps 500 metres away, he thought he glimpsed a shape, moving swiftly and smoothly among the rocks. But then it grew still.

Suddenly three rifle shots came in quick succession, echoing briefly around the hills, then fading into nothingness.

7 Seana

THE POLICEMAN, SOLID-LOOKING with short hair and a thick neck, did not look impressed as Natasha hurried along the corridor, towards the great freezer.

'You are telling me there was a finger in this ice core?'

'Yes, yes.'

'How could it have got there?'

'I've no idea. The sample was apparently taken from near the snout of the glacier but, even allowing for melting, I'd reckon the core must go back to maybe 1800, perhaps a lot earlier.'

'And where was this finger?'

They had reached the clothing store, and Natasha handed the obviously unenthusiastic policeman the requisite coat and accessories, then put on another set herself.

'Where was this finger?' the policeman repeated, a minute or two later.

'About three-quarters of the way down.'

'So you're talking about something that has been there for about 150 years?'

'It looks like it.'

'This does not sound like a matter for the police.'

'I thought that the police should see it first. Just in case.'

'In case what?'

'I don't know.'

The ice core was still lying in the trough, where Natasha had left it after first finding the finger. As she looked at it, her face changed, and frown lines appeared on her forehead. A faint haze of warm exhalations was gathering around her.

'Well?' said the policeman, looking down at the long cylinder of opaque, greyish ice. 'Where's this finger?'

'I don't know.' She scanned carefully up and down the ice, then shook her head. Her voice was muffled by the cup mask. 'This isn't the right ice core. Damn! Someone else must have been in here and moved it.'

The policeman watched as she carefully put the new ice core back into its plastic covering, then slipped it into the long metal tube. The frown on her face deepened, as she glanced at the reference number on the tube.

'People're so careless,' she said irritably. 'This is the tube from my sample, but this ice core isn't my sample. Someone's mixed them up.'

'How can you be so sure there's been a mix-up?' asked the policeman. 'Doesn't one bit of ice look like another.'

'Of course not. They're completely different. This one does have glacial sand in it, but there's far less distortion, and no discolouration at all. And there's no finger in it either.'

'Right,' said the policeman.

Half an hour later, there was still no sign of the original ice core. The policeman questioned Ebbe, the caretaker, who stated categorically that no one except Natasha had requested permission to visit the refrigerated area that day. The policeman turned on Natasha, his face grim.

'Next time you try something like this, you'll find yourself on a charge of wasting police time,' he snapped.

'You don't understand . . .' began Natasha, for the tenth time at least.

But the policeman was already leaving.

'I did see the finger,' she said to Ebbe.

The technician pulled at his straggly, reddish beard.

'You should have told me first, then I could have double-checked,' he said.

'I didn't need anyone to double-check. There wasn't any doubt.'

Ebbe said nothing, but looked at her through thick vari-focal spectacles.

'You're sure no one could have come in here?' she said at last.

'I didn't say that,' he replied calmly. 'Most of the time I was in the electronics building.'

'So someone must have been here. Lots of people have access to the area, and – as I told that stupid cop – I left the door unlocked. Anyone could have come in.'

'Yes,' Ebbe agreed. 'But if they did, it seems that no one saw them.'

That evening an angry and confused Natasha was walking back to her apartment when a young man with long, blond hair and bare feet, wearing filthy jeans and a battered denim jacket, approached her in the street.

'Spare us some change,' the young man said.

She shook her head irritably, and tried to walk on, but to her surprise and alarm, the young man blocked her way.

'Spare us some change,' he repeated. 'Just a few kroner.'

'No,' she said, feeling her heart beating.

'It'll be worth it,' the young man said, his shadowed eyes riveted to her face.

'What do you mean?'

'I've got a message for you. Give me 200 kroner, and you can have it.'

'Bullshit!'

Abruptly, a tall, well-built man in an expensive suit appeared beside Natasha.

'Is he being a nuisance, miss?' he asked quietly.

She looked up at him with a start. Not for the first time in the past couple of days she had a sense that the world had changed. That affairs no longer continued on their usual, straightforward, repetitive way, and that something – or someone – was introducing a random, dangerous element into her life. It was as if everything had been stripped down to the sub-atomic level, and she was suddenly the victim of Heisenberg's uncertainty pninciple – the impossibility of ever predicting anything – that lay at the heart of quantum mechanics. Yet her instinct that her life was slipping out of joint was linked with another sensation, which she remembered from childhood. When she had got into trouble at school, and had had to see the headteacher at the end of the day, the intervening hours had been dominated by a dull cloud of menace. It felt like that now.

With an effort she pulled herself together.

'No, no. It's nothing. Just another beggar.'

The newcomer nodded, then turned on the young man.

'Get out of here,' he said, still quietly, but with suppressed threat in his well-spoken voice.

The young man shrugged, and began to amble off down the pleasant avenue, into the gloom beneath the lime trees.

Natasha took a breath.

'Thank you,' she said. 'But it was not a problem.'

'These people are growing more demanding all the time,' said the man. 'There have been cases of them assaulting people. One cannot be too careful.'

'Yes. Yes, I know. But he wasn't behaving badly.'

'You still seem a little shaken up. Would you like me to escort you home?'

She looked at him, and met his intense gaze.

'No. I'm fine.'

'You're sure?'

'Yes. I'm sure. Thank you. Goodbye.'

Natasha turned and began to hurry away towards her apartment block. But as she glanced over her shoulder, she saw that the man in the suit was still standing there. Watching her.

After a moment's hesitation she walked straight on past her home, to a bar at the far end of the road, where she stayed until the light began to fade. When she finally gathered up her courage and cautiously walked back along the near-empty street, watching all around her, there seemed no sign of the man in the suit. But, as she reached the front door of her block, suddenly – without a sound – a figure materialized close beside her. It was the young man with bare feet.

'I thought you weren't coming back,' he said. 'Who was that creep?'

'I don't know,' she said. Her breath was coming in quick, chopped-off gasps. Half of her mind screamed at her to run, but the other half was paralysed.

'Yeah. Well, anyway. Like I said, I've got a message for you. But now, after all that shit, the price has gone up. I want 300 kroner.'

'I haven't got any money,' she lied.

'Then you don't get the message do you? Maybe I'll find someone else to sell it to.'

Gradually realizing that she was not under immediate threat of attack, Natasha forced herself to be calm. To keep talking. Perhaps someone else would turn up. Perhaps the man in the suit would return.

'Who's the message from?' she asked.

'Fuck knows. Someone came up to me and gave me this message, he described you to me and told me where you live. He said you'd give me some money. If you're not going to give me anything, then you get fuck all.'

'What did this man look like?'

'Fuck knows.' The young man was getting irritated again. 'Give me the money, or I'll throw the fucking thing away.'

He was clenching and unclenching his fist, and his eyes were glazing over. Quickly she groped in her pocket, but there were only a few coins there. The young man looked at her hand full of change and shook his head.

'I don't want that sort of shit. I want 300K.'

Natasha had more than that in her wallet, but if she took it out, surely he would just seize it and run away.

'Now,' he said. His hand was clenching and unclenching faster than ever.

'My friend's coming back,' she said.

'The creep in the suit, yeah. Maybe he is at that. He's been hanging around here ever since I got here. But what's that to me? Give me the 300K, I'll give you what I've got for you, and that'll be that.'

His words fell like stones at her feet. But Natasha's nerve had gone. She took the brown leather rucksack-style bag off her shoulder, unzipped it, and groped inside. The young man's eyes were on her.

After a moment she found her wallet, and pulled out a note.

'That'll do,' said the young man.

He snatched the note from her, shoved an envelope into her hand, and was gone.

Natasha stumbled up into her flat as fast as she could, then sat down. Her whole body was shaking, but gradually she grew calmer. The man had taken a 500K note, but somehow she didn't care. That was all he had taken.

Only after she had made herself a coffee and sat down again did she remember the envelope. She opened it cautiously. Inside was a ticket to the university teaching staff fancy dress party on Sunday evening. She stared at it in amazement, then turned it over in her hand. On the back, in thin spidery writing, were a few brief sentences:

'I must see you, but people're after me. Come to the party. Make absolutely sure no one can recognize you, but wear this. So I can find you. This is really important. If you're not there, you won't see me again for some time. J.S.'

Sellotaped to the invitation was a cheap, glittery silver anklet chain, with a design of interlocking snakes. Natasha looked at it without enthusiasm, then turned her attention back to the message. J.S. must mean Jon Skalli. But what the hell was it all about?

That night she kept all the windows closed, double-locked her front door, then put a chair against it, and another against her bedroom door, but she still slept little. Her mind was dominated by a distant sound of running feet, but when she woke and listened she heard nothing.

Friday passed in a haze. Natasha sought normality by going in to college to work in the library, but she hurried home well before it was dark. And as she entered her block of flats, her heart froze – for there was a figure standing under the trees, a little way up the road. A figure that did not move, and who was still there three-quarters of an hour later, just visible through the dusk, when she peered cautiously out of her window.

Late that evening, her phone rang. Natasha snatched the receiver, her heart thudding.

'Hi, Tash, it's Seana.'

'Where the hell have you been? I've been trying to find you.'

'I needed a job and a flat, but they're sorted now. How are things?'

'I need to see you really badly, Seana.'

'What about?'

'It'd take too long to explain on the phone.'

'Oh. OK then.' It was almost impossible to surprise Seana. 'Come and see me tomorrow, at the place where I'm working. It's on the Kobmagergade, 541. You'd better make it early afternoon, my boss is going out for lunch.'

Next morning Natasha packed an overnight bag, slung it over her shoulder, and set off to Christiania, to the Poppin' café. It was half past eleven when she got there, and as Christiania did not wake up before midday, the only people in the café were a thin man, who looked oriental, or possibly Inuit, eating a smorrebrød covered with chopped ham skinkesalat, and sipping a light lager, and the long-haired waitress, with the same vague, haunted expression.

'Is there any sign of Jon?' Natasha asked. The waitress shook her head.

'He's not coming back,' she said.

'How do you know?'

'The commune voted nineteen to two that he should lose his room. There was smack in it. We don't do smack in Christiania.'

'What about his stuff?'

'Boxed up. If you see him, tell him to come and get it. If he doesn't, we'll sell it off for the commune.'

'That's not fair,' objected Natasha.

'He knows the rules,' said the waitress.

She walked away. Natasha went outside and looked round the back of the building. Jon's motorbike was still there, so he couldn't have gone far. But what the hell was going on? She felt fear, like a foetus, growing and stirring inside her. She was pregnant with raw panic, and it seemed to grow every passing hour.

She walked slowly back through the muddy, weed-scattered streets of Christiania, past an elaborate acidly-colourful mural of the Buddha receiving enlightenment under a bo tree. A door, set in the trunk of the bo tree, opened, and a couple of children came running out, playing with an overexcited mongrel puppy that barked and jumped up to bite their sleeves. Natasha walked on, past the men with dreadlocks down to their waists, sitting on doorsteps and rolling spliffs; past the sharp young men in expensive jackets and sunglasses, hurrying somewhere, anywhere; past the girls with dirty, laughing toddlers; past the couple stretched out on a small, balding area of grass, locked in an embrace, completely unaware of the world; past the motorcyclist, transformed by his sun-visored helmet and leathers into a Terminator-style automaton. The motorcyclist, who turned towards her as she passed him, seemed to watch her walking by with his invisible eyes, so that fear pulsed within her afresh.

After buying a sandwich, Natasha crossed the harbour by the Knippelsbro bridge and walked past the green roofs, tall windows, and grey-brown brickwork of Christiansborg Palace, where the parliament sat. As she crossed the Hojbro Plads, with its pompous equestrian statue of Bishop Absalon, she glanced to one side, and a helmeted motorcyclist, crouched over his machine a few metres away, suddenly roared off. Natasha found herself almost running up the Kobmagergade, desperate to reach the safety that Seana had come to represent.

The two girls had first met when they were nineteen, at university. Seana had been brought up in the unremarkable provincial town of Haslev, set in the gentle hills of southern Sjaelland, but her mother was a Greenlander, and she had a deep fascination for the Arctic. It was this which had brought the pair together, and for a year they had been inseparable. Then Seana had dropped out of university to go to Greenland, to see her mother's relatives. They barely communicated again for seven years, until Seana had returned to Copenhagen to do postgraduate work, after completing a course in polar biology at Nuuk. Natasha had been delighted, and even more so when Seana asked to join the Iversen Land expedition. But the years apart had opened a distance between them, and they had never quite regained the intimacy they had shared as teenagers.

Somehow, Natasha had expected Seana to be working in a dusty second-hand bookshop, of the kind that filled Fiolstraede, but in fact it was a sharp little clothes boutique called Slik at the less expensive end of the Kobmagergade. The window displayed an odd mixture of African-style skirts in brilliant colours, fake fur and leopardskin, pashminas and accessories, and as Natasha went in, her mouth almost fell open in amazement.

The plump, messy, young woman in jeans and T-shirt, who had accompanied Natasha back to Copenhagen just under two weeks ago, had undergone a transformation. Seana's long, dishevelled black hair had been cut back hard and streaked ash-blonde; her round face was carefully made-up with matching purple eyeshadow and lipstick; and she had three earrings in one ear, two in the other. She was dressed in a tight, tiger-patterned top and a pair of black leather trousers, and was selling a red silk T-shirt to a smartly-dressed woman.

Not until the woman had left did she turn to Natasha, and give her a characteristically broad smile.

'You know what she paid for that top? Eight hundred kroner! There are a lot of people in this town with more money than sense.'

Natasha wasn't interested in other people.

'What's happened to you?' she demanded.

'Nothing.'

'Come on. Tell me about it. For a start you look like you've lost about ten kilos.'

'Everyone looks huge in the sort of stuff we wear in Greenland.'

'What about the sort of stuff you're wearing now, then? You'll need paint-stripper to get those trousers off.'

'It isn't easy to get a job if you turn up looking like the broke post-graduate student I actually am. I saw there were a lot of jobs in clothes shops, so I checked out the sort of shop assistants they used, and then got myself a makeover.' Seana raised her hands almost defensively. 'The pay's good, and . . . it's a change.'

'If you're so broke, where did you get the money for the outfit?'

'Actually I hardly spent anything. A friend did my hair, and the trousers are only PVC.' Seana grinned, and ran a hand down her thigh. 'But I think they're what swung the job. As for the top, I hate it. But my boss offered it to me for free, so I made like I was really thrilled. Anyway, the good news is that she went out around eleven this morning, and won't be back for a while. It's the first time I've been left to run the place.'

'How's it been?'

'Brilliant! I've been doing non-stop business. Do you want to buy anything?'

'It's not really my sort of stuff,' said Natasha, looking round.

'So make it your sort of stuff. I can do you a discount. How about these?' Seana picked up an electric blue pair of skirt-trousers and held them against Natasha. 'They're very popular.'

'Not with me.'

'Sshh. No rude comments about the stock, more punters on their way.'

The door of the shop opened with a tinkling rustle from the wind chimes by the entrance, and three Japanese women came in.

'I'll bet you they spend at least 1,000 kroner,' whispered Seana.

'Is anything in the shop less than 1,000 kroner?' responded Natasha.

'Not a lot, no.'

Seana unleashed a faint, sophisticated smile at the customers, who responded with miniscule bobs of their heads, and then gathered around a line of metallic-sheened pencil skirts, talking softly to each other.

Seana turned back to Natasha, a faint frown on her face.

'You know, dressed like that, you don't do much for the aura of this shop.'

Natasha stared at her in disbelief. Then Seana laughed. But a moment later her expression grew sombre.

'I suppose you came to tell me about Frederik. I know about that – saw it in the papers.' She sighed. 'I suppose that's the risk we all run in the Arctic. Things like that happen.'

The door opened and a fresh shopper came in, a well-dressed, professional woman in her early thirties. At intervals of sharing memories of Frederik Dahl, Natasha watched, astonished, as her friend handled the steady stream of varied customers easily, confidently, pleasantly.

'How can you do this?' Natasha whispered, while one particularly difficult woman was trying on a skirt that was obviously not her size.

'Believe me, when you've sold beer on Friday nights in Nuuk, clothes in Copenhagen is baby stuff.' Suddenly Seana dropped her voice to a hiss. 'The boss is coming back. Look like a customer, then drift out to the café over the road. I'll meet you there.'

The shop owner was a stern-looking woman of perhaps forty-five, wearing a smart, understated business suit, rather than the sort of clothes her shop sold. She glanced without interest at Natasha – who was trying to flick casually through a rail of overpriced jeans – then went over to Seana.

'How's it been?' she asked briskly.

'Good, Mrs Eckersberg. Very good.'

The owner glanced in the till, then nodded appreciatively.

'Well done, Seana. It looks as if I'll have to go away more often.' She glanced around with small, quick eyes that missed nothing. 'My God, you've even got rid of that awful pair of fake leopard-skin shoes. I thought I was going to have to give them to someone for a birthday present.'

'Actually, I've got an order for another pair,' said Seana.

'You're a treasure,' said Mrs Eckersberg, almost smiling.

Natasha slipped out. Ten minutes later Seana joined her in the café.

'Extreme stuff,' she said, sifting down and reaching for the beer that Natasha had bought her. 'I just did three times the usual Saturday business in less than five hours. Mega-commission, and I'm well in the boss's good books. She told me I can go home early today, and wear anything I like out of the shop stock while I'm working there.'

'Is there anything you like there?' asked Natasha, looking at Seana's new spiky hairstyle, and pushing a hand through her own shoulder-length mane of curly brown hair.

'Don't get superior on me.' Seana took another mouthful of beer. 'Some of the stuff's fine. And a few weeks of business like today, and I might actually have enough money to live on. Though it'd take a lot more than that just to pay my debts. Anyway, you've got more to say to me, haven't you?'

Awkwardly at first, then with gathering fluency, Natasha told her friend about the trouble with Anderssen, the ice core with the finger embedded in it, and its subsequent disappearance.'

Seana's long eyes seemed to grow and swell.

'You're serious about this stuff?'

'Yes.'

'But how the hell could a finger get into an ice core?'

'I reckon there's a body there,' said Natasha. 'And the drill happened to go through it.'

'Then it must have been there for at least a century.'

'Unless someone fell into a crevasse, which then closed up.'

'Shit!' Seana took a deep breath, then shook her head. 'Is there any more nasty stuff?'

'Maybe.' Natasha told her of the disappearance of Jon Skalli, the note about the party, and the sense she had that she was being watched.

But this time Seana was not impressed.

'Those hippies in Christiania are totally unreliable, Tash. You shouldn't have given someone like that one of our films. I'll bet you the invite's just a pass he's making at you, and as for the feeling you're being watched, well. We all get that sometimes. It doesn't mean a thing.'

'I suppose you're right,' said Natasha. 'But it doesn't feel like my imagination. I'm sure something's going on. Something's happening.'

Seana looked at Natasha's face for a moment.

'OK,' she said. 'You'd better come and stay with me.'

'Are you sure?'

'Sure.'

'Thanks.'

'But I suspect what you really need is a nice, husky boyfriend. A truly fit guy. But then you don't really meet people like that at the university, do you? Or not outside the sports faculty anyway.'

'I hate sportsmen,' said Natasha. 'Their conversation is so dull.'

'True. But one can't deny that they have other uses.'

Seana was living near Hellerup School, in a neat, characterless orange brick house, with a tiny garden patio at the back.

'It's not mine,' she said hastily, answering the question that had not been asked. 'It belongs to a friend who's got a job in Washington for six months.'

She made coffee, then they sat down in the comfortable IKEA easy chairs. For a few moments there was no sound, except the faint hiss of Seana's faux leather trousers as she moved restlessly.

'Well?' she said at last. 'What're you going to do, then?'

'I don't know. I wasn't thinking of doing anything.'

Seana sipped her coffee, then tugged absently at one of her earrings.

'I suppose you could sit around and hope it all goes away,' she said at last. 'But if you really think something weird is going on, then maybe you should try to find out exactly what it is.'

'But I've already been to the police, I told you, and they didn't believe me. What else can I do?'

'Easy answer. Go to this party, and meet your friend.'

'Seana, you know I hate those sort of things – everyone wearing stupid costumes and getting pissed and trying to get off with people they either can't stand, or wouldn't usually have the nerve to talk to.'

'Sounds like fun to me,' said Seana. She reached out and patted

Natasha on the knee. 'It's OK, I'll come with you. And I can fix what we wear too, I've got a friend who runs a costume hire place, so you'll be well sorted out.'

'It's going to take more than a costume to do that,' said Natasha gloomily, with the certainty that, as had happened two or three times in their undergraduate days, Seana was guiding her into doing something that she really didn't want to do. And that it would end in disaster.

8 A Greenlander in Copenhagen

SERGEANT LARSEN WAS tired. He had spent a sleepless night with Risa, making up for the coming time apart, and his whole body felt over-relaxed, heavy and sluggish. So he sat in the office, sipped strong black coffee, and yawned constantly, waiting for the taxi to take him to the airport.

When the telephone rang, it was almost a relief to answer it.

'Nuuk police.'

The line was very poor and crackling.

'Hello, Nuuk? This is Ivtoriseq. We're responding to your enquiry about the Iversen Land expedition, which was led by Dr Frederik Dahl.'

'Go on,' said Larsen.

'It seems that two members of the expedition are in Copenhagen. The other two are still in Iversen Land – they were visited by a supply plane on Thursday, and they're due to be picked up in twelve days.'

'Could you fix for me to talk to them?'

'Not at the moment. We've been having trouble getting through to them ourselves. Shall we keep trying?'

'Do that. What about the two in Copenhagen – have you got names and addresses for them?'

'Natasha Myklund and Seana Arnason. Myklund's a professor at the University, and Arnason's a postgraduate student. Dr Emil Anderssen is the contact name on the expedition's papers. That's all we've got.'

'Thanks.'

Larsen put down the phone with a sense of satisfaction. Now, at least, there was another reason for his trip to Denmark besides trying to track down Steen Sanders. Then he noticed Jette gesturing at the window.

'Your taxi's outside, Tomas. It's time you were on your way to beautiful, beautiful Copenhagen.' The secretary's round, pert face briefly folded into a scowl. 'Why's the chief allowing you to swan off like this? Usually he doesn't allow anyone further than the airport without a major inquiry.'

'Maybe he just wants me out of the way.'

'Lucky you. And don't forget to give my love to the Little Mermaid.'

'You're my little mermaid.'

Jette raised her thick eyebrows.

'Wash your mouth out, Sergeant. I don't want to listen to such things any more.'

'You don't mean that,' said Larsen, with a wink.

'Get in the taxi,' said Jette, pretending to chase him out of the room.

As she did so, Chief Thorold appeared, his face tight and thin and pale, with a small, compressed mouth. Jette mumbled an apology and scuttled back to her desk. Thorold looked at her coldly, then turned his gaze on Larsen.

'You should be gone, Sergeant.'

'Yes, sir. Sorry, sir.'

'I expect results from this trip,' said the chief, his voice dry and brittle, each word sounding as if it had to crawl out between his clamped lips. 'Although you are presently working in collaboration with the Canadian police, you remain an employee of the Royal Greenland Police Force. Do not forget that, Sergeant.'

'No, sir.'

Thorold vanished back into his office.

Jette gave a grimace, and shook her hand as if she had caught it in a door.

'I don't think he likes you much, Tomas,' she said in a whisper.

'You're not wrong,' said Larsen, picking up his bag.

The taxi driver was lounging against his car, smoking a cigarette. As Larsen appeared, he dropped the cigarette and got in.

'We'd better hurry,' said Larsen, glancing at his watch. 'We've only got half an hour before I'm supposed to check in. Will we make it?'

'*Immaqa*,' said the taxi driver, starting the car with an alarming grinding of gears. 'Maybe.'

The Saturday traffic was fairly heavy, and the plane doors were just about to close as Larsen sprang up the steps.

The Dane shrugged. He wasn't the first, and Larsen felt a sense of mounting frustration at continually meeting people who seemed to think a shrug was an adequate response to a direct question.

'Well?' he prompted, irritably.

'Immigration doesn't check Greenlanders coming into the country. Why should we? They're Danish too.'

'Listen,' said Larsen patiently. 'I have checked with SAS, and Sanders was on the Thursday flight from Kangerlussuaq to Kastrup. Are you telling me there's no way to find him now?'

'You could question all the taxi and bus drivers who were on duty that evening, and you might be lucky enough to find one who took him somewhere. Unless he already had a hire car here, or a friend picked him up. But as far as I can gather, you aren't charging this man with a crime . . .'

'Not yet, but there's a very real possibility he might have been involved in the destruction of flight 608 over Arctic Canada last week, and the death of all twenty-three people on board.'

'What degree of possibility exactly?' inquired the officer.

'Obviously I can't say exactly. But the Canadian police, who are co-operating with us in this inquiry, agree we have good reasons to search him out and question him.'

The officer looked at the photograph of Steen again. Larsen could almost hear the banal thought grinding through the man's mind – that most Greenlanders looked the same. Larsen doubted it had ever occurred to the man that to Greenlanders most Danes looked the same, with their pale skin, blue eyes, light brown hair, and the look of casual European self-confidence.

'Wait here,' the man said casually.

Larsen sat on an uncomfortable tubular steel chair in the overheated waiting room. Through the door into the police office, he could hear the murmur of conversation. After a few minutes the officer returned.

'We reckon the best thing you could do would be to visit Vesterbro. You know where that is?'

'Yes,' sighed Larsen.

'If you go a little way past the SAS Royal Hotel – you can't miss that, it's twenty-two storeys high—'

'I know Vesterbro.'

'OK. Well, third or fourth on the right after the hotel, we're not quite sure which, there's a restaurant called Nagtoralik. Apparently it's a popular spot with Greenlanders.'

'That's all you can suggest?'

The officer shrugged.

'If you want to arrest the man, then we'll put out a search order immediately. Otherwise. . . .'

Larsen took a taxi to a small, unpretentious hotel he remembered from fifteen years before. It seemed unchanged – in fact Larsen suspected that the receptionist had barely moved in the intervening time. After checking in, the policeman lay down and dozed for a few hours. Larsen was still tired when he woke up, but a long shower invigorated him, and eventually he went downstairs, collected a hire bike from the nearby stand, putting his twenty kroner into the slot, and cycled off down the Vesterbrogade.

A poorly-drafted painting of a sea eagle over the door marked the Nagtoralik, which was tucked away on the edges of the red light district. Larsen went down some dimly-lit stairs into an even more dimly-lit cellar – a typical Danish combination of bar, restaurant and night club. After buying a Tuborg, he sat down at a small table, scarred with ancient cigarette burns.

A large, very overweight Inuit man, wearing an expensive cashmere coat, was leaning against the bar, holding forth about his successes in the financial market, while the Danish barman nodded politely, and poured drinks for two other Greenlanders, perched on high bar stools. Within a few minutes a noisy group of half a dozen young Greenlanders came in, and demanded drinks and sandwiches.

'Where's the man himself?' demanded one of them loudly.

'Don't you know anything?' put in the large Greenlander. 'Otoochie never arrives down here till at least eight.'

'What does he do the rest of the time then?'

'Looks after his money, maybe.' The large Greenlander lit a cigar. Behind the bar, the barman discreetly switched on an extractor fan.

When Larsen finished his second Tuborg, perhaps forty minutes later, a few more people had drifted in, some music had been put on, and two barmaids had joined the barman. Larsen went up to the bar, ordered a third beer, then looked ostentatiously up and down the bar.

'Waiting for someone?' asked the large Greenlander, who had been talking to another Greenlander, in a dark blue suit.

'Yes.' Larsen summoned up a worried look. 'It's an acquaintance of mine. He agreed to meet me here, but he's very late.'

'What's his name?'

'Steen Sanders.'

'Don't think I know him.'

'Long hair. Big face. About twenty years old. He's only just arrived from Nuuk. Used to work in the airport there.' Larsen became aware that several other people were listening. He turned and appealed to them. 'Does anyone know the person I'm talking about?'

'Why are you looking for him?' demanded a nervous-looking man with small, bright eyes, and a tight mouth that gave nothing away.

'Do you know him?' asked Larsen.

'I might. And I might wonder who you are.'

'I told you, we arranged to meet here, and I'm just worried that he's late.'

'Bullshit!'

'Ah, good old polar courtesy,' said the big Greenlander. 'Just when I thought it was dying out.' He turned back to his friend.

Larsen took another look at the nervous man, then lowered his voice.

'OK,' he admitted. 'You're right. I don't have an appointment with him.'

'Like hell you don't.'

'But I have to see him. It's important. Could you take him a message from me?'

'*Immaqa*. What is it? And who the fuck are you?'

Larsen ran a hand over his recently cropped hair.

'You're asking me who I am, but you haven't told me who you are,' he said, dropping his voice yet further. 'How do I know you have Steen's best interests at heart?'

'What do you mean?'

'I mean he's in danger. Serious danger.'

Larsen's quick, tight-focused eyes saw the momentary flicker that ran over the Greenlander's countenance before the man's face closed up.

'I don't know what you're talking about.'

'Then there's not much point my talking to you.' Larsen stood up, and swallowed his beer in a single mouthful. 'If you see Steen, tell him to meet me here tomorrow evening. Or he can leave a message at the Hotel Copenhagen on Vesterbrogade . . .'

'Wait!' The man put his hand on Larsen's arm. 'Give me twenty minutes.'

He went over to the door and slipped out.

Larsen sat down again. His eyes flickered around instinctively. No one seemed to be taking any notice of him, but the room was filling up, and there were too many people, and the light was too poor, for him to be sure.

Eventually the nervous man reappeared.

'Come on,' he said.

After a few minutes darting in and out of the grubby, poorly-lit labyrinth of little streets towards Dybbelsbro, Larsen had almost entirely lost his sense of direction.

As they reached a large, run-down nineteenth-century house, a black cat darted across the road almost under his feet, an indistinguishable bundle in its jaws. Larsen's guide opened the outer door, then led him through a tiled hall and up the stairs, which grew narrower at each landing, until they were climbing a twisting little staircase to what must once have been the servants' attic. At the top, the man knocked twice on a thick wooden door, paused, then knocked three more times.

There was a moment's silence, then a husky voice said, 'Is that you, Paul.'

'*Immaqa*,' replied Larsen's guide.

There was the sound of a key turning in a lock, then a rattling of bolts and chains. The door opened, and Larsen and Paul entered a dark, low-roofed room. The impression was of a tent, for the walls and roof were covered in wall hangings, and there was a small curtain half around the bed, and another by the window.

Larsen found himself looking at the face he recognized from Salo's Club in Nuuk. But now it seemed to have collapsed in on itself, and the complacency had been burnt out of it. Larsen could not remember ever having seen anyone looking quite as terrified as Steen Sanders. His whole body, from his head downwards, seemed to be shivering, his eyes were empty holes of panic, his mouth was loose and twitching. His hands were knotted together.

'Who is this,' he demanded, as Paul shut and locked the door behind them. 'I don't know who this is. Why did you bring him here?'

'It's all right,' said Larsen, making his voice as calm and soothing as he could.

'No it fucking isn't,' retorted Steen. 'Who are you? What do you know about me?'

'They know,' said Larsen.

'Who? What? What are you talking about? Who are you?' The words sprang from him like gasps of pain.

'The police in Greenland – they're looking for you.'

'The police?'

'They want to talk to you.'

'Talk to me,' repeated Steen, and his voice cracked and shook. Then suddenly he laughed. But there was not a trace of humour in the sound; it was a repeated series of shallow exhalations that sounded like a marathon runner at the wall – the very limit of his endurance – and it made Larsen squirm inside. This was someone who might crack any time. At any moment.

'Keep calm, man,' said Paul.

Steen was still staring at Larsen.

'How do you know this?' he demanded.

'Why should you care?' countered Larsen.

'What if I don't believe you? What if I know where you come from? I'm not a fool. I've seen you before, I know I've seen you before. And that must mean you're one of them.'

Suddenly he groped in his pocket. A moment later a small handgun was pointing straight at Larsen's belly.

'Hey, wait,' said Paul, seriously alarmed. 'You didn't tell me this was going to get heavy—'

'Shut up,' gritted Steen. 'This bastard is one of them.'

'One of who?' asked Larsen softly.

'You're working for Timur, aren't you? *Aren't you*?'

The gun was trembling. Steen's finger was tensing on the trigger. It was not a time to lie.

'I'll tell you exactly who I am,' said Larsen carefully. 'We met at Salo's in Nuuk. Remember?'

'Jesus! You're a cop.'

'Sergeant Tomas Larsen, yes. And I need to talk to you.'

'You're more likely to be picking lead out of your fat belly,' hissed Steen.

'Killing me is not going to solve anything for you,' said Larsen slowly. 'My partner is outside now.'

Steen swung on Paul.

'You fucking idiot. I told you to make sure you weren't followed.'

'I wasn't. I'm sure I wasn't.'

'Look outside.'

Paul scuttled past Steen into the next door room.

He was back a moment later.

'I can't see anyone.'

'Helge will not show himself unless he needs to,' said Larsen. 'He knows what is expected of him.'

Steen's eyes flickered between Paul and Larsen.

'What do you want?' he said at last.

'To talk to you.'

'What about? You must know most of it by now. OK, it's true – I did put an unregistered and unchecked bag in that fucking plane. But you don't know that it was a bomb. You can't know for sure. You can't prove anything.'

His dominance of the situation was withering away, and his voice was breaking up into a begging, panicky whine.

'You can't prove it,' he repeated. 'Jesus Christ in hell!'

'Tell me exactly what happened,' said Larsen softly.

'There's nothing to tell. This guy came up to me, a Greenlander. I'd never seen him before. He said his name was Harald, and he told me he wanted to get this bag on the flight to Iqaluit – and that he was willing to pay me for it . . . 20,000K, no questions asked. Well, Jesus, that's more money than I'd make in four months. It was just a sort of parcel, that's all. How could I guess, Christ, how could I guess?'

Steen reached up and wiped his eyes.

'What did you think it was?' asked Larsen, leaning forward imperceptibly.

'I didn't know. I didn't want to know. I didn't think about it.'

'Drugs?' Larsen suggested softly, offering Steen an escape route.

'Yes. I suppose so. I didn't really think about anything. But a bomb.' He was crying now. The tears running down his face made him look about twelve.

'That's why you ran away to Denmark, isn't it?' said Larsen. 'When you realized what you'd done.'

'I didn't do anything. It wasn't me.' He paused. 'How many people were there on that flight?'

'Twenty-three.'

'All dead. All fucking dead. And I killed them.'

'What did he look like, the man who gave you the package?'

'I don't know. Nothing special. Quite small, black hair, fairly pale skin, round spectacles. I don't know. Just a Greenlander. I haven't seen him again, but when he gave me the money, I remember what he said: "Make sure you do it. Timur doesn't like slip-ups." Timur. Who the fuck is Timur? Whoever he is, his people're after me. I'm sure of it; they've been asking for me, trying to find me. They want to wipe me out before I can put the finger on them. That's what this is about.'

'You need protection,' said Larsen.

'Protection. That's right. That's why I've got this gun. But I know they're out there. Out to kill me. And I don't know what to do. I don't know what to do.' He turned to Larsen, wiping his eyes and nose again. 'What did he want to kill them all for? Why did he do it? It was him, not me. It wasn't my fault, no one can say it was my fault. I didn't make the bomb. I didn't want to hurt anyone. If I hadn't done it, someone else would have, wouldn't they? I mean, Christ, if you get paid shit, then of course you'll take money for doing little things. How could I guess that he was crazy? It's not my fault. I didn't do it.'

His arms dropped to his sides, and he stood there shaking and crying, helpless.

'You'd better come with me,' said Larsen quietly.

But he had misjudged Steen.

Suddenly the gun whipped back up towards Larsen's stomach.

'Oh no,' the young man spat out between clenched teeth. 'I'm not going with you, cop. You're not going to pin those murders on me. No way.'

'But—'

'Shut up! Shut up! If you move, I'll shoot. God help me, what difference will another death make now?' He was breathing heavily, gripping the gun so hard his arm was shaking. 'In fact maybe that's the only safe way. Yeah. Maybe it is.'

'Jesus, man,' began Paul. 'What the fuck are you thinking of. . . ?'

Steen swung towards him.

Larsen struck. With a single spring, he hurled himself forward, lunging straight for the gun. He caught Steen's arm and wrenched it viciously back. The gun fired twice, deafeningly in the small space, and Larsen felt flame scorch his face. Ignoring the sudden pain, like a whip slashing open his cheek, he smashed Steen's arm to the ground, and the gun spun away over the floorboards into the gloom. Desperately, viciously, Steen kicked out, then smashed his free fist into Larsen's face. Larsen grunted with pain, and blocked Steen's next blow with his forearms. Steen lost his balance and lurched back.

Taking the opportunity, Larsen dived to his left, in the direction the gun had gone – but it had vanished under a chest of drawers. As he groped for it, Steen's foot caught him with sickening force on the side of his head. Larsen rolled away, then winced as another kick thudded into his prostrate body. However, he was ready for the third kick, and as it hit home, he seized Steen's ankle, and twisted.

There was a yelp of shock, and Steen crashed to the ground.

Larsen scrambled away, and got to his feet – only to see Steen opposite him, pulling out a long sheath knife, which gleamed faintly in the light of the single electric bulb, and poising himself.

'I'm going to cut you to ribbons, cop,' he snarled, and drove his knife at Larsen's belly.

Larsen dodged the blow, and tried to seize Steen's knife-hand, but Steen was too fast for him, and his follow-up blow only just missed slicing Larsen's shoulder open to the bone. Larsen fell back, and slowly Steen followed him, until the policeman felt the hanging-covered wall at his back, rustling around him.

Steen attacked again, feinting at Larsen's face, then shifting his attack down to Larsen's body, chopping fast and hard, and slashing through the thick anorak, into the defensive arm Larsen had thrown out.

'First blood,' hissed Steen.

Larsen moved a little to one side, one hand feeling behind him.

Abruptly Steen flung out both his hands at Larsen. The right hand, with the knife, was stabbing down when it crossed over with his left hand, and in a blur, so fast it was scarcely visible, Steen shifted the knife to his left hand, which flicked round behind the right, and then thrust straight for Larsen's chest

At the same moment Larsen wrenched powerfully at the wall hanging, which fell on both of them. Steen, intent on his killing stroke, was caught completely unaware, and his lunge slid past Larsen into the hanging. Larsen clubbed down on his knife-arm with every ounce of his strength, so that Steen screamed. A fraction of a second later, Larsen's back-stroke hammered into Steen's face.

There was a sound of choking, then Steen struggled free of the hanging, and staggered away. As Larsen plunged after him, the young Inuit flung himself straight through the attic window, close beside him. It shattered explosively, throwing splinters of glass everywhere, as Steen vanished into the darkness outside.

'Shit!' muttered Larsen. He wiped his forehead, recovering his breath, then turned to find that Paul was holding the handgun. 'What the hell do you think you're doing?' he growled.

'None of this is my fault,' Paul muttered. 'I'm getting out of here. Stay where you are, cop. Don't even think of moving.'

He darted over to the door, and began fumbling with the chain.

'My partner will be waiting for you outside,' warned Larsen.

'Bullshit!' retorted Paul.

'You're being a fool, boy,' said Larsen quietly. 'Just give me the gun, then come down to the nearest police station and make a statement about what you've seen and heard in this room.'

Paul looked at him with eyes over which a veil seemed to have been drawn. His face twisted into a sneer.

'I didn't hear or see anything.'

'Steen put a bomb in that plane,' said Larsen. 'He was the direct cause of the death of twenty-three innocent people.'

'No one is innocent,' retorted Paul.

'Don't be a fool! Of course people are innocent of crimes. But if you help to conceal what Steen did, then you won't be. You'll be taking on part of the responsibility for cold-blooded mass murder. And any court will find you guilty as an accessory. With a crime like this, that'll probably mean a five-year sentence.'

For a moment Paul's resolve buckled, and the sneer crumbled from his face. Then he regained his nerve.

'I don't know what you're talking about, cop. I wasn't in the room when you questioned Steen, I didn't hear a thing.'

'Look, you must help me on this . . .' began Larsen.

But a self-satisfied smile was spreading over Paul's small, round face, as he unhooked the chain.

'I don't see how I can help you,' he said. 'I didn't hear anything.'

He opened the door, slipped through it, then slammed it shut behind him. There came the sound of a key being turned in the lock, then footsteps pattered swiftly away down the stairs.

Larsen tried the door, then swore and savagely kicked over a table beside him, momentarily letting his seething anger burst through. Bitterly he slumped down on to the bed, and held his cut arm, which was burning and dripping blood. Outside there was no sound at all. At last Larsen picked up a wooden chest, and wearily began to batter it against the solid old door. It took several minutes before it finally cracked and sagged open at the hinges.

9 The Party

IT WAS DARK, and Natasha was beginning to get worried, when Seana came in and dumped several bags down on the floor.

'OK,' she said. 'We have ignition.'

'Did you get the stuff from my flat?'

'Yeah, it's in that bag there.' Seana frowned. 'I didn't like getting it though.'

'Why not?'

'Outside your block there was a car with someone in it, and I got the weirdest feeling that I was being watched.'

'I'm not surprised, the sort of clothes you go around in,' said Natasha.

'I'm serious. And you said it yourself too, didn't you? That you felt like that.'

'I think I was just being stupid. You know how it is in the Arctic – no one looks at you for weeks on end, except the odd fox or musk ox. Being back in Copenhagen after an expedition always makes me feel as if I've been thrown into a swirling, sucking, stream of solid humanity. And anyway, I'm paranoid.'

'Maybe,' agreed Seana. 'But maybe someone is out to get you. Just as I was getting your things together, the front doorbell went.'

'I told you not to let anyone in,' said Natasha, giving up her attempt to keep things light. Her face was tense, and the fingers of both hands had interlocked tightly.

'I didn't. But the lights were on, so they must have known I was there. They kept ringing for several minutes.'

'What did you do?'

'I took the fire exit, and sneaked away down the street.'

'You're sure you weren't followed here?'

'Don't worry. I went off to get the costumes, which took ages, and I looked out of the window a few times while I was there. There was no sign of anyone, so let's forget it and get down to the really important business. We don't have long to get ready.'

'I suppose not.' Natasha stared at the remaining bags as if they contained live snakes. 'We're not really going to go through with this, are we?'

'Of course we are,' said Seana. 'For one thing, I've just been to a massive amount of trouble making sure your costume was the right measurements. Secondly, your friend's expecting you, and he must have some really crucial information, or he wouldn't have sent you that letter. And most important of all, I'm looking forward to it.'

'But why do you think Jon said I must make sure no one recognizes me?'

'Because he's nervy, that's all. Don't worry about it.'

'You keep saying that, but I do worry.'

'OK. Worry then. Who am I to say don't worry? Now, let's check out our outfits.' Seana had forgotten her previous tension, and was as excited and enthusiastic as a little girl. 'Shall I do mine first?'

'Do you want me to help you?'

'Of course not. You have to see the whole thing all at once to get the full impact.' She grabbed the smaller bag, and headed out of the room. Then she stopped and looked back over her shoulder. 'You'd better draw the curtains.'

'Why?'

'Just do it.'

Quarter of an hour later there was a sound of footsteps coming down the stairs. Then the lights went out. Natasha started in spite of herself, and let out a gasp of shock as an eerily glowing skeleton walked in.

Recovering, Natasha laughed.

'It's not Hallowe'en,' she said.

'Is it good?' came Seana's voice. 'Where's the mirror? I want to see what it looks like? Oh, brilliant!'

And suddenly she wasn't there any more. There was only a faint green aura, and an indistinct shape.

'Hey, what did you do then?' said Natasha.

'The skeleton is only painted on one side, the other side is all black. Neat, isn't it? In a dark room you can just vanish.'

The light went back on. Seana was wearing a black Lycra bodysuit, with a skeleton painted on the front in luminous paint. A skull-decorated hood completely encased her head and face, so that nothing could be seen of her except her eyes and mouth – with black lipstick ringing it.

'Well no one's going to recognize you in that,' said Natasha.

'You mean you should have had it?' She peeled back the hood. 'I did wonder, but then I thought it was a bit extreme for you. Maybe it's too much for this party.'

'I shouldn't think so. It's been known to get seriously wild.'

'Like how?'

'One year several drinks were spiked with some sort of hallucinogen; another time a couple of tear gas bombs were set off in the dance hall – nine or ten people ended up in hospital for a variety of reasons, and a good-looking young male lecturer, three-quarters out of his head, was rumoured to have been taken into the garden and raped by three masked women.'

'Jesus! What did the police do?'

Natasha shrugged.

'I don't think they were even called. Nothing could be proved, and most people just thought it was a big joke. But the man left soon after.'

'I didn't realize it was going to be that sort of party.'

'I think things have calmed down since then. Anyway, what's my costume like?'

'Fairly discreet.'

'You mean dead boring.'

'No. Just a bit less visible. Especially in the dark.' Seana absently ran a hand down the outside of her thigh. 'Anyway, you don't like wearing tight clothes, do you?'

'If I was in your outfit, I don't think I'd feel as if I was wearing anything at all,' Natasha said wryly.

'Right. So you've got plenty of stuff to put on. I got the idea from your hair.'

'What do you mean?' said Natasha, touching her shoulder-length locks.

'Well, it's just perfect for a seventeenth-century cavalier.' Natasha stared at her blankly, and Seana sighed. 'Don't you see the subtlety of the disguise?'

'No.'

'Gender. Not only will no one be able to recognize you – they may even think you're a man. Especially with that almost flat chest of yours. But don't forget to talk in as deep a voice as possible.'

'I can't go through with this, Seana.'

'If you say that once more, I'll skin you. Listen, I've always wanted to go to a masked party.'

'Why?'

'Because it'd be really different. Wicked.' She paused. 'Someone once told me this story about one of the Russian empresses – Elizabeth, I think. Apparently she had a maid who looked like her, and if she was attracted to someone, she used to get the maid to make an assignation with the man, then have sex with him herself, while wearing a mask. Or else she'd let the maid do it, also wearing a mask, so that she could secretly watch what he was like in bed, and see if she wanted him the next time. The point was that no one except the maid would ever know who the empress had slept with.'

Seana glanced at Natasha, and smiled at the expression on her face.

'That doesn't appeal?' she asked.

'No.'

'I've always thought it was rather erotic.'

Natasha found herself brooding on the practicalities of the tale.

'I suppose the maid ended up blackmailing her,' she said, after a moment.

'Oh no,' replied Seana softly. 'After a year or two the empress rewarded the woman with a large grant of land in one of the more distant parts of Russia. Then, on the way to her new estate, the maid was murdered. Meanwhile, the empress had found another woman to take her place. And maybe the same happened to her.'

Natasha shuddered.

'That's a horrible story.'

'It's probably nonsense. Now, let's get you suited up – we need to be on our way inside the next hour.'

Natasha tried to object again, but she could feel her resistance being swept away. It had always been like that with Seana.

Midway through the costuming, which Natasha endured stoically, Seana suddenly frowned.

'Have you still got that anklet thing you're supposed to wear?'

'Of course. Here.'

Seana bent down and tried to fasten it, then sighed.

'Hell! I forgot about that – it won't fit round your boots.'

'That's OK,' said Natasha, looking with distaste at the thigh-length top-boots Seana had produced. 'We'll skip the boots. I don't mind going barefoot.'

'You will not skip the boots,' said Seana firmly. 'You have to look the real thing. Anyway, the place is sure to be jam-packed, so if you're in bare feet, you'll probably end up lame for life. It's OK, I'll wear the anklet, then when your friend comes up to me, I'll bring him to you. In fact that should make the whole thing even safer.'

Natasha looked down at the boots again, and made a face.

'I'm going to look awful,' she said.

'Oh, I don't know,' said Seana. 'Just now you're demonstrating the tense, wide-eyed, I-never-see-the-daylight looks that go with classical heroin chic. A bit out of date, but not too bad.'

In spite of herself Natasha laughed.

'I mean in my costume,' she said.

'Trust me,' said Seana. 'And have a drink. Or several.'

Seana drove them to the party. Natasha sat in the passenger seat, and huddled her coat round her. Despite the drink, she still felt crucified by embarrassment. The loose white shirt was all right, but the buckskin breeches were too tight and too stiff, and the boots flapped around above her knees in the most disconcerting way. On the back seat, waiting to be put on at the last moment, were a pair of gauntlets, a large feathered hat, a black Zorro-style mask and, perhaps the worst part of the whole costume, a sword belt complete with sword.

'How can you be a cavalier without a sword?' Seana had demanded. And Natasha had been unable to think of an answer. Other than telling herself that she would never go to a fancy dress party again – and if she did, she would never, ever, allow Seana to pick her costume again.

As they stopped at some traffic lights, Natasha put down the passenger mirror, and looked at herself in it. Her face seemed pathetically open and vulnerable, and the heavy eye make-up only made her look even younger and less certain of herself.

The party was taking place in a large house about thirty kilometres west of Copenhagen, not far from the picturesque town of Roskilde. The house had been built a hundred years earlier by a successful clothing manufacturer, who had tried to make it look as much like a seventeenth-century hunting lodge as possible. Some years back the building had been left to the University of Copenhagen by the last of the manufacturer's grandchildren, and now it served as a conference centre, lodgings for visiting dignitaries, and very occasional party venue.

'Nice place,' muttered Seana, as she followed two other cars – both twice the size of hers – through the elaborate wrought iron gates, and up the long, curving drive, lined on one side by an elegant alleyway of beech trees, and on the other by an impenetrable mass of rhododendron bushes. A couple of tracks to the left gave lightning glimpses of the peaceful waters of Roskilde fjord, while the darkness was broken by lines of fairy lights twinkling in the trees, and around the doors and windows.

Although most of the cars were parked under lights near the main door, Seana drew up near the far end of the wide gravelled space, in the deep gloom under a low-branched cedar tree.

'Why are you making us walk so far?' complained Natasha, who was in the mood to object to everything. 'There's plenty of room much closer to the door, and it might rain tonight.'

'Listen,' said Seana sharply. 'You were told to make absolutely sure that no one recognized you. OK? That means we don't want anyone seeing us get out of the car.'

'You're just enjoying the drama, aren't you? It's not really that serious.'

'Isn't it?'

Natasha thought of the vanishing finger in the ice core. Of the flight that had crashed for no reason and the death of Frederik. Of the mysterious disappearance of Jon Skalli.

'Time to go,' said Seana, who was fastening on the silver anklet.

'But what am I going to do?' objected Natasha, nervously strapping the sword belt over her shoulder. 'I mean, I can't just hang around doing nothing, waiting . . .'

'It's a party,' said Seana. 'Your friend said he'd contact you, so you don't need to look for him. Have a drink or two, chat, flirt. Whatever. Try experiencing that strange thing called fun.'

'But—'

'Hurry up.' Seana was pulling the hood over her face.

Natasha tied the mask on tightly, making sure it would not come undone or slip off, and then drew on her gauntlets. As she did so, she felt – to her own surprise – a dim sense of security; at least her costume provided no possibility of recognition.

Seana was already out of the car, and Natasha put on the feathered hat and hurried after her. Her sword swung disconcertingly at her side, and her boots crunched noisily on the gravel.

In the porch a young man with massive shoulders, a black T-shirt, and a shaven head took their invitations, then waved them through the large wooden doors into a huge hall, half-full and dimly lit. There was a high ceiling, a balcony, a carved wooden staircase and several more doors, one of which clearly led to the dance floor, for flashing brilliant colours came from inside, and the beat of disco music was loud.

'Let's get a drink,' said Seana.

They pushed their way through to the bar, where they collected two glasses of wine, before leaning back against the wall and gazing out over a swirling sea of wild, multicoloured costumes. Nearby a woman had transformed herself into a fish with a sheath dress of glittering sequins that must have cost a small fortune. Two people, who made up a pantomime horse, were talking to a Russian in furs. Someone was swathed in bandages as a mummy, while someone else wore a highly expensive, pinstripe suit, topped with a snarling dog's head. Films had influenced many costumes, ranging from *Star Wars* robots, and *Planet of the Apes* outfits, to Marlene Dietrich in *The Blue Angel*. Others had chosen more extreme costumes, including an SS officer in full regalia; and a woman in a rubber dress and stockings, wearing a mask of the Danish Prime Minister.

Natasha turned to Seana, and found herself looking at an unrecognizable, skull-faced, bone-bodied horror. A black pool streaked with fluorescent daubs that glowed with the radiance of corruption. Her eyes, framed by the lurid mask, appeared as holes into nothingness. Natasha suddenly felt sick, and looked away.

After sipping her wine for a few moments, she realized how stupid she was being, and turned to say something to her companion.

But Seana wasn't there.

Natasha looked around for the skeleton, but could not see it anywhere. She gulped down her glass of wine, then reached for another, but knocked it over.

'Shit!' she muttered, and scuttled hastily away.

At the far end of the hall two opposing mirrors, artfully placed, reflected fantastic garish figures into infinity. Natasha stopped, looked, then realized with a shock that she was looking at herself. The embarrassed awkwardness she felt had nothing in common with the striking, unrecognizable creature, who stared boldly out of the mirror back at her. The vision lent her more confidence, and she went over to the entrance to the disco, and glanced inside. The hazy network of flashing lights lit up ancient Romans, Turks in turbans, cats, soldiers, devils, hook-nosed witches, basque-clad prostitutes, Vikings, bishops, dairymaids, and green-gowned surgeons. But no skeletons.

Someone tapped her on the shoulder.

She started and spun round. The clown behind her – his face concealed under thick layers of paint, his hair tufted and dyed crimson – laughed.

'Did I scare you?' he asked.

She didn't answer. The clown's starred eyes looked at her, and she stared back at him, trying to tell if it might be Jon Skalli.

'You're a woman, aren't you?' he said cautiously. 'It's difficult to tell.'

She nodded.

'Good,' he said. 'Let's dance then.'

It wasn't Jon. The voice was wrong.

'I'm waiting for someone else.'

'So am I. So what?'

He put his arm round her and pulled her next door. As they went, he neatly removed her hat and tossed it on to a nearby hook.

They danced together for a while. The clown was a good dancer, and Natasha found she was enjoying herself. Then they got themselves a drink, and stood on the edge of the dance floor, watching. After a few moments Natasha felt his hand on her buttocks. She wondered if she should object.

Before she had made up her mind, he pulled her closer and whispered into her ear.

'I love your boots.'

'They wouldn't fit you,' giggled Natasha. 'You'll have to buy your own.'

'I meant I've always wanted to screw a woman who's wearing long boots.'

'Oh, fuck off!' Natasha pushed him away.

He opened his hands in a pantomime gesture of innocence.

'I was just telling you.'

'Not interested, Coco.'

'OK, OK. I never argue with women who carry swords.'

He laughed again, and vanished into the mêlée on the dance floor.

Natasha went back out into the hall, and collected another glass of wine. To her own surprise, she did not feel ruffled by the clown's pass at her. On the contrary, she felt pleased with herself, as if she had handled the whole thing rather well. She swallowed the wine, then started on another glass, glancing round again to see if there was any sign of Seana.

As she looked out over the hall, it occurred to Natasha that she must know some of these people, even though she could not recognize any of them. The disguises had given them double lives – and as time crawled by, counted by the relentless disco beat, she grew hypnotized, watching the passing of partygoers, and glimpsing the occasional flashes of reality appearing from beneath the masks and make-up. Drunken men and women realizing with panic that they had mislaid their partners; fading beauties trying impossibly to rediscover their pasts; the bored and sophisticated looking for ever-more extreme and exotic experiences; the old and rich seeking, vampire-like, to suck fresh energy from bright, youthful lovers; and the young and naive drawn into a tainted net by the crude drive to have a good time. The interweaving of a hundred different desires, released by disguise, struck her like an icy reminder of mortality. And she had a sudden conviction that the party was evolving into the sliding images of a dream. A dream in which lay the slow-germinating poisonous seeds of full-blown nightmare.

Abruptly her reverie was broken, when an American football player, with huge shoulder pads, and a beard protruding oddly from his barred helmet, tripped over her feet, and fell noisily to the floor.

Embarrassed, she reached down to help him up. And then realized that it was Dr Anderssen. Instantly she froze. There was a sick feeling in her stomach, and she was trembling.

'Thank you,' he said.

She nodded, and turned away. But Anderssen put out a hand to stop her. He was smiling.

'It's a good thing I had this helmet on,' he remarked. 'Or I might have got hurt. Can I get you a drink?'

Suddenly Natasha realized he did not have the slightest idea who she was. At the same moment it also occurred to her that he might know something about the disappearance of the ice core. And she felt an unexpected shiver of anticipation at the thought of discovering more about him, drawing him out, safe behind her own mask. Perhaps there might even be some way of revenging herself on him.

'Thank you,' she answered, carefully speaking in a soft, deep voice, and edging it with a faint Swedish accent.

'What would you like?'

'Surprise me.'

A few moments later he returned, carrying two large glasses of colourless liquid. Thinking it was vodka, Natasha sipped it, then looked up in surprise. After an initial impression of raw, cheap brandy, the drink had a delicate and pleasant after-taste.

'What is this?' she asked.

Anderssen pushed up his barred faceplate, took a sip himself, then smiled.

'Hungarian slivovitz,' he said. 'Plum brandy. The bar seems to serve every drink known to man.'

'It's excellent,' said Natasha, taking another mouthful.

The two of them began to wander slowly through the hall. Anderssen's small, close-set eyes were regarding her curiously.

'Do I know you?' he asked.

'I certainly don't know you,' she answered. 'Isn't that the idea of parties like this – to meet new people?'

'I suppose so,' he agreed. 'What's your name?'

'Rachel,' said Natasha. 'How about you?'

'Call me Emil. What part of the faculty do you work in, Rachel?'

She smiled, her confidence soaring.

'I came with someone else,' she replied truthfully. 'But they seem to have vanished.'

'You look very good in your costume,' he said.

Natasha glanced at herself in the mirror, and intensified the casual swagger with which she was walking.

'I don't think I can say the same about yours,' she replied.

'I suppose not,' he agreed, not offended. 'When you're my shape it's not easy to find something that looks OK. The only alternative I saw was a bear costume, and I thought I'd die of heat in that.'

They walked past the main door, and sat down on a sofa which stood in an alcove, under a muddy painting of a man in tweed hunting gear, holding a shotgun.

Dr Anderssen took off his helmet, revealing a red face. He smiled at her, and then she felt his hand on her knee. She almost started away from him, but somehow found she did not really care that much. Instead she relaxed into the yielding sofa and took another sip of slivovitz.

'Tell me about your work,' she said.

'What do you want to know about it?'

'I don't know.' She waved a hand vaguely. 'Tell me something interesting that's happened recently.'

'Meeting you,' he said. His hand was infinitesimally creeping upwards.

She giggled again.

'I bet you say that to all the girls.'

'None of them are as interesting as you.' He was leaning against her, his breath was coming short and hot on her face.

Abruptly Natasha sat up, and pushed him away.

'I'm serious. What work do you? Has anything unusual happened in it?'

He looked thrown.

'What do you mean?'

'I don't know,' she shrugged. 'I had a . . . friend, who worked in the botany department of a German university, and one day the whole place filled up with armed police, shouting and waving guns. It turned out someone had been refining some obscure Indonesian fungus into a new hallucinogenic drug, then selling it for a fortune.'

'We've never had anything as dramatic as that. Though as it happens the police did pay a visit to my department only two days ago.'

Natasha adjusted her sword belt, setlied back against the sofa, and stretched her booted legs out in front of her.

'How come?'

'You're not really interested.'

'Yes I am. I love stories.'

'Well, a silly young graduate said she saw part of a finger in one of our ice core samples. Ridiculous of course. But she called the police, and there were a lot of embarrassing questions. She's a very hysterical woman, but fortunately her teaching contract comes up in a few months, and we will certainly not be renewing it.'

The complacent way Anderssen spoke of wrecking her career transformed her dislike into steely hatred.

'Isn't that a bit tough on her?' she said.

'If people aren't up to challenges, then it's not fair to them to hide that fact. I'm sure she'll be much happier doing something less taxing – like being a telephone sales assistant or a secretary. Though with the reference I'm going to give her, she'll be lucky if she gets a job at a supermarket checkout desk.'

He laughed, and after a moment Natasha laughed too.

'I think I'd find it very sexy, having the power to control people's lives like that,' she said quietly.

His stubby, pale hand was back, sidling along her thigh. A silver-suited alien, arm in arm with a bewigged eighteenth-century countess, gave Natasha a look out of expressionless almond-shaped eyes.

Suddenly there was the harsh sound of a mobile phone. Anderssen started, swore, then produced his phone.

'Hello?'

There was a mutter at the far end.

'Speak louder,' said Anderssen, 'I can't hear.'

A thought came to Natasha. She bent towards him and began rubbing her gauntleted hand slowly up and down his neck.

'Dr Anderssen?' came the tinny sound of the caller. 'This is Chris Goater.'

'Yes. How can I help you?'

Natasha stroked Anderssen's thin hair, and leant against his padded body, making sure she did not miss a word.

'You kindly sent me the records of the Iversen Land expedition.'

Eagerly Natasha pressed even closer to him.

'Yes, that's right.'

'The records are not quite as detailed as we might have hoped. And I think it would be very helpful if you could see me tomorrow, to discuss some aspects.'

'Yes. Yes, certainly. I am free at eleven.' Anderssen paused. 'But to be frank, I don't really understand why you need. . . ?'

'Goodbye, Doctor. I'm sure you will be delighted by the UNESCO grant I am arranging for future expeditions – provided of course that these last loose ends are cleared up to everyone's satisfaction. I will see you at eleven tomorrow morning.'

The phone went dead.

Anderssen put his phone away with an irritated grunt.

'Everyone seems to think that providing some funds for the faculty means they own you,' he muttered. Then he remembered where he was, and smiled back at Natasha.

'Sorry about that. Now where were we?'

He fumbled for a moment in his padded costume, then produced a cigar and put it to his lips.

Natasha was about to get up and leave him, so that she could look for Seana and tell her what she had just heard. Then, out of nowhere, an idea sprang into her mind. An idea born of the excitement she felt from growing intoxication and the masquerade she was performing. An idea so outrageous, that she laughed out loud.

'What is it?' asked Anderssen.

She shook her head, then finished her slivovitz in a single mouthful. Anderssen was getting out a lighter, when Natasha removed the cigar from his lips, and dropped it behind the sofa.

'I prefer men not to smell of smoke,' she purred, brushing a gloved finger against his lips, then moving her leg against his groin, and letting her breath come deep and alluring.

'Let's find somewhere more private,' he said, a few moments later.

Anderssen clearly knew his way about the house, for within three minutes he was guiding her through a thick wooden door with an intricate key in the lock, and into a small parlour with another, larger, sofa in it. Anderssen flung himself on her, pressing his thin lips on hers, and thrusting his tongue deep into her mouth.

She pushed him away.

'Not so fast,' she said. 'First switch the lights out.'

He did, and the room vanished into deep shadow, except for what little light crept through the windows from the cloud-wracked half-moon. Swiftly, efficiently, she began to strip him out of his costume. Anderssen tried to take off her mask, but she pushed his hands away.

'No,' she whispered. 'We're going to do this the way I want it.'

A minute later he was stark naked. Natasha held him for a moment, then squeezed tightly.

'I've always wanted to wear boots while screwing someone,' she breathed, remembering the clown. 'But first I must go to the bathroom to get myself ready. Make yourself comfortable, and I'll be back before you can count to a hundred.'

She pushed him down on the sofa, and gave him another lingering, erotic caress.

'Close your eyes,' she said. 'And get ready to be fucked within an inch of your life.'

She deposited a last lick on his throat, then slipped away – taking his costume with her.

Once through the door, she gently turned the key in the lock, then removed it. Carrying the key and Anderssen's costume, she hurried downstairs and out into the garden. There were people outside, but no one took any notice of her as she went down to the bushes, concealed the costume deep among the leaves beneath one, then hurled the key into another, larger shrub.

'Maybe it's your contract that won't be renewed now, Doctor,' she muttered viciously, as she returned to the party.

10 Among the Bushes

SEANA WAS STONE cold sober, and very aware of the silver anklet round her ankle. In an attempt to escape her uneasiness, she headed for the disco, danced by herself and waited for something to happen. But the music was old-fashioned and tame, and no one joined her – perhaps they were put off by her costume. Before long she left to get something to eat, but there was a long queue, so she sat down on a bench, crossed her legs, so the chain on her left ankle was easily visible, and waited.

Still nothing happened, so she went back to the disco – and felt a stab of acute jealousy, and some irritation, when she saw Natasha flirting outrageously with a man dressed as a clown. It seemed massively unfair that the staid, repressed Natasha was completely ignoring the reason they were there, and just having a good time, while Seana herself was worrying more and more.

The evening edged past. Two or three people did approach her, but it rapidly became clear that none of them was the elusive Jon Skalli. At last, to her relief, a waiter appeared at her side and presented her with a note. It was short and unsigned.

'*Outside the French windows.*'

At the far end of the hall was a large conservatory lit only by a few candles. A couple were lying entwined on a long seat; several other costumed partygoers were talking, laughing loudly, and smoking cigarettes among the lush plants. French windows looked out into the night.

As Seana entered, she was seized round the waist by a man dressed as a tramp, unshaven and dirty. He grinned at his companions complacently.

'She's not bony at all. In fact she's got some nice curves on her.'

'Let me go, please,' said Seana.

'Not until you give me a kiss. I've never kissed a skeleton before.'

'It's Scully, from *The X-Files*,' shouted a woman in a long black wig, fishnet tights, and red satin bustier. There was a roar of laughter.

'I want her as my skeleton in the cupboard,' said a man in immaculate evening dress, with a monocle and slicked down hair. Or was it a woman? Seana was not sure.

The tramp pulled Seana round towards him, and she tasted his alcohol-scented breath. Rather than cause trouble, she gave him a chaste kiss on the lips, but suddenly his hand was behind her head, forcing her closer to him, and a moment later his tongue, snake-fast, slid in and out of her mouth.

'Now it is her turn to pay homage to the goddess,' came a harsh voice.

The tramp and his two associates gripped Seana tightly and, despite her protests, frog-marched her over to the far side of the conservatory.

In the shadows, Seana found herself in front of a large woman, sitting on a seat and wearing a long, black trench coat, and the thick, white, doll-like make-up of a geisha. She looked at Seana for a moment, then nodded, and suddenly Seana felt a cold pang of fear. Frantically she struggled to get away, but the three people held her tightly, and laughing and cheering, their breath hot about her, they forced her on to her knees.

'Submit to the goddess!' they shouted. 'Grovel before her!'

Seana wondered whether to scream for help. Then the woman lifted her bare foot from the floor. At the same moment Seana found her head forced fiercely down so that, for a second, her lips touched the woman's broad, flat, faintly grubby foot. There was wild applause and more cheering from the watchers. A moment later Seana was released, and staggered away out of the French windows, grateful that nothing worse had happened to her, but burning with anger that she had been so scared by a stupid joke.

Outside, passing clouds had covered the moon, and it took several minutes before she recovered herself, and her sight adjusted to the darkness. Looking around, she saw the great shapes of the nearby trees, the lines of parked cars, and scattered figures moving round the edge of the brilliantly-lit house. Glancing back over her shoulder, she could see the tramp and his friends drinking and laughing. But there was no sign of the woman in the long coat.

As she stood there uncertainly, a tight spear of white light lanced through the night and caught her, then vanished equally suddenly. A moment later a hand took her arm and pulled her urgently towards the bushes.

'Jesus, what a dumb costume you've got,' came a rough voice. 'I suppose you can't be recognized, but anyone can see you anywhere.'

'If I crouch down most of the glow-in-the-dark stuff disappears,' said Seana, taking a breath and trying to calm herself.

'So do it. We must be quick, every moment could be dangerous.'

She could just see a dim shape, half-concealed by a dark, hooded top. Shiny leaves of laurel brushed and rattled against Seana's costume as she bent down, trying to conceal the giveaway luminous lines.

'Why?' she asked. 'What's the problem?'

'What do you think? Those photographs – someone's after them. Seriously after them.' Then he stopped, and his grip on her arm tightened fiercely. 'Wait a minute. You're not Natasha. Who the hell are you? Where did you get that chain?'

'Natasha gave it to me.'

'I don't believe you.'

'It's true. I'm Tash's friend, you can trust me.'

'Trust a skeleton? I don't think so. I talk to Natasha, or no one.'

'I'll take you to her—'

'No way,' hissed the hooded figure vehemently.

'OK, OK. Stay here. I'll get Natasha.'

'Be quick.'

As she ran back towards the main entrance, the conservatory door suddenly flew open, and the tramp appeared outside, blocking her path. From inside there came a cheer.

'You're back for more, my darling death's head,' said the tramp, putting out his arms to embrace her. 'Is it my turn now?'

There was a momentary glimpse of a leering face coming towards her, then Seana dodged. A hand grasped at her, but slid off the slickness of her bodysuit, and she darted away, leaving him groping at thin air, to the accompaniment of the jeering laughter of his companions.

Back inside, Seana could find no sign of Natasha except the feathered hat still hanging on a hook outside the dance floor. She looked around desperately, but saw only a blurred mass of masks, and faces that make-up, indifference or alcohol had turned into masks. When she asked the barmen and waiters, they merely shook their heads, or shrugged discreetly, their faces as mask-like as the partygoers.

At last she saw Natasha, strolling over to collect her hat. She darted over to her and seized her arm, as if her friend might slip away again if not imprisoned.

'Where the hell have you been?' she demanded furiously.

Natasha's face, more than half-concealed under the soft black suede of her mask, revealed nothing.

'Nowhere in particular.'

'I've been looking everywhere for you. What have you been doing for Christ's sake?'

'What you told me,' Natasha answered softly. 'Enjoying myself.'

'We're not here to enjoy ourselves.'

'Sorry.'

Seana looked up at her again, and again learnt nothing.

'Are you OK?' she asked.

'Why shouldn't I be?'

'Well . . . the party's a lot wilder than I'd expected.' Seana laughed nervously, and shook her head. 'Suddenly I find it much easier to believe that story you told me about the tear gas, and that lecturer. I hadn't thought scientists were like this.'

'Maybe everyone's like this when they get the chance,' said Natasha, and laughed.

Seana was about to describe what had happened to her in the conservatory, but suddenly she did not want to. There had been something odd, something un-Natashalike, about the laugh – a casual hardness. And as her friend carefully smoothed out a crease in her breeches, then pulled her gloves on more tightly and flexed her fingers, Seana realized the whole way Natasha was standing, was moving, was different. It had a sexual arrogance about it that was alien to the woman she knew.

'Perhaps,' she said. 'Anyway, he's here. You have to come and see him now.'

Natasha had been looking forward to watching the public humiliation of Anderssen, and she felt a stab of disappointment. But then it occurred to her that there might be too much danger of her own discovery, so she followed the eerily-glowing Seana outside and round the back of the house, to the dark laurel bushes, beyond which a stretch of tree-scattered parkland stretched down to the edge of Roskilde Fjord. The moon had escaped from its covering of cloud, and the water of the fjord shone and moved like gleaming mercury. Seana crouched down, close to the ground by the nearest bush and gave a whistle. After a few moments she gave another whistle.

'Shit!' she muttered. 'Where is he?'

'Where was he?' asked Natasha.

'Just here. Hiding in the bushes. I told him to wait until I came back with you.'

At that moment there was a rustle, and the leaves parted.

'Jon, is that you?' asked Natasha.

'Tash! Thank God! You really screwed me when you gave me those photos?'

'Why? What did they show?'

Jon Skalli was emerging from the bush, and brushing himself down in the moonlight. He glanced across.

'Is that really you, Tash?'

'Sure.'

'You should go about like that more often. It does things for you.' He gave a faint laugh, but it sounded forced. 'Anyway, listen – those remains on the photograph were part of a plane. I'm not sure what sort, but probably a big one. I was also able to work out the serial number – it was in red on what I suppose was the wing – 55-0065.'

'Did you. . . ?' began Natasha.

'Wait. No time for discussion. I remembered you'd said to find out as much as possible, so that was when I made what I reckon must have been my big mistake. I put a message out on the Internet, on a friend's website – with the best of the pictures on it, plus details of what I knew so far – and asked if anyone could help discover what this was about.

'Two days later I came home and found my place had been broken into. All my photographs and discs were gone, and my computer had been wiped clean. I later found out that the website had been taken out too – I didn't know people could do that. Not long after that the police came looking for me, but I managed to get out before they spotted me. Which was just as well, as they searched my room and found several thousand kroner worth of heroin under one of the floorboards. I suppose it was planted in my room by the people who took my stuff, and it was they who contacted the cops. Since then I've been on the run, but tonight I've been promised a lift into Germany, where I should be able to disappear easily enough.'

'I'm sorry to have laid all this on you, Jon,' said Natasha. 'I never guessed . . .'

'How could you? But if I was you I'd tread real careful for the next few weeks.'

'What do you mean exactly?'

'You know how it is in Christiania. Little whispers run round like waves in a lake. This is not just the police; apparently people have been looking for me, nasty people. And if they're looking for me, then maybe it won't be very hard for them to make the link to you.'

Natasha felt a shiver run up her spine, like a long needle of ice. Instinctively she put her arms round herself and hunched her shoulders.'

Jon glanced at her.

'Maybe you should take a runner too,' he said softly. 'Until all this dies down.'

'I can't,' she said, shaking her head. 'I can't.'

Jon Skalli shrugged.

'Suit yourself. Anyway, my lift's waiting for me back along the drive, and I want to be away as quickly as possible.'

'Sure. Thanks for everything, Jon. And sorry again.'

Seana had been listening in silence. But suddenly she noticed that up at the house there was a blaze of lights on the second floor which had not been there before, and the air was full of a loud thumping, and shouts.

'Something's happening,' she said.

Natasha glanced up.

'Perhaps we'll go with you, Jon,' she said hastily.

'Good idea,' said Seana, with feeling. 'The sooner we're out of that party, the happier I'll be.'

'I think I enjoyed some of it,' replied Natasha. 'But not any more. Let's go.'

As they walked down the drive, their feet crunching on the gravel, their moon-shadows long, black and enigmatic, Natasha turned back to Jon Skalli.

'What was the number of the plane again?'

'55-0065. Write it down somewhere.'

'I haven't got anything to write with,' said Natasha, faintly irritated.

'I have. Here's a biro.'

'I'll write it on my hand.' She pulled off one of her gloves. 'What was it again – 65. . . ?'

'55-0065,' said Jon Skalli. 'And don't do it on your hand, it'll fade.'

Natasha hesitated, then carefully wrote the numbers on the soft inside cuff of her left gauntlet.

'My attempts to trace the number didn't get anyplace,' went on Jon Skalli. 'Maybe you'll be luckier, but for Christ's sake be careful.'

'You think it's that dangerous?' asked Seana, who had been walking quietly beside them.

Jon Skalli stopped and looked at the dimly-glowing skull head that stared disconcertingly at him. He shrugged.

'I don't know. And I'm not hanging around to find out. See you in a few months, maybe.' He pointed ahead twenty or thirty metres or so, to where a car was just visible in the gloom under a tree. 'That'll be my lift. Bye.'

He bent forward, gave Natasha the faintest brush of a kiss on her cheek, just below the edge of her mask, then turned away.

As he set off towards the car, there was a sudden eye-burning blaze of light as the car's double headlights went on, trapping all three of them like blinded rabbits. A moment later came a flash and a sound like someone spitting, rapidly repeated.

'Run!' screamed Seana.

She and Natasha hurled themselves off the drive, and in among the thick bushes. Behind them came the spitting sound again, and the crunch of feet on the gravelled drive.

The two women sprinted wildly through the bushes, flung themselves into the heart of a great dark rhododendron, then crawled a little way before stretching out on their fronts, their faces to the ground. Not daring to move, trying to control their panting lungs.

There was no sound, except the distant beat and roar of the party. They lay where they were, branches sticking into their backs, rotting leaves and mud by their faces. Natasha put out a hand, and finding Seana's close by her, held it tight. Seana responded to the pressure. Time crawled past, then the silence was broken by the sound of a car driving away. Somewhere a Little Owl gave its sharp bark, and was answered by a second.

Not until several more cars had driven away along the drive did Natasha put up her head, still listening as hard as she could.

'Do you think they've gone?' she breathed.

'It seems like it,' agreed Seana, getting up on to her knees.

'Jesus, take that bloody skull-face off, and hide it. When you're wearing it, people can see you from a kilometre away.'

'OK. I'll try and cover up the rest of the glow-in-the-dark stuff with mud and earth.'

'Can't you just take it off.'

'It's about all I've got on.'

'Great!' said Natasha, breath hissing through clenched teeth. 'Anyway, we'd better go see if we can find Jon, then get the hell out of here.'

The two women emerged cautiously into the open. The moon was once more behind clouds, but despite her efforts at concealment, Seana still glowed faintly. Nevertheless she went in front as they made their way back on to the drive, then crept towards the place where they had been shot at. Something black lay on the grass by the roadside. Seana took a step towards it. Suddenly there was a rustle of leaves, and a figure appeared close beside her.

'Don't move,' came a man's voice. 'Or you're dead.'

Seana froze.

A moment later there was a faint hiss, a scream, and the man flung up his arms. Something flew through the air and fell to earth behind them in the bushes. There was another hiss, a glint of metal, and the man staggered and fell backwards. Seana felt herself pulled fiercely, and then she was running back up the drive as fast as she could.

Five minutes later, her foot hard down on the accelerator, she was driving her car furiously along the drive, while Natasha crouched low beside her. The headlights showed no one and nothing, and within a minute they were through the wrought iron gates and away. But not until they were approaching Tastrup and the outlying suburbs of Copenhagen did Seana slow down.

'What the hell did you do?' she asked.

Natasha laughed, but this time there was a hysterical edge to the sound.

'I slashed at him with my sword.'

'You what?'

'The sword that was part of my costume. I could see the gun he was holding, and I just lashed out at it with the sword. Luckily he was so surprised, he lost hold of it, then I cut him in the face, and he fell over backwards.'

'I chose you a good costume.'

'I lost the sword though. It sprang out of my hand. And I forgot to get my hat back too.'

'At least we got out of there alive,' said Seana.

'But we still don't know what happened to Jon. Look, there's a phone. Stop, and I'll contact the police.'

'Do you think you should? I mean—'

'Yes. Of course.' A couple of minutes later Natasha was talking to a sharp-voiced policewoman. 'I'm at Hantsholm House,' she said. 'My friend and I have just heard a sound of gunfire, outside by the driveway to the house.'

'Who is this? Where are you speaking from?' said the policewoman.

'My name's Dr Anderssen,' invented Natasha swiftly. 'I'm calling from the house. Please come quickly; we have seen figures moving through the bushes, and a young man has disappeared.'

'Could you stay on the line, please, Dr Anderssen.'

'It is urgent. You must come. He may be injured.'

'If you could just give us some more details, Doctor. Do you know who this missing man is?'

'His name is. . . .' Suddenly Natasha remembered that the police had been looking for Jon Skalli. 'I don't know. Please hurry. There's no time to waste.'

Natasha hung up, and returned to the car.

'Let's get out of here,' she said, an audible tremble in her voice.

'Where to?'

'Back to your place to get out of these bloody costumes. Trying to run in all this stuff was hell on earth – I suppose what I really needed was a horse. And I want a good thorough shower – I feel filthy and my head's coming apart. After that maybe we'll be ready to try to work out just what has been going on.'

She took a deep breath, and collapsed into the car seat. Seana drove steadily back to Copenhagen.

11 Lies

A LARGE FLOCK of starlings descended noisily around the buildings outside the open window, perching on the high balustrades, gutterings and cornices, swaying on the telephone wires. They chattered noisily as they leant, feathers fluttering, into the warm, dusty south-easterly wind. The sky was cloudless, and only a faint yellow haze of pollution veiled the rays of the September sun that baked Copenhagen. Somehow it didn't seem like a Monday morning.

Larsen was not at his best in hot weather, and he sighed and rubbed his forehead, which was dewed with sweat. He had just been on the phone to Chief Thorold, and the call had not gone well.

'What it comes down to, Sergeant, is that you have no real evidence at all,' Larsen's boss had said, coldly and precisely. 'Perhaps this is the moment for me to remind you that nearly all police work is simply accumulating and checking evidence. Not relying on theories, guesswork, and doubtful confessions in front of witnesses who refuse to testify.'

It occurred to Larsen that nearly all major crimes in Greenland were actually solved by confession, but all he said was: 'Yes, sir. Still, at least we now have a good idea of what happened to flight 608.'

'Not necessarily,' retorted Thorold. 'Apparently the Canadian crash investigators have only found scattered flotsam, and the search for the black box flight recorder is likely to take some time. The plane seems to have gone down in one of the less accessible parts of the Davis Strait, where the northern part of the Labrador Current brings down a steady stream of broken pack ice and bergs. In practical terms there is a severely limited time window during which the flight recorder can be found – another three or four weeks at the outside, before the weather becomes too difficult.' Larsen could see Thorold in his mind, probably turning his silver Shaeffer pen over and over in his hand, or gently stroking his pale, thin cheek. 'You understand what this means?'

'I can see there are problems. . . .'

'We are not talking about minor difficulties, Sergeant Larsen. As of this moment, we have absolutely no direct irrefutable evidence that it was a bomb which caused the crash.'

'But, sir – what about Steen's confession?'

'Please permit me to finish. Our country, as you well know, is almost exclusively reliant on air transport. Any suggestion that a flight had been sabotaged could cause panic. At best the airlines would be forced to undertake new procedures, which would add hours to the time of flights, and. . . .'

With a flash of anger Larsen realized where the conversation was going.

'You've talked about this already, haven't you?' he growled. 'You've discussed it with your bosses, and they don't want to see all the extra delay and expense that would come with improved airport security. That's it, isn't it?'

Thorold's response was emotionless. He appeared to be completely oblivious to Larsen's anger.

'The unsubstantiated confession you gained – which would be utterly worthless in a court of law – implies only that an unchecked package may have been carried on to the plane in question. For us to act merely on that possibility would be ridiculously irresponsible.'

'For Christ's sake, what if it happens again?'

'Do you have any solid evidence that there could be a repeat of what happened to flight 608?'

'You know I don't. But—'

'My judgement is that there is no substantive reason to expect a repeat of this unfortunate event. Especially as all relevant companies are undertaking thorough mechanical checks of every plane that flies from a Greenland airport.' Thorold ignored Larsen's attempted interruption, and ground on implacably. 'As for the question of sabotage, even assuming your unsupported theory of a bomb is accurate, there is no danger of Steen Sanders repeating his actions, as he is no longer employed as a baggage handler.'

'What if the people who bribed him bribe someone else?'

'What reason do you have to believe there is a danger of such a thing happening?'

'None. But we should warn people.'

'Precautions will be taken.'

'What the hell does that mean?'

'There is no need to use obscenities, Sergeant. It means exactly what I said.'

Larsen just managed to choke back a more extreme swear-word, and controlled a powerful urge to slam the telephone down.

'Shall I order a search for Sanders?'

'On what grounds?'

'Threatening a police officer would do as a holding charge, until we can get more from him.'

'But you have no witnesses. You should have made sure that when you made the approach to Sanders, you had a second officer with you. It was an elementary mistake for a man of your experience, Sergeant.'

'If I had had someone with me, I wouldn't have been taken to see Sanders,' muttered Larsen.

Chief Thorold ignored his comment.

'However, I think it would be best if you stayed in Copenhagen,' he went on, to Larsen's astonishment. 'I would recommend that you continue trying to search out Steen Sanders, while attempting to discover what, precisely, was in the package, if it existed. If you need further guidance, don't hesitate to contact me.'

The phone went dead.

'Shit!' exploded Larsen. 'It's like talking to a bloody computer.'

Angrily, he stabbed numbers into the phone. After a few moments he was talking to Risa.

'So,' he ended. 'I've got to stay here until . . . I don't know. Until something turns up. Fuck it!'

'How are you finding it back in Denmark?' she asked.

'All right I suppose. If it wasn't that this job is so bloody impossible. Even if I find Steen again, there's no way he's going to admit anything

– not when he knows it will end with him being put inside for a long stretch.'

'But you believe he didn't know what was in the package.'

'I don't see him as a cold-blooded mass murderer, that's true. But he was still responsible, and he might find it very hard to prove anyone else was involved. As for his little friend, Paul, he feels good about defying the police, like some kind of hero of the resistance. If I find him, I can snap him apart, but I don't think that our nice civilized rules are going to give me the chance.'

'Aren't there any other approaches you could take?'

'Like what?'

'Well, maybe Thorold was right. . . .'

'Those last three words contain an impossible concept.'

'What I mean is maybe you should be looking at this from the point of view of *why* it happened.'

'Meaning?'

'Well, if a bomb was put in the plane, why was it done? If you could sort that out, then you'd be well on your way, wouldn't you?'

'It was probably some terrorist group. . . .'

'That's sloppy thinking, Tomas.' Risa's voice snapped down the line at him, like a blow. 'You've no evidence to believe it, have you?'

'Everyone keeps telling me I've no evidence for anything.'

'And don't feel sorry for yourself either. There's never been any terrorism in Greenland, so why should there be now? Anyway, terrorists admit what they've done – they want publicity so that they can blackmail governments. You need to look at other things.'

'Like what? I don't understand what you're talking about.'

'That's because you're still angry with Thorold, and you're thinking with your emotions, not your head. What reasons are there to put a bomb in a plane?'

'To kill people of course.'

'Exactly. So have you considered the list of those who were killed?'

'Yes. But virtually all of them were Canadians or Greenlanders. So I need to leave Denmark to make enquiries, but Thorold told me I have to stay here.'

'So check on the ones who were Danes. That'd be a start.'

'I suppose so.' He stopped, and frowned. The red mist that had filled his head was finally draining away. 'But I still don't understand quite what you're getting at.'

'I'm not getting at anything Tomas, love. You're the smart detective.'

Larsen laughed bitterly.

'Smart!' he repeated. 'I think not.'

'Don't run yourself down, Tomas,' she said intensely. 'You're the smartest guy I've ever known.'

'You don't mean that.'

'Yes I do.' There was a momentary pause, then she laughed. With a warm shiver down his spine, Larsen found he could hear the affection in her tone.

'In fact,' she went on, 'the main problem with you is that you're too bloody clever for your own good. That's why your boss can't stand you.'

'I'll try to be dumber in future.'

'Don't you dare.'

He found he was smiling.

'Feeling better now?' she said, demonstrating her almost uncanny ability to read his moods.

'Yes. Except that I won't be seeing you for longer than I had hoped.'

'And the same back at you. Now, I have to go. Look after yourself.'

Larsen sat down on his bed, got out the passenger and crew list, together with the cargo manifest of flight 608 from Kangerlussuaq to Iqaluit, and began to consider them. After a few minutes he focused on one name: Dr Frederik Dahl, the leader of the Iversen Land expedition. And he remembered the phone call he had taken just before leaving for Copenhagen – two members of the expedition were still in Iversen Land, but had lost contact. Which probably didn't mean anything. But the other two members were in Copenhagen.

Two minutes later he was back on the phone, talking to Helge in the Nuuk office.

'No,' said Helge. 'As far as I know there's still been no contact with the Iversen Land expedition since last Thursday – though that's not particularly unusual. Apparently one of them is a highly experienced mountaineer who's worked in the Stauning Alps, and took part in a crossing of the inland ice five years ago.'

'Anyone can get in trouble anywhere in Greenland,' said Larsen. 'Remember that English explorer who'd worked for three years in the Antarctic. . . .'

'And drowned three kilometres from Upernavik. I remember. But why are you interested?'

'It seems a coincidence that one member of the expedition died in that plane crash, then two days later we lose contact with two others. Could you keep trying to get hold of the ones in Iversen Land for me? Meanwhile, I'll look out the other two members.'

Less than an hour later Larsen was talking to Dr Emil Anderssen's young, blonde, efficient-looking secretary.

'He is in a meeting,' she said. 'I can make an appointment for you tomorrow afternoon.'

'I would like to see him now,' insisted Larsen. 'It will only take a few minutes.'

'I'm afraid that's quite impossible. After this meeting, the doctor has a lecture. . . .'

At that moment the thick oak door to Anderssen's office opened.

'Thank you very much, Doctor,' came a voice from inside. 'You have been most helpful.'

A tall man walked out. He had dark eyes and cropped greying hair, and he carried the aura of success about him, from his strong, confident face, through his expensive and well-cut but unremarkable suit, to his softly-gleaming shoes.

'Goodbye Mr Goater,' said the secretary.

'Goodbye,' he said, with a smile, then walked swiftly away.

Larsen seized his opportunity and darted through the open door. Anderssen, a big, deep-chested man with a small mouth that was almost hidden in his thick beard, looked up irritably, then took off his half-moon reading spectacles.

'Who are you?' he demanded gruffly.

'I am very sorry to disturb you,' said Larsen, showing his ID card.

'Not more questions about last night,' snapped Anderssen, querulously. 'I've already made a statement to the police. A statement that I feel was not treated with enough seriousness, if I may say so.'

'This is not about last night, Dr Anderssen. I am a member of the

Royal Greenland Police, and I am investigating a plane crash.'

Anderssen looked at him with utter incomprehension, then a light of understanding gradually appeared.

'Ah, this must be connected to the death of Dr Dahl.' He shook his leonine head. 'A tragic loss. We are having a memorial service in the university chapel tomorrow morning. Dr Dahl was a most charming and talented man, and achieved much important work. I knew him for many years, and his family have asked me to deliver the eulogy – a great honour. Exactly what do you wish to know about him?'

'Well, it's not directly about Dr Dahl that I have come to see you. In fact, the person I need to see is Professor Natasha Myklund.'

The doctor's hands, on his large, inlaid nineteenth-century desk, bent into claws. The knuckles were white.

'That is . . .' he paused, frowning. 'That is rather strange.'

'What is strange?' asked Larsen.

'Nothing, nothing,' he muttered. The frown lingered a little longer, then he shook his head, as if to clear it. 'Why are you interested in her, Sergeant?'

'I am trying to speak to members of the Iversen Land expedition – which is proving harder than I had expected. . . .'

'Two of them are still in Iversen Land,' put in Anderssen.

'But have not been heard from since Thursday.'

'No, that is not correct. I received a phone call yesterday afternoon, and they are perfectly well. They informed me they had decided to stay out there for another two weeks, that is all.'

'I'm glad to hear it. Perhaps you could contact them again and ask them to make contact with the police in Ivtoriseq.'

'Of course.' Anderssen gave an awkward smile, that seemed at odds with his massive presence. 'May I ask what exactly has this to do with the plane crash, and with Professor Myklund?'

'Probably nothing,' said Larsen. 'But we have to make routine enquiries, you know what it's like – bureaucracy.'

'Quite,' said Anderssen, with visible caution. 'But perhaps I should warn you that Professor Myklund has been behaving rather erratically over the past few days.'

'What do you mean erratically?' inquired Larsen.

'I suspect there must be a degree of shock involved, a response to the tragic death of Dr Dahl, and perhaps overwork, or emotional difficulties, have worsened matters. Not that the incidents have been severe, but they have been troubling.' He sighed. 'On Wednesday she was first overtly aggressive to me during a meeting, and then made a bizarre call to the police, claiming she had seen something ludicrous in one of the laboratories. My attempts to contact her since then have been unsuccessful, and messages left on her answer machine, and at her e-mail address, have elicited no response. Generally Dr Myklund is . . . rather uninspired in her work, but very reliable. For her to vanish, without telling anyone where she has gone, is most untypical.'

Anderssen got to his feet.

'I'm afraid I must leave now. I have a lecture to give.'

'I do need to see Professor Myklund,' said Larsen. 'I was also hoping to speak to Seana Arnason. . . .'

'Naturally. My secretary will give you the home address and telephone number of both women – though I understand Ms Arnason no longer resides at the address we have. She is not a particularly reliable student. And now I must be on my way. If you wish to speak to me again, Sergeant, I would be grateful if you could make a formal appointment. I am a busy man, and my days are scheduled rather tightly.'

A couple of hours later Larsen stood in Professor Myklund's compact, but messy, kitchen, looking carefully at the pinboard. It was covered in photographs, several of which showed a young Inuit woman. After a moment or two he returned to the living room, picked up the phone and dialled ring-back, then wrote down the number.

'If you want to search the place, we'll have to get a special warrant,' said the Danish police officer, who accompanied him.

'I don't think I need to do that yet. Can you find out what address this number belongs to?'

'Sure.' The policeman made a couple of calls. 'It's in Hellerup, a house owned by a couple of university professors. But they're presently out of the country, so it looks as if they must have sub-let the place.'

'I think I will go and see who they have sub-let to,' said Larsen.

Larsen arrived at 149 Ostergarde at four o'clock, walked up to the door and rang the bell.

There was no response, and the curtains were still drawn. Larsen rang twice more. Hearing dim sounds of movement inside, he waited patiently.

'Who is it?' croaked someone.

'This is Police Sergeant Tomas Larsen. May I speak to you please?'

There was the sound of a key turning in a lock, then the door opened a slit, the chain still keeping it fast.

A bleary face, with deep shadows round the eyes, stared at him.

'What do you want?'

Larsen showed his ID card, then glanced at the round, Inuit face, and felt a surge of satisfaction. It was the woman whose photograph he had seen in Myklund's flat.

'I am looking for Professor Natasha Myklund,' he said.

'She doesn't live here.'

'I know that. May I come in?'

'Yes. I mean no.' The woman rubbed her forehead. 'Look, I feel really bad. Do you think you could come back in a few hours?'

'I'm afraid not,' said Larsen, quietly insistent. 'The matter is important.'

'So try her house.'

'She's not there.'

'Well I'm afraid I don't know where she is.'

'Even though someone called this house from her flat just twenty-four hours ago.' He paused momentarily, then went on. 'I appreciate you are trying to help your friend. So am I.'

'Meaning what?'

Larsen said nothing.

Seana rubbed the back of her hand over her forehead again.

'OK,' she said. 'Give me a few minutes to get dressed. Then you can come in.'

The door closed in his face. Larsen waited calmly. Attentively. He had already made sure that there was no back way out.

At length the door opened again. Seana, in a long black T-shirt and leggings, gestured him into the modern, stripped-down sitting room. Her short, streaked hair was standing up in uneven spikes, and her face was ash-white.

'Coffee?' she asked.

'No, thank you.'

'Well I need some anyway.'

She went out into the kitchen, then came back a few minutes later, clutching a mug of strong black coffee. She half-closed the door behind her, and sat down opposite him.

'I was at a party till late last night,' she said. 'You haven't caught me at the best time.'

'Was Professor Myklund there?'

'Why are you looking for her?'

'Was she there?'

Seana looked at him.

'No.'

Larsen did not move. His broad, long-eyed face showed nothing, but his stubby fingers were gently flitting over his knees.

In spite of herself Seana felt a strange respect for him. The policeman had the squat, powerful build of a wrestler, and Seana sensed a massive solidity, a sense of being rooted and certain, that was hard to ignore. It was not that he seemed particularly intelligent, or quick-witted, but there was something more formidable there. She felt a sudden certainty that once he had made up his mind, it would be almost impossible to deflect him, or to put him off the scent. Inexorable, single-minded. Like those terrifying boxers whose faces are reduced to bloody ruin in the ring, but still continue to barrel forward without even pausing, until more skilful opponents are finally destroyed by sheer unbending persistence and willpower.

Larsen relaxed into his chair.

'Is your name Seana Arnason?' he asked.

'Yes.'

'So you were on the Iversen Land expedition with Professor Myklund?'

'Yes. Is this about Frederik – I mean Dr Dahl's accident?'

'What do you know about that?' said Larsen quietly.

'Just what it said in the papers,' she said warily. 'Why?'

Larsen decided to be open.

'The cause of the crash is still not certain. But I have established that a baggage handler at Nuuk airport, who is now hiding here in Copenhagen, was paid to put an unmonitored parcel on that flight.'

There was a pause. Outside a car drove down the residential street. The house creaked slightly as the autumn sun began to sink.

'I don't understand,' said Seana.

'Our attempts to make contact with the two members of your expedition who are still in Greenland have been unsuccessful. However, today I met Dr Anderssen at the university, and he told me that he spoke to them yesterday. And that they were planning to stay for two more weeks.'

Seana looked at him in surprise.

'Are you sure?'

'That is what Dr Anderssen told me.'

'I wonder what made them change their minds. It's not the sort of thing I'd have expected of Jens. He's usually so careful and level-headed, and does everything precisely as it was agreed. And Wendy doesn't have a massive amount of initiative either. Anderssen must have gone nuclear about it – all that extra expense.'

'He didn't seem angry,' said Larsen. 'Have you or Professor Myklund been in contact with Greenland since last Thursday?'

'I haven't. I don't know about Natasha.' Seana looked at him carefully. 'You sound as if you think Dr Anderssen was lying?'

'I have no reason to believe that,' replied Larsen. 'I am simply trying to clarify the situation. Also, Dr Anderssen said that last Wednesday Professor Myklund was involved in a rather confusing sequence of events, which resulted in the police being called. Since then she has not been into the university. In the circumstances it seemed wise to find her.'

He clasped his hands under his large jaw, and looked at Seana. Her initial discomfort had faded, and she looked calm and in control.

'Of course I don't know anything about the horrible accident that happened to Frederik,' she said, with a shrug. 'But I can't see any reason for members of our expedition to be targeted, if that's what you're thinking. It was just a scientific field trip to study ablation rates, summer snow cover, the overall extent of climatic change, and whether the ecology of breeding bird species is showing any changes. Not exactly life or death matters – in the short term anyway. I'm fine, and I'm sure Natasha is too.'

'Really?'

'Yes. Really.'

'When did you last see her?'

'She visited the shop where I work on Friday afternoon.'

'And did she phone you on Sunday afternoon?'

'No.'

Larsen glanced down at his knees, and pursed his lips.

'If my closest friend had left her home and completely disappeared, not leaving me any way of finding or contacting her, then I would be alarmed.'

'I'm not her closest friend,' said Seana. 'We're just colleagues.'

'So you haven't known her long?'

'We've only been working together for a few months.'

'Direct lies are never easy to tell,' Larsen said, without looking at her. 'Ms Arnason, you are unmarried, aren't you?'

'What has that to do with anything?'

'I like to get things right. And, please excuse my rudeness, you're not living with a boyfriend, are you?'

'For Christ's sake, what business is that of yours?'

'I didn't think so. There are no men's coats or jackets in the hall.' Suddenly his eyes were riveted to her face. 'In Professor Myklund's flat there are at least five pictures of you, including a photograph of the pair of you aged around eighteen or nineteen. I think the two of you are old friends. And as you are so certain that she is all right, I think you have seen her very recently indeed. In fact, I suspect she is in this house now, probably outside that door listening to everything we say.'

There was a long silence. Seana and Larsen sat, face to face, saying nothing, unmoving.

At last the door opened, and Natasha came in.

'Professor Myklund?' said Larsen calmly.

'How did you know? Have you been watching the house?'

Larsen shook his head.

'No. But I am pleased to meet you.' He regarded the thin, tall, pale-skinned woman attentively. 'Were you at the university science faculty party at Hantsholm House last night?'

'No.'

'Even though your friend Miss Arnason went to a party last night and, if you will forgive me, you also look as if you are suffering the afternoon after the night before.'

'That's why we didn't go to the faculty party,' said Seana quickly. 'We'd already agreed to go to another party.'

Larsen reached across and picked up a piece of material that was lying on the floor beside the sofa. He put his hand inside it, then held it up, revealing the design of a skull painted in luminous paint.

'Another fancy dress party, it seems,' he said. 'Quite a coincidence.'

'No, no,' said Seana. 'That's left over from Hallowe'en'

'Hallowe'en was ten months ago. Has it been lying round here all that time?'

'This isn't my house – it must belong to the kids. I don't know what it's doing lying around; maybe I've been using it as a duster or something.'

Larsen held the hood up to his nose, then dropped it back on the sofa.

'You were wearing unusually expensive scent while doing the dusting then,' he said, then paused, waiting for one of them to say something. They did not, so Larsen gave a meaningless smile, and got to his feet.

'Perhaps I should be on my way.'

As he reached the door, he stopped.

'There was a tragic incident during the party at Hantsholm House,' he remarked. 'A young man was found in the grounds, seriously injured.'

'Seriously injured?' repeated Natasha, her voice barely a whisper.

'Yes. He had been shot twice, and is in a coma. He is being treated in the intensive care unit at the KAS, Glostrup.'

Larsen's eyes darted from Natasha to Seana, then back to Natasha.

'He was found because a woman, claiming to be Doctor Anderssen, telephoned the police. Of course Doctor Anderssen is a man, and responsible for the Iversen Land expedition, as you both know well. But at the time this call was made, the doctor was locked in a room, as part of some alcohol-induced practical joke it seems. Is that a coincidence, do you suppose?'

There was no answer.

'Have you any idea who the young man in Glostrup hospital might be?' asked the policeman.

Seana shook her head.

'Very well. I will need the names of some witnesses who can tell me where the two of you were last night. As you were at a party that should be easy to provide.'

'What the hell are you on about?' growled Natasha, her pale cheeks flushing red, her eyes glittering. 'Do you think we had something to do with whatever happened to that boy?'

'Did you have anything to do with it?' replied Larsen coolly.

'Of course not. But if someone has tried to murder him, perhaps you'd do better making sure he's protected, rather than hassling innocent people.'

'You think he's still in danger then?'

'Don't you?'

Larsen rubbed his cheek pensively.

'Nearly all murders and attempted murders are done on the spur of moment,' he remarked. 'They are the children of uncontrollable jealousy or blind anger, usually fuelled by drunkenness or narcotics. This attack took place at a party – which no doubt offered the usual cocktail of drugs, alcohol, and casual sex. Why should we suspect anything more than the same old story?'

'People in Denmark don't take guns to parties,' said Natasha.

'I dislike generalizations,' replied Larsen. 'After all, it depends what people we are talking about.'

'What do you mean?'

'I mean there is evidence that the young man is a drug-dealer from Christiania, who was being searched for by the police. Such people live in a world where guns are common. Perhaps he was shot to prevent him revealing anything, or just because he had been careless enough to let the police get on his tail.'

'So now you're saying he wasn't shot on the spur of the moment at all,' said Natasha. 'You're saying it was to do with drugs.'

Larsen shrugged.

'I thought you might be able to help me.'

'Why the hell did you think that?'

'Because the young man was at a party held by your university faculty, and for which your friend here, Ms Arnason, bought a ticket on Saturday.'

'I didn't go,' said Seana.

'Very extravagant of you, to buy a ticket only twenty-four hours before the party, and then not go.'

'It was stupid of me, sure. So?'

'So, Ms Arnason, it is strange that your ticket was used.' Larsen's voice was not loud, but it was hard and strong and it beat at Seana like a hammer. 'We traced the number, and found it in the used tickets box at Hantsholm House.'

'I gave it to someone.'

'Who? Could you tell me their name, please?'

'It was just some kid who wanted to go to a party. I didn't know him.'

'Where did you meet him?'

'At the shop where I work,' said Seana. 'He came in, and started moaning to me about not having anything to do on Sunday evening, so I gave it to him.'

Larsen did not try to conceal his disbelief.

'So you bought a ticket, then gave it away within a few hours? That seems bizarre behaviour, Ms Arnason.'

Seana shrugged. There was another long silence, during which no one moved.

'Is that all?' asked Seana, at last.

'I was thinking of asking you the same thing,' replied Larsen.

'What do you mean?' demanded Natasha.

'Perhaps I should be frank,' said Larsen, entirely unruffled. 'What I mean is that I find it very hard to believe you two are telling me the truth.'

'I don't give a fuck what you believe,' snapped Natasha. 'Our lives are our business – not yours.'

'That is not quite true, because I think I will soon have to insist on your making a formal statement. And if you have been lying, then there is the strong possibility of a charge of obstructing the police in their investigation of a serious crime. If nothing else.'

Suddenly Natasha choked, and hid her face in her hands. Seana put her arms round her friend, then turned to Larsen.

'Get out,' she said angrily. 'Get out now.'

Larsen realized he had overplayed his hand.

'There is a small piece of advice I would like to give you,' he said, instilling a placatory tone into his voice. 'It seems to me that both of you may soon find yourselves in serious difficulties. Perhaps even in danger . . . .'

'Trying to scare us won't work,' retorted Seana.

'I am not trying to scare you,' said Larsen. And for a moment his intense, controlled voice took over the room. 'I am warning you that if you persist in trying to deal with this matter without help, then things may become very bad for you.'

Natasha looked up.

'What do you mean?' she asked.

'As of this moment, I don't know,' admitted Larsen, shaking his head gently. 'If I did, it would be easier to give you advice. But I do not think this is a simple matter, and I feel certain that there is more to come. Are you quite sure there is no more that you wish to tell me?'

Seana glanced momentarily at Natasha, but her friend was staring fixedly at the floor.

'Go away,' she said.

Larsen took out a small pad, scribbled his name, and mobile phone number on it, then put it on the table.

'If you need me, or want to talk to me, you can always get me on this number,' he said. 'I hope I will hear from you soon.'

As the door shut behind him, Larsen stood still for a moment, and just managed to stop himself swearing, before walking swiftly away. Ten minutes later, his mobile rang. He answered it with a flash of hope, but it was only Poulson, his contact with the Danish police force.

'Sergeant Larsen, some fresh news I thought you might like to know.'

'Yes?'

'The ID of the man at Glostrup Hospital has been definitely confirmed. As we thought, his name is Jon Skalli, and he's a photographer from Christiania.'

'And last week his apartment was raided, and found to contain heroin,' said Larsen. 'Do we have anything at all on who gave the tip-off?'

'No. But that's often the way in these drug cases.'

'Did he have any previous convictions?'

'No.'

Larsen thought for a moment.

'I'd like to see Skalli's photographs,' he said at last.

'There wasn't much in his apartment. It looks as if he might have been about to make a flit.'

'No photographs of Greenland?'

'I don't think so. Most of the ones I saw were arty pictures of walls and windows and murals, together with a few obviously commercial shots. I wouldn't have said Mr Skalli did a roaring business. We have a detailed breakdown on what we found, which you can look at if you want.'

'Thanks,' said Larsen. 'I will. How is Mr Skalli?'

'Still in intensive care.'

'Poor bastard.'

'He was a heroin dealer.'

'He's still a poor bastard. Any family?'

'Not that we've managed to trace yet, though we're still looking. The doctors may need authorization from someone to turn off his life-support.'

'Is it that bad?'

'It could be.'

'Shit!' muttered Larsen.

'What did you say?'

'Nothing. But I think perhaps I will go and see Mr Skalli myself.'

'It'll be a waste of time.'

'Probably.'

The doctor nodded.

'We've just decided to operate,' she said. 'The patient is showing several signs of the onset of deterioration.

'What are the chances?' asked Larsen.

The doctor, pale, hawk-nosed, slashed lines around her mouth and shadows veiling her eyes, shrugged.

'Not good. And I would guess that even in a best-case scenario, some permanent damage will have been done.'

'What sort of permanent damage?'

'Medicine is not an exact science, Sergeant,' replied the doctor. 'And anything involving the brain is even less precise. Slickly-written newspaper pieces about the Human Genome Project, and such things, may imply that we now know practically everything there is to know about human physical make-up, but that's trash. To be frank, when I go into major brain surgery, your guess as to how the patient will react is not a lot worse than mine.'

'You don't sound very hopeful.'

The doctor shrugged again.

'I'll do the best I can. The hospital will contact you the moment there is any news.

Larsen remembered something Natasha had said.

'There's no way that anyone could get in to see the patient, is there?'

'They wouldn't find out anything if they did,' said the doctor dryly. She gestured to the door beside them. Through the glass window, Larsen could just see Jon Skalli, barely recognizable as human under the mass of drips, tubes, respirators and monitors that made up his life-support system.

'It was an attempted murder, Doctor,' said Larsen.

'Oh. I see. You think someone might try to finish the job. Don't worry, there's always at least one nurse on duty at the intensive care staff base, just through there. Now, if you will excuse me. . . .'

'Thank you for your time,' said Larsen.

The doctor nodded, and vanished. Larsen looked through the glass at Jon Skalli again, then sighed. He had a sudden desire to get some fresh air.

A few minutes walk from the great, white sprawling hospital, with its massive car parks and its signposts, was a small park – immaculately neat, with clean benches, waste bins, weed-free flower beds, tarmac paths, well-pruned trees and hedges, and signs forbidding dogs, except when they were on a lead.

Larsen sat down on a bench, and watched the sun sinking in a red and orange glow. Suddenly the colour was reflected close by in a flash of brilliant salmon-pink, and sharp white. A male bullfinch flew from a nearby bird-cherry tree. Flocks of sparrows were bustling about, looking for scraps, pigeons and crows flew overhead, and a blackbird prospected a sterile-looking area of well-mown grass. It suddenly occurred to Larsen that there were probably more species of bird in this dull little corner of suburban Denmark, than there were in the whole wilderness of Greenland.

Eventually he got up, and tried to burn off some of the frustration that surged round his veins, and glowed sullenly in his head, by striding rapidly along characterless, modern, tree-lined roads. He passed street after street of 1960s houses, each with their identical garage, their tidy little hedges walling off inviolable front gardens, their net-curtained windows, and their security systems. All of them ringed by invisible but overpowering '*Keep Away*' signs. They nauseated him, and he felt a great yearning for the messy, dirty, dilapidated houses of his own country, ringed by the flotsam and jetsam of a life outside, doors always open, inhabited by people who did not regard every single stranger as a threat.

12 In the Net

THE FIRST TOUCH was light as a feather. Scarcely to be noticed, save that her senses were strained to breaking point, taut as wire, sensitive as freshly-flayed flesh.

It crept round her neck, then began to tighten. She tried to run, but her legs dissolved into shivering gelatine, and she fell forward on her face. There was pressure on her back now, even as the grip on her throat tightened yet more. The pillow before her face closed in around her nose and mouth, clinging as tight as skin-thin rubber, leaving no space for even the tiniest air pocket. The blackness thickened, and the pressure on her throat grew irresistible. She struggled and writhed, but she was helplessly pinned to the bed of her death. She could not escape. There was no escape. Blood thundered in her ears, her heart was a mass of swelling, gut-clawing pain beneath her left breast. She tried to scream, but she could not.

And then, like the slash of a scalpel, cold air burst into her lungs in a wave that almost choked her.

She was sitting upright in the gloom, panting, her heart crashing, staring about her blindly, clutching at her throat, her mouth wide open to scream – if only she had had the breath to do so.

Gradually Natasha recovered control of herself. There was nothing to fear. There was nothing there, it had only been a dream. She turned on the bedside light, and reassured herself that she was safely in Seana's spare bedroom. The gleam of sun through a gap in the curtains, and the distant murmur of traffic, told her it was morning.

But the aftershock of blind terror was not so easily shrugged away. It still washed to and fro within her, so that her breath continued to hammer in her lungs, and her brain seethed.

She looked down at her quivering hands, and saw she had torn her thumb nail. Angrily she pulled at it, then winced as the nail tore deeper.

After a moment she got up, pulled on the blue and white cotton kimono that served as her dressing gown, and went to the bathroom. She cut her nail with clippers as she sat on the toilet, then washed her face and hands, feeling the normality of her actions soothe her twitching emotions. At last she went and knocked on Seana's door. There was no answer. Natasha opened the door.

The room was empty, and fresh panic struck, then she saw the clock. It was after eleven – Seana must have gone to work hours before.

'It's OK,' she said to herself. 'The windows are all locked, and the door's on a chain. There's nothing to worry about.'

After a moment she went back to the bathroom, had a shower, then got dressed, and went downstairs. On the kitchen table was a note: '*I'll be late tonight, maybe seriously late – Mrs E. needs me for stocktaking. Don't worry. If you want to go out, there's a spare key hanging by the door. S.*'

Natasha cooked herself a late breakfast, then glanced at the loudly ticking kitchen clock. It was midday – which meant that it was nine in the morning in east Greenland. A good moment to contact Jens or Wendy, and find out why they had decided to stay on for another two weeks.

The phone rang, half-concealed by the hiss of distance. It rang, and rang. There was no answer.

At length she gave up, went over to the front window and peered outside, through the net curtains. A couple of people walked by in the sunshine. A car drove along the street. Everything seemed normal, dull, safe. But still, fear pulsed deep in Natasha's veins.

As she sipped her coffee, a thought struck her, and she hastily went into the hall. The large bag was still there, and she began to burrow inside, throwing aside first Seana's bodysuit, then the breeches and boots she had worn at the fancy dress party. She could scarcely believe that, for an hour or two, she had actually enjoyed wearing them, enjoyed the new personality they had lent her – and the freedom to behave badly. Now they nauseated her. A condom may carry the charge of erotic excitement before sex, but afterwards it is a limp and repulsive thing. Natasha felt the same about her costume, but she was relieved Seana had not yet taken it back.

After a minute or two, she found the left gauntlet, pulled it out, and looked inside the cuff – at the numbers she had written down during the party: 55-0065. She noted it down on the telephone pad, then in a sudden attack of caution scribbled over the faint letters on the glove, until they were illegible. Almost guiltily, she put the glove away, zipped up the bag, and went upstairs.

She sat down on the bed, turned on her laptop, and began to search the Internet.

Looking for plane registration numbers turned out to be a grinding, seemingly endless, task. After well over an hour, during which she visited thirty or forty useless websites – most of them apparently set up by the sort of sad people who were actually interested in plane registration numbers for their own intrinsic fascination – she at last began to make progress.

Half an hour later, she had established that her number might identify an Ariana Airlines Ilyushin, last noted flying from Herat to Tashkent a year ago. Which made no sort of sense. So she returned to net-surfing, and the numbers next led her to East African Airways, which seemed equally improbable. However, a series of links progressed her to a site entirely devoted to military planes.

Natasha did not like the site. There was a lip-smacking satisfaction in the details on the weaponry available, and the massive destruction they could wreak. Contributors had added copious notes: gloating over the bomb weight delivered in Kosovo or Chechnya or Vietnam; going into graphic detail on what cluster bomblets could do, or the advantages of plastic shrapnel; comparing the MK 60 Captor mine and the MK 56 OA 05; considering the success rate of the AGM-142 Popeye missile, and the CBU-89 Gator bomb. One section especially made Natasha's skin crawl – a detailed discussion of the modifications that permitted planes to use chemical and biological weapons, together with cases when such weapons were rumoured to have been used. Natasha wished she could leave the site, but it was useful. In fact it was pay dirt, for it included an

Ancient History section, which contained an extensive index of the ID numbers of USAF planes back to the Second World War. And as Natasha scrolled through the seemingly endless pages and pictures, the number 55 sprang at her. Her fingers tight on the mouse, she looked for more, but the entry was brief:

'*The 55 designations were used for some of the early models of the B-52 Stratofortress, up to, but not including, the B-52G, developed in 1958. Links~.*'

Hurriedly Natasha tried the links, but they all took her to the B-52G, and its specifications, describing at length the integral fuel tanks in the wings, the remote-controlled tail-gun turret, the underwing attachment points for GAM-77 Hound Dog missiles, and the precise specifications of the eight Pratt and Whitney turbojet engines, later replaced by the TF-33 turbofan. There was nothing at all about ID codes of the early models, but at least Natasha now had something to work on.

She returned to the search engine and typed in B-52. The usual mass of alternatives followed, ranging from a cyber-cafe in Thailand to innumerable sites devoted to an American cult rock group. Determinedly she began to investigate any references to the plane. Fairly soon she had learned that the early B-52s had been stationed at all US airforce bases with a sufficiently long runway to accommodate them. That included Keflavik in Iceland; and Narsarsuaq, Kangerlussuaq, and Thule in Greenland. Natasha sensed she was closing in on her quarry, and a few minutes later she had it: the very plane – 55-0065. It had been a B-52D-20-BW, and it had first flown in 1957.

A further chain of links led her to one section of a massive US Air Force website, which focused exclusively and extensively on the history and details of the B-52. However, before being allowed to enter the part of the website she was interested in – a detailed gazetteer of all decommissioned planes up to 1980 – Natasha had to fill out the visitors' book, and explain her interest in the particular information that she wanted.

After a some thought she typed in that she believed a relation of hers had flown on a B-52 with the registration number 55-0065, and she was trying to track down exactly when it could have been. She didn't really believe that the feeble lie would be enough to open the website to her, but clearly the security blocks were not stringent, and after just two or three minutes, she found more details of that specific plane were – miraculously, it seemed – appearing before her. The 55-0065 had been built at Wichita, Kansas, and had initially been based with the 42nd Bombardment Wing at Loring air force base, Montana. It had been moved to the Eaker air force base, Arkansas, in November 1957, and also visited Andersen air force base, Guam, before crashing during trials near St Paul, Wisconsin, on 16 September, 1958. That was it.

Natasha considered the information, frowning. It seemed that she had come to a dead-end. But if the plane had crashed in Wisconsin, what was it doing in north-eastern Greenland? Natasha was not the sort of woman who gave up. There was an obsessiveness about her that had often contrived to get her in trouble, and that might perhaps have been the main reason that her love-life had been so unimpressive and unsatisfactory. One of her boyfriends had once told her that she wasn't really a people person.

The next thing was to probe local records in St Paul, Wisconsin. It was only after a few minutes that she realized there was no such place as St Paul, Wisconsin. Which seemed strange. Further research took her to St Paul, Minnesota, close to the Wisconsin border. Presumably that was the city that had been meant. But then she met a further problem: despite going through the records of first the *Star-Tribune* newspaper, then the Community Press Association, she was not able to find any reference to a plane crash on or around 16 September 1958.

It was now mid-afternoon, Natasha's eyes were aching, her right forefinger had cramp, and her head felt light. However, after making her fifth cup of thick black coffee, Natasha began a careful runthrough of the service history of all the B-52Ds. Eventually she had tracked down one hundred and sixty-six B-52Ds, of which twenty-six were on display in various places, and most of the rest had been scrapped, tested to destruction, mothballed, or used as ground instruction machines. However, twenty-eight had been destroyed by fire or crashed, including two mid-air collisions, and thirteen had been shot down in Vietnam, or so damaged by enemy action that they had to be scrapped. It seemed that the Air Force was open enough about losing B-52s. But then why did there seem to be a mystery about 55-0065?

While Natasha brooded afresh, her screen suddenly offered her an invitation to talk. Her instinctive response was to refuse, but then it occurred to her that whoever it was might be able to help her. She punched in her agreement.

'Hi cyber skiver,' came the typed message. 'You must be like me, really fascinated by these sexy big birds. Bobby.'

'You said it,' replied Natasha, after a moment. 'Actually I am trying to trace one of them, but somehow not getting what I need on her anywhere.' She signed it Matt – the male username she sometimes adopted.

'What is the sly bitch?' came the return message.

'Her serial number is 55-0065. She was a B-52D. The lady's said to have crashed in September 1958, but there are no details on the crash that make any sense.'

'Give me a few minutes. I know my way round this site pretty well.'

Natasha waited curiously. At length a fresh message came up.

'OK, Matt. You got a good one there. No details on the crash, nothing about what went wrong, nothing about anything. The bitch seems to have vanished off the earth. Something weird here, and I feel like spending some time looking for her. Give me your e-mail and I can come back to you. OK?'

Natasha looked at the message warily, then typed out her reply.

'Bobby. Thanks for your help, but I got reasons for not handing out my e-mail. Know what I mean? You got any news for me on the woman we been talking about, post it up on the University of Copenhagen biology site, under the heading Thayer G. If I get anything new, I will put it same place for you. OK? Matt.'

'OK Matt. No questions. I understand. The truth is out there. Keep checking – you will hear from me. Bobby.'

Somehow Natasha did not feel particularly encouraged by the exchange of messages. If anything, the reverse. Suddenly sick of the Internet, she quit. She wanted someone real to talk to, but Seana might not be back for hours.

'Perhaps I should go for a walk,' muttered Natasha to herself.

She yawned massively, then peered outside. The morning sun had completely vanished, and the window was speckled with ten thousand little freckles of rain, and the tiny, snaking streams that ran down from them. A big sandy-grey coloured car was parked thirty or forty metres away, and Natasha stared at it for at least a minute, then shook her head irritably.

'I'm starting to see ghosts,' she muttered to herself.

When she stepped outside, a few minutes later, into the steady drizzle, she was wrapped up in a battered brown jacket of Seana's, and she carried an umbrella. On reaching the road, she turned away from the big car, and hurried off along an unpredictable route through the suburban streets, every now and then turning to make sure that no one was following her. No one seemed to be.

She stayed out for a couple of hours, browsing in a large bookshop, then stopping for a beer and a leisurely sandwich. Leaving the café, Natasha briefly wondered whether to go into the university, or perhaps to Seana's shop. But it was still raining, the straight, unforgiving rain that does not feel too heavy, but is guaranteed to soak you to the skin. Seana's jacket was already dyed black by the water, and Natasha reluctantly decided to return to the house. It was growing dark when she got there, but Seana was not back yet. Natasha went upstairs, stripped off her wet clothes, pulled on her spare jeans and a sweatshirt, then sat down at the desk, and turned on her laptop. She went straight to the department e-mail, and checked under Thayer G. There was a message there, and as Natasha opened it, her heart beat a little harder.

'From Bobby G for Matt. You got a real interesting bitch, man. How did you come to it? This has to be more than a hunch. I got one cross-ref mentioned that means nothing to me. How about you? Just one word – Pituffik. Help me?'

That, at least, was easy.

'Bobby. Pituffik is the local name of the USAF base in north-west Greenland, usually called Thule. Does that help?'

She signed off, then found herself wondering briefly what the mysterious Bobby G looked like. Probably he was a sad and spotty geek who spent hours every day surfing the Internet on a vain search for conspiracies. The sort of person who believed there was a US base on Mars already, and that government-sponsored aliens were living amongst us. The sort of person, it struck her, that she seemed in some danger of becoming.

She reassured herself. The death of Frederik; the attempted murder of Jon Skalli; the strange lack of contact with Jens and Wendy – and their sudden decision to stay in Greenland for two more weeks; and now the plane without a history. It was enough to build a very real conspiracy theory on.

Her thoughts were broken by the sound of the telephone. She snatched it up.

'Hi, it's Seana. Look, Tash, we've just finished the stocktaking, and it appears that things are going really good, even better than the boss thought. So, would you believe, she's just invited me to dinner at the Spiseloppen.'

Natasha was impressed. The Spiseloppen was a seriously fashionable restaurant in Christiania, all greenery and modern paintings and top class food. She had only been there once, but she could still remember exactly what she had eaten.

'Great,' said Natasha. 'Enjoy. And don't miss out on the nougat cheesecake, it's out of this world.'

'OK. I won't be too late. Don't worry.'

Natasha hung up. A moment or two later there was a sound outside the house, round the back. A loud rustling, then a dull thump. Natasha started like a frightened six-year-old, then remembered Seana had told her that foxes often raided the local dustbins, ripping open rubbish sacks in their search for scraps. She went over to the window and looked out, but she could see nothing through the darkness and driving rain.

Perhaps half an hour later there was a knock on the door.

Natasha froze. There was another, louder knock.

'Hello,' called a muffled voice from outside. 'This is Sergeant Larsen. Could I speak to you for a moment.'

With a feeling of relief, she opened the door. A figure in a hooded jacket stood in the rain. Then suddenly Natasha saw the squat gun in the gloved hand, pointing straight at her belly.

'Turn round and go back inside,' said a soft voice. 'Do not make any sound or sudden movement, or I will have to kill you.'

Dully, Natasha did what she was told, and heard the door close behind her.

'Good. Now, Doctor Myklund, lie down on your face.

Natasha was barely able to move – despair had sucked all the energy from her limbs. As she lay there, she felt her hands strapped behind her back. A few moments later, her legs also were tied together, then something that felt like a scarf was fastened tightly over her eyes, so that not even the tiniest spark of light crept through.

'Good,' came that soft voice again. 'Now, I think it is time we had a talk, Professor Myklund.'

'Who are you?' said Natasha.

'You don't need to worry about that. What I wish to know is what you have discovered about 55-0065.'

'I don't know what you're talking about.'

There was a laugh.

'Then why is the number written on this note-pad?'

Natasha said nothing. Her stomach was an empty pit. Her mind curdled with fears she dared not face.

There was a minute or two's silence. The scarf that blindfolded Natasha also half-covered her ears, and she could not hear anything. She wondered if she had been deserted. Then that soft, calm, confident voice spoke again.

'All life, people say, is made up of decisions, and there is always a choice. That's existentialism – the belief that we are all free and responsible creatures who determine our own development. But of course sometimes the choices can be stark. The Jewish woman pushed into the gas chamber of Treblinka, unable even to fall to the floor because of the pressure of others around her, only had the choice between dying in blind panic, screaming, or dying in silence and relative dignity.'

Natasha realized the words were carefully chosen to feed the fear in her soul, but even so her throat tightened, and she could feel her skin rippling over her bones in the terror that came from complete helplessness.

'The choices facing you are not quite as limited as that wretched woman, or her sister in Rwanda fifty years later,' went on that relentless voice. 'But limited, they certainly are, Professor Myklund. I shall detail them for you. One: you can tell me everything you know about 55-0065. Everything. Two: you can lie or conceal things from me. Three: you can refuse to say anything. Now, let us consider the direct consequences of each of these decisions. Choices Two and Three lead to the same result. A few minutes of life, to provide the opportunity for you to change your mind, then a bullet in the back of the head.'

As he spoke, Natasha felt something cold and solid pressing against her neck, just below the base of her skull.

'Choice One will lead to my departure. However that will, as in all existentialist thinking – except when death ends the sequence – open up other choices. Choice A is for you to forget everything that ever happened connected with the plane in question, and that will lead to a recommencement of what might be described as your normal, day-to-day life, and the near-certainty that we will never meet again – because you are of no importance to me at all, except for a few fragments of knowledge you presently possess. Choice B is for you to inform people what has happened to you. Oddly, the consequence of Choice B will, in the long term, prove to be exactly the same as the consequence of Choices Two and Three. You understand me?'

He let the question float in mid-air for a little while, before going on.

'Of course you do. You are an intelligent, highly-educated woman. A simple flow diagram of action and consequence, such as I have just outlined, is child's play to a person like you. Now, I will give you five minutes to decide what you are going to do. Starting from this moment. . . .'

The room fell graveyard silent. Only that ever-present cold metallic pressure near the back of Natasha's ear reminded her what was happening.

'What if I tell you everything I know, but you don't believe me?' asked Natasha, her voice shaking.

'I want to believe you, Professor Myklund. Believe me. I really want to. But if I don't, then that counts as what we might call a subdivision of Choice Two, with the consequent results.'

'That's not fair.'

'Fairness is an overrated, rather superficial, and of course, entirely subjective and therefore impossible, concept. You have four minutes.

Silence fell again. Natasha's mind whirled, but she could see no alternative, no way out.

'I'll tell you what I know, but it isn't very much.'

'Don't say that, please, you're worrying me. Now, go on, Professor Myklund. Go on.'

13 Kidnap

NATASHA LAY ON the floor, trussed up like a chicken, blindfolded and gagged with parcel tape, aching from where her unseen captor had, without warning, kicked her in the ribs. Suddenly she heard keys rattle in the lock. The front door opened, then closed.

'Hi, I'm back,' came Seana's voice.

A moment later there came sounds of an exclamation, what might have been a slight scuffle, muttered words, then silence. Fear for her friend rose in Natasha's throat, like a bubble of high-pressure air, but it was at least ten minutes before she sensed someone close beside her.

'Professor Myklund,' came that hateful, soft, confident voice. 'I am leaving now. But before I go, I want to remind you not to speak to anyone. And to underline the point, I am taking your Eskimo friend with me. If I have any reason to think you have broken our agreement, then no one will see your friend again. Otherwise, I will release her when the time seems right. Oh yes, one other thing. If you crawl roughly in the direction you are facing, you will find some scissors on the ground. You can use them to free yourself. Goodbye, Professor. Thank you for your help.'

The door closed, and silence fluttered down like an autumn leaf. At last Natasha gathered the courage to begin to wriggle awkwardly forward. It took her perhaps ten minutes to find the scissors, then another quarter of an hour of awkward twisting before she had finally freed herself. Having done that, she staggered over to the sofa, collapsed on to it, and began to cry.

When there was a knock on the door, Natasha did not move. But the knocking went on, so she dragged herself up, turned on the outside light, and cautiously opened the door on the chain. This time it was Larsen.

'May I come in?' he asked.

She nodded and unchained the door. He came in, and sat down opposite Natasha in the neat, clean sitting room.

'Why are you here?' Natasha asked him, after a moment.

'Because when I tried to phone you, I was told the line was out of order, which seemed strange.' He nodded towards the telephone, which had been ripped from the wall. 'Are you going to tell me what happened?'

'Nothing has happened. It was just an accident.'

Larsen's slow gaze scanned her thoroughly. Her face was stretched and monochrome, as if a chemical had bleached all the life and colour from her skin, except for blotches of lurid red around her eyes and her nose, and what looked like dirt around her mouth. Her hands were trembling uncontrollably.

'Take a look at yourself in the mirror,' he said. 'Then say that to me again.'

Natasha hid her face, and her shoulders shook with sobs. It was several minutes before she had recovered enough to sit upright.

'I'm not allowed to say anything,' she whispered. 'If I do, he'll kill Seana. He'll kill me.'

Larsen put an arm round her.

'It's OK,' he said gently. 'I won't tell anyone.'

Natasha looked at him through wide, pale, tear-blurred eyes.

'I don't know if I can trust you.'

'No,' agreed Larsen. 'You don't. But you need to.'

'Why? What's the fucking point of my telling you?' she retorted, suddenly shoving him away. 'What the hell do I care about all this crap? I just want my friend back – and the only way that will happen is if I keep my mouth shut. I promised to keep my mouth shut.'

Larsen choked back his answer. This was a girl – no, a woman, he corrected himself – who needed delicate treatment. Whose instincts were to suspect and resist the police. Which meant that he needed to appear as something of an outsider himself.

'I respect your promise,' he said, after a moment. 'And maybe you're worried that everything you tell me will get passed on. Well, I've got enough trouble with the Danish police myself already, added to the fact that my boss in Nuuk hates my guts, but I'll risk making things even worse by promising that I won't tell anyone else anything at all, unless you agree. OK?'

Natasha stared at him nervously, suddenly aware that she was alone in the middle of the night with a man she knew almost nothing about, a man who had something hidden about him, an apart-ness that she found disturbing. On the other hand, she had to talk to someone. And that at this moment, her only choice was this squat, solid looking Greenlander, with the gentle manner.

'It's Seana's life,' she said. 'We mustn't do anything, or he'll kill her.'

'OK,' Larsen said again.

There was a brief pause, then without even making the decision to talk, suddenly everything, every detail, was pouring out of Natasha – from the moment that she had gone to look for Jon Skalli in Christiania, through the party, to the events of the past few hours.

Larsen listened in almost complete silence, only putting in the occasional small question when he sensed Natasha was beginning to run down, or if there was a detail he needed to confirm. He wrote nothing down. He knew any sign that he was recording what she was telling him would stop Natasha instantly, but he tried to hammer every point into his mind. Like pitons into the face of a precipice.

At last she finished, and slumped back into her chair, exhausted. Larsen sat in silence for at least a minute, then he scratched his head.

'You didn't see what this man looked like?'

'No, other than that he was tall. His face was completely hidden in his anorak hood.' She opened her hands. 'I could meet him now, and never guess it was him. Except for one thing. I'm pretty sure I'd recognize his voice again; it was soft and had a faint sort of accent, though I suppose it could have been disguised.'

'And what exactly did you tell him about this plane?'

'Everything I'd found out – which wasn't much. But he seemed happy with it.' Natasha sighed heavily, then clasped her hands behind her neck. 'There was one thing I didn't tell him though – but only because I was so scared that I forgot.'

'What?'

'I'm waiting for an e-mail about the plane. Maybe it'll have something in it – but then so what?'

'So we need everything we can find, if we are to sort this out and release Seana.'

'OK' said Natasha dully. 'Let's go see then.'

They went upstairs. On one side of the landing the door was open into Seana's bedroom. Larsen glanced inside, and saw clothes everywhere: on the floor, on the chest of drawers, hanging on the cupboard handles, draped over chairs, even on the bed. Jackets, T-shirts, tights, trousers, shoes, boots, belts, trainers, jogging pants, skirts, knickers, bras, socks, scarfs and shirts. Clean and dirty. New and old. Black, white, red, blue, green, yellow, and more and more black. It reminded Larsen of his daughter. That was exactly how her room had been.

Natasha led the way into the spare room where she was staying. In sharp contrast to Seana's room, there was almost nothing inside. Just a single soft bag, one set of clothes on the back of a chair, a laptop on the desk, and a faint perfume in the air.

Natasha sat down on the bed, then gestured to the laptop.

Many young Greenlanders used computers constantly – they were ideal for a thinly populated country where getting around was difficult and expensive, and there was little in the way of indoor entertainment. But Larsen had resisted computer literacy, and he looked at the laptop as if at an alien being.

'Well?' said Natasha wearily. 'Don't you want to have a look?'

'The privacy laws don't allow me to,' he replied, thinking on his feet. 'You have to do this.'

'OK.' She got up, sat down at the desk close beside him, then turned on the computer, her hands fluttering efficiently over the keyboard. A couple of moments later they were looking at the Thayer G file on the Biology department noticeboard.

'What does Thayer G mean?' asked Larsen.

'Thayer's gull,' said Natasha briefly. 'And here's what we're looking for.'

Larsen read the e-mail over her shoulder.

'Matt, my man. Things are hotting up. I pushed on with the

Greenland theme, like you said, and I got a hint that your bird was stationed very briefly at Bluie West One – which must be some base or other. I don't like this crash in Wisconsin either. Only brief references to it in the records, and nothing at all until about three months after it happened – which makes no sense. Anyway, since we spoke, I get this feeling someone is trying to track me, so this computer has to close down for a while. Bobby will be back when he can find himself somewhere secure, believe it. But you take care too. There are motherfuckers who no like it when you rattle their cage. Take care, man, and make sure these messages are good and properly shredded. Know what I mean? Remember to expect the unexpected. There is something out there.'

'What does it mean?' asked Larsen.

'I'm not sure about the last bit,' replied Natasha. 'But the rest is to do with the plane ID number Jon Skalli gave me.'

Larsen frowned. The phrase Bluie West One had a dim familiarity, but he could not place it. He brooded for a while, then shrugged. His mind felt slow and stupid.

'What's the time?' he asked.

'Half past ten.'

'I'd best be on my way then.' He got up to go.

'Wait,' said Natasha.

'What is it?'

She hesitated.

'I don't want to be alone tonight. Not after what's happened.'

'Aren't there any friends or family you could contact?'

Natasha's mind skated swiftly over people she knew at the university. None of them was the sort of person you could phone at midnight and ask a favour from.

'Could you . . . would you mind staying?'

Larsen looked at her suspiciously.

'The sofa's quite comfortable,' she said, with an almost pathetic air. 'Please. I'm scared.'

'OK,' he said, reluctantly.

Ten minutes later, Natasha had vanished upstairs, and Larsen was stretched out on the sofa, under a couple of blankets. It was one of the times that he was pleased he was not a tall man, for he was able to curl up where he lay with relative comfort. The lights were out and his eyes were shut. A huge wave of tiredness had swept over him, and he could sense himself going to sleep – yet a small part of his mind remained wide awake and alert, struggling to make links between disconnected items, dates, places, people. Working out the questions he needed to ask, if he was to get where he needed to go. And it was that which reminded him what Bluie West One was.

As the thought came to him, sleep suddenly vanished. He got out his mobile phone, and dialled the police HQ at Nuuk. Jette answered.

'You're working late,' said Larsen.

'Tuesday's my evening on,' she replied. 'Anyway, it's only seven here. What can I do for you?'

'Do we have anything in the files about what happened after the old US air base at Narsarsuaq was closed down?'

'You don't feel you should be a bit more contemporary, do you?' said Jette. 'I mean we're talking about the time that my mum was born.'

'This is serious.'

'OK. I'll have a look, but don't expect much.'

She rang him back an hour later.

'There's not a lot. The base was closed in November 1958, and after the Yanks left, a Norwegian firm, Wegner Engineering, got the contract to strip down what was left. Apparently there was some trouble about it – they made a lot of money, and local people thought they should have got a cut.'

'Does Wegner Engineering still exist?'

'I had a feeling you were going to ask that. The answer is no – they were taken over by another Norwegian firm, Ølssen Brothers, in the late 1980s.'

'Shit!'

'I haven't finished. Gustav Wegner, the founder of Wegner Engineering, became a non-executive director of Ølssen Brothers, and – incredibly – I've found an address and telephone number for him in Stockholm, Sweden.'

'Jette, you're a gem.'

'You said it.'

Larsen copied down the address and telephone number.

'I owe you a meal out when I'm back.'

'I'll take you up on that. But before you get too excited, I should warn you that the address is eleven years old.'

'If he's there, I'll find him.'

Jette laughed.

'Have fun.'

Larsen tried to settle down again, but sleep had entirely left him, and he lay on his back and let thoughts race through his mind as time ground past. Suddenly there was a faint creak and a rustle close by. Larsen pushed himself upright, so the blankets fell off him. A breath of cold air told him that one of the doors was open. Swiftly, almost soundlessly, he rolled off the sofa and poised himself a couple of metres closer to the door, where he could now see a dim silhouette. Unmoving. As if frozen.

Aware that the blackness of the sitting room hid him, Larsen edged closer to the shape, even as he slipped away from the sofa. Still the shape did not move. Larsen crept forward, then sprang.

As he landed, there was a crack as something broke under the weight of his heel. At the same moment came a startled gasp. The figure tried to run, then crumpled and fell without resistance as Larsen pinned them to the ground.

'Who are you?' demanded the policeman harshly.

'It's Natasha,' responded a choking voice.

Larsen started violently, then got up. He turned on the hall light. Natasha, wide-eyed, shaking, wearing only a long T-shirt, was still lying on the ground, staring up at him.

'I'm sorry,' said Larsen. 'I didn't realize. . . .'

'No,' replied Natasha. She summoned up an unconvincing attempt to smile.

Larsen reached down and helped her up.

'I thought you were an intruder,' he explained.

'Yes. Of course. I . . . I don't know what I was doing. Standing there. It was stupid. Stupid.'

Larsen's own embarrassment faded as he realized that hers was much greater.

'Was there something you wanted to say to me?' he asked.

'Yes. I suppose there was.' She walked past him, turned on a light, and sat down on the sofa, where he had just been sleeping. The lower half of her strong, well-toned thighs gleamed a little in the light. 'How much danger do you think Seana is in?'

Larsen glanced down on the floor, then picked up his phone, and examined it. It was cracked and shattered. He scowled, tried a number, then a second, and finally lobbed the mobile neatly into the wastepaper basket.

'There goes one piece of Royal Greenland Police Force property,' he said. 'My stupid fault for leaving it lying on the floor.'

He looked up, caught Natasha's eye, and sat down at the other end of the sofa.

'I'm sorry, what did you say?'

'I was asking if Seana is in real danger.'

'I don't know,' he admitted. 'But we have to take it very seriously.'

'I thought that too.' She was still shivering. 'Do you think that man will come back here?'

'Probably not.'

'Probably,' she repeated. 'That's not a very encouraging word.'

'What do you mean?'

'I mean that I'm still scared. Very scared.' Then she gave a weak laugh. 'But the way you sprang on me and knocked me down is sort of encouraging really. It makes me feel safer knowing you're there.'

He said nothing. Slowly she got back to her feet, but she did not leave. With flaring eyes, she watched him. But Larsen found his own gaze turning on her small, neat breasts, topped with erect nipples, which pressed through the thin fabric of the T-shirt.

'Why do you think that man took Seana, not me?' she asked at length. The same question had occurred to Larsen also.

'You were both on the expedition.'

'Yes, but Seana was the most junior member. If he wanted to find out more, it would have been smarter to take me.'

'Except you would have been missed. Doctor Anderssen had already commented on your disappearance. No one besides us knows about Seana.'

'Yes,' said Natasha, after a moment. 'That must be it.'

'But I think I ought to arrange police protection for you.'

'No, no. If you do that, he'll kill Seana. You mustn't. Anyway – I think I'm going back to Greenland next week.'

'Why is that?'

'Mainly to check that all the expedition's equipment gets safely put on board the ship. But also to see what's happening with Jens and Wendy. I haven't heard a thing from them for nearly six days.'

'Doctor Anderssen spoke to them on Sunday.'

Natasha said nothing.

Larsen looked at her shrewdly.

'You don't believe him, do you?'

She shook her head.

'I think they're dead,' she said in a voice that was no more than a whisper.

Suddenly, without warning, she sat down again, close beside him and put her arms round him. The warmth of her body seeped through to his skin, and hungrily, he kissed her. She neither joined the kiss, nor resisted, but simply relaxed softly in his arms. He pulled her closer to him, and slipped his right hand round under the T-shirt and on to the smooth, enticing curves of her back and bottom, barely concealed by the knickers she was wearing. He ran his hand eagerly up and down, pressing his forefinger against her spine, so that she arched her back a little and her breasts pushed warmly against his chest. He kissed her again, thrusting his tongue deep into her mouth, feeling desire grow hot and urgent within him.

Still she barely reacted. Larsen's left hand ran down on to her thigh, stroked the outside, and then slid round to the inside. He kneaded the flesh a little, then stroked higher and higher, feeling the first strands of wiry pubic hair at the very top of her leg. He kissed her again. More fiercely this time. Then looked down at her. Her eyes were shut, and her face seemed almost lifeless, grey-tinged, dull-skinned.

Gently he let go of her, and she lay back against the sofa. After a moment she opened her eyes and looked at him.

'It's probably just bad communications,' she said. As if nothing had happened. 'I knew we should have spent more on radio equipment – satellite phones aren't reliable enough, not that far out in the wilds. But I can't help feeling something bad has happened to them.'

Larsen said nothing. After a moment Natasha yawned massively.

'Anyway if I'm going to be good for anything, I'd better get to sleep. It's late.'

She went out, closing the door behind her. Then Larsen heard her stop on the stairs, and come back down again, like a child that does not want to go to bed. The door opened again, and her face appeared.

'Would you mind if I left this open?' she asked.

'OK,' he replied.

'Good-night.'

'Good-night.'

She vanished again, but Larsen noticed that she had left the upstairs landing light on, and he guessed her bedroom door was open also. He turned off the lights in the sitting room, lay down on the sofa again, pulled the blankets over him, and closed his eyes.

In spite of himself Larsen found himself wondering what would happen if he went upstairs. But there was nothing between him and Natasha. And he knew that if she did accept him into her bed, it would only be from fear, or the desire for comfort, not from her true feelings. So he stayed where he was, and remembered Risa back in Nuuk.

But he could smell Natasha's perfume on the cushions, and on his own hands. And he lay awake and restless deep into the small hours, trying to fight off the all-pervading aura of women that the house carried.

14 Almhult

THE TRAIN FROM Copenhagen to Helsingør, and the ferry over to Halsingborg, had gone smoothly, but then there was a train breakdown on the main line north, and Larsen's carefully calculated connections fell apart. Eventually, with the help of an earnest and balding desk clerk at Halsingborg station, he worked out an alternative, but the result was that he had to catch a slow-moving local train to the spacious, broad-avenued little town of Lund, then wait for three more hours, before catching the Malmo–Stockholm express. At least it gave him the opportunity to get a good meal – an enormous pizza, topped with artichoke hearts.

Sweden felt very different from Denmark – less approachable, slightly self-important and humourless. Although people pretended not to look at him, he knew they were, and some seemed to find his Danish hard to understand. Certainly he found their replies difficult.

The Stockholm train was full, but he managed to find a seat in an old-fashioned-looking compartment, where several people were already asleep. No one spoke to him, barely anyone even moved, except when the ticket inspector passed through a few minutes later. Outside, the softly rolling farmland of Skane passed by, with its neat villages of large wooden houses; its crops; its rich green meadows, grazing cows and horses, and flocks of busy starlings and pigeons. Larsen stared out of the window, and thought of cliffs and stony promontories; shoals of rich blue icebergs and secret mountain valleys; glaciers, cruel grey sea, sharp-bladed wind, and the unending white snow. Suddenly he felt helpless, almost despairing. He would never understand people who lived in this peaceful, tamed world, where the weather was just a mild inconvenience, and their comfortable little lives were planned out before them like railway tracks. He would have a better chance of comprehending the inhabitants of the Amazon rainforest, or Tibet, or Ethiopia.

As the light died, and the train steadily made its way north, the land began to change. The farmland grew more broken up, and small patches of deciduous woodland were replaced by conifers – great marching waves of evergreen trees, that swept forward like an invading army from the rolling hills to the west. Larsen watched for some time, but the compartment was warm, and eventually he dozed off.

He woke suddenly, but except for the fact that the western sky was almost entirely dark, there seemed little change. The train pounded away northwards, into the province of Smaland. Dark forests rose on every side now, broken only by the occasional flashes of yellow light which told of small towns. In the compartment everyone still seemed to be asleep, but Larsen no longer felt tired. He sat up, and waited.

The station at Almhult was almost deserted. Three or four people hurried away into the darkness, and the air was full of the rich, scented smell of pine. A guard briefly descended, checked no one was boarding, then climbed back on to the train, and it continued on its long journey north. Larsen, his bag over his shoulder, felt a little lost. He had not expected to arrive in the town so late.

At the far end of the platform a teenage couple were sitting on a bench, kissing. Two bottles of Falcon beer were on the ground beside them, but they were completely engrossed in each other, so tangled up it was hard to tell where one began and the other ended. Larsen looked at them for a moment, and envied the unselfconsciousness and energy of their youth. The ability to blind themselves to everything but the moment. Maybe he had had it once, but it seemed less and less likely. His mind floated back to Risa. They got on well most of the time, but both of them spent too much time worrying. Worrying about what things implied; about what their real feelings might be – whatever real meant; about the dull realities of day-to-day life, and deadening fears of an unpredictable future.

Such things did not concern the entwined couple at all. They simply followed their desires and instincts, and a battery of clichés supported them: let tomorrow take care of itself, don't look a gift horse in the mouth, don't cross bridges till you come to them. But Larsen's precise, controlled mind dismissed such concepts. The whole essence of his life lay in foreseeing what would happen, trying to react to situations even before those situations had arisen. Guessing that the drunk would draw a knife before he actually did. Assessing when the thief might strike again. Predicting the behaviour of a killer. He could not let himself drift with the current, even though sometimes he desperately wanted to. And Risa was the same. It had been that which had attracted him to her, but sometimes he feared it was also that which could poison their relationship – he dared not use the word 'love', even in his own hidden thoughts.

'Hey, oxygen's becoming an issue here,' came a girl's voice.

Larsen saw that the kissing couple had detached from each other, and the girl was getting up. Seeing Larsen, she gave an easy smile, and flicked back her long fair hair.

'Hi.'

The man – tall, with similar longish blond hair, and an inexpressive, blunt face – still had his arm round his girlfriend.

'Are you lost?' he asked, looking at Larsen with open curiosity.

'Thank you. No.'

'He's not lost,' said the man, turning to his girlfriend. 'It's 10.30 at night on Thursday 12 September. He's in Almhult station, and he's not lost. Some things are too hard to believe.'

She laughed. The man turned his attention back to Larsen.

'But what are you doing here?' he persisted, and Larsen sensed that he was slightly drunk, though whether on alcohol or sex was hard to tell.

'I think that's my business,' said Larsen calmly.

'Sure, sure. I don't want to be nosy. It's just that no one ever comes here, except people with holiday homes in the woods. And they always come in cars.' He paused, then added. 'Except for a few Danes and Germans, and one English couple who camped here last year, we don't get anyone who isn't Swedish.'

Larsen did not reply, but the man still seemed determined to talk.

'It's a small town, Almhult. Some time in the eighteenth century a famous man was born here, but he was the sort of famous man no one's heard about. Now there are maybe 5,000 people, and nothing ever happens here. Once every year or two a moose appears, walking along one of the side streets, and that's front-page news. Everyone says to each other: 'Did you see the moose? What was it doing?' Like Almhult is so dull, people can't understand why even a moose would want to visit. So that's why I wondered if you're lost. Are you Vietnamese, maybe?'

Larsen shook his head.

'I think you're an Eskimo,' said the girl suddenly. 'You speak Danish, so I think you're an Eskimo from Greenland.'

'I'm from Greenland, but we don't like being called Eskimos. It's like calling a black man a nigger. We are Inuit.'

'Oh. Right. Sorry.'

'That's OK. Is there anywhere to stay here?'

'There's the Haga Park Hotel, but it's pretty expensive for what it is. Why not try Harlund's bed and breakfast. We'll show you where it is.'

'That's OK. Just tell me the way.'

'No, no,' said the man. 'Don't deprive us of the pleasure. You're one of the most interesting things to happen to Almhult this autumn. Not that that's saying much.'

'We do have rather a good IKEA,' remarked the girl vaguely.

Next morning, Larsen got out of bed and pulled back the cream-coloured curtains. It was sunny, and he found himself gazing out on to the half-wooded Nicklabacken park, and beyond to the town hall. The bed and breakfast was a modern house, white, with neat windows and shutters, steps up to the wooden door, a balcony at the far end and tumbling geraniums in hanging baskets. Pleasant, yet oddly characterless. It was a description that also applied to his bedroom – with its cream-coloured bed, cream-coloured chest of drawers and cream-coloured flower vase holding an unconvincing display of golden rod – and to the house's owner, Mrs Harlund, a Swedish woman in her fifties who said almost nothing, and was also vaguely cream-coloured.

At breakfast, Larsen asked Mrs Harlund the way to the address that he had.

'It is about five kilometres,' she said carefully. 'On the far side of the lake, off the road to Pjatteryd. You will need a map.'

Half an hour later Larsen was walking through broad, airy streets of comfortable detached houses towards Lake Mockeln. It was further than Larsen expected from looking at the map, but eventually he reached a camping site, which looked out over the lake, its many small bays picturesque with reeds and waterlilies. Scattered boats were visible, and there were one or two fishermen, otherwise everything seemed deserted – the camping site already closed down for the winter. He took the small road that ran round the south of the lake, darting in and out among the pines and spruces that covered much of the area. The forest was broken up by many clearings: fields, where hay lay drying on long lines of fences, or a few cows grazed absently; intensively farmed vegetable patches; and occasional stretches of crops. There were also frequent unsurfaced turnings leading off to hidden houses.

Keeping a close eye on the map, without which he would soon have become hopelessly lost, Larsen walked on. As he got further from Almhult, the forest grew thicker and almost impenetrable, but in places there were huge empty spaces, covered in a thick skin of woodshavings, where the trees had been clear-felled, and a mass of undergrowth had sprung up among the great wheel-ruts and the piles of logs waiting to be carried away to the lumber yards.

Hot and sticky, pursued by a halo of flies, midges and mosquitoes, Larsen reached the turning he was looking for. It looked exactly like thirty other turnings, except for a battered wooden sign marked Wegner in faded letters. Larsen took the track, which dived into the forest, heading back in the direction of the lake. There was a flash of russet as a red squirrel darted in and out of pools of sunshine. Further on, near the side of the track, he saw a huge mass of pine needles, almost two metres high, and then realized that the ground around the pile was alive with red-black wood ants.

The track drifted on idly through the forest, which changed from evergreen to birch woodland, then swung left and north, past a small stony beach which looked out on a quiet enclosed bay, hemmed in on the far side by reedbeds. In the open water a pair of black throated divers fished peacefully, while the shores were lush with seeding purple loosestrife and rosebay willow herb. A few invisible birds were calling in the trees, and a late-staying tern flew elegantly and unexpectedly overhead, its angled white wings and blood-red beak reminding Larsen of the Arctic terns of Greenland. It hovered briefly, then flew on.

At last, without warning, the track swung round a group of tall conifers, and stopped in front of a large, rather battered, double garage. There was no sign of a house, just a muddy Volvo estate in one half of the garage, and a wood pile together with an assortment of tools and abandoned household belongings in the other. Larsen looked around, then followed a small, overgrown footpath. It led through a copse of birches, then a gap in a drystone wall, to a lawn, lined with immaculately kept flower beds, rich in dahlias. Beyond rippled a broad vista of Lake Mockeln, reaching away to the east.

At the end of the lawn was a small, cedar-red house, two storeys high, with a covered porch painted sky blue, and a front door the same colour. It looked unoccupied – all the windows were tightly shut, and several had curtains drawn across them. Larsen went up to the door and knocked.

There was no reply.

He knocked louder, and after perhaps a minute, to his relief, he heard a distant shuffling. It was at least another minute before the door opened.

An old man stood there. He was small – shorter than Larsen, and much thinner, with skin that seemed little more than a wrinkled covering over his prominent bones. His hair was wispy and white, but still covered his head, and fell almost to his shoulders in rat's tails. He had a scrubby grey beard, a sharp-featured face half-hidden behind massively thick spectacles, and a determined manner. Despite the fine weather, he was dressed in a thick grey cardigan, with the collar up around his scrawny neck, and grubby-looking woollen trousers. There were down-at-heel slippers on his feet.

He peered at Larsen.

'Who are you? Where do you come from?' His voice was high-pitched, cracked and querulous.

'My name is Tomas Larsen. . . .'

'Where do you come from? What do you want here?'

'Are you Mr Gustav Wegner?'

'What is it to you? What do you want? How did you get here? Answer my questions.' The man's pointed chin stuck out aggressively.

'I am Sergeant Tomas Larsen of the Royal Greenland Police Force,' said Larsen, showing his ID card, which Wegner perused suspiciously. 'I would like to ask you some questions about your company, Wegner Engineering, if you don't mind.'

'Why should I mind? But you don't want me. I sold out fifteen years ago – more fool me. If I'd hung on another five or six years, I would have made four times the money – and I would have been in the South of France not here. Anyway, I sold out to Ølssen Brothers, and they've since merged with some American combine, I don't remember the name. It doesn't mean anything to me. You've come to the wrong place, Mr Larsen. And why didn't you just phone me? It would have saved you a lot of time.' He laughed.

'Mr Wegner,' replied Larsen calmly. 'As you know perfectly well, you don't have a telephone here – the only number you are listed with is your flat in Stockholm. I tried it repeatedly before, and with some difficulty, I finally discovered that you had this summer home in Smaland.'

'I like the feeling I'm completely cut off from everything when I come here. No phone, no television, no radio. Just a fortnightly drive into Almhult to buy food, and barely a word exchanged with anyone for weeks on end. I like that, Mr Larsen. No one visits me, no one troubles me, no one even sends me letters. The worst I have to put up with is occasional fishermen, and they don't say anything, or stay long. There's no fish worth catching round here.' He laughed again, then stopped abruptly. 'You take the point, I'm sure. I like to be alone, and you are interfering with my privacy, so I would be pleased if you would leave.'

He began to close the door.

Larsen stopped him with his foot.

'I have not come this far to be sent away like an unwanted salesman,' he said.

'You'll do what you're damn well told,' retorted the old man, his skinny hand folding itself slowly into a useless little fist. 'This is Sweden, and people have rights. What are you doing here anyway? If you are a policeman, why isn't there a Swedish policeman with you? Explain yourself.'

'I am trying to,' replied Larsen. 'But it may take a little time. Could we perhaps sit down somewhere. I am feeling rather hot and tired.'

'You're not coming into my house,' snapped Wegner. Then relented a little. 'There's a garden bench.'

'Thank you.'

Wegner grunted, and emerged on to the sunlit lawn. He carefully locked the door, then put the key into his pocket.

'Round there,' he muttered, gesturing.

Larsen walked along a well-kept gravel path, and found himself on a stretch of daisy-starred grass that reached down to a thin line of rushes, with the lake beyond. A sturdy home-made bench, screened on one side by a trellis, thick with honeysuckle, looked out over the lake, where a great crested grebe drifted.

Larsen sat down. The old man shuffled past him, his slippers slapping against his thick-socked feet, and settled on the far end of the bench.

'Well?' he said.

'It's about your old firm, Wegner Engineering.'

'You told me that already. I may be old, but my mind hasn't gone yet. Get on with it.'

'You set up your firm in 1957, and your first big contract came the next year.'

'Are you asking me, or telling me?'

'Is that correct?'

'Obviously you've done your homework, but I have no idea why you should be interested.'

'Could you tell me about the contract in late 1958?'

'Why?'

'I am investigating a plane accident in Greenland two weeks ago.'

The old man rubbed a bent finger over his dry, cracked lips, and stared at Larsen through his thick spectacles, which somehow dehumanized his eyes, made them inexpressive, and dimly fish-like. Larsen had no idea what he was thinking.

'It sounds to me like you are talking nonsense, young man,' said Wegner. 'What could my work over forty years ago have to do with a plane crash in the last two weeks?'

'It appears to be a possibility that there is some link between a plane serial number and the accident. That plane number is 55-0065.'

'If you think that number means anything to me, you are much mistaken.'

'The number identifies an American B-52 Stratofortress, which vanished, or crashed, in late 1958, shortly before the time that your firm was undertaking its contract in Greenland.'

'So what?'

Larsen realized he was losing Wegner's interest. Changing his approach, he lowered his voice, and injected an air of urgency into it, leaning towards Wegner as he spoke.

'Has anyone else come here recently? Has anyone else asked you about the autumn of 1958?'

Wegner stifled a yawn.

'Of course not. Why should they?'

'They may come any time.'

'Who?'

'There are other people out there who are very interested in precisely what it was that happened to 55-0065. And before long they will certainly learn that your firm was given the contract for clearing up Bluie West One. Then they will come looking for you.'

Wegner's attention was sharply back in focus. A faint emotion, which might have been fear, flickered on the man's face.

'What do you need to know?' he snapped. 'It was just a job, that's all it was. A job.'

'How did you come by the job?' asked Larsen sharply. Wegner shrugged.

'We tendered for it. The USAF and the Danish government accepted our offer.'

'I thought it was the Norwegian government that took on the responsibility of cleaning up the base.'

'You have been doing your homework, haven't you?'

'I spent yesterday morning researching your firm, Mr Wegner.'

'I suppose that's as good a way of wasting time as any. Well, for what it's worth, I suppose you're right. My memory isn't what it was. So the Norwegian government gave us the contract then. We fulfilled it. End of story.'

He's lying, thought Larsen instinctively. Then his confidence faded, and he took another approach.

'Was it profitable?'

'Fairly. But we were only the sub-contractors, and most of the profit went to the Norwegian government.'

'Nonetheless, your firm did very well out of it, didn't it? Your taxable profits went from zero to half a million dollars in a year, and the share price quadrupled between October 1958 and March 1959. People might say that single contract made your fortune.'

'Fortune!' repeated Wegner dryly.

'Yes. In those days, it was a fortune. But there's something that worries me about the whole thing. Why did the US and Danish governments both back off decommissioning the base, and why was the contract sold to Norway for just quarter of a million dollars? That's a ridiculously low price, when there was the potential for such massive amounts of salvage.'

'You're on the wrong track, son. The Americans aren't fools. They'd already removed all the high-tech gear.'

'Of course, but there was a lot of other stuff. The Norwegian government's figures show them profiting to the tune of at least a million dollars worth of salvage, and I doubt your company did much worse. So it was good deal. A very good deal. And that's surprising too. Your firm had only been in existence for fifteen months – why should such a small concern win such a big contract.

'It's what happened.'

'I couldn't find the records of what other firms tendered for the contract, but maybe they were all small firms too. Is that right?'

'How can you expect me to remember? Ask these questions to the people who awarded the contract, don't ask me. And I still don't see what it has to do with you, or with anything that's going on today.'

Again, Larsen sensed that Wegner was hiding something, and again he switched his line of attack.

'How was the contract?'

The old man shrugged.

'Straightforward, though a lot of work. The Americans had stripped the place of everything they thought would be useful, so it was up to us to clear out the rest. It took several months, and we had to take on a lot of extra workers but, as you say, we did pretty well. It set the firm up.'

'Were you involved in the base before the Americans had left?'

'Of course. We had to ensure the terms of the contract were being fulfilled, and that they were leaving intact those areas they had specified, that sort of thing.'

'And?'

'There wasn't a problem.'

A cold breeze had sprung up from nowhere, and was rustling the trees. Clouds were racing overhead, blotting out the September sun, and Wegner pulled his cardigan closer around him.

'Have you any more questions?' he demanded harshly. 'I've had enough of being out here. There's no warmth in talking.'

'Just two or three more minutes. How did the Americans clear out the base?'

'What do you mean?'

'Did they use ships?'

Wegner shrugged.

'Maybe.'

'You're sure?'

'Why?'

'Narsarsuaq is on Eriksfjord, and in November the inner sections of the fjord are virtually always frozen. Furthermore the Qoorqut glacier means there are always bergs in the fjords – at any time of year. And while Narsarsuaq has a harbour, large vessels generally stick to Qaqortoq or Narsaq.'

'Are you trying to trap me?'

'No,' said Larsen soothingly. 'Just to find out the truth.'

'Maybe it wasn't ships then. I can't remember much, except how bloody cold it was, and that the wind was so loud I couldn't even tell when planes were coming in.'

'So the Americans cleared the base using planes?'

'Yes. Yes, they did. Huge great things, I remember them now. They looked too big to fly, but fly they did, making the ground shake as they passed over. B-52s. They were built as atomic bombers, you know. Used to make me laugh – the idea that those clumsy great things could destroy the world.'

'B-52s,' repeated Larsen. 'That's what they used to empty Narsarsuaq base? You're sure?'

'Yes.'

Wegner's face was creased, and his eyes were looking far away. The distant past, with its hypnotic attraction for the old, had caught him in its meshes. He might find it hard to remember things that had happened last month, or last week, or even yesterday, but that was not how he judged himself. If he could still summon up a clear memory of something that had happened over forty years ago, then he knew his mind was as sharp as it had ever been.

'Is there anything else you can remember? inquired Larsen.

'Yes. It's coming back to me. The weather had been bad, that's why we were let into the base late – it was supposed to be the beginning of November, but the Americans couldn't clear their things in time. It was that massive great hospital which was the problem, though it wasn't our business – I never could understand why not.

'Anyway, things suddenly improved, the snow stopped, and it got bitterly cold, but very beautiful. I can still see that last plane talking off, the evening before we started work. It was late, and growing dark, and the northern lights had begun. I had never seen them before – first there was a sort of fuzzy shimmer, and then it gradually changed to these transparent, green ribbons of light, like seaweed almost. And the strange thing was that you can hear them, I hadn't known that. As the plane thundered down the runway, I could just hear a muffled swishing, like the sound of heavy velvet curtains moving. Or some material being waved in farewell. And I looked out over the airbase, in that green glow, and I thought that for the next few months it was mine. That was the strangest thought I've ever had.'

The old man fell into silence, looking out over the soft green and blue of Lake Mockeln, but he was not seeing the gentle image of rural European peace which lay on his retina. Instead he was gazing at an image etched deeply into his brain – of the aurora borealis glowing over the newly-deserted airforce base, thousands of miles and tens of years away. A memory that was unique to him, that could never be caught or understood by anyone else, and that would die and be lost for ever with him. His face sagged, infected with a deep sorrow for the past that he could not share, except through the crude, unsatisfactory medium of words.

Larsen said nothing, hoping more nuggets of memory might be dug from the old man's mine, but the silence only stretched on and on.

'Do you think that the last plane could have had the serial number 55-0065?' he asked at last.

Wegner looked at him grimly.

'How would I know?' he said. 'Is there anything else you want?'

'Did the American planes come back later?'

'No. They didn't. Why should they? After that it was just a salvage job. Clearing up the dormitories, the kitchens, the living quarters, and all the rest.'

'Nothing different, or unusual? Nothing that made you stop and think to yourself?'

Wegner shook his grizzled head.

'How long did it take?' pressed Larsen, without much hope.

'About four months I think. Maybe longer – after all it was winter. Anyway, I only oversaw the first few weeks, then I left the rest of it to my partner and went back to Oslo. I never went to Greenland again, though we did win one or two more small contracts out there in the following years.'

He looked at Larsen coldly, blaming him for being brought face to face with the relentless passage of the years.

'You don't know what the US planes were taking away?'

Wegner shook his head.

'I wasn't allowed to see. I suppose one can guess the sort of stuff – communications and guidance equipment; anything linked to weapons; files; records; medical resources – plenty of them I should think; radar and tracking equipment. All those things that obsess military men and that we aren't allowed to know about, even though we pay for them through our taxes.' Again his misty eyes turned to Larsen. 'Like the police,' he added derisively.

Larsen gave a smile, but felt as if it had been launched at a brick wall. Above them the sky was now completely cloaked in low, hanging, grey clouds.

Wegner got up.

'I'm tired,' he said. 'And as I told you, I come here to be left alone. I've had enough of talking.'

Without another word he walked back along the path, round the side of the house, unlocked his front door and went in. A moment later the door slammed shut, and there was the sound of the key being turned inside, then the rattle of a chain.

Larsen turned to face the long walk back to Almhult. As he did so, he thought that a curtain in the house twitched, but he could not be sure.

Lightly at first, then steadily harder, it began to rain. Larsen sighed and resignedly pressed on. There didn't seem much else to do. As he walked, he wondered whether he had achieved anything, and found that he wasn't sure. But perhaps there was a narrow twisting path beginning to emerge through the undergrowth that surrounded him.

Shortly after reaching the road, a large and expensive car passed him on the other side of the road, driving slowly, its windscreen wipers making a staccato slapping sound. It swung round a corner, then the sound of the engine seemed to stop.

Larsen frowned, and wondered for a moment if he should turn back. But the rain was pouring down now, dripping from the surrounding trees, and he pulled the hood of his anorak further over his head, and trudged on.

When he got back to Copenhagen, that evening, there was a message waiting for him.

'I'm leaving for Greenland next Wednesday. If you need me, you can contact me there. Or leave a message at the university. Don't look for me at Seana's, I've gone to stay with my mum. Natasha.'

Larsen read it twice, sucking in his cheeks in thought.

'Maybe it's time I went home too,' he said quietly to himself.

15 Back in Nuuk

IT WAS RAINING outside. One of those thick, heavy depressions, that sometimes settles on Nuuk for days at a time, had arrived, and the water that had soaked everyone on their way to Salo's was evaporating sluggishly. Coiling steam mingled with cigarette smoke, alcohol fumes, and the muggy breath of seventy or eighty young Greenlanders, to make the air barely breathable.

As usual the club video and its soundtrack were out of synch, and as usual no one seemed to mind – or even notice. Meanwhile, the light show and glitter ball sent luminous multicoloured pinpoints racing round the peeling, stained walls, slashing through the foggy atmosphere like Darth Vader's light sabre.

Edvarth had arranged to meet a couple of his friends at ten, but it was already half past and there was no sign of them. He wondered briefly whether to go home, but it was Friday night – the night for having fun, so he doggedly resolved to stay. With no live band booked, most of the customers were clustered around the bar, and he spent ten minutes edging and jostling his way through the hot, damp, sweat-scented crowd before he was finally able to buy a can of beer.

As he emerged from the crowd, he found himself in front of the dance floor. 'Under a blood red sky . . .' sang U2's Bono, and the thudding beat mingled with the dancers to make the floor shake. Edvarth was not usually fond of dancing, but he had a sudden desire to use up some of the excess physical energy that pulsated in his body.

Forgetting just how much the beer had cost him, he threw back his head, swallowed it in three mouthfuls, put the the can on a table, and began to dance. Wildly. Unpredictably. With an undertone of suppressed violence that the repetitive beat brought out in him.

Suddenly, as the music changed, he realized there was a girl dancing sinuously opposite him. He had not seen her arrive, but there she was – and she seemed dimly familiar. His eyes ran over her helmet of black glossy hair, cut jaggedly just above the nape of her neck, then took in her heavily made-up face, with its black-lined slanting eyes, the battered leather jacket over a purple crop-top and short skirt, and the spike-heeled shoes. She intercepted his look, and her dark-lipsticked mouth gave a smile. She came a little closer, and his hopes soared.

'Forget it, boy,' she said casually, her voice just audible above the music. 'I don't go in for cradle-snatching. I want my men to be men.'

But Edvarth had her placed.

'You're Katinka,' he said.

She stopped dancing, and looked at him closely.

'I don't know you.'

'I know you.'

She shrugged.

'So one of your friends has taste. Or maybe I was just feeling sorry for him. Now run off, because I can give you a cast-iron guarantee that what I'm not interested in is a kid like you.'

'You would be if you thought I had money,' growled Edvarth, remembering the circumstances in which he had last seen her, and feeling a sudden flare of anger.

Katinka reacted instantly, walking up to him, her eyes hot, her small, lightly-built frame hunched pugnaciously. Light caught the rings on her right hand as she raised it to push him backwards.

'You've no right to talk to me like that,' she spat out. 'I'm free to do what I want, when I want, with who I want.'

'And I know just who you want,' retorted Edvarth. 'The sort of dumb, pissed no-hoper who drops a wad of thousand-kroner notes all over the floor, giving you the chance to grab a couple.'

He tensed, unsure if she would attack him with words or a slap. To his surprise she seemed to relax.

'So you were there that night, were you?' she said calmly. 'Well, that was then, and this is now. OK? And let me tell you, just as a piece of friendly advice, that your pick-up lines are not going to score you a lot of girls.'

'And there I was thinking my main problem was that I haven't got more money than sense.'

'I'd say that was arguable,' said Katinka, then laughed. 'Buy me a drink and I'll sit down and talk to you for a while. The talent here just now is so zero-rated, even you'll do until things liven up.'

Edvarth opened his mouth to tell her where to go, but Katinka reacted more quickly than he did. She reached forward and put her forefinger, with its well-varnished nail, the colour of dried blood, over his lips.

'Listen, I think I quite like you. In fact I'm even willing to give you the money for the drink. How about that?'

'I can get my own drinks,' retorted Edvarth, and plunged back into the crowd, using his elbows mercilessly to drive his way through to the bar.

When he finally fought his way back out, holding two cans of Carlsberg that had cost him most of the money he had left, he was certain he would see Katinka fluttering her thickly mascaraed eyelashes at someone else. But there was no sign of her at all.

'Shit!' he muttered, sat down at a table and opened the first can.

It occurred to him that at least he still had both drinks.

He was brooding sullenly, when someone tapped him on the shoulder. He started.

Katinka grinned, leant her bony elbow on his shoulder for a moment and gazed straight into his eyes, then sat down opposite him, and neatly collected the untouched beer.

'You were quicker than I expected,' she said. 'You must come here quite often.' She took a sip, then looked at him calculatingly. 'So you don't think I behaved well that night?'

'No.'

'I suppose you're right, though that dumb ox was going to get ripped off whatever happened, so why not by me? I'd give him as good value as anyone else, and better than some. Anyway, I've remembered you now – and maybe you can tell me something.'

She paused, and gave him a sharp, questioning look.

'Stashing away information can always be useful. So I do it a lot, even about things that don't seem to mean much.'

'What are you talking about?'

'There was a policeman that broke up the party, right? And I noticed that he talked to you for a while. Quite a while, considering that you didn't seem to have anything to do with anything. Now I'm seeing you again, I find myself wondering why should he do that?'

'I've had dealings with him before,' said Edvarth, trying to adopt a hard, cool manner.

Katinka's look was cynical.

'Don't tell me what those dealings were, will you?' she remarked. 'I might be disappointed. Isn't that right?'

Edvarth took another drink.

'International man of mystery,' teased Katinka, wagging her finger at him.

'You said it,' said Edvarth, beginning to enjoy the conversational fencing. It was not like any conversation he had had with a girl before. 'And here I am facing the femme fatale of Nuuk.'

She opened her eyes wide. 'You what?'

'French,' said Edvarth casually. 'What happened to the dummy with the wad anyway?'

Katinka leaned forward, put her elbows on the table, and elegantly linked her fingers under her chin.

'If you want to know, he's back. And I'm waiting for him now. But I have the feeling there are things going on – he seems different from before, twitchy, always looking over his shoulder, that sort of thing. And why was that policeman there that night anyway? I reckon Mr Steen has something nasty tucked away somewhere.'

Edvarth shrugged.

'I don't know him.'

'Neither do I. But seeing that the prime purpose of life is to make sure Katinka is OK, it looks like maybe I should tread carefully, right?'

'If you feel like that, why see him at all?'

'You have to take a few risks. And maybe he's going to start spouting more thousand K notes, I wouldn't want to risk missing that. Anyway, I'm curious. Just like a pussy cat.' And she ran that blood-red nail on her forefinger down Edvarth's cheek, as if threatening to slice his face open.

'Why are you telling me all this?'

She considered the question.

'Maybe because my girlfriend, Leah, has gone off back to Sisimiut. Imagine! Why would anyone want to do that – what's in it for her up there, other than a few half-starved, out-of-work sledge dogs?'

'Her family?' suggested Edvarth mildly.

'Family,' she repeated, and for a moment it was as if something had been torn open. The vivacity died in her, and her body seemed to shrink. Then she was herself again. 'Anyway, to get back to the point. One reason I'm telling you this is that I might be interested in someone who has links with the cops. Another is that I might want someone to talk to now and then. Someone who I maybe quite like, and who. . . .' She stopped again, then made an indeterminate gesture. 'And maybe the real reason is just because I always sort of wanted a little brother.'

Her long, rich brown eyes flickered smoothly away from Edvarth, behind him and upwards.

'Hi, Steen,' she said casually. 'This is my baby cousin, Jørgen.'

Edvarth would not have recognized the man who sat down beside them. His black hair had been cut tight to his skull, and his big chin was gleamingly clean-shaven. But his broad face was somehow stretched, his breath was coming fast, and he constantly glanced around him with short, staccato movements.

'You got a drink'?' he said, entirely ignoring Edvarth.

'Sure.' Katinka pushed her can over to him, and he drank from it heavily.

'That's better.'

'I still think I preferred you with long hair,' remarked Katinka.

'Yeah. Well. Did you do what I asked?'

'Sure, I called up Leah. Though I can't imagine why everyone's getting it into their head that it's a smart move to head off to Sisimiut. There must be something there that's really fascinating, and that I don't know about. What is it – can you tell me?'

'Get on with it, for Christ's sake. What did she say?'

'She said OK. You can stay with her, provided you've got enough money. How much can you pay?'

'Not much just now. But I'll get work in the shrimp processing factories. She needn't worry about money.'

Katinka gave a laugh of disbelief.

'Talk sense, Steen. There's no one who doesn't worry about money. Anyway, like I said, her spare room is yours, if you pay a fair price.'

'Thank Christ for that, at least!' Steen was staring at the table, making patterns with his finger in the spilt beer and cigarette ash, swirls and jagged lightning strikes.

'There's just one problem,' said Katinka, putting her head to one side and surveying Steen critically.

'What's that?'

'When are you going to turn up?'

'As soon as I can.'

'There's a flight from Nuuk to Kangerlussuaq tomorrow morning, which links with Sisimiut.'

He looked up from his patterns.

'How do you know?' he asked, with sudden suspicion. 'And why are you so bloody interested anyway?'

Katinka made a gesture of exaggerated innocence.

'No need to bite. Leah told me about the flight – she wanted to know if you'd be on it.'

He grunted, and his attention turned back to the table. Not looking at her.

'Well?' said Katinka eventually.

'I won't be able to make that one,' he replied.

Katinka produced a cigarette, lit it, took a drag, then reflectively made the burning tip describe a circle.

'What are you not telling me?' she asked. When he did not reply, she went on. 'Is it that you haven't got enough money for the fare, maybe?'

Steen gave an almost imperceptible nod.

'Yeah,' he muttered.

'So how the hell do you plan to get there?'

'I'll get the money. Don't worry.'

He took another mouthful of Katinka's beer.

'Why should I worry?' she answered. 'But Leah won't keep the room for you. If someone else turns up, she'll give it to them.'

'Tell her I'll be there within the week.'

'OK. But why don't you explain to me why you're not just staying with some of your friends in Nuuk – someone like Harald.'

For a moment Steen did not react.

Then he turned on her, face contorted, hands gripping the edge of the table like talons.

'What the fuck do you know about Harald?' he asked, his voice like the hiss of a snake.

Katinka looked suddenly younger, vulnerable, frightened by the raw ferocity of his response. She held up her hands, as if in surrender.

'Nothing, nothing,' she gabbled.

'Tell me,' he demanded, snatching her wrist, and holding it as if he would snap it clean apart.

'It was nothing. A few days ago a man came up to me—'

'Where?'

'Here. In the club. He came up to me, and said his name was Harald, and he was a friend of yours and did I know where he could find you. That was all.'

Steen still stared at her.

'What did you say?'

'I said I hardly knew you. That I'd only seen you that one night. So he said if I did see you again, I was to tell you that he wanted a few words.'

'Why the fuck didn't you tell me that before?'

'I forgot.'

'You stupid, stupid bitch.' Steen sprang to his feet, and vanished towards the exit, pushing roughly through the crowd.

'See,' said Katinka, after taking a moment to relight her cigarette, and recover herself. 'Twitchy. And not just twitchy – out of his fucking mind maybe. What was all that stuff at the end? And who wants to live in Sisimiut, for God's sake, when they could be here in Nuuk? He had a good job too – working at the airport, and plenty of money that he'd got from somewhere. Then he throws it all up for work in the shrimp processing factories. Like I said, out of his skull – unless maybe he's got a fetish about aprons, head-nets, rubber gloves, and the stink of fish.'

'I think he's scared of something,' said Edvarth. 'Very scared.'

Katinka nodded judiciously, blowing smoke in a long stream from between her reddish-purple lips.

'Looks like it. Most of the time he's got one of those blank open faces that don't show much except stupidity, but he did get seriously stressed, didn't he? I reckon you're probably right. Maybe he's running away.' She picked up her beer, discovered it was empty, and reached for Edvarth's can. After taking a mouthful, she frowned. 'What do you think he's frightened of?'

'It seemed like it was that man, Harald.'

'But he was just another Inuk. Quite little, not much hair, prissy little hands, and cheap wire-rimmed spectacles. Like the kind of teacher no one takes any notice of.' She frowned. 'It must be something to do with all that money. A lump of mud like Steen doesn't get masses of money without doing something he shouldn't.'

Edvarth shrugged.

'You're right,' nodded Katinka. 'It doesn't matter. Let's dance, little brother. Maybe I can find myself some good time amusement for tonight – and who knows, we might even discover some pretty young thing for you.'

'How old are you?' demanded Edvarth, stung.

'Much older than you, little brother. Much, much older.'

'I don't think you're more than seventeen or eighteen,' he said.

She gave a smile of pure amusement.

'Listen, let me explain something to you. Dummies think that the passing of time is about years and months and days. It isn't. It's about what you put in those years and months and days. Some people never get beyond seventeen in their whole lives, and others have lived through fourteen winters and several lifetimes.'

'I don't understand.'

'That makes you somewhere short of twelve. Come on, let's dance.'

She got up, dropping the cigarette butt on the floor, and crushing it with the sole of her shoe. He followed, half-reluctantly. To his surprise, she put her hands on his shoulder and began to dance, moving her broad hips smoothly, temptingly, a sexual charge sliding over her whole body, as if she had sheathed herself in it. Edvarth could feel himself being aroused.

'If I'm your little brother, you ought to give me your phone number,' he said. 'Otherwise I won't know where to find you.'

'I don't think so,' she said.

'Why not?'

'Because little brothers are only useful now and then. But maybe you can give me your number – just in case.'

Excitedly he scribbled out his number and address on a piece of paper and gave it to her. She looked at it, then slipped it inside her jacket, and lent towards him. Despite the cigarette, her breath was unexpectedly sweet.

'Listen, I don't know how far you're thinking we might go,' she said softly.

'Try far,' replied Edvarth.

She laughed, then grew serious again.

'I don't want you disappointed, so perhaps you're due further explanation. There's nothing that flatters and fools a man so much as the belief that he's taken a woman from another man. So someone here is going to think he's a tough, sexy son-of-a-bitch, because he took me from you. But you and I know that you're just my little brother, and this dancing is just a scam. Right?'

'Right,' said Edvarth, trying to hide his disappointment.

'Good boy. And when I find what I'm looking for, it might be worth your while checking out that little thing over there. The one who must be wearing her first high heels, seeing as how she keeps falling off them. She looks about your age and style, little brother, and she has a cute round little face, and masses of hair. I know you young kids think loads of hair is sexy.'

Her hand ran enticingly through her own carefully-styled black helmet.

The phone went harshly. Edvarth groaned and clutched his throbbing head, through which a nauseating disco beat still pulsed. His throat felt as if it were lined with ash, there was a stale gaseous taste in his mouth, and his stomach was heaving.

He crawled out of bed, glanced at the clock, which showed 9.30 in the morning, then reached for the machine with a shaking hand.

'Yes?'

'I'm trying to find Police Sergeant Tomas Larsen,' came a woman's voice.

'He's not here,' croaked Edvarth. 'He's in Denmark. . . .'

'Yes, yes. I know he's supposed to be in Denmark. That was the last place anyone saw him, but we haven't been able to contact him there, and the Danish police don't know where he is either. His mobile phone isn't answering, and no one's seen him since Wednesday. So I thought maybe you'd have an idea of where he is.'

'You could try his home in Nuuk.'

'He's not there either. I was told he might be reachable at this number.'

'It's no good talking to me,' mumbled Edvarth, with an effort. 'I suppose you want to talk to my mother. But—'

'Listen, this is really important,' the woman interrupted. 'I've got a very important message for him. Could you or your mother give it to him?'

Edvarth tried again.

'I'm not sure when she's likely to see him or talk to him,' he began. 'You see. . . .'

She still wasn't listening.

'Have you got a piece of paper handy to take this down?'

Edvarth scrabbled about, found a biro and the back of an old shopping list, and sighed heavily.

'OK,' he said.

'Right. My name is Jette, and it's about Chief Thorold, Tomas's boss at the station. Yesterday he was in contact with the Canadian police about flight 608 to Iqaluit. With winter coming on, they've decided there's no realistic chance of getting the black box flight recorder up until next spring. . . .'

'Hang on,' said Edvarth. 'You're going too fast.'

'Don't worry about the details. The point is that the crash investigation is being put on hold, so Tomas is wanted back in Nuuk. If he's not back for work the day after tomorrow, then he'll be heading for suspension and disciplinary proceedings.' She dropped her voice. 'I don't know why, but Chief Thorold seems to have it in for Tomas, and if he gets the chance, he'll be down on him like an avalanche.'

'So, what he needs to know . . .' began Edvarth uncertainly.

'Is that he must get the first plane back, and be in for work on Monday morning.'

'OK. But—'

'Just make sure you contact him – it's important. I mean, it could be his job on the line. I must go now.'

She rang off abruptly.

Edvarth slumped back into his bed, and tried to lessen the sickening sense of constant movement inside his skull, as if his brain was being shaken slowly and thoroughly from side to side.

After a few minutes he decided it was even worse lying in bed than it would be getting up, so he dragged on a T-shirt and pants, both of which stank of smoke and sweat, and staggered uncertainly to the kitchen, where he found some paracetamol and took them, then poured himself three glasses of water, and made himself drink them straight down.

The pills didn't seem to have any impact on the throbbing ache in his skull, and as he went back to his bedroom his head whirled afresh. He slumped on the bed, rubbed his temples, and tried to remember what happened the previous night. After a long period of dancing, everything went hazy, except where it was broken up by a few sharp images – of long, hot kisses with a girl he did not recognize, a girl who had great thick veils of hair, flashing over her face like zebra stripes – or was that the club light show? Of drinks arriving in front of him, again and again; and of Katinka whispering something that he could not hear above the music. The rest of the evening seemed to have fallen into blackness.

Never mind, he said to himself. I'll ask Katinka what happened. Then he realized that he had no way of contacting her, except the chance of meeting her again at Salo's. But the thought of another night in the club sent nausea rushing through him like a wave.

His mother came back at eleven, after the end of her shift at the hospital. Risa's face was grim.

'I met old Mrs Arvidsson outside,' she said, looking at her son, who had retreated back to bed after all, and was wondering if overdosing on paracetamol might be a good idea. 'She says you didn't come back until abut 3.30 last night, and that you were singing, and laughing, with a girl.'

Edvarth looked at her blankly, shook his head, and then wished he hadn't.

Risa sighed.

'Did you have sex with the girl?'

Edvarth shrugged helplessly.

'Well?' she probed.

'I don't know, Mum,' he confessed.

'Bloody hell!' exploded Risa. 'Haven't you got even half a bloody brain cell? You mean you got so pissed, you don't even know what you were doing? That is just so stupid, Edvarth.'

'Sorry.'

'Sorry! Jesus Christ, you're not six – sorry doesn't make things OK.' She sat down on the bed beside him, took a deep breath, then spoke more quietly.

'Look, I know that young people of your age often go off and get drunk. But there's drunk and drunk. You mustn't let yourself get to the state where you haven't a clue what's going on. For one thing, it's seriously expensive. How much did you spend last night?'

'Not much.'

'Really?'

'Yes. Really. I only took 200K out with me. That's all gone, but there wasn't anything else. I promise.'

'So how did you get so drunk? Two hundred isn't enough to get so pissed you lose time.'

'Someone bought me drinks.'

'Who?'

'I'm not sure,' he admitted. 'A girl maybe.'

'Maybe,' she repeated cuttingly. 'And who is this girl? What do you know about her?' She waited, but he didn't reply, so she leant forward. 'Look, Edvarth. There's a second reason you don't get helplessly pissed. A big reason: you're gambling with your life.'

He stared at her.

'Do I have to spell it out?' said Risa. 'OK then. HIV and AIDS are becoming commoner in Nuuk every day. If you don't even know who this girl is, how the hell can you be sure that she hasn't infected you?'

Edvarth still said nothing. His brain seemed to have crashed.

'Well?' she said. 'What happened?'

'I don't think I went to bed with anyone last night,' he replied at last. Hesitantly. 'I'm sure I'd remember it. I'm sure I would.'

'So who was this girl then, who came back with you?'

He tunnelled back in his mind again, and still found only emptiness.

'Did Mrs Arvidsson say what the girl looked like?' he asked. 'Like how long her hair was, or. . . ?'

'For Christ's sake, Edvarth. Don't you have a clue?'

He backtracked hastily.

'Yes. Yes, of course. Her name's Katinka, she's someone I met at the club. A friend.'

'Maybe not the sort of friend you need, Edvarth. I can't live your life for you, but when you're only sixteen, you haven't got much of an idea about what really goes on. I try to help you all I can, but if you're determined to make stupid mistakes, there's nothing I can do about it.' She paused, then reached out a hand and put it on his shoulder. As if curtains had been drawn back, he could glimpse the huge deep lake of concern that lay behind the stream of her anger.

'Listen, Edvarth. You know I've got to go to Kapisillit this afternoon.'

'I thought you said it wasn't going to be necessary.'

'That's what I thought. But it seems the bloody hikers aren't getting any better, and the people there don't know if it's safe to move them. I'll be gone at least a day – but if they can't be moved, or if the weather gets worse, as they're saying, then it could be longer. Are you going to be all right on your own?'

'Sure, Mum. No problem.'

'It's hard to trust you, if you behave like you did last night.'

'I'll be OK, Mum.'

'I hope so. Now I need to get some rest. I feel wrung dry.'

She went into her room and closed the door. When Edvarth looked in on her a few minutes later, she was fast asleep on the bed, still in her clothes. Edvarth gazed at her for a while, then closed the door again, taking great care not to make a sound. Then he quietly slipped outside, and knocked on the first door on the left. There was no answer. He knocked again, louder, and an old woman opened it.

Her face was thin and frail, crossed with thin, deep lines of bad temper – like razor cuts in her parchment skin.

'Well?' she said, scowling.

'Mrs Arvidsson,' said Edvarth, summoning up an ingratiating smile. 'I'm sorry to disturb you, but. . . .'

'Well?'

'I'm just going out to the KNI. I wondered if there was anything I could get for you.'

'Maybe,' she retorted ungraciously. She vanished into her apartment, leaving him in the doorway, then reappeared a minute or two later with a list, which she pushed abruptly towards him. 'Here. These things.'

'Of course.' Edvarth smiled again. 'I'm so sorry about last night, Mrs Arvidsson.'

She grunted.

'Drunk is one thing,' she said. 'But girls are another.'

'Of course. I realize that it must have looked bad, but in fact she was just a friend, helping me home.'

'Then why didn't she leave when she'd got you home?' snapped Mrs Arvidsson, unappeased. 'And a girl like that – she didn't look like anyone's friend.'

'You mean her hair. . . ?' probed Edvarth cautiously.

The old woman snorted again.

'If she wants to hack most of her hair off and look like a fool when the winter comes, that's her problem. But those clothes weren't the sort of thing worn by any decent girl. Especially that skirt – so short you could scarcely call it a skirt. It's disgusting what they wear today, shameless! When I was a girl women always wore trousers. And we looked good enough in them, I can tell you. Better than these skinny things today, flashing their thighs at everyone, and shivering like shaven dogs.'

'I'll get you your shopping,' said Edvarth hastily.

He hurried away, with a confusion in his heart that he could not remember having felt before.

When he got back, his mother was up, hastily throwing clothes into a bag. She looked up as he came in.

'Where've you been?' she demanded, but did not wait for an answer. 'Not that it matters. I've just had a phone call – there's a storm on its way, so I have to leave now.'

'Be careful, Mum.'

'You too.' She snatched up her coat, slung the bag over her shoulder, and patted him briefly on the cheek. 'Make sure you're sensible while I'm away. I'll ring you when I can. Bye.'

'Bye, Mum.'

The door shut and she was gone. Ten minutes later Edvarth realized that he had forgotten to tell her about Larsen.

'Fuck!' muttered Edvarth to himself.

But a moment later he was thinking about Katinka again.

16 The Agency

CHIEF THOROLD STOPPED by Jette's desk, and looked down at her.

'Did you say you had had contact with Sergeant Larsen?'

'Yes, sir. He'll be arriving at the airport at midday. He apologizes for being late, but he had to spend last night in Kangerlussuaq because there's no connecting service here on a Sunday.'

'He should have thought of that before. Inform accounts that I am authorizing them to penalize him by withdrawal of his next day off.'

'Yes, sir.'

'And send him to me the moment he arrives.'

'Yes, sir.'

Thorold retired to his office, where he ran a comb through his thinning hair, adjusted the photograph of his daughter on his desk, then glanced at the crime report for Saturday and Sunday. It had been a quiet weekend, just three fights, and a liquor store broken into. Nothing worth taking much time over. He signed a couple of forms, then began to draft a department memo about late arrival for work. He had scarcely begun when the telephone rang. He picked it up, frowning.

'It's a call from America,' said Jette, her young and misleadingly artless voice sounded almost excited. 'For you, sir.'

'Who is it?' asked Thorold.

'I'm sorry, sir. I forgot to ask. But the man definitely wanted to speak to you, sir. He knew your name.'

Thorold sighed, and reminded himself that at the next budget meeting, he intended to request funds to cover the salary of a full-time secretary. Jette was perfectly adequate as a general receptionist, and had the advantage of being good-looking. But as a secretary she was a walking catastrophe.

'Put me through. Hello?'

'Hello, Mr Thorold,' came a thick mid-western accent. 'This is James Herrera, calling from Washington. We're making enquiries about a certain Timur Medari. Does that name mean anything to you?'

'No, Mr Herrera. I'm afraid not. Should it?'

'Well, we were hoping. We've received some pretty solid information that he's been seen in Greenland in the past two weeks or so. Added to that, we have some cause to believe he may be interested – for a reason we cannot yet uncover – in a research expedition presently investigating the north-east of your country.'

'I'm sorry, Mr Herrera,' said Thorold cautiously. 'Perhaps I am being obtuse, but I do not understand. Who exactly are you, and what organization do you represent?'

'Fair question, and you're due an apology that things weren't made clear earlier, Mr Thorold. This is an enquiry on behalf of the Scandinavian Bureau of the Central Intelligence Agency.'

The CIA! It was so unexpected that Thorold felt his composure rocking.

'How do I know that you are who you say you are?' he demanded.

Herrera chuckled.

'Feel free to make any checks you wish, Mr Thorold. The relevant PIN you will be concerned with is SBG479/S2. I'll call back in a couple of hours or so – would that be convenient?'

'Thank you, Mr Herrera. I'm sure you understand the necessity for confirmation.' Thorold cut off the outside line, and called Jette. 'I want you to contact the Scandinavian Bureau of the American Central Intelligence Agency, and see if they have an operative named James Herrera, employee number SBG479/S2.'

There was a long pause.

'Well? What is it?' asked Thorold testily.

'I don't know the phone number, Chief,' she said.

'Look it up, girl. Look it up.'

'Yes, Chief.'

Twenty minutes later Thorold came into the reception room. Jette was sitting at her desk, staring blankly at the telephone.

'Well? Well?' asked the Chief.

Jette looked up at him with wide eyes. 'I don't know, sir,' she said.

'What do you mean you don't know?'

'I can't find the telephone number, sir. It's not in any of our directories.'

Thorold ground his teeth.

'Use the bloody computer, girl. Type up CIA on the search engine, then look for the Scandinavian section.'

'Yes, sir.'

'And get on with it. I'm going out to get a sandwich. I want the answer on my desk when I get back.'

'Yes, sir.'

Half an hour later Thorold returned. Jette did not seem to have moved.

'I've just put a report on your desk, sir,' she said.

He stared at her.

'Report? What report?'

'A young man found dead this morning, sir, in a disused shed near Blok P.'

'Do we have a name?'

'No sir. Not yet. But Helge's up there now, and when he called in, he said it looks like a fairly routine suicide. No sign of anyone else being involved. No one seems to have heard anything, the gun's on the floor beside the victim, and there's a sort of farewell note.'

'What do you mean a sort of farewell note?'

'It's a torn bit of paper that was lying on the ground.'

'What does it say?'

Jette almost looked embarrassed.

'It says "Fuck you all".'

'I see.'

Thorold looked bleak. But suicides were not uncommon among the young men who lived in the poorer parts of Nuuk, especially in the autumn. And this one didn't sound any different from a dozen or so that would probably take place in the next eight or nine weeks.

'Tell Helge to contact me when he has any more information. Now, what about that telephone number I told you to find?'

'Yes, sir.'

'What does that mean?'

'I did find it, sir. Eventually.'

'And. . . ?'

'I phoned them up, sir, and said what you told me to. But they said. . . .' She referred to her note-pad, then carefully read out what she had written. 'It is not agency policy to name operatives, except on a need-to-know basis.'

'Well?'

Jette shrugged.

'They didn't think I needed to know, sir.'

'Give me the number,' gritted Thorold.

After the best part of three quarters of an hour, the police chief had achieved little more than Jette. The contact office refused to confirm or deny either the number, or the name.

'You must realive, Mr Thorold,' said a stone-voiced woman, 'that we receive many calls, and that we cannot possibly give out privileged and confidential agency information to just anyone. It is essential that we receive cast-iron confirmation of your ID and credentials before we can even consider taking this matter any further. I'm sure you understand.'

'No, I don't,' fumed Thorold. 'The man telephoned me.'

'So you said, sir.'

'Obviously I need to double-check on his identity before I can take the contact any further. But now you're saying that you won't let me do that until you have double-checked on my identity.'

'That is correct, sir.'

'But presumably Mr Herrera must have already checked on me before he contacted me.'

'That is an assumption, sir. We have no substantive evidence to that effect.'

Thorold dosed his eyes, and tried to calm himself, without much success. He felt as if he had walked into a land of mirrors, where everything he did would be reflected back at him.

'How the hell do I prove my identity to you?' he asked.

'Well, sir. There is a formal process which I can e-mail you details of. . . .'

'And how long will that take?'

'I could not say, sir. It requires that two people who are already known to the agency provide you with bona fides, and that a level 7J security check is undertaken on—'

Jette cut in.

'Mr Herrera is on the other line, sir.'

'Fuck!' exploded Thorold. A moment later his pale face flushed deep red. Hastily he cut off the CIA number, chewed his lip violently for a few moments, then took several deep breaths, and tried to recover control of himself. Eventually he felt calm enough to accept the incoming call.

'Herrera?'

'Yes, Mr Thorold. Done your checks OK?'

'What is all this about?'

'Well that, Mr Thorold, is precisely what we are trying to discern. We'll fax you through details on Medari via our secure line, but what it comes down to is that he's a man we've been interested in for a couple of years. Very interested. And if he's involving himself in something in your country then you can put your mortgage on the assumption that two things are kicking in here. Firstly that it's going to make waves, and secondly it's something most people wouldn't touch with two pairs of gloves on.'

'But. . . ?'

'Up until a few days ago, he was apparently claiming to be a representative of UNESCO named Christopher Goater, from New Zealand. Does that help?'

'No. Who is this man?'

There was a pause at the end of the phone.

'OK. You've got the right to ask that, so I'll tell you what I can. Which isn't a lot. Medari first came to our attention when he was working out of Australia about eighteen months ago. He's in his forties, tall, thin, quiet, fairly Western looks, but tough. Where exactly he comes from, we're not sure – his trail goes cold before 1997. He does have a New Zealand passport, which he was given as a political refugee from Iraq, but our betting is that he is not an Iraqi at all. We think he's from somewhere in the Caucasus region, maybe Azerbaijan, Dagestan, Georgia, Chechnya, or Armenia. Possibly Turkey or Iran. We have considered putting some pressure on the New Zealand authorities, but for one thing we want him to stay in sight, and for another we have no direct evidence against him.

'As far as we can gather, he's a wild card who works by and for himself, but in a very short time he seems to have made himself a big operator. In fact, he doesn't seem to take off his night-shirt until the seventh digit appears on his bill. Which means that to get him up to your part of the world, which is right off his usual track, there must be something seriously sexy on line.'

'Like what?' asked Thorold, with a spinning sensation in his head.

'That's what we're trying to find out. Mostly he appears to specialize in arms dealing, with a possible sideline in drugs – but neither of those seem too likely in Greenland. So we were hoping you might be able to help us. Look, we'll send you through what we know – give it some thought, then come back to us. But it's urgent, that's for sure. Medari is not a man to waste time. He lays his way carefully, works with as few people as possible, keeps things tight, then strikes fast. Like a mountain lion. By the time you see him, it's often too late – it was only luck that got us this latest contact.'

'Are you sure. . . ?' began Thorold weakly.

'We're sure as we can be,' came the immediate response, before Thorold had even finished speaking. 'But the crucial question here is precisely what help you can offer us.'

'What sort of thing are you suggesting?' said Thorold, with his habitual caution.

'The point is that we don't have a lot of first-person input on the region we're talking about here.'

'What region is that?'

'Your north-east coast. What's it like?'

'Wilderness,' said Thorold. 'Less than a thousand inhabitants, who live chiefly by hunting. Only one real settlement, and that's almost deserted in the summer. Transport links by helicopter and plane, except for maybe three months a year when a ship can get in. Almost all law and order problems, of which there are many more than you might think, are linked to alcohol. Added to the fact that everyone has guns.'

'Can you think of anything, anything at all, that would draw an ambitious, big-money man like Medari there?'

'No. Absolutely nothing.'

'Neither can we.' It was faintly disturbing the way Herrera never referred to himself, except in the plural. 'That's what we don't like. But there has to be something.'

'Most of the area, just under a million square kilometres, is a national park. Access is fairly tightly controlled, limited to scientific expeditions and registered companies that arrange carefully monitored, small-scale visits. There's also one permanent weather station, and a couple of temporary ones. That's about all there is to say.'

'Which broadly confirms what we came up with. But there's no question that the man is interested. And we have to know just why that is.'

'Why exactly?'

There was a pause at the end of the phone.

'Well, Mr Thorold, you must appreciate that there are confidential details here that will have to be kept under wraps. In fact, some aspects of this case are so high on the security ratings that we cannot possibly reveal them to you. However, we are authorized to confirm that one of our operatives, working for a different bureau, has logged two conversations between Mr Medari and . . . best we're not too specific here – a leading representative of a third-world government. Not a government that the United States is particularly close to, if you take our meaning. To develop that point a little further, you can safely assume that we are talking about a government with a powerful strategic position in what might be loosely described as one of the world's premier hot-spots.

'OK. Now, we were unable to discover the substance of these conversations, but there is no question that this particular government, in the past, has cast around for some method to adjust the local and regional balances of power in its own favour. In other words it is just the sort of government that we at the Central Intelligence Agency are extremely interested in, and concerned about. Furthermore, we know from past experience that Medari is not a man to take on more than one major project at a time, so that points directly to his visit to Greenland being linked with these conversations. In such circumstances, you can understand why we have registered this affair as a most serious cause for concern.'

Thorold felt as if he was swimming through liquid mud.

'I don't understand. What do you want me to do?'

'OK. Well, in the first instance, obviously, to make sure your department is alert to this matter, and to give us any information at all that you might think even faintly relevant. In the second instance, we would be very grateful if you could perhaps send a team to the relevant area.'

Thorold frowned.

'I don't have many officers,' he said. 'And there are staffing shortages at present. What exactly do you mean by a team?'

'Maybe three operatives.'

'I'm afraid that is completely impossible. But I might be able to release one officer.'

There was a long silence at the far end of the phone.

'It's true that Medari's team – if it returns to the area – is likely to be a small one,' came Herrera's voice at last. 'It may even be him alone – we have known that happen. But our recommendation would be strongly against the premise that you should use a lone operative in this case.'

'Are you saying it could be dangerous?' Thorold inquired.

There was another extended pause.

'Mr Thorold, it is probably necessary to inform you that we have no direct evidence of Medari being linked to violence of any sort. However, there have been cases of accidents that appear to have been connected to his work . . . conveniently connected. In fact. . . .' Another hesitation. 'Two of our operatives have either died or disappeared while being assigned to Medari. We appreciate that this may cause you to have second thoughts, and we would naturally understand if you kept your co-operation with us to the level of a simple information-gathering exercise.'

'So you would prefer that I did not send a single man?'

'That was not exactly the thrust of the statement. All assistance is naturally welcome, and we would be most grateful for it, but we are required to inform you that there may be a degree of risk attached to such an operation.'

'I see,' said Thorold noncommittally.

'However, it may become necessary for our operatives to visit north-east Greenland. If so, then we may possibly request some form of guidance in the area. But no doubt you need time to consider things further. We'll be back in contact shortly.'

An hour and a half later Thorold returned from his lunch and sat down at his desk. Cautiously, he began to look through a budget report, when abruptly his computer printer began to spit out paper.

Thorold picked it up. It was the information from the CIA, and he read one sheet after another with his eyes bulging.

It appeared that Timur Medari was suspected of links with the Taliban in Afghanistan, Hamas in Lebanon, the Chechens, the Kurds, anti-government forces in Tajikistan, and two fledgling independence movements in far-eastern Russia. It also appeared that several men and women closely connected to him had died in a variety of accidents. Including in two cases, plane crashes. Thorold's tight little lips pressed closer together at this news, then he read on.

Medari's fortune was estimated at perhaps $70 million, but no one was sure – nor had he ever shown any sign of conspicuous wealth. He was wanted in six countries, including Russia, was rated by the CIA as extremely dangerous, and there were three symbols beside his name that Thorold could not understand. No one was known to work with him regularly, and he was thought to prefer a very hands-on approach to his jobs. The picture that came with the report showed an unremarkable middle-aged man, thin-faced, grey-haired and long-eyed, with a straggling black beard. It wasn't a face that stood out in any way, or that many people would bother to look at twice.

It seemed ludicrous that someone with this history would be even remotely interested in Greenland. Surely it must be a mistake. But what if it wasn't? Thorold's fingers beat a tattoo on the desk.

At that moment there was a knock on the door.

'Yes?'

It was Helge. Big, slow, thorough, with a face that almost never lost its smile.

'Well?'

'It's about the suicide up by Blok P, sir.'

'Well?' repeated Thorold impatiently.

'We still haven't found out the name of the victim, sir.' Helge paused. 'I've seen a lot of suicides, sir. But this one is a little different. For one thing he's got absolutely nothing on him that would help us identify him – his pockets were totally empty. It's almost as if he was trying to stop us finding out who he was. Added to that, it was done with a handgun – there aren't many handguns in Greenland.'

'They're not so difficult to get hold of. Have you checked the gun?'

'Yes, sir. It's not in our licence records.' He looked uncomfortable.

'You mean you think this might not be a suicide?' asked Thorold.

'I don't know, sir. It's just that, like I said, it all seems a little strange, sir.'

'Well, keep on trying to identify the dead man.'

'Yes, sir. Oh, and Jette told me to tell you that Sergeant Larsen has arrived at the airport, and is on his way.'

'Good. Tell Jette that I want to see Larsen the moment he comes in.'

'Yes, sir.'

17 The Apartments

IT WAS TEN on Monday night. Edvarth had just got back from buying some ribs for his supper, and was eating them while staring blankly at a TV quiz show, when there was a loud knock on the door. He started up, got uncertainly to his feet, and then went over and unlocked the door as a second volley of knocking began.

'Is your mother here?' demanded Larsen, bursting in.

'No.'

'So where is she then?'

'In Kapisillit. A couple of hikers were caught in a landslide on Nikku mountain, and apparently they've got pretty severe injuries. Mum was flown out there on Saturday afternoon, and she phoned yesterday to say it's too risky to move one of them, and she'll be there at least another day or two.'

'Oh.'

The energy seemed to drain out of Larsen, and after a moment he sat down. Edvarth looked at him, and realized how tired and stressed the policeman looked. Momentarily he felt sorry for the older man.

'Do you want a coffee?' he asked.

'Thanks. That would be good.'

While Larsen sat in the chair, his eyes shut, barely seeming to breathe, Edvarth went into the kitchen.

'How was your trip to Copenhagen?' he asked, coming back with two steaming mugs.

'A waste of time, I think,' said Larsen.

Edvarth looked at the policeman with a serious face, then returned to finishing off his ribs.

'Did you get a message from Jette?' he asked eventually. 'She was worried that you wouldn't get back here in time.'

'I didn't.' Larsen sighed, then sipped at his coffee. 'But it doesn't really matter.'

Edvarth looked at the powerful form of Larsen, which gave the impression that the years had slowly and painfully hacked it out of granite. He was the first man in several years who had managed to give a feeling of stability and confidence to Edvarth's mother. Yet now Edvarth sensed a brittleness, perhaps even a pain, in him that he could not remember having seen before.

Time edged reluctantly by. The clock on the mantelpiece ticked loudly. Edvarth finished his food, and cleared it away, then returned to watching the television. Larsen sat and stared into nowhere.

'How is your mother?' he said at last.

'OK.'

'Good.' Larsen summoned up a faint smile. 'Have you been back to that club again?'

Edvarth hesitated, then realized that his hesitation had already given his answer, so he nodded.

'Last Friday.'

'How does your mum feel about it?'

'I'm not sure she knows.' Hastily Edvarth changed the subject. 'When I was there, at the club, I saw that man again.'

'What man?'

'The one who was throwing money everywhere – you remember. . . .'

In a moment the policeman sprang alive. Exhaustion slipped from him as if it had never been there, and he leaned forward intently.

'You mean Steen Sanders?'

'Yes, I think Steen was his name. I was talking to one of the girls I'd seen that night, and suddenly he turned up.'

'Go on.'

'Well he seemed a bit weird. Kind of nervous. Said he was about to go off to Sisimiut and get a job there, but he hadn't got enough money to pay for the flight. I wonder how he managed to spend so much in the past few days.'

'I can tell you that,' replied Larsen. 'By flying to Copenhagen, and then coming back.'

Edvarth looked at him in surprise.

'Did you go there to look for him, then?'

'Among other things. I caught up with him too, but he did a runner. So he's back here is he? I suppose you don't have any idea where I could find him, do you?'

'No. But you're not the only person looking for him. The girl said someone called Harald had asked where he was, and Steen totally freaked when he heard that.'

'What do you mean?'

'He seemed really scared. I thought maybe he'd swindled this Harald guy out of all that money.'

'Something like that probably,' said Larsen, but his eyes were far away, and there was the keen, focused expression of a hunter on his face.

At that moment the phone rang. Edvarth answered it, expecting it to be his mother checking he was safely at home, and about to go to bed.

'Thank Christ you're in!'

'Who is this?'

'Katinka.'

Edvarth felt a leap within him, as if his stomach was trying to reverse itself. It was the phone call he had spent three days waiting for, and that he had never really expected to come.

'Oh,' he said, almost stammering. 'Hi. How are you?'

'Forget the social stuff. Listen, Steen's dead. I was due to meet him this morning, but he didn't show. Then I saw a cop car parked nearby, so I went to have a look. They were bagging up a body, before taking it away, and it was Steen. I'm sure it was Steen. I caught a glimpse of the clothes, and they looked just like the ones he was wearing at Salo's. But he'd been shot in the head. I asked one of the cops, and he said it was just another suicide. But Steen was murdered. I'm sure he was murdered.'

'How can you be sure?'

'He was scared. You said it yourself. Seriously scared. But scared people don't kill themselves. What's the point of being scared if you're about to kill yourself? Someone stiffed him, then made it look like suicide. And now I'm the one that's scared, Edvarth. Because if it was that man I mentioned, Harald, then he asked me where to find Steen. So that means I know what he looks like, and he'll be after me next.'

'I'm sure you're panicking unnecessarily,' said Edvarth, trying to be as reassuring as he could.

'I'm not. I'm panicking necessarily. I gave the guy my number, in case he wanted to phone. He can track me down any time, and I don't intend to be there when he comes round. I've been keeping on the move all day, waiting for you to get back. Where the hell have you been?'

'At school, then I. . . .'

'Don't bother to tell me. Just stay right where you are, OK?'

'Sure, but Katinka—'

She had already rung off.

Edvarth hung up with a dizzy feeling. He found Larsen looking at him thoughtfully.

'A friend of mine,' he said hastily.

'With an unusual name,' said Larsen.

'I'm sorry?'

'It wasn't only you I questioned that night at Salo's,' said Larsen. 'Among the others, there was a girl called Katinka. A girl who was mixed up with Steen Sanders too, and who managed to get some of his money off him. And maybe you saw her at the club on Friday too?'

Edvarth hesitated, glancing at the TV as he did so. Larsen waited with his customary patience.

'OK,' admitted the boy at length. 'That's true.'

'Would you mind telling me what the call was about? I got the feeling she had been scared by something.'

'Yes. She says Steen was found dead this morning, and that the police are treating it as suicide.'

'What?' Larsen sprang to his feet, then sat down again. 'Go on.'

'I don't know anything else.'

'You mean she thinks it wasn't suicide?'

'Yes. No. I'm not sure. She just—'

'So we could be talking about murder,' interrupted Larsen sharply.

'But. . . .' Again Edvarth ground to a stop, and glanced at the TV, as if he could not keep his eyes away from it.

Irritated, Larsen turned it off.

'Murder,' he repeated.

'There's nothing really I can tell you, until she comes.'

'You mean she's coming here? Now? How long will she be?'

Edvarth realized that he had let slip what he had intended to hide. Sullenly he stared at the ground, and said nothing.

'This is important, Edvarth,' said Larsen, with barely suppressed vehemence. 'When is she coming here?'

At that moment there was a knock. Slowly Edvarth went and opened the door.

Outside stood Katinka, breathing heavily. Over her cropped hair she wore a black baseball cap, sprinkled with fast-melting sleet, its peak low over her pale face. A thick, fleece-lined brown leather jacket was huddled round her, its high collar turned up against her cheeks, and she was wearing jeans tucked into mud-spattered knee boots.

'Thank God,' she said, giving him a hug and a fleeting kiss on his lips. 'I phoned you half a dozen times during the day. I was beginning to think you'd gone away some place.'

'You got here very quickly,' said Edvarth, feeling foolish and uncertain.

'Sure. I phoned from just up the street.' She pushed into the room, tossed her cap on to a side table, started to take off her jacket, then saw Larsen.

She froze.

'Good evening,' said the policeman, quietly.

After a moment she pointed a long red-tipped forefinger at him.

'You're the cop from Salo's, aren't you?'

'That's right.'

'So it seems I'm not the only one to move fast,' said Katinka, in a cold, level voice. 'I wouldn't have thought it was possible for you to get here so quickly.'

'I was here already,' said Larsen.

'Sure,' said Katinka. 'I remember. The kid here said he'd had dealings with you before. What is he – your pretty little boyfriend?'

Edvarth's jaw tightened, but Larsen was unmoved.

'Of course not. And now let's concentrate on you, and Steen Sanders.'

'I'm not talking to a fucking cop.' Katinka zipped her jacket back up, reached for her cap, then turned to go.

'He's OK. Really,' said Edvarth desperately, taking a step forward, and putting his hand on her shoulder.

Katinka pushed him away.

'Don't even talk to me, you little shit.' She shook her head, and her heavily-made-up eyes flared with fury. 'To think that I trusted you, and all the time you were just another fucking sea-slug, only too keen to go squealing to the cops. You make me sick.'

Edvarth's face was paper-white. His body was shivering visibly.

Katinka put her hand on the door handle.

'There's nowhere to hide out there,' said Larsen grimly.

She stopped, but did not turn back.

'What do you know about it?' she demanded.

'Enough to realize that if you're right, and if Steen Sanders was murdered, then walking out of this door could be exactly what the murderer wants you to do.'

No one moved. Outside a car hissed past, its wheels spraying up the slush.

Katinka looked over her shoulder at Larsen.

'What the hell do you mean?' she demanded.

'I have good reason to suspect that Steen Sanders was being used by a man who deliberately planned the deaths of over twenty people. Under those circumstances, he is unlikely to worry about another death or two.'

Katinka turned to Edvarth.

'What is this?' she asked. 'What is he talking about?'

Edvarth shook his head.

'I don't know.'

They stood close to one another, not quite touching, but gaining strength from each other's presence. Like two five-year-olds waiting for a telling-off, thought Larsen. But this was much worse.

'I need your help,' said Larsen gently.

'Not till I know what this is about,' retorted Katinka.

'Do you want the details then?'

'Yes.'

Abruptly Katinka went over to the sofa, and sat down on it. After a moment Edvarth joined her. Larsen sat opposite them. His concentration was focused on the girl, and he looked at her carefully, trying to estimate how honest he could be with her. His initial feeling that she was basically untrustworthy had faded. And if she really was in danger, then he owed her some help and information.

'It's important that you don't discuss this with anyone else.'

'I don't squeal,' said Katinka. 'Unlike some people I could name.' And she threw an acid glance at Edvarth, who looked away.

Larsen hesitated a moment longer, then instinctively decided to take the risk.

'Two weeks ago, as you must know, a plane from Nuuk to Iqaluit went down into the Davis Strait, killing all twenty-three people on board. Sea conditions, and the onset of autumn, mean it hasn't been possible to prove anything yet, but it is highly probable that the plane was carrying a bomb. Furthermore – and here we are going into the realm of theory – I have reasons to suspect that the bomb was aimed at killing just a single individual among the passengers, a Doctor Frederik Dahl.'

'Who. . . ?' began Katinka. Then she stopped. 'Don't let me interrupt. Wait – let me interrupt. If someone wanted this doctor dead, why not just shoot him?'

'Fair question, I asked myself the same thing. I imagine the idea was that killing so many people would conceal who the target really was. And, of course, the idea of a bomb causing the disaster probably wouldn't occur to many people. The Arctic is a dangerous place, and planes have been lost before.'

'You're talking about someone seriously ruthless,' said Katinka, her eyes wide and dark, her voice subdued. 'Someone willing to murder twenty-two innocent people just to make sure they get the one they want.'

Larsen nodded, and went on to explain who Dahl was, while the two teenagers listened warily.

'This is nasty stuff,' said Katinka, at last, 'but I don't see what the hell it has to do with me.'

'Steen,' said Larsen simply.

'What?' Then a thick layer of fear and understanding spread over her face. 'Fuck! Of course. He was a baggage handler at Nuuk airport, and suddenly he mysteriously equipped himself with loads of money. You think he was paid to put the bomb in the plane?'

'There's no real doubt about it,' said Larsen heavily. 'Though I'm sure he didn't know what he was doing. Anyway, he's been on the run since then, and it sounds as if maybe someone caught up with him last night.'

'But what's it all about?' asked Edvarth.

'I'm not yet sure,' admitted Larsen. 'But it seems that all the rest of the Iversen Land expedition are in some sort of danger also. The two members still in Greenland have been strangely hard to contact, and may even be dead, while one of the two in Copenhagen has been kidnapped, apparently to ensure the silence of the other. Furthermore, a young man employed to develop the expedition photographs was shot, and is still in a coma.'

Larsen stopped, then glanced down at his watch.

'Midnight already,' he said. 'And tomorrow morning I have to leave.'

'Where are you going?' asked Edvarth, failing to conceal his uneasiness at the news.

'This afternoon the chief told me I must go to north-east Greenland, to try to sort out this business. I'm booked on a plane first thing tomorrow to Kangerlussuaq, and from there three more flights, spread over twenty-four hours, will take me to Iversen Land. It's not the most accessible place in the world. Anyway, I need to sort a couple of things out fast.'

Larsen reached for the telephone and dialled police headquarters.

'Hi. Is that you Helge?'

'Yes. I'm the unlucky one on night duty. What can I do for you, Tomas?'

'Any more information on that suicide you were looking at this morning?'

'No, nothing.'

'Where's the body?'

'At the morgue. Why? Do you want a look at it?'

'Yes. And tonight, if possible. You see, I'm pretty sure I know who it is.'

'OK. I'll fix it with the hospital.'

Larsen rang off, then turned to Edvarth and Katinka.

'I have to go,' he said abruptly. 'You two had better take care – and it would probably be best if Katinka didn't go back to her place.'

'So where do I go then7' the girl asked.

'Don't you have any family, or friends, in Nuuk?'

'Why do you think I came here?' retorted Katinka.

As she glowered at him, he was reminded irresistibly of his elder daughter, Mitti. But Katinka was much younger, smaller, frailer, and despite her surface sophistication, it was easy for him to see just how frightened she really was. And he felt a sudden deep pang of pity for her.

'OK then. You can use my flat,' he said, almost without thinking.

The girl raised her plucked eyebrows in astonishment.

'You can't be serious.'

Larsen was briefly tempted to agree, but then he remembered Steen, and Jon Skalli, and twenty-three people tumbling to their deaths in the Davis Strait.

'It would be best,' he said quietly.

'And you're really willing to risk leaving me alone in your place?' said Katinka. She shook her head in total disbelief. 'That's more than my parents ever did – and you don't even know me.'

'Edvarth can keep an eye on you,' said Larsen. 'He knows where I live. Here's the key, I must go.'

'Wait,' said Katinka.

'What is it?'

She stood up, put a tentative hand on his arm, then smiled.

'Thanks. Thanks for trusting me.'

'Goodbye. Be careful, and keep all the doors locked.'

Two minutes later Larsen was out in the street, hurrying through the sleet towards the hospital.

'I must be out of my mind,' he muttered to himself.

He was taken down to the morgue by a hospital porter, and then left there by himself. The body was in the refrigeration unit, and Larsen saw instantly that Katinka had been right. It was Steen, and the left side of his head had been blasted away at point-blank range. Larsen looked at it grimly, but felt no pity, nor any of his usual revulsion to dead bodies.

After a few moments a thought struck him, and he went back up to the hospital reception.

'Is there a doctor I could speak to briefly?'

Eventually a young, blonde Danish woman came to see him.

'How can I help you?' she inquired.

'Is it possible to tell if someone is right- or left-handed?'

She shrugged.

'Ask them, or give them a pen and watch them write.'

'I meant if they were dead,' said Larsen.

The doctor chewed her lip.

'There's a chance that the muscles in one arm would be slightly better developed than the other – but it wouldn't be a big difference. And it might not be there at all. Why?'

Five minutes later the doctor stripped off her gloves, and nodded down at Steen's body.

'Yes. I would say there's clearly greater muscular development in the right arm.'

'And yet he used a handgun to shoot himself on the left side of his head,' said Larsen. 'That seems strange.'

The doctor looked at him, then nodded again.

'Yes,' she agreed. 'It does seem strange.'

'Thank you,' said Larsen. He glanced down at his watch again. 'I must go.'

There had been a long pause after Larsen left. For some reason neither Katinka nor Edvarth dared to meet each other's eye.

'I suppose I'd better be away,' said Katinka at last. 'Where's the flat?'

'I'll show you.'

'Don't worry. Just tell me the way.'

'It's a bit difficult. I'll come with you.'

They left Risa's apartment and walked silently down the stairs. Outside the sleet had lessened, and a cold east wind, straight from the ice-cap, was blowing through the muddy streets. Katinka pulled up her high collar, and then took Edvarth's arm.

'There's something I need to ask you,' said Edvarth at last.

'There's nothing to know,' she answered.

'Yes, there is. Why did you bring me home on Friday night?'

She made a casual gesture, as if throwing away his question.

'One has to look after one's little brother, and you weren't in any state to look after yourself.'

'I suppose not. What happened with that girl?'

'Those girls you mean,' said Katinka dryly. 'You were passed from one to another like a baton in a relay race. Until I picked you up from where you'd been dropped.'

Edvarth glanced at her, but her face was in shadow.

'Thanks,' he said. 'it was kind of you.'

'You said it. I turned down a couple of offers to do it.' Immediately she regretted what she said, and patted him almost clumsily on the cheek. 'Don't worry, they weren't good offers.'

They walked on a little further. The streets were almost empty, and the wind was blowing steadily harder. Edvarth gathered up his courage.

'There's something else I want to know too,' he said.

'You mean why did I spend the rest of the night in your mother's flat? Well, it was a long way back to my place, and I was a little worried by what Steen had said, so I thought I'd stay where I was. And if you've got dim memories, then yes. It's true you and I shared your bed. I was bloody cold.'

Edvarth stopped, and swung her round to face him. In the yellow light of a street lamp, she scowled at him.

'No,' she snapped instantly. 'Absolutely nothing happened. Nothing! If you and I had screwed, then you'd remember it. Believe me.'

'Thanks,' said Edvarth again. To his own surprise he felt a wave of relief, and suddenly he grinned at her. 'I'm freezing, and Tomas's place is only round the corner. Let's run.'

Edvarth did not go to school on Tuesday morning, nor did he go home to his mother's flat that evening. But some time on Tuesday night, he lost his virginity.

It was not at all like he expected. Not the slam-dunk sex that boys boasted about at school. Not athletic, sweaty, noisy, untamed, like in the films. Nor did it resemble the jagged, hard-edged, almost painful lust that struck him at times without warning. For this was nervous, then reassuring, gentle and tender, prolonged and sweet. He and Katinka lay on Larsen's spare led, and held each other, and caressed each other, and kissed and wriggled and laughed and said inconsequential things to each other, even as they made love throughout the night, and far into the next day.

'I love you,' said Edvarth, as he lay in glowing pleasure, feeling her body pressed down upon his.

'No, you don't,' replied Katinka, kissing him lightly on the eyelids, then on the nose, then on the chin. 'You love making love.'

He ran his hand through her spiky hair.

'I love making love with you.'

She smiled, then pulled herself off him.

'I'm hungry,' she remarked.

'Perhaps I should ring home, in case mum's back.'

When Risa realized who was phoning her, she exploded into blazing anger.

'Where the hell are you?' she demanded. 'I've been worried sick. The school said you hadn't been in today, and the flat looks like a bomb's gone off in it – dirty plates and mugs all over the place, bed unmade, lights still on. What the hell's been going on?'

'Sorry, Mum,' said Edvarth, uncomfortably aware of Katinka close beside him, listening to every word. 'There's nothing to worry about. We're at Tomas's.'

'What are you doing there? Let me talk to Tomas.'

'Well, actually he's away at the moment.'

'Then what the hell do you mean by 'we'? It sounds like you have a lot of explaining to do.'

So Edvarth explained as best he could.

It did not go well.

'I don't want you with a girl like that, Edvarth,' Risa said firmly. 'I know all about them. I see them in the hospital most days – girls of sixteen, seventeen, eighteen, nineteen, who look ten years older. Girls who smoke and drink too much, who already have drug problems, and a history of promiscuity and abortion. Girls who catch and spread syphilis and AIDS, without even knowing they've done so – until it's too late!'

'You just can't say that, Mum. You don't know a thing about her.'

'I think I do,' said Risa, immovably. 'She's just out for what she can get.'

Edvarth felt the phone snatched from his hand.

'If I was only out for what I could get, Mrs Poulson, I'd never have bothered with your son,' snapped Katinka.

'Get off the line,' retorted Risa. 'I want to talk to Edvarth.'

'You're not talking to him, you're just telling him what to do. He's too old, Mrs Poulson. You can't shove him around like a kid any more. He's old enough to make up his own mind.'

'You mean you're old enough to make up his mind for him. Now, let me speak to my son—'

'It's time you got real,' interrupted Katinka. 'This is when you step aside, get back to sorting your own life out, and let your kid handle his own.'

She didn't listen to Risa's reply, but handed the receiver back to Edvarth.

'Mum. I'm sorry you're taking it like this,' he said, as soon as Risa grew quiet. 'But I'll call you again soon.'

'Edvarth, I'm coming over.'

'Don't, Mum. It would just be embarrassing for all of us. I'm fine, and there's nothing to worry about. I'll see you soon. Bye.'

He hung up.

The phone rang within moments, but Edvarth quietly got up and unplugged it.

An hour later Katinka and Edvarth, their fingers interlaced, were lazily, almost absently, playing footsie with their bare feet, and looking out of the window at the quiet street, and the low grey clouds that lay over Nuuk. Suddenly Katinka clutched Edvarth's hand in a savage grip. He looked at her, and saw her face was ice-white, fixed with terror.

'What is it?' he asked.

She pointed at a small, bespectacled man, wearing a large, rather dirty overcoat, who was making his way slowly up the street.

'I think that's him,' she said, retreating from the window, and pulling Edvarth after her. 'Harald – the man who was looking for Steen. And now he's looking for me. Jesus!'

'But—'

'Sshh. For Christ's sake, don't make a sound, or show yourself. He's coming here. I know he's coming here.'

Both of them stayed where they were, holding each other.

Suddenly, harshly, the front doorbell rang.

The teenagers did not move, or make a sound. Only their hearts crashed fiercely in their chests. The bell rang two more times. Time slithered agonizingly past. At last, through the silence, they heard steps going away down the corridor.

Edvarth darted over to the window, and keeping himself behind the curtains, looked cautiously down into the street. After two or three minutes he saw the small man emerge. He took his spectacles off, wiped them carefully, then put them back on and looked up and down the street, before walking away.

'It's all right,' said Edvarth, taking a deep breath. 'He's gone.'

'Don't you believe it,' replied Katinka.

'I could go downstairs and check if he's out there.'

Katinka took a step after him and pinned him in her arms.

'No,' she said.

'But—'

'Remember what happened to Steen.'

Edvarth hesitated.

'Lock the door,' whispered Katinka. 'Lock and chain the door, put a chair up against it, then come back to bed.'

'OK.'

Two hours later Edvarth took another cautious look out of the window. There was no sign of the little man. But opposite the block of flats, leaning against the wall, was a thick-set Greenlander with a can of beer. As Edvarth looked down at him, the Greenlander looked upwards, and their eyes met.

18 Returning to the North

NATASHA WAS EATING her breakfast in the Leif Eiriksson airport self-service cafe, staring out through persistent rain at the massive sculpture of metal birds outside the Keflavik terminal, when her neck prickled. She looked around.

Larsen sat down next to her.

She stared at him in disbelief.

'What on earth are you doing here?' she asked.

Larsen looked at her cautiously. In the past six days she seemed to have lost weight, to have shrunk in on herself. Her shadowed eyes had retired into deep hollows, and her flesh and hair looked tired, dry and uncared-for.

'I was looking for you.'

'What are you talking about? You didn't even know I'd be here.'

'Yes I did,' he said. 'You told me you had to return to Ivtoriseq to sort out the expedition equipment, and with only one flight a week, it wasn't hard to confirm that you were booked on this one.'

'Why didn't you phone me?'

'I tried. But you haven't been back to your home, or to Seana's, have you?'

'No.'

'Have you seen Seana?'

'No. But she spoke to me on the telephone the day before yesterday. She must have guessed I had gone back to my mother's. She said she didn't know where she was, but the man who had seized her had promised her that she'd be released in the next few days. Provided I didn't do anything stupid. Then she rang off before I could say anything.' She looked at Larsen with something close to desperation in her face. 'I feel that I'm running away, but. . . .' Her voice trailed away.

'I told the Copenhagen police all about Seana's kidnap,' said Larsen quietly.

'Shitl You promised you wouldn't. . . .'

'They've been watching your house and tracing all your calls for some days now, but they thought it was better that you didn't know. They're confident that she's in no danger.'

'How the hell can they be so sure?'

Larsen did not answer. She stared at him.

'And what are you doing here anyway?' she asked at last.

'I've been posted to Ivtoriseq. I'm to see if I can find any trace of a man named Timur Medari, and to help a team of Americans who may be arriving there shortly.'

'In Ivtoriseq?' Natasha dragged up a weak smile. 'That'll set the place by the ears. Who's this Medari? The name doesn't mean anything to me.'

'Apparently he sometimes calls himself Christopher Goater, and a Mr Goater was in Copenhagen last week, seeing Doctor Anderssen. Before that, the same man seems to have been in Ivtoriseq, and also to have visited the remaining members of your expedition in Iversen Land.'

'I don't understand. Who is he? What is it all about?'

'Have you managed to contact Iversen Land yet?'

'Yes, I have actually, which was a massive relief. I was starting to get seriously worried about them. But I got through to Jens last Friday. He said things were going fine, and that – weather willing – they'd be on the return flight from the weather station tomorrow evening, to help me do the final sort out and loading in Ivtoriseq.'

'Oh.' Larsen concealed his surprise. 'And he sounded OK?'

'Sure. A bit, sort of. . . .'

'Sort of what?'

'Sort of fuzzy. Not really there. But people're often like that when they're about to go home.' She shrugged. 'I still don't understand what made them suddenly decide to stay another two weeks, without talking to me. Jens just doesn't behave like that. And it's not as if Seana was with him.'

'You mean because she's a bit unpredictable?'

'I suppose she is, but that's not what I meant. We all suspected Jens and Seana were sort of on the edge of having an affair, or at least thinking about it – though of course that sort of thing is almost impossible when everyone is living so close together. Anyway, we'll know the answers soon enough.'

'Exactly. That's why I also want to check out the plane at the lake, the one Dr Dahl took those photographs of.'

'You still think that's important?'

'I think it could be.'

'Those fucking photographs,' she said quietly, and took a deep breath. 'Jon's still in a coma, you know. I went and saw him yesterday. He didn't seem to have moved, but it was weird, he looked somehow younger. The hospital had tracked down his mother, and she was sitting beside him, knitting. Just knitting. They don't know how long he's going to be like that.'

'I'm sorry.'

'It's my fault. If I hadn't given him those photos, it wouldn't have happened, would it?'

'That doesn't make it your fault.'

'I know, it's the fault of the person who shot him. But it doesn't feel like that.' Her eyes turned abruptly away from the barren lava hills that surrounded Keflavik, and drilled into Larsen. 'Have you any idea why the hell it happened?'

'Perhaps,' said Larsen cautiously.

'But you're not going to tell me.'

'I'm just guessing at the moment. But I need to visit Iversen Land.'

She frowned.

'You can't just trot off to Iversen Land as if it's a day trip up the fjord. It's hard enough to get there in the first place, and if you go alone and without proper preparation, you'll probably just get yourself killed.'

'I've got supplies and equipment for a few days, and the fortnightly run to the weather station coincides with our landing at Nerlerit Inat. I've already confirmed that they can drop me off in Iversen Land this afternoon, then pick me tomorrow evening – which gives me just over twenty-four hours there. It's not long, but it's something.' He paused. 'I had hoped you might help me.'

'Help you?' She looked at him dully, and he seemed to see a sudden enlargement of her pupils, which made her eyes look faintly disturbing. Too receptive, like someone under the influence of drugs. Then she turned away.

'It's strange,' she mused. 'We may have found a wholly new bird species, which is far more than we ever guessed was possible. I suppose we could name it Dahl's gull – larus Dahliensis – but somehow it doesn't mean anything anymore. Not since Frederik died. I'm sick of this whole thing. I want it over as quickly as possible. It's as if, I don't know, as if. . . .' Her words ran down.

Larsen watched her sympathetically.

'Shall I get you a coffee?' he asked, but she didn't seem to hear him.

'Maybe I'd better try to get a job in America, or Britain, or anywhere that's hundreds of miles from Copenhagen, and Dr bloody Anderssen.' Her eyes slitted suddenly. 'At least I got the chance to shaft that bastard. People aren't ever going to forget what happened to him at the party.'

Five hours later the plane from Keflavik, having crossed the Davis Strait, at one point passing over a pod of thirty or forty white whales – clear to see in the aquamarine sea – began a cautious descent towards the great, iceberg-speckled gash of Kangertitivaq. Leaving lvtoriseq concealed by the crescent of mountains that hemmed the settlement in, the plane swung sharply north and followed a deep fjord, six or eight kilometres wide, lined by black rocky heights.

'I've never seen so little snow this far north,' Natasha remarked.

Larsen, who had been dozing, woke suddenly, and looked out.

On the left, barren hills, rising slowly and evenly from west to east, came to a sudden end in three-hundred-metre-high cliffs. On the far side of the fjord, out to the east, great glacier-capped peaks soared to more than four times that height, walling the fjord off from the ragged island-lined coastline, and the open sea. The airstrip was built on a stretch of flat, sandy ground, where two rivers flowed together, and were busily building a delta out into the fjord. There was little to see, except radar masts, and a few buildings – some abandoned when the oil company that had built the strip gave up its search. Ahead of them rose a single isolated hill, while away to the right, stretching north, was a deep, glacier-carved valley, interlaced with many yellowish, silt-laden rivers.

A Bell helicopter was waiting on the strip, to take the passengers the thirty-seven kilometres to Ivtoriseq. It swiftly began to fill up, but Natasha, somehow reluctant to get on board, stayed beside Larsen, talking of nothing. The helicopter pilot, a Greenlander in sunglasses, his fingers yellow with nicotine, emerged from the accommodation block, and nodded to Natasha.

'Your plane's just coming in.' He pointed up to where a small prop plane was flying up the fjord, then laughed. 'Rush hour at Nerlerit Inat! I'd better make sure everything's being loaded OK. See you.'

As he strolled away, Natasha turned back to Larsen.

'It's not my plane,' she said. 'It's yours. But I'm coming with you.'

Two hours later the Piper Navajo, loaded with supplies for the weather station at Danmarkshavn, and piloted by Mathias, was on its way north towards the isolated wilderness of Iversen Land. The weather was clear and they flew low, so Larsen was able to look out over a seemingly endless mosaic of bare rock, water, ice and snow, broken by rare patches of green – Arctic oases in the shelter of south-facing cliffs, or beside rivers and lakes.

Natasha tried to contact her companions with her satellite phone, then asked Mathias to use his radio, but neither of them got anything but white noise.

'Often the way when high pressure settles in,' said Mathias.

'I suppose so,' agreed Natasha.

'I'd arranged to pick up you and the other two on Thursday afternoon,' remarked Mathias. 'But my schedule's been rearranged – there's some fly-by they want me to do up at Danmarkshavn tomorrow. That means I won't be able to make the collection until Friday morning now, God and the weather willing.'

'What is the forecast?' asked Larsen.

'Not bad. Though there is some question of a depression that's edging eastwards, straight over the inland ice. If it keeps going, it'll arrive on the coast somewhere between here and Ivtoriseq in about forty-eight hours.

In other words I won't want to hang around. So if you're not on the strip Friday morning, and I haven't heard anything different, I'll assume you're sorting your own way out.' He shook his head. 'I can't believe this is my last flight up this year. Stockholm, here I come!'

The plane landed bumpily on the long strip of dark grey glacial gravel, which ran by the side of a thin ribbon lake. Several large metal tubs, painted red and white, showed where fires had been lit to serve as landing markers, but they were cold and empty now. On a small knoll above the strip was a medium-sized prefabricated hut, tied down with iron cables, battered by the Arctic winters, and clearly unoccupied.

'No sign of anyone,' said Larsen, opening the door and shivering as a breath of cold air washed over him.

'No one was expecting us,' said Natasha.

'On your way,' said Mathias briskly. 'A head-wind slowed us down, and I want to be at Danmarkshavn in time for dinner.'

Natasha and Larsen pulled on thick anoraks, and got down. Then Natasha began double-checking their packs, making sure they had everything they needed: several days' supply of food, a cooking stove with solid fuel, matches, a small lightweight tent, sleeping bags, and a complete change of clothes and waterproofs, together with a miscellany of other objects, including binoculars, camera, notebook, compass, satellite phone, sheath knife, ice axe, alpenstock, a flare launching tube and cartridges for firing.

'We're only going to be here for thirty-six hours,' remarked Larsen.

'We hope. But it's never wise to take risks in the Arctic. Just because the weather up here's not usually very changeable is no reason to get overconfident.' She raised her hand to Mathias. 'OK.'

'OK.'

Mathias nodded, reached over to close the door, then taxied the plane round in a tight circle, and gunned the engines. Within thirty minutes of landing, he was airborne again, heading off north-west. Larsen had never been so far from habitation before, and he felt a shaft of pure fear lance through him as he looked up at the little plane, a last tiny lifeline, vanishing into the distance. However, Natasha shouldered her pack contentedly, checked her boots, then set off eastwards. Larsen followed.

'Wait!' he called out. 'Where exactly are you going?'

'To our camp, of course,' said Natasha, still striding steadily onwards.

'But I need to visit this lake, where the photos were taken.'

'Sure. But it was Jens who went to the lake.'

'Don't you know where it is?'

'On the map, yes. But I've never been there. Jens'll know the best approach. Come on, we haven't got much time.'

'How far is it?' Larsen asked, unenthusiastically.

'Only about ten kilometres. But we have to cross the glacier.' Natasha laughed at the expression on his face. 'Don't worry, it's not so hard.'

For once Natasha was telling the truth. The expedition had found the shortest route over the glacier, and created what amounted to a well-marked track across the grey, cracked ice, with pitons hammered in to help with the more difficult climbs and descents, and poles marking crevasses. Natasha went first, and Larsen followed carefully in her foot-steps, taking exactly the same path as her. They were over the three kilometre-wide river of ice in only an hour and a half.

After crossing a muddy stream that ran beside the glacier, they stopped for hot vegetable soup, with pumpernickel bread, biscuits, and coffee, then set off again at a steady walking pace. A steep scramble up the side of the valley was followed by a plateau of bare, hard, rolling rock, carved and gouged by great glaciers in the past, and interspersed with small, clear lakes and tumbling, stony streams. They continued over a land that showed little signs of changing for the best part of an hour. In places Larsen saw a few cushions of moss campion, covered in dry brown seed heads, and once a raven flew high overhead; otherwise there was no sign of life.

Eventually they stopped for ten minutes, and a bar of chocolate.

'Are you sure we are going to find your partners?' said Larsen, looking around warily at the silent, empty wilderness that surrounded them on every side.

'Of course,' answered Natasha calmly. 'They still think that they're due to meet Mathias, with all their stuff, tomorrow afternoon. That means they'll have to cross the glacier first thing tomorrow morning. Actually I'm quite surprised they didn't elect to spend tonight in the hut. Anyway, they'll certainly have packed up the base camp today, and be planning to leave before sunrise tomorrow.'

'What if they're on their way now?'

'Then we'll meet them.'

'But supposing they take another route?'

'You're very twitchy. Don't worry. This is the way they'll use.'

Larsen looked about him, but could see no clear reason why they should follow this precise route, and not walk a kilometre to one side or the other – or almost anywhere.

He shrugged, and lay back for a few moments, feeling the early evening sun on his face. When he sat up, Natasha was already preparing to press on.

The ground was sloping more and more upwards, and directly ahead of them, their tops hidden in mist, the hunched shoulders of thousand-metre-high mountains gradually appeared. There looked to be far higher peaks out to their left, and a cold, fresh wind blew down off the ice into their faces, and whispered hissingly through the stones.

Half an hour further on they had to pick their way over a long, wide slope of boulder scree, scattered with patches of hard old snow and great rocks. At one point a snow gully cut clean across their way, and Natasha went first, carefully cutting steps with an ice axe. The sun was growing weak and low, and impossibly long shadows stretched out over the land, as they finally scrambled down the hillside, into a deep valley.

To the left, snow-born streams came bounding from the highlands, and ran on down the valley, joining with each other into arrowhead-shaped lakes, then separating out again, so that the whole floor of the valley was a complex braiding of water and land. It was by far the most fertile area they had seen. Great spongy masses of moss and lichen, brilliant green, red and yellow, dominated the wetter areas, while higher up lay grassy, flower-rich Arctic meadows, with seeds ripening everywhere in the last heat of the summer, before the nine-month winter descended afresh.

'The camp's just the far side of that outcrop,' said Natasha, pointing at a steep, rocky hillock that stood out from the far side of the valley. 'But it looks like we'll have to be a bit careful getting there.'

'Why?'

She pointed.

Over to their left, on an area of gently undulating grassy hillside, were some closely clustered brownish mounds.

'What are they?' asked Larsen.

'Haven't you ever seen a herd of musk oxen before?'

'No,' said Larsen, irritated. 'There aren't a lot living in Nuuk.'

Natasha laughed.

'I suppose not. I always assume that Greenlanders know more about their own country than I do.'

'We do. But that doesn't include creatures that only live in the most isolated parts of the land. Are they dangerous?'

'Not generally.'

'That's reassuring.'

They continued almost directly towards the musk oxen. As the creatures grew aware of the advancing humans, they hastily gathered in a tight defensive mass, looking down suspiciously at the intruders.

Natasha swung right, and headed for a gap between the steep ridge and the river. Larsen looked at her, and saw her expression had changed, and her thin face was frowning and worried.

The sun had vanished behind the western mountains, and the light was fading when they came round the shoulder of the rocky outcrop. In front of them a pleasant slope ran down to a small, clear stream, lined with gravel banks and cotton grass. A curving stretch of rugged bare rock on the far side of the stream provided protection to the north and west, and there were several wiry, half-metre-high Arctic willows, their silvery leaves bright amidst the boulders.

Natasha looked about her with confusion.

'They're not here,' she said after a moment, unnecessarily. 'I did wonder why a musk oxen herd had taken up territory so close to our camp – it must have done so since they left.'

'So where are they?' demanded Larsen.'

'I don't know.'

'Are you absolutely sure this is the right place. I mean I can't see any sign that people have ever been here. . . .'

'This is a national park,' interrupted Natasha angrily. 'We take as much care as we possibly can to leave no trace. Nature in the Arctic is at the very limit of survival, and even the smallest damage can harm it irreparably. And yes, of course I'm sure this is the right place. I camped here for eight weeks.'

She pointed at an almost imperceptibly faint oblong square, on a stretch of flat ground.

'That's where one of the tents was. There was another over there, and a third here.'

'So where are they then?'

'I don't know. I don't understand it. But we can't look for them tonight – you'd better help me get this tent up as quickly as possible.' She began burrowing into her pack. 'After we've done that, you can cook us some hot food, and when it gets dark, I'll use one of the flares. If they're within a few kilometres, that should alert them.'

An hour had passed when the flare hurtled high into the deep indigo sky, then exploded into a starburst of brilliant yellow, lighting up the area around them and casting sickly shadows in all directions. Twenty minutes later, Natasha fired a second.

'I'll keep the last one,' she said. 'In case.'

'How are they expected to find us?' asked Larsen, handing her a steaming bowl of rice, dried vegetables and meat that called itself risotto. 'Seeing as it's almost dark.'

She settled down in the bell of the little tent.

'By taking a compass bearing to the flare, then following that, probably first light tomorrow. We'll stay here until around midday.'

'But we have to visit the plane wreck.'

'We're not doing anything until I find Jens and Wendy,' she retorted firmly. 'Now, we need to get some sleep. I hope you don't snore.'

'I don't,' said Larsen, untruthfully.

'I'm told that I do,' said Natasha.

She went to sleep almost immediately, but the ground was hard and unforgiving, and Natasha did snore. Larsen lay awake, and listened to her for some time before sliding into a light, unrefreshing doze full of active dreams and semi-wakefulness. Only towards the end of the night did he finally fall deeply asleep.

He was woken by a sound of movement.

He opened his eyes, and saw that Natasha's sleeping bag was empty.

At the same moment he heard a quiet voice.

'What?' he said, then yawned massively, and wriggled to get the stiffness out of his body. 'What did you say?'

The voice spoke again, from just outside the tent.

'I said come out of there very slowly. Carrying nothing, and with your hands where I can see them.'

19 The Elephant

LARSEN EMERGED TO find that a thick, cold mist had fallen over Iversen Land during the night, and the rising sun was a barely visible white ball. The tent was dripping wet, and the two men outside, rifles in their gloved hands, were well wrapped up in anoraks, thick woollen trousers, and tall boots. Natasha, her face white as the snow-fields, was in front of the men, standing stock-still.

'Jens!' she said, looking at one of the two men. 'What are you doing?'

Jens, burly and bearded, wearing a fur hat, looked straight back at her, and said nothing.

'Hurry up, search her,' said the second man, lean and angular, his face shadowed by the thick lumberjack's cap he wore.

Jens began to go through her pockets. The warmth of his breath, slightly tainted, brushed her cold cheeks. After a moment he produced the satellite phone. His companion took it, dropped it on the ground, and crushed it beneath his foot.

'I'm sorry, Tash,' Jens said, in a voice like shaken gravel. 'But I wasn't going to turn down a chance like this.'

'What the hell are you talking about?'

Jens turned away, and began a perfunctory search of Larsen's pockets.

'Where's Wendy?' asked Natasha, who was still looking as if she could not believe what was happening her.

'There was an accident,' said Jens. 'I'm sorry.'

'You mean she's dead?'

'She fell, and broke her neck. There was nothing we could do.'

'I don't believe you,' said Natasha, breathlessly. 'I. . . .'

'We need to get to the lake as soon as possible, so could you please hurry,' said the second man.

'You bastard, you fucking shit!'

Without warning Natasha flung herself at Jens, lashing out at him with her fists. Jens reeled backwards, holding the stock of his gun up as a protection. Natasha knocked it aside and clubbed him savagely in the face. Jens staggered, and dropped his rifle.

'Get the gun,' shouted Larsen.

He had a glimpse of Natasha snatching up the rifle and swinging round, then he launched himself full at the other man. The man side-stepped neatly, and tripped Larsen, who sprawled forward on the ground. The man kicked Larsen, so that he rolled on to his back, then put a booted foot on the policeman's chest and deliberately aimed a rifle at his head.

'Put your gun down,' came Natasha's voice, shaking a little.

The man with the cap laughed softly.

'It's true that you have a rifle pointing at me, Miss Myklund,' he said. 'But for one thing I don't believe that you're really going to use it. Secondly, I cannot see how you can keep me and my companion covered at the same time. Especially as I am on the point of putting a bullet into this man's brain. So I think it is you who had better put your gun down.'

Natasha stared at him. Her face was set, like a tragic mask.

'I know you,' she said at last. 'I recognize your voice. You're the man who kidnapped Seana. Where is she? What have you done to her?'

'I couldn't say where she is,' answered the man easily.

'You've killed her, you bastard.'

The rifle she held was shaking. But her opponent did not seem concerned.

'Of course not,' he said, smiling.

'What do you mean? You're lying. You've murdered her.'

He almost laughed.

'Of course I haven't killed her,' he repeated. 'On the contrary. I have paid her an advance of a hundred thousand dollars. With substantially more to come when we've realized the assets we are on our way to collect.'

'What the fuck are you talking about?' Natasha's voice was a monotone from which every trace of emotion seemed to have been drained.

'Do you mean you still don't understand?'

'Understand what?'

'About Jens and his little friend.'

Natasha glanced at Jens, but he did not meet her eye.

'You mean. . . ?' she stopped.

'Cut it out, Chris,' said Jens suddenly. 'Let's do what needs to be done, and get away from here.'

Natasha stared at him, and the air sighed in and out between her teeth.

'I think maybe I don't need to ask any more questions, do I?' she said, suppressed fury filling her words, so that she spat each of them out as if they hurt her. 'Perhaps we're talking about my closest friend, the girl I thought I was trusting with my life. Darling Seana.'

She let out a bitter laugh. The gun was still tight in her hands, and her eyes burnt.

'No wonder everyone always knew exactly what the fuck I was doing. Seana was telling them. No doubt she was the one who cleared out the ice-core with the finger too. And that fucking kidnap was just a fake, wasn't it? How does she feel about all this lying and betrayal? How do you feel, Jens, you little shit?'

'It was a lot of money,' said Jens. 'You don't understand. Seana worked hard to get to university, really hard, but she'd never made money. In fact, she still owes a bloody fortune. And I've got nothing in the bank either, and no pension. If I smash up my leg tomorrow, I starve. Then suddenly this came along.' He paused. 'I'm sorry, Tash. But that's the way it is.'

'That's the way it is,' repeated his companion, quietly. 'Everyone has a price – and most people are far too cheap. Now, Miss Myklund, return that rifle to my friend Jens. Quickly. Otherwise I will have no choice except to put a bullet into this fellow's head.'

There was a long moment's silence. Larsen felt numb, helpless. A seal in the jaws of a bear. Every second stretched into hollow emptiness.

'A rapid decision is necessary, Miss Myklund!' said the man, in the same level, unhurried tone. His finger tightened perceptibly on the trigger.

There was a clatter as Natasha dropped the rifle to the ground. Jens stooped and picked it up.

The gun remained where it was, within a centimetre of Larsen's head, not even wavering.

'How did you get here?' demanded the man.

'We were flown in,' said Natasha.

'And how are you going to get out again?'

'The plane will be back at the strip tomorrow morning.'

'Not today? I think you are lying.'

'It's probably true, Chris,' put in Jens. 'I know the return flight was supposed to be this afternoon, but it often gets delayed for one thing or another.'

'And what will the pilot think if no one turns up?' asked the man that Jens had called Chris. The man that Larsen realized must be the very person he had been sent to look for – Timur Medari.

'Mathias won't wait if there's no one there.'

'So, there's no problem?'

'No.'

'And of course we have no room for passengers—'

'That's not part of the deal,' said Jens instantly. Heatedly. 'Listen, they can help us load up – it could be heavy. Then we'll leave as we planned, no problem. They'll be picked up in a week or two, when we're well away.'

Medari laughed. An easy, almost infectious laugh.

'Of course,' he said, as if soothing a recalcitrant child. 'I wasn't serious.'

The mist barely lifted all day, and progress had been grindingly slow. But as the four of them spent twelve hours making their way across the barren uplands and deep valleys of Iversen Land, there had not been the glimmer of a chance to escape. Natasha and Larsen, their hands tied efficiently behind their backs, had to concentrate constantly if they were not to fall – and their captors watched them unceasingly. Scarcely a word was spoken.

It was not until late afternoon that they stood on a grey, stony fell, and looked out at their destination. The sinking sun had finally escaped below the mist, but the great peaks to the west were already swallowing it up, casting long, grasping shadows over the cold, oil-black waters of Lake Sølveig. Half a kilometre away a great glacier came crawling down between two ragged, bare peaks, to end in a humped grey snout, slick with meltwater, slashed by great black lines where silt-lined precipices were etched deep into its weakening surface. Beyond that it crumbled away into the lake in tumbled masses of ice that varied in colour from filthy grey-black, through yellow ochre and pure white, to the rich swirling turquoise of ancient, decades-old deposits.

Natasha and Larsen were sitting wearily on a lichen-stained rock.

'It's further than I thought,' muttered Natasha. 'We'll never make it back to the airstrip by tomorrow morning.'

'No,' said Larsen.

Medari was a few metres away, on a steep little hillock, surveying their surroundings with a thorough, careful eye, and a critical frown.

'You're sure this is the place?' he called down.

'Yes,' said Jens.

'It had better be.' The disinterested tone the words were spoken in barely seemed to carry any threat at all.

He scrambled back down.

'Tell me about that area there,' he said, pointing below them to a stretch of relatively level ground, green with coarse grass, and intersected by the shining lines of two or three small streams, like snail trails in the low beams of autumn sunshine.

'I don't know,' said Jens. 'Dr Dahl and I kept to the high ground. There's too much danger of blundering into a marsh if you follow the valley bottoms, and the mosquitoes are always worse too.'

'You led us here with remarkable ease and confidence for someone who has only been here once before.'

Jens threw him an angry look.

'I don't understand,' said Natasha suddenly. 'Why are you all so interested in the remains of a plane that's more than forty years old? What's so important about it?'

Medari glanced at her with contempt.

'Most people can't recognize a platinum-edged business opportunity if it kicks them in the mouth.'

'Is that what you thought it was, Jens?' asked Larsen quietly. 'A business opportunity?'

Jens looked back at him.

'One of my friends was killed last year, up in the Stauning Alps. A group of rich American climbers wanted to climb a peak that hadn't been climbed before – but it turned out to be much tougher than anyone expected. That was when I decided this business of helping cash-strapped scientific expeditions up and down the mountains of Greenland was a sucker's game, and I was getting out. And then came that trip with Frederik. He was so stupid, he couldn't see what it was. But I saw, and suddenly there was my way out.'

'Don't you mean "our way out"?' demanded Natasha. Suddenly the dammed-back emotion flooded out. 'You and that treacherous bitch, Seana? I can't believe she's done all this. Every fucking moment that I thought she was helping me, she was selling me out. And what about Jon Skalli? Did she put a bullet in his brain?'

'Of course not,' said Jens. 'It was an accident. If he'd done what he was told, nothing would have happened.'

'There have been a lot of accidents,' said Larsen softly. 'But the money we're talking may be enough to justify quite a few deaths.'

'That's what I don't understand,' said Natasha. 'What money? What the hell are you all talking abut? How can anyone make money out of some old plane?'

There was a silence.

'That plane in the glacier is a B-52,' explained Larsen at last. 'And B-52s were – and still are – nuclear bombers. Our friends here are hoping to take the bombs out of the plane, and sell them. That's what this is all about.'

Natasha gaped.

'Nuclear bombs! You can't be serious?'

'Oh yes,' said Medari. 'Absolutely serious.'

'But countries don't just leave atomic weapons lying around.'

'Actually they do,' replied Medari. 'There are quite a few abandoned in the world's seas and oceans. It was assumed that this particular plane was lost in the Denmark Strait, and therefore its bombs would be unreachable. It seems the truth is different, which is very fortunate.'

'But nuclear bombers are not allowed to overfly Greenland.'

'Maybe the US doesn't always tell the truth about where its nuclear strike force goes,' said Medari. Then unexpectedly he laughed. 'And maybe the Danish government knows perfectly well that the Americans, whatever their promises, have always used Greenland bases for their nuclear strike force. After all, in January 1968 a B52, carrying four H-bombs, crashed on sea ice near Thule, but the joint Danish–American commission of investigation hastily covered up by assuring the world, completely untruthfully, that there was no danger to anyone or anything. Yet virtually none of the people who helped in the clean-up are still alive.'

Natasha looked at Medari, then at Jens.

'How much money can you sell an atomic bomb for?' she asked softly.

There was another silence.

'A few million dollars perhaps,' said Larsen at last.

'A few million,' repeated Medari, shaking his head pityingly. 'No wonder you Greenlanders are so out of touch with the modern world that your idea of capitalism is selling whale and seal meat to eco-tourists. To let genuine atomic weapons go for a few million! You obviously have not the slightest concept of what certain regimes – not to mention certain organizations – would pay today for a working atomic weapon. I already have expressions of acute interest from five different sources – and there will be more. When the bidding is over, I have no doubt that it will pass well beyond a hundred million.'

'A hundred million?' Natasha shook her head in disbelief. 'That's crazy. You'll never get that. The bombs can't possibly be still in working order after sitting in a glacier for forty years.'

'You think not? Well, maybe you're right. Either way that's our problem, isn't it? Not yours.'

'Either way it's just the usual, sordid little game of greed,' said Larsen, edging his words with as much scorn as he could muster. 'Though perhaps played with slightly higher stakes than is usual.'

Unexpectedly Medari swung on him, his face colouring, his hand clenching around his rifle.

'Greed,' he snarled. 'What do you know about greed? I tell you, I would do this for nothing. I would pay to be able to do this. I have the right to do this.'

'Of course,' said Larsen, doggedly persevering with his attempt to needle Medari into making a mistake. 'Of course you have the right to enrich yourself, to fatten your Swiss bank accounts, and to forget all about the innocent people you have murdered.'

The rifle butt swung out, and knocked Larsen to the ground.

'Murder and innocence,' hissed Medari. 'What do you know of such things? Yes, I have the right to do what I am doing. I have the right of my son whom they murdered before my eyes. I have the right of a raped and tortured country. I have the right of one who has suffered agonies, and fought for his life. It is you – fat, complacent westerners who live like parasites, draining the lifeblood of the poor to support your own luxury, it is you who have no rights.'

All three of them were staring at him now.

'You think I do this for money?' he said. 'Every dollar I make, every dollar I will ever make, I give to my people. Everything is for freedom – and for revenge.'

'You're a Palestinian,' breathed Larsen, in spite of himself.

'I am a Chechen. And I know what is happening to the Chechens every day.'

Suddenly he turned on Natasha. And his voice fell to barely a whisper.

'It started with the bombing,' he said. 'Before the Russian troops arrive, they send in the bombers. Have you ever been bombed? No, I did not think so. Let me tell you what it is like. There is a nerve-shattering shriek of noise that seems to come from all around you. The earth shakes, and then you see the bomb strike. It seems to explode without sound, and for a micro-second it is beautiful. A trunk of fire rising up, huge, twisting, writhing, as if made up of a thousand red, orange, and yellow serpents, all interlocked. It arches over you, and from its great searching boughs fall fruits of liquid fire, like a curtain of deadly raindrops. Then the sound and the heat strike you, a rolling wall of pain, which stuns your ears and mind, rips the air from your gasping lungs, and flings you backwards as if you weigh no more than a dead, autumn leaf. Flings you into the inferno.'

Medari was still standing, a tight hold on his gun, but his face was etched with pain.

'That is just the beginning,' he said softly. 'When I recovered consciousness, with the smell of my own scorched skin thick in my nostrils, I was a prisoner. And after a little while the Russian officer came and taunted me with how many of my people were dead. And then he asked me questions, that I would not answer. But that only made him smile. He gave me to his soldiers, and they kicked me, and beat me, until every part of my body was numb – numb because every single square centimetre was crying out in agony and faced with that blanket of pain, my brain had shorted out and removed my feelings from the compass of my body. I seemed to float above the twitching, blood-smeared, wracked mess that was myself, and like a fool I thought the pain was almost over and I had nothing to do but die. Then the officer came back, and told the men to wash me down, for it was time to get down to business. It was time to face the elephant. Do you know what the elephant is?'

His gaze flickered from Natasha to Larsen to Jens.

'I did not know either. And I did not know why the watching men cheered. And I did not know why one of them wrote numbers on the wall with a piece of chalk. Numbers that started at fifty, and went up in fives to five hundred. Nor why the soldiers got out money and put it on the ground, while the one with the chalk marked letters beside the numbers. Then at last the officer said, "OK, people. Time to play Elephant." And he sounded just like a game-show host. But before it started, he explained to me that the men were betting on how long I would stay conscious. Then he showed me the elephant.

'It was the gas mask from a chemical warfare suit, thick, black rubber, with huge round eyepieces and a long air tube attached to the filter, which looked like a trunk. That is where the name came from. They turned off the radio inside the mask – so that they would not have to listen to the noises that I made – and then they strapped the mask tightly over my face. So tightly I could feel my skin stretching as if it would snap. And for a moment I could hear my breathing, a great heavy panting as the air passed in and out of the gas filter. Then they closed the air valve, and I could not breathe.

'I told myself that they weren't going to kill me. I told myself that even if they did, it wouldn't matter, it would just be a handful of seconds of pain. But it wasn't like that. I could hear someone counting out the seconds, and they crawled past, while my head and chest seemed to grow red hot, shuddering, on the point of tearing apart. My eyes pulsed as if they wished to burst from their sockets, and my body was entirely taken over by the desperate, the manic insane desire to breathe air that was not there. I felt my lungs collapsing, while my whole body seemed to be half-exploding outwards, half-imploding into an agonizing nothingness. Only with a slowness that came from Satan did unconsciousness finally creep over me. And the last thing I heard, as emptiness took me, was a roar of triumph from the soldier who had betted on the correct time.

'Afterwards they took the mask off me and woke me up with a combination of cold water, cigarette butts, and kicks to the ribs. Then they gave me the Elephant three more times, and each time it was worse. For each time I knew a little more of the agony, and each time I knew that this would not be the death that it seemed to be, but just a brief pause before I would die again, and again, and again. And when the officer came towards me with the mask again, for the fifth time, I begged him with tears in my eyes. I grovelled like a cur. And he smiled, and fastened the mask over me. But this time he turned on the radio, and tightened the air valve just a little, so that I had some air, but not quite enough. To remind me what would happen if I did not behave. And I told him everything he wanted. Everything. I betrayed my neighbours, my friends, my family. Only the fact that I had nothing more to tell stopped me. But to make sure that I really had told them everything, they brought out my fourteen-year-old son and put a gun to his head. And after I swore to them by every God that ever was that I knew nothing else, then they shot him in front of me. And his blood spattered my body.

'A few months later, some UN human rights delegation came visiting, to see that the Chechen people were not being mistreated, and I was one of the prisoners that the Russians freed – to show how liberal and fair they were being. But ever since that day, I have sworn that I will do all that I can to gain revenge. Dare any of you say that I do not have that right?'

Larsen, Natasha and Jens looked away before his blazing glare. And Medari gestured with his rifle down the barren reddish slope before them. 'Now get on.'

20 Like a Dog

THEY APPROACHED THE snout of the glacier cautiously, along the marshy edge of the lake. A cloud of mosquitoes danced over the water, making the most of the last few days before the first hard frost of autumn killed them. On their right, towering rugged heights soared darkly up, to be lost in the hidden, mist-concealed, sky. The wind had dropped, and the only sound was the shuffling, cautious footsteps of the four invading humans. To Larsen their very presence seemed somehow a desecration of that silent land.

'Where's the plane?' demanded Medari, staring ahead.

'I don't exactly know,' said Jens.

'What?' Medari spun round, the rifle gripped tightly in his gloved hands. 'What do you mean you don't know. . . ?'

'I told you,' said Jens. 'I never saw it. Frederik took the photographs, and it wasn't until afterwards that he told me what he'd seen. But I know roughly where it was – under that tall cliff on the left-hand side of the glacier. . . .'

'So how do we cross the river?'

'Just down there. There's a glacial sill we can follow.'

A tongue of slightly raised land cut across the bottom of the valley, and where the river crossed it, the water was fast-flowing but shallow, and the four of them were able to wade across with little trouble. On the far side, they entered an extended region of hummocky, coarse grass, spotted with a few late yellow flowers, like tiny stars, and interwoven by the worn paths and tunnels of lemmings, and scattered half-concealed pools of brownish water. The grass felt like thick, wet, pile carpet as Larsen walked over it.

Medari stopped, took out his binoculars and scanned the area in front of them, then summoned Jens over to him. They spoke together in hushed tones. Natasha shuffled a cautious step closer to Larsen.

'What do you think they're going to do to us?' she asked in a shaky whisper.

'I don't know.'

'You're just saying that, aren't you? We all heard the sort of man he is, and the sort of money that's at stake. He's going to want to kill us – once they've found the plane and taken what they've come for. That's what you think, isn't it?'

'I don't know,' repeated Larsen.

'But Jens won't let him, will he? I'm sure Jens won't hurt us.'

'Jens is not the leader. And I think he will do what he is told.'

She stared at him with wide eyes, and he swore silently at himself for his truthfulness. He could see her chest moving sharply up and down, her mouth was half-open – as if she was about to scream – and her body quivered.

'Don't worry,' he said hastily. 'I always see the worst in everything.'

'No. You're right.' Despite her words, he saw with relief that she was slowly regaining control of herself, suppressing the blind, insane panic that had briefly threatened to take her over. 'Is there anything we can do?'

He said nothing for a long moment, his eyes on the two men, who were talking intently perhaps thirty metres away.

'We must try to get away somehow,' he whispered at last.

'How?'

'I don't know. But you must be ready to run if there is the smallest chance of escape. OK?'

She looked at him, fear returning to cover her face like a rippling veil.

'Is it that bad?'

'It may be.' He thought for a moment, then changed his mind. This was not the time to let her have any illusions. Only the truth would do. 'That man's real name is Timur Medari, and he's the person I was sent to look for. He's wanted big-time in a lot of countries – for a lot of things.'

'You mean, like murder?'

'Perhaps. But don't let him realize you know who he is.'

She said nothing.

'Basically we need a diversion,' said Larsen, after a moment. 'Something, anything, to turn their attention away from us.'

Without knowing what he was looking for, he stared out over the surrounding countryside. There seemed to be nothing there, no sign of life except scattered spreads of green and brown. Not a bird was visible in the sky. Rugged boulders were all that broke the skyline, and the mountains that hemmed them in were bare rock, broken only by precipitous cliffs, snow fields and glaciers.

Their captors were still talking, gesturing at each other, then at Larsen and Natasha, but it was impossible to understand what they were saying.

Suddenly Natasha drew in her breath with a hiss, and gestured with her head, out to the left, close to where a river emerged from the lake.

'What is it?' asked Larsen.

'Look.'

Larsen suddenly realized that what he had thought was a dark brownish rock, jutting out of a stretch of rolling grass perhaps a hundred metres away, was moving.

'What is it?' he repeated.

'A musk ox.'

The animal was much closer than the herd they had disturbed the day before, and as it emerged from a dip in the ground, and gazed straight at them, Larsen was able to see it clearly. Its stumpy, off-white legs were bright in the sun, and the thick, shaggy, blackish-brown coat was moulting, giving the creature an impression of dishevelled thinness. However, its high hunched shoulders, and the heavily armoured and scythe-horned head that was lowered towards them, added a distinct air of menace. Small wide-set eyes, under a brow of orange horn, looked down over the long, broad muzzle. The steam of its breath rose into the sky.

'It's strange,' said Natasha thoughtfully. The arrival of the musk ox seemed to have drained away all her fear, and she had become a scientist once again, only interested in the object of her study.

'What is?' asked Larsen, not really listening, but casting another watchful eye towards their captors.

Medari was half-sitting against a rock, completely still except for his hand, which ran up and down the stock of his rifle, as if he were stroking a cat. Jens was standing in front of him, talking vehemently, and shaking his arms. Larsen wondered if perhaps they should simply make a run for it now – there might never be another chance as good as this. The light was fading, the mist was showing signs of thickening, and it would surely be better at least to make a try for freedom rather than to be shot down in cold blood.

'There don't seem to be any more.'

He turned back to Natasha.

'You mean any more musk oxen?'

'Yes.'

'Does that matter?'

'Well. . . .' Natasha frowned. 'As you saw yesterday, a herd is no problem. The lead male may make a few short charges, but basically the animals will either run away, or get into a defensive circle and stay there until we leave the area. But if this is a lone bull.. . . '

Suddenly Larsen was interested.

'You mean it could be dangerous?'

'If he's had his herd leadership taken from him by a younger animal, then yes, he could be a problem. Such animals are often very morose and aggressive.'

Again Larsen's eyes flickered towards Jens and Medari. They didn't seem to have noticed the thick-set animal that was advancing slowly towards them. Then, just as his hopes were rising, the musk ox stopped, and began to graze.

'It looks as if he's not going to attack after all,' said Natasha.

'Shit!'

'What?' Slow realization lit up her face. 'Oh. You thought if he charged, it might give us a chance to get away.'

'Of course.'

She shook her head.

'He's not going to.'

'Is there any way at all that we can make it attack?'

'Not without running at him – and even then he might just lumber off. Though of course if we had a dog, it would be different.'

'What do you mean?'

'Musk oxen can't bear dogs. Their only natural enemy is the wolf, and they will always attack a barking dog. Apparently. . . .'

Larsen saw that their captors had finished their discussion, and were beginning to walk back towards them. Jens had his head hanging low, but there was a certainty in the way Medari walked, in the casually proficient way he handled his rifle. An instinctive fear rippled down Larsen's back, and at the same moment he was sure the decision had been made. That even if it did not happen immediately, they were certainly going to be killed.

'Get down and howl like a dog,' he hissed at Natasha.

'What?'

'Like a dog. Quick!'

Larsen flung himself to the ground, and tried as best he could to imitate the howling of the Greenland husky. A moment later Natasha did the same thing. Desperately, the two of them howled and barked as loud as they could.

Their captors, just twenty metres away, stopped and stared at them in astonishment.

But beyond them, the musk ox had looked up. It took a step forward, then a second, and began to paw the ground. Its snorting breath carried clearly through the crystal-cold Arctic air. Larsen and Natasha were still barking as loud as they could. Suddenly the animal tossed its great horned head, dropped it low and charged straight towards them on its short, powerful legs. Its accelerating hoofs crashed a staccato rhythm on the stony ground, and its coat flew in the wind of its onset.

Even as Jens and Medari spun round towards this unexpected threat, Natasha and Larsen sprang to their feet and ran up the rugged slope behind them, driving themselves as hard as they could.

Two shots rang out abruptly, then a third. There was the vicious spitting sound of breaking rock. The snorting of the musk ox still rang through the air, and there was a fresh thudding of hoofs, then a sudden scream. More shots rang out.

Larsen, darting from one side to another to make himself a difficult target, felt Natasha close behind him. Ahead of them the slope banked steeply up towards a great razor-backed ridge. Larsen could feel his breath rasping in his throat, his heart crashing, as he forced himself on with every scrap of muscle he possessed. Stones rattled at his back as Natasha struggled after him. Distantly, through his own breath, he could hear shouts.

The ridge was only twenty metres away. Fifteen. Five.

In a massive burst of adrenalin, Larsen hurled himself full-length over the top, then slid helplessly, in a chute of pebbles, down the steep slope on the far side. A moment later Natasha tumbled down to join him.

'What now?' she panted, her pale eyes wide, her face taut.

Larsen was fiercely rubbing the rope that tied his wrists up and down against a sharp rock edge. After a minute, it began to fray, and with a wrench of his powerful arms, he broke it apart. Hastily he untied Natasha, then both of them wriggled back up to the top of the ridge and peered cautiously back into the valley they had come from.

The first thing Larsen saw was Medari, his rifle levelled. A few metres from him was the musk ox, and to his astonishment it was still standing. Facing the armed man head on. A little way away Jens lay on the ground.

As Larsen watched, the bull tossed its head again, snorted loudly, and then suddenly dropped its head even lower, and crashed forward straight at Medari. There was the sharp crack of a shot, but the musk ox seemed barely to notice it, and the gunman was forced to spring aside, and take shelter behind a large rock pillar. The musk ox swung round to face him again.

'I don't understand,' breathed Larsen. 'How can that creature still be alive?'

Natasha was beside him.

'When a musk ox charges straight at you, then the rifle bullet will hit it in the head, and nearly all of a musk ox's head is bone and horn, so most bullets just bounce off it.'

The animal was lowering its head again, moving slowly towards Medari, who was sheltering behind the rock. But at that moment Jens, still lying on the ground some way to the side, began to crawl slowly, painfully, across the ground. The musk ox took no notice, intent on Medari. After a few moments Jens had reached his rifle. He picked it up, and steadied himself by leaning back against a boulder. Carefully he took aim, and fired, once, then again.

The musk ox shuddered, and half-spun round. There was a third shot, then a fourth. Slowly the great animal keeled over and collapsed.

'Jens knew that he had to get it in the side,' said Natasha. 'Poor thing.'

'Let's go,' said Larsen urgently, pulling her back down the slope.

He led Natasha at a steady trot along the shallow valley they found themselves in, swung round a curve in the hillside, then rapidly up another stony, barren slope. As they climbed a second ridge, there was a sudden burst of fire. A bullet whined past Larsen's head, sounding like a huge mosquito. Other bullets crashed and skipped on the rocks around them. Then they were away, out of sight over the hill crest.

Twenty minutes later they stopped in a well-concealed hollow, at least three hundred metres above the valley floor, and with a narrow, almost invisible, cleft in the rocks behind them.

'Now,' said Larsen, after he had regained his breath, 'you make sure we're not being followed, while I phone for help.'

'But they took our phone.'

'I had another,' said Larsen, producing it from a hidden pocket inside the waistband of his trousers. 'I just pray to God that it's still working, after all the punishment it's had to put up with.'

But the phone was dead. No sound came from it, but a faint crackling hiss.

'Hell!' swore Larsen. 'What do we do now?'

'I would say that we don't have any realistic choice,' said Natasha, glancing down from the edge of the hollow.

'What do you mean?'

'We have to follow them.'

'That's crazy.'

'No it isn't, it's the only thing we can do. They've got the food, the radio, the map, the warm clothes, the equipment. Everything we need to survive. Without them there is not the slightest chance that we can get back to the airstrip in time to meet Mathias tomorrow morning. And without them there is no way that we can summon help. So they are our only chance of survival.'

But they are far more likely to be our killers, thought Larsen.

'OK. We'll wait and watch for our opportunity then,' was all he said.

'That means staying here overnight,' said Natasha grimly. 'And it will get seriously cold. You try to build up some protection against the wind, I'll get us some bedding.'

'Bedding?'

'That's right. But what we really need is snow.'

'Snow?'

'The best insulator there is. Unfortunately, there looks to be no chance of any, so we'll have to do the best we can.'

She slipped down into the dip, and started ripping up every scrap of vegetation there, while Larsen began to build up walls of broken stone and rock around the cleft. Three-quarters of an hour later night had fallen. Larsen and Natasha, almost entirely concealed from outside, lay upon a thin layer of cotton grass, Arctic willow, and moss, pressing against each other to preserve as much heat as they could.

Both of them were shivering.

'Shouldn't we use the darkness to try to launch a surprise attack?' whispered Larsen.

Natasha shook her head.

'Jens is a brilliant hunter. However quiet we are, he'll hear us coming at least half a kilometre away. Probably more.'

'Then what chance have we got?'

'Wait until they've forgotten about us. Wait until tomorrow morning, when they're more interested in the plane.'

The shadowed, indigo dark of the Arctic, with no sound but the hiss of the ever-present wind, had faded away. The sun, small and white, was rising in the east, casting a thin illusion of heat over the ice-hardened mountains and barely liquid lakes of Iversen Land. Still shivering, their very bones aching from the vicious cold, Natasha and Larsen watched from above as two men, one of them limping noticeably, scrambled along a ridge on the north side of the great, crawling, greyish river of ice.

'There,' hissed Larsen, pointing.

They could both see it now.

The glacier had melted and withdrawn further in the weeks since the photographs had been taken, and now the fragments of a plane were clearly visible – a huge torn and twisted wing, missing its ailerons. There was no sign of the other wing at all. But close by was the crumpled nose cone, with its high cockpit, at the tip of the long tunnel of the fuselage, the upper-half grey and green with camouflage paint, but also glinting with the silver of scarred metal, the star and stripes of the USAF symbol still just visible on the side. Two huge double wheels, crushed and distorted, jutted out like sprawling broken limbs. Much further back, still half-encased in ice, towered the huge great tail, painted dead black. On it, marked in red, were the numbers Natasha had written inside her glove back in Copenhagen – 55-0065.

Larsen and Natasha stayed where they were, until the two men vanished round the far side of the plane.

'What do you think?' asked Larsen, beneath his breath.

'We don't really have any choice,' she replied unemotionally. 'No food. No shelter. No gun to hunt with. No way of contacting the outside world. And when the weather turns colder – as it very soon will – we'll be facing a rapid death from exposure.'

The two of them slipped down the hillside, using every curve and fold of the land, every area of shadow, to make their way towards the fragments of the plane. It took them quarter of an hour to reach an outcrop of glacier-worn and broken rocks, perhaps thirty metres from the side of the plane. There they stopped.

A few faint sounds of distant movement drifted through the still air. After a moment Larsen gestured at Natasha to stay where she was, then he scuttled along behind a low ridge, until he was able to see a great gaping hole in the far side of the plane, surrounded by torn and twisted metal, and fragments of limp fabric like banners. Medari and Jens were standing by the gap, peering inside. Larsen hesitated, then used the body of the plane as cover to dart down towards the left-hand side of the plane. A massive broken wheel lay on the ground, elegantly stained with grey and yellow lichen, and above it was a great, frost-rimed flap. Cautiously Larsen took shelter underneath it, looked around at the complex mass of hinges and wires in the gloom above him, then saw a lightless square in front of him – the hatch into the forward part of the plane. After a moment he gathered up his courage, and clambered cautiously up.

21 55-0065

IT WAS DARK inside, but not pitch dark. As his eyes adapted, Larsen realized that whitish-blue light was seeping in through a variety of jagged rips and holes in the skin of the plane, where the fuselage had been semi-crushed, compressed and distorted by the weight of the ice that had encased it for more than forty years.

Crouching, Larsen took a few careful steps inside, feeling as if he was entering a cold, twisting tunnel. A murmur of nearby conversation made him pause, but then he slipped on forward, just managing to squeeze through a twisted metal door into what had clearly been a cabin. He stopped again. Below him and in front he could see out through the broken fuselage, cracked glass, and the empty spaces where the glass had been. Above was a solid ceiling, and all around him belts, wires, tubes, levers and cables hung dangling from above, or lay curled on the floor, like branches and creepers in a rainforest. In front of a broken and rusted instrument panel, with line after line of ancient-looking dials and screens, were two silver metal seats, almost like boxes, with a mass of white-handled levers between them. Half sticking out from underneath the left-hand seat was a misshapen kit-bag with a few illegible letters on the top.

The sound of voices was coming closer, echoing oddly, almost unrecognizably, in the cold dead air.

Larsen looked around frantically for somewhere to take shelter, but the whole small cabin was so packed with equipment that there was nowhere he could go. Nowhere to hide. Even as he groped around for something, anything, that he could use as a weapon – it seemed that Jens and Medari had stopped to talk.

'Have you contacted the chopper to pick us up?'

'Not yet.'

'Why not? I'd feel a lot happier if it were here now, outside, waiting for us.'

'We're not doing this to make you feel happier.'

'But it's going to cost us a lot of time, and—'

'Listen, Jens. Think smart. The end of the Cold War may mean that the US base at Thule has been run down, but it's still operational. And that means northern Greenland is still thoroughly scanned by radar, and no doubt all sorts of other, satellite-based systems. If they want to, they can probably pick out lemmings they don't like the look of. So, from the moment the helicopter approaches this area, there's every likelihood it'll be spotted and tracked, and if it is, then it is not going to take them very long to realize that we've got no clearance to land here. At the most it will only be an hour or two before a plane from Thule is overhead, seeing just what the hell is going on. That means we have to make absolutely sure we're on our way as fast as possible. And that means that we should be looking for what we want, not standing around here talking.'

'There's no sign that I can see. Are you sure. . . ?'

'Of course I'm sure. Didn't you notice that the whole underpart of the plane, and of that broken wing, were all painted bright gloss white, without any markings or letterings in sight at all?'

'So what does that prove?'

'It's anti-flash paint, intended to reflect away some of the thermal radiation from a nuclear detonation – so the crewmen wouldn't be fried by their own H-bomb. Obviously, that was only done on aircraft which carried nuclear weapons.'

'Oh. I see.'

'Listen, you go and check out the navigator's area – maybe there's some clue up there. If you can't find anything, then climb up into the main cabin, and look around the back chair – the one that's not facing the windows. That was where the electronic warfare officer sat – there could be something there.'

'What do you mean, something?'

'I don't know.' Medari's voice was sharp and irritable. 'Just look. I'll check out some more of these weapons' bays. All these massive piles of steel cases must contain something or other.'

'I've already looked inside them.'

'How many?'

'Three. They broke open fairly easily – the ice has made the metal brittle. They're nothing but records I'd say, medical ones maybe. I don't know. Basically all the ones I opened were just filled with masses and masses of paper, most of it impossible to read.'

'There are some larger containers over to the back there. I think I'll have a look at them.'

'OK. But-'

'Check out the cockpit, like I said.'

There was a sound of steps coming closer again. But from the conversation Larsen had already realized that there was a route of escape – to another, upper section of the cabin. More important still, he had spotted the ladder, almost concealed in the shadows. Swiftly he darted over to it and began to climb. There was a creak, then he pushed his way through a narrow access hatch into the upper cabin. This was larger and the front, where the pilot and co-pilot had sat, was much lighter.

Larsen glanced at the two chairs, similar to those downstairs, but with half-wheel controls in front of them, together with yet more dials, and levers, and yet more pipes, tubes and cables. Just behind him, in deep shadow and facing the opposite way, into the body of the plane, was another chair. Hearing the sound of movement immediately below, Larsen crept over towards the third chair and, to his relief, found that the buckling of the fuselage had created a dark hole under what must have been another ruined control console. With a burst of relief he edged himself slowly into the space, then almost slipped and put his hand out to save himself. The edge of the seat beside him was bone-chillingly cold, but the metal had a strange flaccid feel, underneath what seemed to be a leather covering.

Suddenly Larsen wrenched his hand back, as he realized that he was touching a corpse. Slumped bonelessly over to the far side, but still held in place by a strap round the waist, was a dead man. A long-dead man.

In the dim light Larsen could just make out the old-fashioned flying suit. The head, dangling unnaturally, was almost entirely concealed under a flying helmet, tinted goggles, and oxygen mask. Larsen looked closer, and realized that he must be beside one of the original crew of the plane, the body perfectly preserved by the glacier ice in which the plane had been entombed for over forty years. The man's legs were crushed between the instrument panel, the chair, and the deeply indented wall of the plane, and both arms were missing.

At that moment, there was a sound of someone coming up the ladder. Larsen pressed himself back as far as he could into his hiding place, closed his eyes, and held his breath. There was a sound of someone moving just two or three metres away from him, then a sudden half-strangled yelp. Jens, if it was Jens, must have just noticed the dead man.

At that moment there came a shout from downstairs.

'Come and help me open this thing.'

'OK.'

A minute or so later, Larsen allowed himself to breathe, and then, very slowly, began to emerge from his concealment.

Jens and Medari were back together, by the weapons' bays. There was a sound of grunting, a sudden crack and a tearing, screeching noise, then finally a savage curse.

'What is it?'

'There's a stiff inside.' Jens's voice was shaking.

'Let me see. Oh, right.' There was a half-laugh. 'So what's the problem? Didn't you notice what was left of the tail gunner, blocking up that crawlway to his lonely little place in the arse of the plane?'

'Sure. And the warfare officer up top. I wonder what happened to the rest of the crew?'

'Who knows. Maybe they survived, and managed to get out, only to die of exposure and be eaten by foxes and ravens. Maybe the ice or meltwater swept them away. Does it matter?'

'I suppose not. But I'd still like to know what the fucking hell is a body doing in this box?'

'The Americans are sentimental about cadavers. It's probably an airforce man who died while he was working on the base, and whose body they were taking home.'

'Except that there are about twenty of those containers. Why should a base in the middle of nowhere suddenly have twenty men die on them?'

'We don't know that they do all contain bodies. But if they do, then it was probably some sort of accident.'

'What sort of accident would that be?'

'How about a nuclear one? They've always covered those up.'

'Shit. I don't like this at all.' Jens's voice was breathless and frightened. 'That would mean there's a chance these bodies might still be radioactive, wouldn't it?'

'Do you plan to live for ever? Get a grip, Jens. You have to take a few risks for this sort of money. And anyway, it was over forty years ago.'

'Yeah. I suppose so. But it looks like the weapons' bay is full of these containers. Maybe the plane wasn't carrying any bombs. . . .'

'Listen, Jens, let me sketch this out for you in words of one syllable.' Medari sounded like an irritated teacher, dealing with an exceptionally slow pupil. 'This is a B-52 we're standing in. The Danish government may have said that they didn't want nuclear weapons in Greenland, but the B-52s stationed here were strategic nuclear bombers. That's why they were here. That's what they were for. So there has to be at least one bomb aboard, almost certainly several.'

'They didn't always fly armed, did they?'

'Maybe not. But we are talking about late 1958 – the Cold War was never closer to turning into a hot one than in the late fifties and early sixties. The Americans were scared shitless because Russia had just tested the first intercontinental ballistic missile, and put the first sputnik into space. Everyone thought atom bombs were about to start raining down on them from outer space. Over the next four years there was the U-2 business, the Berlin Wall, and the Cuban Missile Crisis – when the world was one short phone call from all-out nuclear war. The whole point of having B-52s constantly cruising the skies was to make sure the Russians couldn't hit all America's weapons in a sneak attack. And that meant every plane in the air had to have atomic weapons aboard – ready to retaliate. We know for a fact that the only other B-52 that crashed in Greenland was carrying nukes, and that was ten years later, when things weren't so dangerous, and when the US was also protected by its new long-range missiles. There's another point as well – this plane was the last to leave Narsarsuaq, so the chances are very high that it was carrying extra nuclear stock from the US airbase there. . . .'

'OK, OK. I'm convinced. But then where are the bombs? Perhaps someone got here before us.'

'Impossible. No one even knew this plane was here until you and Dr Dahl found it a few weeks ago. The bombs must be here – hopefully several. I would like to be able to save one.'

'What? What do you mean, save one?'

'It would please me very much to be able to keep one for the use of my own people.' There was a faint laugh. 'It would be a fine irony if a bomb built to devastate Russia may finally be called on to do its job half a century later.'

'You mean you're planning to explode one?' came Jens's voice, breathy and frightened.

Again, the faint laugh.

'No, no. It will simply be used as a threat, to make sure the cursed Russians realize that this time they must get out of Chechnya for good. And don't worry, there will still be plenty of money. More money than you can even dream of. You took a shrewd decision when you contacted me.'

'It doesn't feel like that at the moment. That bloody animal outside has left me feeling as if my right leg was caught between a hammer and anvil.'

'At least you killed it.'

'Yes. But I'm more interested in these fucking bombs, and where they are. I mean, the tail end of the plane is still embedded in the ice. What if they're in there?'

'No. I've studied many blueprints of the B-52D. The bombs weren't kept in the tail section. They were always in the weapons' bay – which is where we are now standing.'

'OK, OK. But all I can see are all these weird containers – some with papers in, some, it seems, with bodies in. And no sign of any bombs.'

'We'll find them.'

'Sure. But I think maybe I'll just go outside and check that Natasha and her friend aren't creeping up on us.'

'As you wish.'

Larsen pressed himself back against the wall, making sure he was not visible through the windows. Below, steps echoed faintly along the metal, and faded away. There was a fresh sound of hammering from the rear of the plane, where Larsen guessed that Medari was either trying to break into another of the containers, or into another of the weapons' bays.

Uncertain what to do, Larsen stayed where he was. Then a few minutes later, Jens's voice suddenly and abruptly came from close outside.

'So, here you are again. I did wonder. That's right, hands nice and high. Now, get into the plane.'

Larsen fought back panic and stayed where he was.

Again, steps crunched on the stones, then splashed through a pool, just outside the plane.

'See what I've caught outside.'

Natasha's voice cut through.

'You fucking, unspeakable bastard, Jens! There were moments when I thought you were dead. Jesus, I even wept for you one night—'

'Shut up!'

'What the hell do you think you're doing here, anyway? You cannot be seriously planning to sell atomic weapons to terrorists and dictators, to the very sort of people who might use them—'

'I said shut the fuck up.'

'The money you make could be paid for in thousands, millions of innocent lives. Kids burned up alive – maybe as much as a death for every filthy, blood-stained dollar you make. . . .'

There was the thud of a savage blow striking home, and a grunt of pain. Then a second blow.

Larsen bit his lower lip. But he dared not move. Not yet.

Medari's voice came echoing out of the depths of the plane. For the first time his drawling, controlled tone was tense with excitement.

'I've got them. I've fucking found them.'

'What are you talking about?'

'Here. Look, it's the bomb storage racks – they aren't where they were shown in the blueprints, but there's no question. And six of the sods. Six of them.' There was a high-pitched laugh. 'Six! We're about to become seriously rich men.'

'Thank God for that. Now let's get out of here. This place gives me the crawls.'

'It shouldn't. It's the most beautiful thing you'll ever see in your life – a solid platinum mine, or should I say plutonium? But you're right, we must move fast. Let's get outside and start to sort things.'

Carefully, Larsen began to climb down the ladder, back into the navigation and radar cabin. Once there, he ducked down, then peered out of a slit in the cabin wall. The two men were standing close beside that gaping tear in the side of the plane where the wing had been, both of them holding rifles. Natasha was crouched on the ground in front of them. There was a swelling bruise under her left eye, and a thin trail of blood running down from the side of her mouth.

'Right,' said Medari, quietly. 'Where's your companion?'

'He's gone to get help,' answered Natasha sullenly.

'How is he planning to do that?'

'By getting to the airstrip, and linking up with Mathias.'

'That'll take him at least twelve hours,' muttered Jens. 'We've got plenty of time.'

'Except that she's lying.'

'How do you know?'

Medari took a menacing step towards Natasha.

'Your story's got more holes in it than that plane. Why did your companion set off and just leave you here?'

'I told him to go. I twisted my ankle running away, so I would have slowed him down, and he wouldn't have got to the airstrip in time.'

'Good answer. But you told me the plane was coming in this morning – and that if you weren't there, it would simply fly on. So how exactly could your friend reach the airstrip in time?'

And suddenly, with no warning, he hit her with the stock of his rifle, so that she doubled up, gasping for breath. Then he bent down beside her, his gun hovering over her temple. Behind him Jens started forward, then stopped.

'Why do I have to keep persuading everyone that I am not a fool?' said Medari softly.

Slowly, almost imperceptibly, Larsen began to creep back towards the hatch, and the square of light that came through it.

Natasha's interrogator was still talking.

'First point, that man would not just leave you here, and even if he had, why should you stay? Far more sensible simply to follow after him as quickly as you could. Or at least dig yourself a nice, safe hole somewhere that we wouldn't find you. Second point, that man was not part of your expedition, and has almost certainly never been here before, so he wouldn't have a chance in hell of finding his way across Iversen Land without any equipment. Third point, you are telling me all this much too easily – there's still plenty of time for us to catch up your friend, if he's really on his way to get help. But I don't think he is. I think he's a lot closer than that. I think he's hiding around here somewhere, waiting for a chance to jump us.'

Natasha said nothing.

Medari put his gloved hand under her chin, and forced her to look him in the face.

'You are going to tell me,' he said.

'I have told you.'

'I think not.'

Suddenly he bent down and slammed Natasha's face straight into a puddle of meltwater that lay at his feet. After a moment she began to struggle, but he held her down in the water. Seconds ticked by. Jens's face was white. Natasha was kicking wildly.

At last Medari pulled her up, then watched with uncaring eyes as she coughed and choked.

'Not as bad as the elephant, but still effective,' he said quietly. 'Now, tell me the truth.'

'I have—'

He drove her head back down into the puddle. This time he held her even longer. When he allowed her back up, she retched agonizingly and was unable to speak for at least two minutes.

'Final chance,' he said at last. 'I've found what I came here for, so I don't intend to waste any more time. You have precisely twenty seconds to tell me the truth.'

It was impossible to doubt him.

'Fifteen seconds.'

'All right,' gasped Natasha, water still dripping from her face. 'I'll tell you. There's a tourist group in Iversen Land, climbing one of the peaks, he's gone to look for them. . . .'

'I don't believe you.'

'It's true.'

With a swift movement Medari slammed his rifle into her face, knocking her to the ground, her mouth and nose gushing blood.

'I have seen the planning documents for Iversen Land this year. There were no scheduled visits between 10 August and next January. Time's up, Miss Myklund.'

The rifle was levelled at her head, and there was a click as he released the safety catch. Natasha closed her eyes.

'No, wait. You can't just kill her,' protested Jens, grabbing the other man's arm, and pulling it back.

'Let go of me.'

'I'm not going to let you shoot her down in cold blood.'

'What the hell else can we do with her? There's a hundred million dollars at stake here. And my people's freedom—'

'No. No.' For a moment the two men swayed to and fro, struggling.

At that moment Larsen jumped down on to the ground, ducked under the doors of the wheel bay, and flung himself at the two of them, snatching at the rifle as he did so.

There was an extended timelessness of vicious, uncontrolled struggle. Hands twisted and strangled, nails ripped skin open, fingers clawed and gouged at eyes and mouths, elbows lashed out, feet kicked blindly, fists slammed into flesh. Each of them fought savagely, desperately, against the other two. The three wrestling men were insane with fear and anger, locked inextricably together in a squirming, grunting mass, that surged to and fro over the rough, rocky ground.

As they lurched towards Natasha, she dragged herself out of the pain and despair that had claimed her for their own, and sprawled forward. A blindly-swung boot caught her in the ribs. Instinctively she grabbed it, and wrenched and twisted as hard as she could. There was a shriek of pain, and a moment later the whole group staggered, then crashed to the ground.

Larsen was at the bottom. His head smashed against a rock, and his clutching hand was jarred free of its hold on the gun. Black nausea overcame him, and he almost lost consciousness. Something hit him in the face. Wildly he lashed out. His boot struck someone, and there was a grunt of pain. He kicked again, then tried to get to his feet. A crashing blow on the side of his head sent him rolling over the stones, until he struck the side of the plane. He lay there for a moment before, with a massive effort, forcing himself up on to his feet – only able to keep his balance by leaning back against the cold fuselage of the plane.

It was too late.

Natasha was crouched on the ground a couple of metres from him. Her face was the dirty grey of glacier ice, except where overlain with smears of drying blood, but she was not looking at him. Standing unevenly above her, all his weight on his left side, was Jens. An unreadable expression on his lean, wind-scarred features. Beyond, on a small knoll of rising ground, stood Medari. The rifle was in his hands.

'Right, Jens,' he said, gradually recovering his breath. 'Go over and pick up your rifle. Carefully! Remember, it won't take much to make me shoot you down, not much at all. Good. Now unload it, please. Quickly. And throw it over there. As for the bullets, they can go in the opposite direction – behind you into that pool. All of them. Good, that's much better.'

He surveyed his captives.

'What are you going to do to us?' demanded Jens.

'Don't look at me with that stupid, dumb, accusatory expression,' growled Medari, raw anger suddenly breaking through his façade. 'You and your Eskimo girlfriend were the ones who came to me, who contacted me about that plane. It was you, not me, who sold out your colleagues for easy money. Well maybe you should have remembered that this sort of thing comes with the territory.'

'What do you mean, this sort of thing?' said Jens. 'If you mean murder, I'm not going to have any part in murder.'

'You already have,' said Medari coldly.

'No. No, I haven't. It was you who killed Wendy, not me. I didn't touch her, I never guessed what you were planning. If I had. . . .'

He stopped.

'If you had – then what?' Medari's face was a sneer. 'God in hell! It is a constant source of amazement to me how weak people fool themselves. When I told you to take her off to the lake, what did you think was going to happen? That we would show her the plane? That we would tell her what we were planning?'

Jens looked at him for a long moment, then turned to Larsen and Natasha.

'No one was supposed to get hurt. I never thought that this is what would happen.'

'What about Wendy?' retorted Natasha.

'I never realized he was going to shoot her. I. . . .'

'What about Jon Skalli?'

'No one told me anything about that either. Just that someone panicked, and there was an accident.'

'An accident. Like the death of Dr Frederik Dahl, and twenty-two other people?' said Larsen quietly, spacing out his words as if they were bullets.

'That really was an accident. We all know that flights in the Arctic can be dangerous. It could have happened to any of us at any time. Just bad luck.'

'Bad luck?' repeated Larsen. 'Have you asked your companion there about the crash?'

Jens glanced at Medari, his expression a turmoil of conflicting emotions.

'He's paranoid,' said Medari, with a shrug.

'With reason, I think,' said Larsen. 'Dr Dahl's death was not an unfortunate, if convenient, accident. There was a bomb in his plane. It was put there by a young and stupid Greenlander named Steen Sanders, who was bribed to do it by an associate of your companion, a man apparently named Harald. Steen Sanders, you will not be surprised to hear, is also dead. He apparently committed suicide last Sunday night, but there seems no doubt that his death owed a great deal to the presence of Mr Harald.'

Jens stared, then shook his head.

'No. I don't believe you. I don't believe there was a bomb. . . .' His voice trailed away. 'And who are you, anyway?' he asked at length.

Larsen said nothing.

'I can tell you,' said Medari calmly. 'He's a Greenland cop named Tomas Larsen. Our friend Seana had already told me about him, but it wasn't until after our trouble with that stupid ox creature last night that I realized this must be the same man. Otherwise I might have been a little more careful. Not that it matters now.' He looked from Jens to Larsen to Natasha, then back again. 'I think the time has come to radio for the chopper. After all, it's good weather, isn't it? And it would be foolish of me not to make the most of it. Meanwhile, if anyone tries anything that makes me even slightly uncomfortable, I will instantly, and without any warning, shoot them. Probably dead, but even that is not guaranteed.'

'What are you going to do to us?' asked Jens again. But this time his voice was weak, uncertain, with more than a hint of trembling.

'You three will get out the bombs from the weapons' bay where they are stored, and load them into the chopper, when it arrives.'

'And after that?'

There was no answer, but an abrupt gesture of the rifle.

Three hours later Jens, Natasha and Larsen were all sitting outside the plane. Their captor, rifle in hand, a second by his side, was watching them with eyes that did not waver, barely even seemed to blink. No one had spoken for some time, and Larsen was beginning to feel growing pangs of hunger, but there was nothing that could be done.

Suddenly he realized that the air had imperceptibly begun to vibrate with the sound of rotors. After a couple of minutes, the noise grew suddenly much louder as the helicopter appeared over the edge of the valley, and started to drop down towards them.

'What if the bombs are unstable?' said Larsen suddenly. 'There must be a good chance that they are, after such a long time. They could explode when we try to move them.'

'They could,' agreed their captor judiciously. 'But in my opinion, and thinking of what the profit will be, it is worth taking the risk. And we do have a nuclear physicist on his way to help us. Anyhow, either way it's not going to make much difference to any of you three, is it?'

'You're going to kill us,' said Jens.

It was not a question, and Medari did not answer it.

Larsen had long-since realized what was going to happen. When the helicopter was loaded, they would be shot down, and left; their bodies joining the frozen bodies of the crew, and the mysterious corpses in the containers. He knew he should make one last desperate effort, but a dull hopelessness, a grey resignation, sat inside in his head and sucked all the energy from him. They were 400 kilometres from the nearest settlement, completely cut off and at their captor's mercy. It was over. The End. Nothing could be done about it.

He looked across at Natasha, but she was staring at the ground, her bruised face showing nothing.

The helicopter was descending slowly and cautiously on to a wide, flat area of bare stone and rock, spotted with a few sparse cushions of plant growth. The thunder of its engines filled their ears, and the wind blew glacial dust in their faces. Larsen felt his eyes sting, and blinked away the salt water that trickled down his cheek.

Briefly he remembered his children. Vigdis – still and always a tiny, miraculously blonde baby, smiling toothlessly and waving her arms, although she was now a teenager. Mitti – tough, independent, able to look after herself, so briefly found and then lost again. Except for a few ragged, soon-to-fade memories among his work colleagues, his two daughters were all that he was leaving to the world. And neither of them were really his – had never truly been his. The image of Risa rose up also, but it seemed far away and long ago. Only the pain of loss struck at him like fire in his throat. His isolation was overwhelming. Unanswerable.

From some long-forgotten scrap of his memory came a vision of the time a neighbour of his had given his six-year-old son a lemming as a pet. When the little creature died after four or five months, the child had cried for half an hour, weeping with total grief, as if his heart had broken apart. Now Larsen found himself pointlessly wondering if anyone would offer him the great gift of such sadness. Without feeling sorry for himself, for he was beyond that emotion, he accepted that it was more likely that his death would pass without even a few short tears by one single person. That it would barely raise any emotion except surprise.

And back in Nuuk, Chief Thorold would breathe more easily.

With a great effort, Larsen tore himself free of the cloying, clinging loneliness that cut at him, and looked up at Medari, who was standing, rifle in hand, gazing down the slope to the landing place, perhaps a hundred metres away.

The helicopter landed perfectly, with the lightness of a feather. It rocked a little on its skis, and the rotors began to slow.

Medari took a step down the slope, then stopped.

Abruptly the door of the helicopter opened, and half a dozen men sprang out. They were dressed in blue, white and grey polar camouflage fatigues, and they carried automatic weapons.

'Shit!'

Medari fired his rifle twice in quick succession, then turned to run.

Larsen just had time to recognize the irony. Medari himself had also been double-crossed.

A moment later, through the sound of the slowing rotors came a deafening burst of fire. Bullets cracked and skipped among the stones. Larsen felt a searing pain in his skull and slumped to the ground. But his eyes were still open. And from somewhere close by he could hear screaming.

There was a fresh burst of gunfire, deadly, filling his head so that there was no longer room even for thought. But somehow he was still alive when it stopped. The screaming had stopped too.

Larsen lay without moving, sprawled on the rocks. There was a crunch of feet close by his head, and something blocked out the sun.

A nightmare face looked down at him. Black and shiny, mouthless, inhuman, with a bulging pig-like snout, and enormous, shadowed, insect eyes.

Somewhere in his brain Larsen wanted to scream, but nothing happened.

Hell, thought Larsen. I am in hell.

A black shiny hand, huge, inexorable, descended towards him, seized his jaw and pushed his face to one side. The goggling eyes came closer, peering at him. At the same moment Larsen realized what it was – the man above him was wearing a gas mask.

That realization seemed to unleash his power of movement. He seized the man's arm and wrenched down with every ounce of his strength. There was a muffled grunt of surprise, then the man's face crashed into a jagged rock close to Larsen's face. Larsen hurled himself free, ripping away the man's gun as he did so, then rolling over twice before springing to his feet.

He spun round, the automatic rifle in his hand. The man beside him was writhing on the ground, clawing at his face. Larsen kicked him ferociously in the side of the head, then again in the kidneys. As the man slumped and lay inert, Larsen crouched and looked around him. There were other shapes on the ground, not moving. But four more masked men were turning rapidly round towards him, raising their guns.

Larsen's finger tightened on the trigger. But before he could fire, something hit him a crushing blow on the back of his head.

Even as his legs turned to jelly, he just had time to remember that six men had got out of the helicopter. One of them must have come up behind him.

Stupid, he thought. How could I have been so stupid?

Overwhelming darkness was a welcome relief.

22 So far . . . and no further

FOR WEEKS LARSEN was kept in a single room. He had no clothes to wear – not even underwear; no blankets – though the temperature remained at an unchangingly comfortable level; and no concept of time passing – for the room had no clock and no windows, and the lights remained on all the time. Nor did he have a scrap of privacy, for he was constantly watched by three closed-circuit cameras – mounted out of his reach on the ceiling – and less frequently through the reinforced double glass panel in the door. His food, microwaved and on paper plates, arrived at regular intervals via an automatic dispensing machine: hamburgers, pizza, lasagne, breaded fish, baked potatoes, french fries, insipid vegetables, fruit with juice but no taste, cheese with the consistency of plastic, danish pastries that seemed ninety per cent syrup, and soggy doughnuts that oozed fat. Drinks, too, came in paper containers: sugary orange squash, black tea, water with a metallic hint of chemicals, and the highlight of the day – a cup of strong coffee.

He washed in a searingly hot shower, which stung his skin with the power of its needle-thin spray, and he had to use a liquid soap that smelt like bleach. The toilet was like a sophisticated chemical one, but with no flush that he could control, though it did clean itself occasionally and unpredictably. The very air he breathed had a strange aftertaste, there was a constantly humming draft from two ventilators at the top of the room, and Larsen felt constant faint air pressure in his ears, as if he was in a plane.

There was no telephone, no television, no newspapers, no contact with the outside world at all. For amusement he had a library of American thrillers, and a slow, old-fashioned computer with a few games – though no Internet connection. He soon grew bored with patience, hearts, spin doctor, maze wars, and minesweeper, but fortunately the computer also had a chess programme. Oddly he found the machine easier to beat when it was set at the higher levels – and played a cautious defensive-minded game – than at the lower ones, when it launched an all-out attack on him.

At periodic intervals he was checked over by men and women, wearing head to toe chemical-biological protection suits that did not expose a single millimetre of naked skin – not unlike that worn by the man he had attacked. They entered through what appeared to be a pressurized airlock, and asked him, in voices made inhuman by their self-contained breathing apparatus and respirators, how he felt. Then they checked over his naked, vulnerable body with their well-gloved hands, gave him an injection or two, removed blood and tissue samples, sometimes checked his eyes, mouth, nose, ears, penis and anus, or attached him to one of the various medical monitors that stood on a trolley near the bed. And all the time they looked at him through their masks with cold, scientific interest. As if he was a specimen. The first few times he tried to talk to them, but they were no more communicative than the computer, and eventually he gave up, and returned sullenly to playing chess. He briefly considered attacking them, and trying to escape – but the idea was obviously impossible.

Thankful for just being alive to begin with, Larsen soon began to wonder exactly how long he would be kept in these conditions. Weeks. Months. Years. But he had no idea how long had already passed. Eventually even chess bored him, and he spent more and more time simply lying on his bed, staring up at the white ceiling – the same brilliant, anti-flash white, it seemed to him, that had been supposed to protect the crew of the B52 from a nuclear blast.

Then at last, to Larsen's astonishment and disbelief, there came the day when a woman entered the room. A woman who wasn't wearing a protection suit; just a dark blue suit that looked like a uniform, and sensible shoes. She was about thirty-five, quite short, with cropped mouse-brown hair, dark green-framed glasses, and a long oval face.

There was not a scrap of make-up on her pale skin, no earrings in her ears, no rings on her strong fingers. She carried a black plastic bag, zipped up tight.

'Good day, Sergeant Larsen,' she said, in English, with an American accent. 'I'm Doctor Stypinkski.'

'You've decided I'm clean then?'

She handed him the bag.

'Some clothes for you.'

'Thanks.'

'My pleasure.' She stood calmly, watching him as he pulled on the pants, jeans and sweatshirt. 'You must be relieved this is over.'

'Is it over?'

'Sure. You've been put through every test that we can think of – including some new ones we haven't tried before. Just about every cell in your body has been monitored, and every scrap of air you've breathed and food you've eaten, right down to your waste products, has been split down into its component atoms. We can't find a trace of anything. You're clean.'

'Are you going to tell me what this is all about?'

She looked at him through her thick spectacles, calculating.

'I thought you would have worked most of it out by now.'

'So tell me, and let me see if I'm right.'

Was that a trace of a smile? He didn't think so.

'Very well. In 1958 one of our B-52s crashed out in Iversen Land, but no one was able to trace it. It was way off course, the last recorded position we had for it was out by hundreds of miles, there was a severe magnetic storm at the time, and Iversen Land was into its winter darkness. We sent out search planes over a period of several months, but found nothing, so we assumed the plane had been lost somewhere in the Denmark Strait. Of course, in fact we were looking in the wrong place. Not that we would have found it anyway, it seems that it crashed straight into the glacier above Lake Sølveig, and was swallowed up in the ice. So there it stayed, until this summer, when the retreat of the polar glaciers, combined with a warm summer, exposed the plane for the first time in over forty years, and it was accidentally found by the Copenhagen University Iversen Land Expedition.

'A member of the expedition realized the possible value of the plane's cargo, and somehow made contact with Timur Medari, who had close links with the Chechen rebels in Russia, and planned to sell any atomic weapons he could find. However, we were tracking him, so we turned up and that's it, really.'

'Have the others all been kept in isolation too?' asked Larsen.

She said nothing, and only then did he realize.

'They're all dead then? Medari. Jens. Natasha.'

'There was no way our team could tell that two of you were unwillingly present,' she said.

'But Natasha hadn't done anything wrong. . . .'

Even as the words escaped him, he realized how pathetically naïve they sounded.

'It was not a situation when any risks could be taken,' the woman said, without emotion. 'To be frank, Sergeant Larsen, you yourself were exceptionally lucky not to have been killed, especially after you severely injured one member of the team – a man who has not yet been released from hospital. He had to endure the same precautions as you, but with the added complication of needing an operation on his face – to rebuild his nose, and deal with severe scarring. Your assault on him was a very savage one.'

'I thought he was about to kill me,' muttered Larsen.

'On the contrary, he was certainly hoping that you were still alive, for the team had been given a specific order to ensure that they brought back at least one living person. An order that, no doubt, was what saved your life subsequently. However, you'll be pleased to learn that an associate of Medari was also arrested in Nuuk, after a tip-off.'

'Was his name Harald?'

'I do not know. No doubt you will be able to find out later. I would now like to move on to more immediately relevant matters. You will clearly understand how essential it is that this business is kept entirely secret. We will, of course, completely deny anything that may appear in public, but it would be best – for you as well as us – if nothing did appear and no one at all was told . . . under any circumstances whatsoever. We have prepared a report for you, which we expect you to sign, and which will cover, I think, every eventuality. Stick to the letter of that, and it will save all of us a lot of trouble.'

She handed him a sheet of paper.

Larsen looked at it, and admired the professionalism that did not produce a perfectly word-processed report, but instead this roughly-typed document, with a couple of misspellings. It was written in Danish, and did not go as far adrift from the truth as Larsen had expected, until the end – where it told many lies of omission.

'Could you first explain to me why, until this moment, everyone has treated me as if I have the plague?' he asked.

This time she definitely did smile. But it was a cold little expression, that barely twitched her small, tight, pale mouth.

'Would you sign the report please,' she said, producing a biro.

He hesitated.

'Listen, Sergeant,' she snapped. 'The essentials of this are right down the line. Medari was after nuclear weapons, weapons that he would have sold in some of the most dangerous places on earth. We made sure he didn't get them. That's it. And if it cost a few lives, well, it was worth it. Try thinking about what the Chechens, or the Kurds, or some of the extreme Islamic organizations might have done with a nuclear device. Or for that matter, even some of our own American survivalist fanatics. When you've thought about that, I think you'll find it hard to deny that the world has become just a little bit safer as a result of what we did. Maybe an awful lot safer.' She paused, then softened her tone. 'You helped us, and we're grateful. Now sign the statement.'

It suddenly occurred to Larsen that perhaps Natasha, Jens and Medari had been killed on purpose – but that they had needed one living person to do tests on. Or was he just being paranoid?

'Why all these precautions anyway?' he demanded again. 'You haven't explained anything.'

'Need to know,' was all she said.

'I nearly got killed by your men in Iversen Land, and three other people did. I'd say that gave me a right to know.'

'I'm afraid not. You have no rights. I am, in point of fact, authorized to clarify the situation to you, but only after you have signed this statement. Could you please do so?'

'What if I refuse?'

Her face tautened, and in a second her voice had become as bright and sharp as chrome.

'Sergeant Larsen, no one knows you are here – except our people. No one else even knows whether you are alive or dead.'

'You're threatening me.'

'I am pointing out that you are in no position to bargain, because we can do whatever the fuck we want to do with you.' The tone was even and controlled, yet the obscenity was somehow profoundly shocking, coming from that neat, prim, conventional-looking woman. 'In fact, I could have you gradually sliced down to your component DNA, if I gave it as my professional opinion that it was necessary, and no one would say a word against it. And none of your people would ever be any the wiser.'

Larsen glanced down at the statement again, then up at her colourless, indifferent face. With a shrug he signed.

Even as he did so, he realized she had outwitted him. That the people who were holding him here must have known about his congenital inquisitiveness, and then used it, most delicately, to control him.

'OK,' he said. 'What is this all about then?'

She made a casual gesture.

'Not as fascinating as you maybe think. Basically, there is some cause to believe that the bodies which were being transported by the crashed plane had died of a virulent strain of pulmonary tuberculosis, which was attacking Greenland at the time. In the circumstances, we thought it wise to leave nothing to chance – especially considering the recent spread of antibiotic-resistant strains of the disease. However, no infection has resulted, so you are free to leave here.'

'TB?'

'That's right.'

Larsen said nothing for a moment or two, then shrugged.

'Where am I anyway,' he asked.

'Thule Air Base,' she said. 'We'll send you back to Nuuk in the next few days.'

'After you've had a chance to use my statement – so that I can't go back on it.'

'You can't go back on it,' she said with utter certainty, and turned to go.

'What happened to my things?' Larsen asked suddenly.

She did not reply. The heavy, airtight door hissed and then clicked shut behind her.

Larsen realized that they must have destroyed everything. Dully he returned to his bed and lay down on it, his hands behind his head. He wondered if they had caught Seana, and found that somehow he did not care either way. The closed-circuit cameras were still on him, but at least they could not see inside his head. For there, strange ideas were flowering.

Like a lightning strike came the thought that perhaps the whole thing had been nothing more than an elaborate trap, hatched by the CIA – and maybe involving the Russians also – to catch and kill Medari. That the existence of the plane had long been known, and that there had not been any nuclear weapons on it, or anything else important. Which would in turn mean that he himself had simply been part of the smoke-screen, set up to deceive the Chechen. The more he looked at the theory, the more possible it seemed. But if it were true, then many things flowed on from it.

Perhaps Seana had not been working for Medari at all, but for the CIA – that would certainly explain the apparent ease with which she had vanished. And did that mean Jens was working for the agency as well? In which case he might easily still be alive, probably with a new identity. Or were the deaths of Jens and Natasha not unfortunate mistakes at all, but deliberate, cold-blooded murders? And for that matter, was he quite certain it had been Medari who had started the whole thing, by arranging for the bomb to be placed in Dr Dahl's plane?

Larsen put his hands over his face, and closed his eyes. He felt old and tired and sick.

Even for him, there had come the moment when he no longer had the energy, or the desire, to consider any more questions.

It was sleeting in Nuuk. The town had the dull and colourless feel that it always carried at the end of autumn, weighted down by the oppression of coming darkness and winter.

A taxi took him to the police station, where Chief Thorold read the report with an uninterested face, and barely bothered to ask any questions at all.

'See you tomorrow,' he said coldly.

Larsen went home. His flat was cold and empty. Four and a half weeks had brought him no post at all, except a few circulars. Not even one of Mitti's brief postcards. He glanced at his watch. It was six in the evening. He made himself a cup of coffee, then suddenly threw the coffee into the sink, grabbed his anorak and went out. The sleet had turned to snow, and there was a thickening white and grey layer on the road.

Edvarth opened the door, and gaped.

'Hey, you're back,' he said at last. 'Where have you been? What's been happening? We kept trying to contact you, but it was like you'd been wiped off the face of the earth.'

'It felt like that too. Is your mother in?'

'No. But she should be back soon. Come in.'

To Larsen's surprise, Katinka was there, curled up like a cat on the sofa, watching TV. She flicked off the remote control, then grinned at him.

'I'll be gone in a few minutes,' she said. 'Edvarth prefers that his mum doesn't see me. But listen, where have you been? We have some really weird stuff to tell you.'

'That's right,' said Edvarth, sitting down beside her.

'Go on,' said Larsen.

'OK, it was about the old US airforce base at Narsarsuaq. We got interested, so we went along to the Cultural Centre, and looked it up in the Groenlandica library.'

'It was really weird,' said Katinka again, her liquid eyes wide and black. 'Apparently the hospital north of the base was secretly used for severe American casualties during the Korean War. But not a single one of the wounded brought there ever left. Not one. Also the hospital was incredibly strictly guarded – even more than the airbase itself. There were no visitors for the sick – ever; no one was allowed in without passing a whole load of security checks; and none of the local people were allowed to work there.'

'Mind you, some of the books did give a completely different story,' put in Edvarth. 'They said the hospital was never really opened at all, just used for a few American personnel from the base, together with the occasional Greenlander with severe TB. Then it was abandoned, together with the base, in 1958.'

'I don't believe that for a moment,' said Katinka. 'The hospital was vast – it had 250 beds. Why so big? Why should they spend millions and millions of dollars to build such a massive place out in the middle of nowhere, then never use it? And there was something else too: the US documents on the Narsarsuaq airbase have all been declassified, but the ones on the hospital still haven't been. So something must have been going on there – germ warfare stuff, or maybe weird medical experiments. Did you find out anything?'

Larsen shrugged.

'It was a long time ago.'

'And they still don't want us to know about it,' said Katinka. She frowned, and put her finger on her lower lip, so that she looked momentarily like a small child. 'I wonder why?'

'We'll probably never find out,' said Larsen.

At that moment there was the sound of a key at the front door.

'Shit!' said Edvarth. 'It's mum. She's early.'

Risa came in, and stopped dead.

'You've been having a little party here then, Edvarth' she said. Larsen could read nothing in her wide face.

'Tomas has only just turned up,' said Edvarth. 'I mean. . . .'

'I think I'd better talk to him alone,' she said. 'Perhaps you – and your friend – could go for a little walk.'

'But it's snowing . . .' began Edvarth. Then he caught his mother's eye, and hastily pulled Katinka up, and bustled her out. 'Let's go.'

'See you soon,' said Katinka, stopping in the doorway, and casting a dazzling smile at the two adults.

Edvarth pulled her outside and closed the door.

There was a long pause.

'I stopped expecting to see you,' Risa said at last.

'I need to explain.'

She considered for a moment. Her face did not change.

'OK,' she said. 'Explain.'

'It could take some time.'

'Then I'll make some coffee.' She went into the kitchen, leaving Larsen nervously regarding his short, thick fingers.

At that moment the door opened again. It was Edvarth. He looked around, then followed his mother into the kitchen.

'Mum, could you lend me a couple of hundred kroner for tonight.'

'You've had your allowance for this month.'

'I'll pay you back.'

'Why should I give you money to spend with that girl?'

'Maybe to buy yourself some peace. Come on, Mum. You're going to say yes, aren't you?'

Risa shrugged. 'What the hell! Here you are.'

Edvarth pocketed the money, kissed his mother enthusiastically, and headed for the door, grabbing his jacket. On the way out, he passed Larsen.

'It's OK,' he whispered, raising his thumb encouragingly. 'She's been worrying herself sick about you. As long as you've got a good explanation of where you've been, and why you didn't contact her, it'll be fine. If you play your cards well, maybe you'll even have as good a night as I expect to. See you!'

He clenched both his fists exultantly, and shot out of the front door.

Larsen glanced at the door to the kitchen, and saw Risa standing there, holding two cups of steaming coffee.

'I've given up trying to keep him apart from that slut,' she said. 'After all, the brains of sixteen-year-old boys lose out to their pricks every time.'

'I'm sure she's not as bad as you think she is. And she makes Edvarth happy.'

'At the moment, yes. But I'm thinking in the long term.'

'Perhaps you think too much of the long term.'

'You think so?'

'Yes. I do.'

'OK,' she said, sitting down opposite him. 'We'll forget that for the moment. Now, you can explain why the hell I haven't heard from you for over a month.'

'It's going to take time.'

'I've got time.'

Larsen broke his word to Doctor Stypinkski at Thule, and told Risa everything. Starting from the moment he had left to go to Copenhagen. And gradually her chilly manner faded, and she became totally engrossed. At the end, after his description of what had happened at Thule Air Base, she shook her head.

'They were lying to you,' she said, with complete certainty. 'They don't take those sort of precautions for TB – especially not over forty years later.'

'So what was it then?'

'I don't know. But there's a Danish virologist I've met who would be interested, I think.'

'It doesn't matter, Risa,' said Larsen, suddenly feeling faintly nervous.

She took no notice. There was a look of acute, intellectual curiosity on her face.

'You go and lie down,' she said briskly. 'You look as if you haven't slept for days.'

Not expecting to, he fell asleep within minutes. When he woke up some hours later she told him what she had learnt from a series of phone calls to America and Denmark.

'What we're talking about here is a link between the Korean War and the hospital at Narsarsuaq. During the war a lot of American soldiers – no one's quite sure how many – were struck down by a mystery illness, which caused fever, bleeding, and kidney failure, with a death rate running at ten per cent, or more. It seems that some of the cases were flown to Narsarsuaq Hospital, which because of its remoteness had been set up specifically to study contagious diseases. Anyway, the patients were carefully studied and kept strictly isolated. Meanwhile, all information about the illness was suppressed, and the bodies of those who died from it were sealed up for future research. The disease they were suffering from actually took over twenty years to identify. It was called Hantaan virus, the very first example of a new and highly unpleasant family, the hantaviruses, which give rise to a condition known as HFRS – haemorrhagic fever with renal syndrome.'

'OK,' said Larsen. 'I see where this leads us. The plane that crashed in Iversen Land was carrying the sealed bodies of those who died from Hantaan virus. Which explains all the precautions. End of story.'

'Not quite,' said Risa, and her face was grave. 'For one thing it appears that none of the USAF B-52s were missing.'

Larsen frowned.

'You mean they covered the crash up too? That's no big surprise, is it?'

'Except that, as you and the woman Natasha discovered, they claimed the particular B-52, which they lost in Iversen Land, had actually crashed in the northern United States about ten weeks earlier. Which might make some people think that more of this had been planned than it looks like at first sight.'

'What else?' asked Larsen, watching her face.

'Well, returning to the disease aspect – in recent decades the hantaviruses have been spreading, with periodic outbreaks in many different countries. Most alarming was a new form of the virus, hantavirus pulmonary syndrome, which appeared almost from nowhere in the USA, inflicted death rates of up to seventy per cent, then equally suddenly vanished. It is interesting, incidentally, that the doctor at Thule mentioned pulmonary TB. However, what you endured at Thule is far more thorough than what is considered appropriate for Hantaan virus. The combination of doctors wearing total protective bodysuits, self-contained breathing equipment and respirators, with a maximum security environment, and what sounds like negative airflow, all confirm the fact that they were taking precautions for a Biosafety Level 4 Germ.'

'What's that?'

'A top of the range killer. Something like Ebola Fever, for which there is no vaccine and no cure, and with a death rate that starts at twenty-five per cent, and goes up to one hundred per cent. There are probably only about forty or fifty places in the world where they could provide that sort of secure environment.' She sighed. 'Whatever they were worried about, for sure it wasn't TB, and nor was it just Hantaan virus.'

'What do you mean?'

Risa hesitated.

'It seems significant that the precautions they took with you at Thule went from extreme one day, to non-existent twelve hours later. That implies they knew exactly what they were looking for, and exactly how long the dormant period of the disease was.' She looked at him.

'It does seem possible that the Narsarsuaq hospital may have been linked to a biological-warfare facility . . .' she added reluctantly.

'You mean. . . .' Larsen stopped.

Neither of them spoke for several minutes.

'One of these days,' he said, at last, 'something like that will escape.'

'I hope to God not,' whispered Risa.

Abruptly, harshly, the telephone rang. Risa got up and answered it. She listened for a few moments, and her face grew drawn and stiff. Then, without a word, she handed the receiver to Larsen.

'Mr Larsen,' came an American voice. 'This evening a friend of yours has been making enquiries that seem to be connected to your recent experience. I would advise most strongly that such enquiries cease. Immediately and totally. For the sake of both of you.' The voice paused, then went on, clear and heavy with menace. 'This is the only warning you will receive, Mr Larsen. Any further sign whatsoever that you have broken confidentiality will result in immediate action on our part.'

'What sort of action?' asked Larsen.

'There is no necessity for you to know that.'

The phone went dead.

Larsen and Risa looked at each other, then together their eyes turned back to the telephone.

'It seems they're listening to your calls,' said Larsen softly.

It was well after midnight when the front door opened, and Katinka and Edvarth came in. They found Risa and Larsen sitting in silence on the sofa, their arms round each other.

'Hey, you're still here,' said Edvarth, with the beaming good nature of someone who has had just the right quantity of alcohol. 'And you've sorted everything out. Excellent! I knew you would. You don't mind if Katinka stays the night, do you mum? Sure you don't. Brilliant!'

The two of them vanished into Edvarth's room. But as the door closed, Katinka frowned.

'They didn't look very happy, did they?' she remarked softly.

'Adults don't know how to be happy,' said Edvarth, rolling on to his bed. 'But I do. Come here, beautiful.'